Starting Over

59

Starting Over

Sue Moorcroft

Copyright © 2009 Sue Moorcroft

First published 2009 by Choc Lit Limited
Penrose House, Crawley Drive, Camberley, Surrey GU15 2AB
www.choclitpublishing.co.uk

The right of Sue Moorcroft to be identified as the Author of this Work
has been asserted by her in accordance with the Copyright, Designs and
Patents Act 1988

All characters and events in this publication, other than those clearly in
the public domain, are fictitious and any resemblance to actual persons,
living or dead, is purely coincidental

All rights reserved. No part of this publication may be reproduced,
stored in a retrieval system, or transmitted in any form or by any means,
electronic, mechanical, photocopying, recording or otherwise, without
the prior permission of the publisher or a licence permitting restricted
copying. In the UK such licences are issued by the Copyright Licensing
Agency, 90 Tottenham Court Road, London, W1P 9HE

A CIP catalogue record for this book is available
from the British Library

ISBN-978-1-906931-22-3

Mixed Sources
Product group from well-managed
forests and other controlled sources
www.fsc.org Cert no. TT-COC-2063
© 1996 Forest Stewardship Council
FSC

Printed in the UK by CPI Cox & Wyman, Reading RG1 8EX

For Carl
Forever singing in our hearts

Acknowledgements

With thanks to Det. Supt Mark Lacey,
Dr Adrian Perkins, Fig Taylor, Laura Longrigg,
Mark West, who read an early draft and
persuaded me to stop using the word 'piratical',
and all at Choc Lit.

Also to the Romantic Novelists' Association, in this,
the Association's fiftieth year. It's such a brilliant
organisation and has provided me with both friends
and writing opportunities. What else could I ask for?

Prologue

☐ (Priority)
Subject: Wedding …
From: Olly<ollygray@ollygray.co.uk>
Time: 18:14
To: Tess<tess@tessriddell.co.uk>

Tess,
No easy way to say this so will be direct.

Given it loads of thought and the idea of moving in with you & your messy workroom has got to me. I've gone cold on the wedding.

You're normally the first to walk away from a bad situation but this time it's me that's recognised the issues & I think you'll be glad I did, some day.

I've spoken to the travel agent re the honeymoon. I expect you will want to see to the return of the prezzies & whatnot, as I won't be around. Am taking a contract in Scotland for a couple of months – good opportunity. As soon as I send this I'll be out the door.

No point talking, anyway. My mind's made up.

Sorry.

Married bliss is just not me.

Love
Olly x

Chapter One

Tess's vehicle stopped as if a giant had slammed a door in its face.

Metal screeched, glass crashed, the seat belt wrenched the breath from her body and the airbag thumped her in the face.

Then, slowly, the bag deflated.

And everything went quiet apart from the ringing in her ears.

She found herself gazing into the flatbed of the breakdown truck she'd been following for the last two miles. Her windscreen had dissolved into a million crystals twinkling in her lap, on her chest, on the floor, on the dash and on an Izmir Blue bonnet bent up like a broken beak. One wiper twitched in mid-air. The rain that, until now, had been pounding on her windscreen, began to pound on her.

'*Shit*!' she croaked.

A man ran from the breakdown truck, dark curls swinging around his eyes as he leant through the space where the windscreen used to be. 'Are you hurt?'

'My face is hot,' she mumbled.

'Yeah, airbag. But you seem to be breathing and thinking. Sit still.' He fished out a phone.

'Don't ring anyone. I'm fine.' She swivelled her head from side to side, flexed back and legs, then pushed at the driver's door. It groaned outward, allowing her to fumble out of the seat belt and slither gingerly onto the road where the rain burbled into a gully.

The man glared, phone still poised. 'What are you *doing*? You could have a spinal injury!'

She pointed to her legs. 'Working!' Checking her nose for blood, her hand came away wet only with rain. She didn't think it was the rain that was blurring her vision, though.

'You need checking over.' He seemed not to feel the torrent that flattened his hair and rolled down a hard-cut face and into blue eyes. If he needed two shaves a day it looked as if he seldom bothered.

Tess tried again to flex. Her back felt as if she'd just done a bungee jump. She hunched her shoulders. 'I don't like hospitals. Look, sorry I didn't see you stop, I turned on the heat and the windscreen misted. My insurance will cover your truck OK.'

He glanced at where her Freelander was gnawing at his breakdown truck. 'Doubt you've done more than add a couple of new scratches to the wrecker. It's your Freelander that's bent.' He narrowed his gaze on her once more and his voice softened. 'Better go to hospital, you know.'

She shook her head. And winced. 'You're from a garage, right?' She indicated the sign on the side panel of the truck. 'MAR Motors is the garage in Middledip, isn't it? At the Cross.'

'Yes. You're not local, are you?'

'Just moving in – to Honeybun Cottage.' Not that it was any of his business. 'Can you give me a tow?'

He grimaced. 'You'll sue me if it turns out you've got a cracked neck.'

'I won't because I haven't!' she snapped. 'But the Freelander's undrivable. I'd appreciate a tow. If I have to call someone else I'll be sitting here in the rain for hours.'

He hesitated. Then sighed. 'Come on, then!' Ungraciously, he installed her in the passenger seat of the wrecker before spending ten minutes clanging around at its rear, while Tess sank her swimming head on a seat that smelt of old oil and closed her eyes.

Finally, he climbed back into the cab, shook the rain off his hair and drove her the remaining mile or so to Middledip village. As the breakdown truck began to rumble along, he flipped his thumb in the direction of her poor Freelander. 'Were you fond of it?'

'Loads. Everyone said it was a posey vehicle – I was living in London. But I love it. What's left of it since it hit your truck.'

'Nobody forced you to run it up my backside,' he pointed out, disagreeably.

Tess's head was pounding and sudden tears pricked her eyes, blurring the already blurred raindrops that drummed on the windscreen and hissed beneath the wheels, bouncing and bubbling off the expanse of tarmac at the centre of the village, where three roads converged at the point known inaccurately as the Cross, and where there was a building with the sign: 'MAR Motors'.

Wordlessly, she eased out of the cab and squelched across the forecourt, following her disagreeable saviour out of the deluge and in through a long run of folding doors. The floor was painted grey, like the pit garages at the motor races on television.

An office chair stood in front of a computer. He nodded at it. 'Sit there while I have a look at your car, then we'll talk about what to do.' He raised his voice to a masked figure welding under a ramp at the back of the garage. 'Jos! Can you get her a cup of tea? She's had a prang. Pete! Give me a hand, will you?' A man uncoiled himself from under the bonnet of a little red sports car, pushing back floppy fair hair, smiled at Tess and ran to help at the back of the breakdown truck.

Aching and shaking too much to object to being ordered about, Tess gazed out through the hammering rain to where an old-fashioned van in baker's livery graced the forecourt along with two old cars. Not banger-type old but 1950s old, all grinning chrome grills, candy colours and swiping tail fins. The forecourt looked like a classic car show.

She let her chin sink onto her fist and once again closed her eyes. What a crappy beginning to her fresh start.

Jos, welding mask discarded, wiping his hands on his overalls and stamping about in motorcycle boots, rattled cups and filled the kettle. His long dark hair was pulled back in a ponytail and he had a beard like Hagrid, not the trendy goatee worn by so many men she'd known in London. He brought her steaming tea in a mug with the MG logo on the side and an open pack of sugar with a spoon sticking out.

Through the strands of dripping hair she managed a smile, even as she shivered. 'Thanks.'

His eyes were gentle. 'Ratty'll soon get you sorted.'

Presumably, he meant the disagreeable man. She made a face. 'Ratty? Yes, he is, a bit.'

The eyes smiled. '*Ratt*enbury.' And pointed to the 'M. A. Rattenbury' sign on the wall.

'Oh. I get it.' The owner of the blue eyes and black curls was the boss. She should've known.

In a few minutes, he was back. Draining a mug of tea, he bent over the computer, so close that Tess could feel the chill of the rain from his arms and shoulders. The sleeves had been cut from his T-shirt to exhibit small tattoos. Sculpted by physical work, he was a different breed from Olly with his designer labels and career in IT.

She jerked her gaze away.

She was done with men. She was here to concentrate on getting better, on freeing herself of the lassitude that had left her vegetating these past months.

He tapped the computer screen. 'Want me to book it in?'

Her mind flipped to Channel 4 documentaries about tow bandits. Maybe he'd stick her with a £500 bill and she

5

wouldn't be able to argue because she'd *asked* him to bring the Freelander … 'Wouldn't it be better at Land Rover?' she enquired dubiously, through her headache.

He tapped the screen again, harder. 'Yes! There's their number – ring and arrange for it to be fetched.'

Belatedly, she realised that what he'd called up on the computer was the contact details of the Land Rover main dealer in Bettsbrough.

He turned to a toolbox, obviously having a hundred better things to do than deal with her any further.

She didn't need his tight expression to tell her she'd been out of order. Having run up the arse of his truck and demanded he rescue her, she supposed it would, actually, have been polite to put the resultant business his way. And starting at square one with another garage suddenly seemed exhausting. 'Actually … I'd like to book it in here for the repair.'

A flash of those hard eyes. 'Probably better at Land Rover.'

She propped her head back on her hand. 'So you can't do it here, at your garage?'

'I can do it, but it'll be *best* at Land Rover.'

He was annoying, scraping through his tools and not wanting her business. 'It'll be *convenient* to have it done here.'

'Oh shi— Book it in, Pete. Sheet it up until we can bring it inside.'

In silence, Tess watched as Pete and Jos fixed a faded blue tarpaulin over where the windscreen used to be, to direct the rain away from her front seats.

In silence, Ratty worked at the bench.

The Freelander looked so forlorn all bashed, squashed and abandoned on the forecourt. Tess groaned. 'All my gear's in the car.'

He glanced up. 'Anyone you can call?'

She sighed. 'Not really.' It sounded so sad.

Silence. Then, 'OK! Just to Honeybun Cottage? I'll bring the van round.'

It was shameful, really. The situation was all her fault and yet she sat in the echoing chill of the garage and watched the three men like ants in the rain, transferring her sacks of clothes and boxes of books into the back of a van. But concrete was setting into her muscles, her head clanged and she felt so sick.

Boxes, cases, bags, a behemoth of a computer and an awkwardly large printer … Finally, Ratty had everything transferred to the van, what seemed to be all the worldly possessions of the accident-prone owner of the Freelander.

Impatiently, he loped back over to the doorway. 'Anytime you're ready ...'

He watched the woman hunch her shoulders against the rain and clamber stiffly into the front seat, obviously prepared to endure the tortures of hell rather than admit that she was hurting. Her hair was a sodden rope and her T-shirt clung interestingly. During the short, rattly journey she stopped shivering only long enough to offer, 'It's this road.'

'Yep, this is Little Lane all right.' He nodded. 'What happened to the commuters who had Honeybun after Herbie died? Mortgage rate get them?'

'I suppose. I bought it as a repo. My father's field of expertise.'

'Profiting from someone else's bad fortune.'

'Like you, fixing breakdowns?' Her face was tight with irritation.

He half smiled. 'Got me. But repair's not my market.'

'Really? But you are going to fix my car?'

7

'When you get the OK from your insurance company.' He turned in between the gateposts of Honeybun Cottage and pulled up as close to the kitchen door as possible, beside a lawn full of clover and daisies. He knew these cottages and the way the door opened straight into the house. 'They'll probably tell you that it has to be done by Land Rover. I'll dump all this crap in the kitchen, shall I?'

For the first time she smiled, and it lit her face like a sunbeam on a stormy day. 'You're a regular Sir Galahad.'

Trotting to and fro from van to kitchen, he got wetter and wetter, until he was really tired of it. He didn't suggest the woman should help, though, because she was so pale that a dusting of freckles was standing out across her nose. Then he saw her rubbing her eyes and blinking. 'I think you're concussed,' he said shortly, piling four black bin bags, round and puffed with clothes, beside the kitchen table.

She pressed her palms to her forehead. 'Probably.' She turned both her palms into a *Halt*! sign. 'But I'm not going to hospital.' She picked up one bin bag and one overnight case. 'This is all I need for the first night. I'm going to be incredibly rude and ungracious but do you mind if I go to bed?'

'No prob.' He waited until she'd clambered up the twisting staircase before adding under his breath, 'You seem pretty good at being rude and ungracious.'

Chapter Two

A bottle of milk. Then a pot of jam. Now a bunch of chrysanthemums, incurved yellow petals silky under Tess's fingertip.

Somebody, a reader of too many magazine stories maybe, was leaving daily gifts on her doorstep.

The sun lit the reddening leaves drifting on the brisk breeze into Little Lane and suddenly she wanted to move, go, get into the fresh air instead of hiding like a mole in its hole. Out. It wasn't as if she was accomplishing much indoors, fiddling with the arrangement of her new workroom instead of actually producing any work. After two days her headache and swimming vision had improved, but her neck still felt as if she had an overdose of Viagra stuck in her throat.

As an illustrator, she was used to working from wherever she lived but Honeybun Cottage didn't feel like home, yet. Her new home. Her new hidey-hole.

Her parents' house in Middleton Stoney was once home, also her garden flat in Finchley. The house she'd owned with Olly in Brentwood should've been home.

She was away from Olly.

And away from her parents, James and Mari.

She especially wanted to be away from her father, who had taken an uncomfortably philosophical view of what Olly had done, saying, 'He must have had his reasons.' James had always got on well with Olly.

When Olly changed his mind about loving her forever, her first instinct hadn't been to run to her parents; but she had wanted to be just about anywhere except that house where every empty room reminded her of what Olly had done.

And then she'd been ill and her parents' house had been the obvious place for that, good or bad, depending how you looked at it. But now she was living in Middledip where she knew nobody. And she was glad.

Honeybun Cottage was small and sweet with its uneven walls, black doors, wonky lattice windows and mossy tiled roof. James had negotiated for much of the furniture, which The Commuters had bought in turn from the estate of the previous owner, no doubt the 'Herbie' that the garage man, Ratty, had referred to. Desperate to discharge frightening, escalating debt, they'd settled for a stupid price for the carved oak furniture.

'But,' she warned the old walls, as she listened to her footfalls on the quarry-tiled floor, 'don't get too used to me. I don't always stick around. Sometimes, I like being away from prying eyes.'

The first time had been when her looming A levels stressed her out. She'd reappeared in time for the exams; but had been where no one knew or cared why she was there, long enough to acquire the taste for the delicious, naughty distance from real life. Four days in the Cotswolds, here. A month in France, there.

She found her purse and gave into her compulsion to escape the house. She'd go shopping; she'd enquire about who might have been leaving kind offerings. Village shop proprietors were omniscient.

At the Cross, opposite MAR Motors, the sign over the shop door read 'A. & G. Crowther'. The door pinged open to reveal shelves to the ceiling, a middle-aged lady and a girl with twin enquiring expressions above smart grey smocks.

'You're from Honeybun! Seen you going in and out.' *Gwen Crowther* the lady's badge declared.

Tess hovered on red and grey vinyl tiles. 'That's right.'

'Settling in all right? Nice little place, Honeybun. What can I get you, duck?'

'Apples, please, a bag. And oranges.' She didn't look at the biscuits, waiting to seduce. Away from Mari's sugar-stocked kitchen she was going to make room in her waistbands. 'Tomato soup. And a loaf.'

Before parting with the change, *Julie* – said the other name pin – and Mrs Crowther closed in adroitly on the subject of Tess. 'And do you work, duck? An *illustrator*! An artist, really, then? Never known an illustrator, have you, Julie? What do you illustrate?'

Tess shuffled. 'Folk tales, animals and dragons. Kids' stuff, whimsy.'

'Books 'n' that, then?'

'And cards.' Looking over at the racked cellophaned greeting cards, Tess recognised some of Crowther's stock. She pointed quickly. 'That's one of mine.' Little wolves dressed in breeches and aproned frocks, with toothy grins and feathered ears. The card company was a useful source of income, providing bits and pieces between commissions of book work obtained by Kitty, her agent. The wolves had recently been reproduced on mugs as well, another fee.

Olly had wanted her to design something funky, had urged her to try and break into CD covers, implying that her chosen market must be of a lesser quality. CD covers came under design, not illustration; there were few openings and little money in it – but trust Olly to ignore little things like that.

Mrs Crowther gaped. 'Get away!'

'Really? *You* drew that? Oh, sign one for me!' Julie, flicking back her long blonde bunches, snatched up a birthday card and stripped away the wrapping. 'Where's a pen? You don't mind, do you?'

"Course not.' Tess wiped her palms on her jeans, scribbled *Best wishes, Tess Riddell* self-consciously on the front, alongside the T inside the little star that she added discreetly to her illustrations.

She was out of practice at being sociable, felt worn out by such beady interest. But, as supposed, Mrs Crowther could pinpoint the likely giver of gifts. 'That'll be Lucasta Meredith at Pennybun Cottage, I'll bet! That's her style.'

'Where's Pennybun?'

Mrs Crowther snorted with amusement. 'Next door to you!'

'I didn't know there was anything but trees next door to me –' She scurried aside as Mrs Crowther rushed to the door to help drag in a tandem buggy, disregarding Tess instantly. 'Hello Angel! *Hello* Toby, hello baby Jenna!'

The little boy in the front seat of the buggy looked up at Tess. 'My daddy's in prison.'

His mother corrected him gently. 'Preston.'

Tess smiled politely and made for the door.

Breaking off simultaneous conversations with the pretty mother and sturdy son, Mrs Crowther called after her, 'Fifty steps past your gate, my duck, you'll see old Pennybun Cottage.'

As the door swung behind her, she heard, 'Is that the new one from Honeybun?' She grinned. Looked across at the garage; scowled.

Last night, Jos had dropped in an invoice for the tow into the village. Jos was nice, she couldn't stay wary with him for more than the two minutes it took him to pull out a chair and invite himself for coffee. The biker gear disguised a real sweetheart.

Must pay, next stop.

That abrupt, sarcastic man. Yuk. She could always write a cheque, pop it through the door when they were shut?

Yes, she'd do that.

'No, you won't!' she muttered crossly to herself. 'He doesn't worry you! You can deal with annoying gits, you're not a wimp.'

Crossing the forecourt, she took a good look at her Freelander, still under the tarpaulin, and almost bowled into Ratty, right by the door. Damn, the surly pirate. She'd hoped to deal with one of the others.

She whisked out her credit card. 'I've come to pay my bill.'

'Great.' He glanced up from the falling-apart manual in his oily hands. 'So your insurance company insisted on the repair being done by Land Rover? They're picking it up later.' His voice was clipped, accentless.

She flushed. 'You were right about that.'

He grinned. He looked more relaxed today. 'They'll do a good job. And if your policy allows for a courtesy car ... well, I haven't got one. But there was no chassis damage and the engine still runs. It's just cosmetic stuff, bolting on the new panels and lights – looks worse than it is. Feeling OK, now?'

She pushed back her hair that was blowing out of its clasp. Flushed, self-conscious under his intent gaze. 'A bit stiff. Nothing to worry about.' Then, as an afterthought, 'Thanks for asking. And for delivering my stuff.'

'No prob.' He returned to his reading.

He gave her time to march away across the forecourt.

Then, 'She paid,' Ratty told Pete's legs. 'Funny woman.' He turned a page that was no longer attached to the manual. 'Amazing colouring, hasn't she? When her hair was wet it looked nothing special. But it's extraordinary – kind of amber.'

'Who?' Pete's hollow voice floated up through the engine compartment and out of the open bonnet of an MG Midget.

'The funny woman from Honeybun who pranged the wrecker.' Not auburn, not blonde, somewhere between. Long, long hair swung carelessly in a thick ponytail. *Turquoise* eyes, like in a romantic novel. Alive, those eyes, in a face bearing the slightest sprinkling of freckles. Unusual, she was. A pair of studs in one ear, a pair of big hoops in the other, gold bands, some patterned, some plain, all without stones, on every long, upturned finger but not the thumbs.

'But "funny"?'

A pause. 'Interesting.'

Pennybun Cottage proved to be snuggled into the trees only a few yards from the end of Tess's garden. A mirror image of Honeybun Cottage in a teeming garden of big white daisies, golden rod, the last hollyhocks taller than herself, papery old laburnum pods rustling as she wandered to the door, obligatory deepest red rose around the doorway ...

'Good morning, dear! You're the new one –'

'– from Honeybun,' she agreed. Before she'd lifted her hand to the door, before she'd completely made up her mind to knock, even, the door was opening and Lucasta Meredith was waving her in like an old friend. A silvery chignon complemented a dress patterned in eight shades of blue, a stick propping up a walk that had become a jerky dance. Lucasta scarcely looked capable of walking round to Honeybun with her little gifts.

Tess was ushered into a parlour of hanging plants, glass and ivory ornaments, with a floral cottage suite nestled in the middle.

'Tea? Coffee? Sometimes you younger ones prefer ...?' Lucasta swung open a spindly-legged black japanned cabinet, exhibiting a fine selection of bottled lagers and alcopops.

Tess grinned to see club-trendy booze where she'd expect sherry. 'Tea's fine.' She flicked a glance at her watch. She hadn't meant to get involved in a tea ceremony. If she'd thought at all, it was that she'd offer quick thanks for the doorstep gifts and go home.

To do what? Wander round in circles achieving very little? Maybe think about a card illustration but not begin it? She gazed at the dull sheen elegance of a Liberty pewter tea set complete with raffia handles. She must start work. Over the past year she'd lost the habit.

Along with the tea in tiny cups of eggshell china, Lucasta produced crudités and cheese dip, chips of carrot, celery and red pepper. One old lady who'd broken away from petticoat tails, evidently.

And she admitted happily to being the doorstep-gift giver. 'Just to make you welcome, dear. Are you meeting people?'

'Not really.'

'I said to Miles that the young lady had moved into Honeybun. Do try the peppers, I grew them, Miles watered them for me. Or do you prefer biscuits? I always worry that they clog the heart.'

Tess let Lucasta shoulder the bulk of the conversational burden as she munched and sipped, Lucasta lifting the pot in both knobbly knuckled hands, wincing, to refill the dinky cups. 'Are you feeling better? And is your vehicle mended now?'

Oh God. A nosy neighbour.

She fidgeted. She didn't need to be overseen, explanations expected, she shouldn't have come. How long before she could slink away? 'Not yet.'

'Miles said, when I asked if he'd met you, he said your motor needed to go for repair.' From Lucasta's twinkle, it seemed likely that she knew how the Freelander had come to grief.

'Miles?'

'Miles Rattenbury. It's so nice, don't you think, people restoring those old cars? Come from all over to MAR Motors so Miles can sort their precious MGAs or Cadillacs.'

Ah. The old American cars on the forecourt, the ageing Jaguar. 'So he specialises in old cars?'

'Old cars, fast cars, funny cars. It's where the money is, Miles says. Fascinated by anything with an engine when he was young, always hanging round Carlysle's place to have a go with the tractor or mess around with someone's car.' Lucasta waved a matchstick of carrot. 'Making a complete nuisance of himself whenever he could get into the paddock at Silverstone.

'His parents, Lester and Elisabeth, they would've liked him to follow Lester into law, perhaps, or accountancy. But no.' She tipped out the final few bronze drops from the teapot.

'And Miles did a year of an accountancy course but he hated it, dear. *Hated* it. Used to come home and be simply miserable when it was time to go back. So one day, he didn't.'

Crunching celery, Tess considered. Miles Rattenbury; Ratty, sarcastic grumpy guts. But her impressions were shifting slightly. Strip away the tattoos, the sleeve-discarded T-shirts and the oil stains and the well-spoken, educated son of a solicitor began to come into focus.

The anniversary clock on the china cabinet rang the hour softly. Interrupting herself, Lucasta reached for an ivory box and took out a tablet. 'Mustn't forget.' The last draught from her tiny cup. 'Stupid thing. Getting old.'

Before she'd realised she was going to, Tess said, 'I had to take tablets for ages ...' An uncontrolled bleed, that's what the hospital had called it, that terrifying, consciousness-sapping deluge of blood. She waited for a stream of questions but Lucasta just tutted sympathetically.

'Horrible for you.' A frail-boned hand bestowed a momentary, butterfly touch. Then Lucasta launched into a dry monologue about the trials of growing old. 'It's such a bore! I was quite lively, in my day, but I need to write everything down, nowadays.' She flipped open a floral-covered pad of lists and notes in gorgeous script. 'I don't know where I'd be without my notebook. Look here, "put chicken in oven by 10.30 a.m.". How silly can you get?' More pages. 'And here, debating whether to move to sheltered accommodation.' A sudden creaking laugh over a page split into 'plus' and 'minus' columns.

Tess looked, waiting politely for when she could make her excuses.

Lucasta smiled, skin as soft as rose petals, eyes faded to nearly grey, smiled gently. 'I've rattled on! I won't keep you.'

On her feet like a dog hearing its lead clinking, Tess paused at the front door. In the interests of graciousness, she ought to offer something in return for the little gifts. 'You know where I am if you need anything.'

Lucasta creaked another laugh, tapping her stick. 'Miles keeps an eye, though I've *told* him there's no obligation. I'm used to looking after myself, my husband and I kept separate establishments.'

Wrong-footed, Tess managed only, 'Really?'

Grey-blue eyes gazed across the garden. 'It's what we did in those days. Live apart, remain married. Pointless. Wasting our lives.' Another touch of the fragile hand. 'At least there's Miles.'

Tess escaped, wondering what Miles Rattenbury had to do with anything.

And then, as she walked the few yards home, there he was, black curls swinging across his forehead, turning into

17

the lane. A raised hand, perfunctory. She returned the smallest possible wave and bobbed through her own gate.

Workroom. To kid herself that she was doing some work she opened two new files, side by side, on her Mac. The first headed *Every Day*, the second *Overall*. Under *Every Day* she began a list, just like Lucasta's: *work, correspondence, walk, shopping, read*.

Moving to *Overall* she typed: *be positive, stop looking back, relax, phone home sometimes, go out, give in to the Curse when you have to, don't eat sugar, don't buy a television, get on with your life*.

Back to *Every Day: eat sensibly*.

A burst of energy, another new file, *To Do*. A quick glance around the workroom. *Roughs for book jacket, ideas for two new wolf drawings*.

Back to *Overall*, and *finance*. Royalty cheques had come in whilst she'd been ill. Funds were accumulating. Grandmother leaving her capital had helped start the ball rolling; James's dealings had improved her position. And, of course, she was successful. She sometimes forgot that.

Under all three headings she added, *SURVIVE WITHOUT OLLY!*

With the lists stuck up on the wall, she got down, finally, to sorting the boxes, pads, portfolios and spilling folders.

At bedtime she wrote *begun* by *roughs*, and ticked *phone home*.

'Did you realise ...?'

Tess woke from her dreaming study of the rippling countryside's geometric browns and late dusty yellows and greens. Shook her head to clear the image of the baby that never was, that had never focused or grasped puffs of air with starfish hands. Never cried. Never fed. Never been a warm weight in her arms.

The baby that had quit her body and, minuscule and unformed as it had been, left an awful, gaping hollow in its place.

The man, striding up the hill in waxed jacket and green gumboots, glared from under a mop of brown floppy hair. Tess rose, warily. He didn't seem too pleased to see her.

'You've left the footpath.'

'Oh, I'm sorr—'

'I'll have to ask you to leave. My father thinks all walkers are hell-bent on ignorant destruction.'

She flushed. The morning's sketches had eaten the day until she'd dashed out to grab a last slice of autumn daylight. She'd so enjoyed the walk, the wind whisking her spirits, that she'd forgotten that large bits of countryside belonged to people.

Embarrassed, she turned to battle through the long grass up the hill. Then, realising the entrance into the copse lay to the right, changed direction. Or did it? She changed again. Halted.

Then the man was at her side, brown eyes kinder. 'I've startled you. But we've had such a packet of trouble recently, my father gets so infuriated! We've had travellers on the land, crops spoilt, place turned into a furniture dump.'

He had an attractive smile. Tentatively, smoothing stray hanks of hair back behind her ears, Tess tried out her own smile in response. 'I didn't mean to trespass.' Watched, with satisfaction, his eyes become interested. Nice eyes, too.

He seemed now to be recovering his manners. 'Let me walk you a little way.' He led her towards an opening that Tess now recognised quite plainly as the way home. 'Are you visiting the village? Oh, *you're* the new one from Honeybun!'

By the time they'd stumped back along the uneven

footpath, pace slowing as conversation quickened, and he'd delivered her to the edge of the village, she was laughing and chatting as if they were old friends. She'd learnt that his family, the Carlysles, owned the estate, and that he, Simeon, helped with the management, 'mainly by keeping out of everyone's way'. He let his arm brush against hers as they walked, and made shameless use of his terrific smile.

And, somehow, she found herself agreeing to let him take her to the bonfire night on the estate later in the week. 'All the village'll be there, beer and hot dogs, great night.' He glanced at his watch. 'Must go! Pick you up at six on the fifth?'

Marching up Port Road and Cross Street, Tess assessed Simeon Carlysle. Pleasantly friendly compared to Miles Rattenbury, he'd liked her, had been aware of her body, she'd caught him peeking. When she'd glanced back as she walked away, he'd been staring after her. Balm to her flattened ego.

He seemed harmless. Having a Seriously Nice Man interested in her would cheer her up a bit.

Absorbed in these thoughts, she stopped abruptly when she reached the bronze stone and slate roof of the village pub, The Three Fishes. She'd managed to turn the wrong way up Main Road.

But the pub looked inviting. Tubs of ivy, lights shining into the dusk, the sound of a guitar. *In you go, then. Mmmm ... is it a good idea? Yes, no one's going to bite you!*

Initially, the buzz of after-work drinkers seemed welcoming enough. Someone was playing the guitar and singing a song that she'd heard Sting sing. But, as she stepped resolutely into the front-room atmosphere, she saw that it was Ratty, cradling the guitar, perched on a stool with his back to the bar. When he saw her, he stopped singing. The buzz halted as sharply.

Every head turned. *It's a bad idea.*

She froze. *Smile! Order a drink, nod at the men from the garage.* The sudden silence had not been – could not be – planned to make her feel like an intruder.

But ... Spinning suddenly, she ducked her head and blundered back through the door, hands clammy, heart bumping. She wasn't ready, yet.

Chapter Three

'You're not having a good day, are you?' Tess studied the house spider as it floated, despairing legs spread, in her bleach-laced floor-washing water. 'Drowning and poisoned. I wonder which will kill you?'

'D'you generally talk to buckets?'

Tess jumped. The young mum she'd seen in the shop with the buggy was hovering by the open door, enquiring eyes smiling.

Carefully, Tess scooped up the casualty. 'I'm counselling a dying spider.'

The intruder grinned like a pixie. 'Kind of you. A big dog hasn't come in here, has he? Springer?' She dangled an empty collar.

Tess wiped damp hands. 'Don't think so.'

Rapid remarks carried the visitor into the room. 'We haven't met properly. You know Pete Sissins, from Ratty's garage? We're married, I'm Angel. Stupid name, isn't it – Mrs Sissins. Missississins. Mustn't be long, I've parked the children at your gate.' A backward step, a peep to check. 'It's Ratty's wretched dog, anyway, whenever he's at an auction good old Angel gets stupid dog McLaren to mind, McLaren the escape artist. As if I haven't got enough with two tiny kids!'

'Absolutely.' Tess wiped her hands again, wondering whether to invite Angel to stay. Or to offer to help find the dog.

But a fresh subject was already on Angel's lips. 'I want the kids to sleep so they won't be grizzly this evening. Simeon says he's invited you to the bonfire bash?'

Tess nodded, unsurprised that Angel and Simeon knew each other. Such was village life.

A laughing-faced springer appeared casually at the door, head on one side, much like Angel. '*Here's* McLaren, look!' Angel lunged with the collar. 'Don't put your dirty paws on the nice lady's floor!'

'Doesn't matter.'

'He's like his master, never knows when he's not welcome.' Angel laughed, the comfortable laugh exchanged between friends. Tess felt a warmth awakening in response.

Backing towards the door with the dog, Angel kept up a stream of chat. 'So shall I see you tonight? Oh, *stupid* dog!' Angel giggled as McLaren, applying the brakes, slipped collar and lead again to have another look at Tess, tongue lolling. Tess laughed, too. 'Yes, I'll see you at the bonfire party.' Simeon seemed easy, amiable company, Angel open to friendly overtures. Maybe a few friends would lift her, make everything fall into place. Middledip could be a kind of emotional Wonderbra.

'Tess, if you're there, pick up! It's Kitty.'

Kitty, forthright, brisk, clear-sighted, was Tess's agent, working from a large desk in a small office in the King's Road, flicking through work submitted on spec by 'supplicants' and caressing a marmalade cat. Her enthusiasm, when Tess finally announced her readiness to return to full book work, had been reassuring. Kitty valued a good illustrator.

Tess snatched up the phone, frowning at her hair in the mirror. It needed to be washed before the bonfire party. 'Hi Kitty! Been to Bologna?' Kitty would've spent a hellish, frenetic few days at the children's book fair discussing the agency portfolio with a different publisher every half an hour, stirring up interest in her artists. Tess was hoping to benefit.

'Haven't I just and haven't I got *such* a job for you!' Kitty's enthusiasm rang down the line. '*The Dragons of Diggleditch* is being relaunched – possibly the whole series – and they want a new illustrator!'

Tess forgot her hair, bonfire night, Middledip and Simeon Carlysle. *The Dragons* series had been legendary, stories from ancient Britain; of Slider skating on oversized feet, Winder slithering like an enormous worm, and Slinker, a sort of dachshund of a dragon. In a time long before this, these mischievous dragons had inhabited Pennine caves above a hard-working village, stirring up trouble between the villagers and other forest creatures. Always, the dragons, naughty rather than bad, after a rampant adventure of greed and magic, ended up satisfactorily bested by the honesty and intelligence of the villagers.

'The original illustrations are dated. They like your work!'

Tess's mind began to fill with visions of grinning dragons, pot-bellied and gorgeously coloured. She picked up a pencil, drawing a spiky tail with quick, sure movements. 'Wow, will they use me?'

'Can you hack it?'

'Positively!'

'The first anthology will be nine stories, two full pages, a half and two decorative borders to each story, plus end papers, plus jacket. Probably at least two further anthologies later.'

'Definitely.'

'I can't recommend you if you feel any doubt. Particularly in view of the further anthologies in the pipeline.'

'Didn't I get those jacket roughs to you on time? Honestly, don't worry, I want to do this.'

Kitty's friend-voice replaced her business-voice. Theirs

was about the only friendship that had survived the Olly Age; Kitty, not only necessary to Tess's career, was not easily put off by a possessive man skilled in separating his woman from influences other than his own.

'I don't want you going backwards health-wise because I suggest a commission that's too much for you. Olly rather put you through the wringer.'

Tess closed her eyes, wishing she could shut her mind so easily against the chilly knowledge that she hadn't been strong when she'd needed to be. 'I don't know how I could let a man *submerge* me like that. Why I tried to be his idea of what I ought to be.'

'First love's meant to be painful. You get over it and make way for something genuine and lasting and totally beautiful.'

'But what if second love turns out to be painful, too? At the moment I feel as if I'll never even want sex again, because ...' The words jammed in her throat.

Kitty's voice softened. 'Because of the miscarriage? That's going to hurt you for a long time.'

Tess looked away from the mirror. 'Every day. Just because the baby wasn't planned doesn't mean I wanted it to die! I should have known it was there, protected it. I must've done something to cause what happened.'

'You didn't!'

'Then why did I haemorrhage? That doesn't *just happen*.'

Kitty sighed. 'Come on, Tess, we've been over this. What did the doctors say?'

Silence. Then, 'Sometimes it just happens.'

'That's right. It doesn't matter how careful the mother is. Sometimes it just happens.'

It just happens. Tess could see the hospital ward, cheerful lemon-yellow curtains around the beds full of empty women. Hear the doctor's voice, 'I've no neat explanation to offer, it just happens'. Words said a thousand times to a thousand bewildered women. Savagely, she changed the subject. 'Tell them yes to the *Dragons* commission.'

Buoyed by such fabulous luck, she strolled up to Gwen Crowther's crammed shop for hair conditioner and a face pack.

Forget Olly and the crippling disappointment; leave behind the brief pregnancy, rise above the illness. She had a great commission and there was a party to look forward to.

But, later, at the party, in the dark night, Tess was having a horrible time.

The muddy field was an oasis of bobbing orange light from a bonfire built to burn all evening. Stalls sold beer, hot dogs and lanterns to the inhabitants of Middledip, who churned the mud as they waited for the fireworks.

What had become of the sweet man who'd escorted her courteously off the Carlysle estate? He'd vanished, to be replaced by a drunken arse. Simeon had dived into the hot rum punch the moment they arrived and then swilled beer by the gallon. Tess had begun to hate everything about the big, dizzy lump with his insistent, heavy arm dragging on her shoulders.

The evening had promised better.

In jeans, boots and a long black coat, newly conditioned hair slithering in a curtain down her back, she'd been fairly satisfied with her reflection.

Simeon had arrived promptly in a tiny, dark-green sports car. 'Frog-eyed Sprite, Ratty got it for me. Let me help you with the seat belt.' He'd adjusted the sliding buckles of the belt, the old fixed kind, the backs of his fingers brushing her shoulder, her chest, finally her lap. That should have rung the first alarm.

But the bonfire party had been fun, at first. Simeon knew everybody. Angel and Pete had stopped to chat, Jos waved and Ratty raised a brief hand, passing his gaze over her. Everyone, mingling with easy familiarity, was jolly and friendly.

But it hadn't lasted.

Simeon's arm became an intrusive fixture as he drank, dragging her from group to group, his cheek meatily against hers as he roared with loud, beery-breathed laughter. Miserably, Tess lifted her face to the metallic rain of fireworks as all the children went, 'Ooooooh!', wishing that she'd brought her own vehicle so that she could scarper.

Angel reappeared after the firework display, frowning, clasping a sleeping toddler. Pete carried Toby on his shoulders. 'We've got to take the kids home. Simeon's well oiled, isn't he?'

Tess attempted again to escape the possessive arm while its owner honked at a conversation she was ignoring. 'Can I have a lift with you? I'm not going to get in a car with this drunkard!'

Angel made an agonised face. 'There's no room in our car between the two kiddie seats. Ratty will have space, though.'

She might prefer to ride home bare-arsed on a porcupine's back than ask Ratty. But, 'Right, thanks,' she said.

Watching Angel and Pete pick their way to their car, a happy family with their sleepy offspring, she felt a settling of disappointment. Light and friendliness seemed to drain away as the families departed, leaving only adults indulging in serious drinking in the bonfire's sinister dipping light.

The crashing of Simeon's conversation was unrelenting. A headache pounded between Tess's eyes, her feet were cold to the bone.

Maybe she ought to sidle over to Jos – or even Ratty as she was getting desperate – and cadge a lift? Simeon was in no fit state to drive. Yes, she'd pick her moment and do that. In fact she'd do it now.

But her effort to escape the insistent arm seemed to focus Simeon's attention. He paused at last, staggering and beaming. 'C'm'over here a minute. Before we go.'

'You're drunk. I'll get a ride back to the village.' She made another attempt to free herself.

He smiled as his arm tightened, crooning with drunken emphasis. 'You're very *nice* and I want to *show* you *something*.'

'Get lost, Simeon! I'm getting a lift.'

'OK, OK!' He swayed, dolefully. 'Take you to the car park.'

Glad to be heading in the right direction, she allowed herself – actually allowed it, she must be *thick* – to be steered through the mire towards the darkness of the parking area.

Simeon slid to a halt by a parked camper van, propelling her towards the denseness of the shadows. 'Just a minute.' He balanced his beer carefully on the van roof. And with unexpected precision swung her expertly between his body and the van side.

'No!' Too late. Her squawk was snipped off by the accuracy of Simeon's plunging mouth. Strong arms pegged hers to her sides, his weight pinning her to unyielding metal.

Unprepared, she was trapped. She couldn't avoid his tongue thrusting into her mouth, nor his body pushing against her. It was abrupt, overwhelming, awful! Could she bite him hard enough to make him stop? *Stop,* she should scream, *no*! Her nails should be finding his eye sockets, her knee jabbing into his groin. But his mouth kept hers propped unwillingly open, her body locked by his weight.

The tongue intruded unrelentingly in her mouth as Simeon proved his kissing stamina. If it could be called kissing.

He broke away eventually to pant, 'You sexy handful!' Tess turned her face to avoid his lips, struggling for breath and, fruitlessly, to yank her arms free. 'No!'

Leaning harder, Simeon bit her neck sharply. 'Yum!'

'*Stop!*' The protest was again choked off by his wet, returning mouth.

His greater height blocked her vision, his weight engulfed her. She couldn't even free a hand to slap him. Leaning heavily on her chest, he panted, 'It's OK.'

Her frantic wheezes, 'No!' and 'Don't!', were lost as he crushed her against the van, blocking her airway with his repulsive mouth and tongue until her ears rang.

It was going on, on forever! No breath, no voice. Dizzy. Suffocating, she was suffocating under the mouth mashed over hers, panicking, no air, God-God, no air, screaming inside. Would nobody notice? A heart-chill. What if he tried to go further?

Simeon's teeth scraped her lips, her chest heaved on empty, unconsciousness waited with the black swarms edging her vision.

'Having a good time, Simeon?' Those hard, accentless tones, she'd never dreamt of being so glad to hear them. Relief! Simeon would back off with Ratty watching. Twisting, reducing the burden, ignoring Tess's pained whoop as sufficient oxygen finally entered unwillingly deflated lungs, Simeon rested his forearm casually across her chest. 'Ratty! Just the man! Got a condom?'

'What?' What was intended as an enraged scream emerged as a croak. '*What?*'

'Some in the car. Struck lucky?' Ratty laughed, shortly.

Tess's fear turned to bloody red fury.

'Think so! Gorgeous armful, don't you think? Love –'

'*Basta-a-a-rd*!' Rage and relaxation of Simeon's grip gave Tess's knee such upward impetus into his softest parts that she was free before his shrill howl had died. Bursting past Ratty's smirk and Jos's puzzled frown, humiliation, rage and mortification fuelled her jerky, slithering strides. 'Keep away!' she flung hoarsely behind her. 'Keep right away, you shits!'

She heard, behind her as she floundered, away, away, must get away, a sudden cold snap in Ratty's voice. 'Things getting out of hand, Sim?'

And Simeon groaning sulkily. 'Only a bit of fun. Only what she'd expect.'

'Don't think she liked it.' The last word coincided with a dull, metallic clang.

Tears blinding. Slipping feet running. Pausing, retching. Brushing past the parked cars and puffing into the lane. Sniffing, stumbling. Bastard, bastard men. Three miles home behind the hedges, shrinking into the hawthorn every time a car passed.

Bastard men.

Chapter Four

She fell out of bed, the carpet burning her knees, fumbling for the lamp, heart banging, ears rushing. It's OK, OK. OK. Safe in her bed, bedroom, Honeybun Cottage, Middledip.

Trembling, she slid into her robe, wiping her clammy face with the cuff, heart still galloping.

Astounding after Simeon's pass, so brutal and ruthless, that her nightmare should feature e-mail. E-mail! The age's most popular method of communication. E-mail and Olly.

Wadding her hair into a scrunchie, she padded down the twisted staircase, thinking about Olly, his passion for computers, his sensual lips caressing words like *virus* and *network*.

Olly never turned off his mobile. Even lovemaking could be interrupted by a client's call. And why should Tess feel insulted? It was Olly's *work*.

And Tess's work? Well ... it was a job. Its demands weren't so precise, if the deadline was a month away, she had today, tomorrow, whenever, to work.

He never saw her argument that a month's work, after all, took a month.

When she met Olly she'd just moved from a shared house into her own flat in a leafy street in Finchley, off the main road and under the railway bridge. Olly specialised in systems for private clinics and hospitals; they seemed in a position to afford him. None of her previous relationships had prepared her for what she'd feel for Olly. She'd been infatuated. Obsessed, even.

Olly was gorgeous. Olly was popular, glad-handing his way across a favourite pub. Olly was exhilarating.

Tall with a squared, cleft chin, curtains of Nordic-blond silky hair, ice-blue eyes to sweep down to fix on Tess. Before she was ill, of course. Olly was lustful.

A lustful, exhilarating, gorgeous ... control freak. With a temper.

Initially, Olly's intensity had been flattering. 'I just want to be with *you*!' It must have been obsession that prevented her from resisting as her friends gradually faded away. How could she have tolerated it? Or his attitude that, neither creativity nor kids being his thing, illustrating children's books was a risible occupation.

He and his friends had *careers* in IT. Real work.

Despite the permanent question mark she felt she wore in her relationship with Olly, she was flat on her face in love with him. And in lust. Something else he used to manipulate her.

Olly couldn't bear not to get his way. She shuddered as she made herself tea. Once or twice ... well, he'd slapped her face. Not a heavy blow, no bruise to show, just a short cut to Olly winning his argument. And then he'd be horrified and remorseful.

She sipped the tea, drawing her chilled, bare feet under her cotton robe as she looked out into the moonlit garden of Honeybun Cottage.

Even now that she could see Olly Gray for the self-orientated phoney he was, she understood that there had been plenty good in the relationship. They'd had a blast with Olly's friends and their girlfriends, clubs and dinner parties – usually at Tess's flat. Olly wasn't keen on having his space invaded, the apartment with one bedroom and a grey office. Then a diamond ring, the proper announcements, the unusual and expensive presents from Olly's clients. The house hunt; Olly settling, eventually, for the town house in Brentwood through James's contacts. (Olly liked James; he'd never tried to get between James and

Tess.) Tess's flat was sold to provide the deposit, and Olly's rented flat kept on.

'It'll be easier for you to move first,' he said, 'with me working from home.'

'But *I* work from home!'

Olly laughed and kissed the sentence from her lips. 'I know you do but it's not the same. I'll need time to organise the relocation.'

So she moved into the new house alone for the months leading to the wedding that would be in a smart hotel frothing with spring flowers. And it was a lovely bay-windowed house of lofty, airy rooms.

Olly hadn't been able to contribute to the mortgage payments, with rent still to manage along with his everlasting finance company commitments. 'Keeping up with technology is expensive! All right for you technophobes.' He talked as if funds just fell into her hands and her work wasn't a valid earner. She knew she was good in her field but it was difficult to access the appreciative part of Olly.

'Technophobe or not, I can manage the mortgage alone!' she hadn't been able to resist.

He'd glared, and then decided to smile, running his knuckles down her back. 'Yeah, who'd have thought you'd be so good with dosh?'

With two days to the wedding, Tess was in the midst of chaos as she tried to find places for presents. Was Olly ever going to get on with his move? Unlikely though it seemed, was he in the grip of pre-wedding nerves? These days he was preoccupied, absent-minded or just plain absent. Where was he?

She unwrapped their third non-stick wok, telling herself not to worry. He'd turn up any minute, with a plan of the way his hardware was to be organised in his new office, downstairs to give him space. Tess's workroom, upstairs, had been fully functioning for ages.

Unfairly, Olly was now grumbling that Tess was lucky to have moved first and have the entire hassle behind her. Hadn't that been his plan? Anyway, unpacking things she didn't want wasn't her idea of relaxation. She added the wok to the others hanging from the rack, wondering how many stir-fries people expected them to have.

Sod it, she'd finish later.

In a moment she was at the table in the deep blue of her workroom, picking up a pencil. The next book commission wasn't to begin until after the honeymoon that Olly was organising. Somewhere hot and exotic, he'd promised, somewhere beautiful to walk entwined as lovers do. Bahamas? Scilly Isles? With a happy little hop of the heart, she sketched a cat in a wedding dress woven with ribbons, the dress she'd designed herself. Perhaps Africa?

She checked her e-mail. One new message: *Tess, no easy way to say this so will be direct. Given it loads of thought and the idea of moving in with you & your messy workroom has got to me. I've gone cold on the wedding ...* But probably not as cold as her heart as she read his words.

But the casual *I expect you will want to see to the return of the prezzies & whatnot* had evoked a despairing, 'I've only just finished unpacking all the bloody prezzies!'

And, then, a whoosh of reality, as if she'd gone down too fast in a lift. Olly was *jilting* her, to use a melodramatic, old-fashioned word. How could he? Why? What was wrong with her? Was she messy? What had changed for the tall, sexy god who until the last weeks had held her and murmured about love? OK, things had been a bit cooler recently, she'd noticed that – but surely they were just wound up in anticipation of the big day? Was it she who'd wanted the greater commitment?

If so, why had *he* proposed?

And then her parents arrived, ready to attend her wedding on the following Saturday, and she had to confess with floods of tears her failure to keep Olly, to howl out the ruins of her wedding day.

'The *bastard*!' Her mother clasped Tess too tightly to the cushions of her chest.

Her father, James, said very little to Tess, but he spent hours on the telephone dealing in a hushed way with guests and caterers, photographer and cars.

Tess lay on her bed, very still.

But later she overheard her father remark to her mother, 'Olly must have had his reasons.' He must. He must! And they must be down to Tess.

And then she'd miscarried her baby.

It had been safe inside her body and she'd let it seep out.

Steaming cup in hand, she trod back up Honeybun's winding stairs, opening her wardrobe door for the full-length mirror, shrugging out of her robe and nightshirt. She examined her nakedness objectively.

Still a bit generous and soft.

When she'd been thinner and tauter, Olly had gone from lust to indifference in a month.

Last night, in distorted appreciation of her body, Simeon had snogged her half-senseless in a big muddy field.

Men. She shook her head as she dragged out a fresh sweater and jeans. Who could understand them?

She worked for the remainder of the night and into the day on a new wolf illustration, breaking only for coffee and a toasted sandwich.

She watched from the window as Angel came knocking and she explored shades of blue for Slider from *The Dragons of Diggleditch*.

Jos wandered up the drive and shouted for her. But hadn't Jos, however worried-looking, stood by as Simeon Carlysle invaded?

In anticipation of the delicious, plum *Dragons* commission she played with the opacity and fairy-tale colours of gouache and ink. A very thin gouache mix for fragility and delicacy. Ink for emphasis and line. She washed out her pens, turning on the lamp as daylight levelled out to create shadows.

Even when Ratty escorted a sullenly hunched Simeon to rap the door, she paused only to watch them arrive and watch them leave.

She was working. Working like she used to before her life took on the tacky quality of a 'reader's own story' magazine confession – maybe she could sell her story some time, and make three hundred quid?

But, just now, she was working.

'Bloody Sunday. Fine day of rest.' Face burning from the oven, Tess turned the joint, basted the potatoes and slammed the oven door. Her parents, judging from the piddling about she could hear going on in the drive with coats, bags and car keys, had just arrived for their first visit to Honeybun Cottage since she'd moved in. Like having a tooth out, it had to be done, but she wasn't looking forward to it.

She suddenly realised she hadn't given the red wine time to breathe and snatched it up, flinging open the back door at the same time.

Her father patted her shoulder. 'Well, Tess!'

'Hul-lo!' Her mother, smelling of face powder and her brown hair blow-dried back from her face, kissed her cheek, glancing around. 'The table looks nice! Are those Grannie's glasses? Aren't the chrysanths going on a long time, this year?'

Her father tried to take the wine bottle from her hands. 'Shall I do that?' His hair, too, silvering now, was also combed straight back. The pair of them looked as if they'd been in a wind tunnel.

Tess pushed down the twin levers of the corkscrew. 'There, done it! Let me take your coats so you can sit down. Dinner will be about half an hour. Go through to the sitting room.'

The sitting room looked lovely. She'd polished, and vacuumed – even the lampshade, even the cobwebs from between the beams. The fire burned behind the guard and more chrysanthemums glowed from the low table. She managed to settle her parents into the turquoise moquette chairs with sherry and coffee and more or less keep them there whilst she whizzed around in the kitchen. She hated it when Mari hovered, saying, 'Should you be turning the meat?' two seconds before she was going to turn it anyway.

So she made the gravy, poking her head around the door to keep up her end of the conversation then rushing back to catch the gravy before it clamped into jellified lumps, until she could call, 'Come through! Dad, can you pour the wine?'

And the meat was tender and the potatoes crisp and everything was under control, except when Tess knocked over her wine. '*Shit!*'

James blotted his shirt with kitchen roll. 'Doesn't matter.'

Biting her lip, she picked up her glass. 'Sorry, Dad, it has to be red wine, too!'

'Don't worry.' He patted her shoulder and went on with his meal as if he always wore a maroon patch over his heart on his honey-coloured golf shirt. And she knew that her parents really did want the best for her, even if they irritated her like toast crumbs in bed.

Mari cut into her pork and said, 'Red meat?'

Tess gulped her wine. 'If it is, it needs to go back in the oven.' Then she laughed, to show she was joking. And suddenly remembered that James was supposed to be eating mainly white meat and fish because of his cholesterol.

Over dessert, crumble made from apples from Lucasta's garden, it was Mari who asked, in a suitably solemn, measured voice. 'And have you heard from Olly?'

'No. Would you like more custard?'

James took up the baton. 'Ever consider getting in touch?'

'No. I'll make more coffee in a minute. Or tea.'

Mari laid down her spoon, having cleared her plate in a way that was ladylike but deadly efficient. 'We were thinking – you mustn't blame Oliver for everything.'

Tess felt her throat dry. 'I didn't ask him to jilt me and run away.'

James reached across the table and covered her hand. 'We do appreciate how you feel over that, but don't blame him for … *everything*. Everything else. He didn't make you lose the baby. Nor make you ill.'

Mari looked anxious. 'What we mean, Tess, is we'd be happier if you'd talk with him and get rid of some of your bitterness. Then you might not feel this need to seclude yourself over here. You might move nearer home again, to us, then we needn't worry so much.'

Tess began to gather the plates, knowing her hand movements were too fast and uncoordinated; in a minute one of the dishes would crack. 'You needn't worry at all and I'm hardly the globe's diameter away. Let's have a walk before you go.'

It was a brisk walk because Tess set the pace and she needed exercise before she *exploded* with frustration. God, must they be so *bloody* reasonable about Olly? If she wanted to blame him, she would!

Rain flung odd spots against their faces, golden leaves spinning around their ankles and the wind in their ears as they marched to the Cross and up Main Road towards Bettsbrough.

And Tess wondered how quickly she could point her parents towards home.

'Guy, you're a pain in the arse.' Tess sighed down the phone. Wintry rain skittered against the kitchen window like handfuls of gravel. Hardly had she got her parents out of the door and Guy was on the phone! She'd wanted to chill out. Well, that was out of the window!

'Just for a week, Tess, I'll pay you straight back.'

Tess wondered how many times it had happened now; Guy finding himself short and, reluctant to share the information with his wife, Lynette, approaching Tess for funds. Which, when Lynette discovered it as she always did, would make her resent Tess even more.

She sighed again. But Guy was her cousin. All those climbed trees and teenaged exploits counted, the learning together, the lying for each other.

'The bank is being bloody,' he explained apologetically.

'And you're mystified that there's no automatic unlimited overdraft for an unspecified period without collateral? Particularly as you're on their staff?' Tess couldn't help a gurgle of laughter. Poor old Guy, life was tough on disorganised self-servers, sometimes, but Tess loved him. And it wasn't his fault her mum and dad had made her feel stressy. She capitulated. 'I'll send you a cheque.'

'Thing is,' – she could picture Guy rubbing his angular nose at having to go into boring detail – 'I need a couple of hundred cash straightaway or I can't meet the mortgage. I was hoping you could transfer it online ...'

She laughed. 'I'm not hooked up to the Internet here, yet.

Out of luck, Guy.'

He wheedled, 'I'll take you to the cash machine.' She pictured the beginnings of his triumphant grin.

'You do that,' she agreed. Let Guy come out of his way. If she was going to be two hundred pounds out of pocket and in Lynette's bad books again, let Guy drive the necessary miles.

Waiting for the sound of his car in the lane an hour on, she finished her salad and cheese and thought about her *Dragons* illustrations. They were going well; it had seemed a big commission to dive into, but hadn't it been ideal? A project that carried her along into a different world where she needn't worry about people.

People. After the Simeon Carlysle debacle they'd lain in wait for her. Angel to commiserate, her pretty mouth an O of dismay. 'Ratty and Jos just *standing* there like imbeciles! "We didn't realise she was in trouble!" Would you believe it?'

'I'm not sure I do.'

Angel half grinned, lowered her voice. 'Did you know Ratty went for him? Smacked his head on the side of a van! But he wouldn't have left you in that situation intentionally – he said it just looked like a bit of passion, from behind. He's sorry you were ... upset. He did go looking for you but you seemed to disappear.'

Disappearing was something she was good at.

But all of this was irrelevant when Tess, two hundred pounds poorer, sat in the passenger seat of Guy's car feeling the wheels spin impotently beneath them in soft, saturated soil. 'You just about take the bloody biscuit,' she sighed flatly, plaiting the front of her hair. 'Doesn't your brain ever engage? "Let's stop, I need to talk,"' she mimicked. '"Here will do." Straight through a gateway and into a ploughed field, regardless of the fact that my warm, dry home is only a couple of miles away!'

Biting his lip, every emotion typically visible, Guy looked glum. However attractive he was, with his sandy hair and flat-planed face, he had an unparalleled affinity with trouble. After almost an hour of confidences, where Tess learned all about his expensive girlfriend and suspicious wife, they were stuck fast in good English farming soil.

'If you ever *thought*,' she griped, 'it would make the national press.'

Guy sighed. 'Now what do we do?'

Ratty backed the breakdown truck into the gateway, glancing left-right at each post half-hidden by the hedge. He secured the chain, checked clearance and, in a minute, had heaved Guy's car backwards onto solid ground. He grinned through the window at Tess standing in the lane, shoulders hunched against the weather. The funny woman had a talent for calamity.

'*Another* incident in a muddy field? At least I was here for you this time.' The wrath in the startling eyes made him laugh out loud.

'My cousin has the intellect of donkey crap.'

He leant his elbow on the sill. 'Are you continuing your journey with your friend, ma'am, or do you require a ride to the village?'

Indicating her choice by suggesting a bizarre route home to her sheepish-looking cousin, Tess climbed into the cab of the breakdown truck. Ratty watched her fight the seat belt with tight, angry movements.

'Thank you,' she said coldly, ignoring Guy as he waved goodbye.

Ratty put the wrecker in gear. 'Cousin, eh?'

Tess nodded, gingerly fishing long skeins of damp hair from her collar.

Ratty grinned. 'Usually when I have to fish couples out

of muddy fields they're –'

'Well, we weren't! With a wife, a girlfriend and an overdraft, Guy's pretty busy already!'

Chapter Five

Angel, one of the least artful people Tess had ever encountered, had been quite open about her mission to winkle Tess out of her shell. 'Come round!' she insisted. Often. 'I get so fed up stuck at home with the children.'

Slowly, it had become routine for Tess to call at the cottage in Rotten Row at one side of Cross Street, a home full of sunshine colours and children's things. She felt at ease there, and sheltered. The children were easy, too young to judge, speculate, expect. Jenna, walking properly now, was happy with cuddles, food, the noisy entertainment of clapping songs.

As she was asleep now, Tess played with Toby on the floor with Duplo, listening to Angel, ever busy in the wholesale, harassed way of mothers of two small kids, wielding her iron or filling the freezer and churning out cameos of the village into Tess's receptive ears.

'She'll have you broke, that really blonde woman. Lives up in the new village, always at your door for donations.' Or, 'You know Tubb from the pub? You *do*, he's got that wiggle of hair at the front, here ...'

The iron would clatter back onto its stand as Angel shook a pillowcase out with a snap and folded it briskly. With a sigh, she turned to the awful task of ironing work jeans. 'Don't you think Jos is lovely? Quiet compared to the others, but lovely. Poor soul, when his parents split up *neither* of them wanted him! He's been brought up by his grandmother. He keeps geese in his garden, they're ferocious.

'You couldn't be horrible to Jos. He's not as close to Pete and Ratty as they are to each other – it's buy one, get one free with them.' Having conquered the jeans she began folding sleepsuits. "Course, it's cars, cars, with the lads. No, cars *and* women. And the women are the lesser commitment – except Pete and me. Ratty says our marriage is the only half-decent one he knows. He's good as gold, really.'

Tess looked up from the Duplo castle she was creating for Toby. 'Really? Ratty?'

'Generous, funny. Quite balanced.'

'Presumably by a chip of equal size on each shoulder?'

Angel laughed delightedly, no doubt saving that one up to share with Ratty later, flicking a shirt round the ironing board. 'When he's good, he's great; when he's bad, he's dire. But he can be really, extraordinarily kind – look how he is with Lucasta. He's amazingly successful with women but he doesn't involve Pete – probably because he knows I'd kill him. Apart from the garage and his place up Ladies Lane, he owns three houses in the village. Buys them, rents them out. He's a right moneymaker and he says he'll leave it all to Toby and Jenna if he never has his own offspring. He loves the kids.'

Tess began to select square blocks for her castle's crenellations. 'They're gorgeous children. I'm becoming one of those sad singles who tag themselves onto a family.'

'Oh well. I'm glad you picked this family.'

'Don't want a castle any more,' said Toby, yanking Tess's careful crenellations off again. Just returned from playgroup, he really needed a nap but was resisting.

'Draw him something,' Angel suggested, stowing the ironing board away. 'There are crayons and things in that yellow box.'

'What shall I draw?' Tess looked enquiringly at Toby, his sturdy blondness, peachy skin and intent expression.

'My pig.' Toby carted a toy pig everywhere by a string

that once used to activate a voice. 'Draw Nigel.' And he posed the soft toy, flaccid and drunk with too much hugging, on the carpet.

Full-length on the itchy smoky greyness of Angel's woollen carpet, head supported on hand, ponytail looped over a shoulder, Tess took the pad that Toby plonked in front of her, feeling the familiar smoothness of paper under her fingers, and drew Nigel with swift, minimal strokes of soft blue crayon. Snout, trotters, wiggly tail, one bent ear.

Toby hotched closer. 'Draw Nigel playing football!'

And, wax crayon, blunt pencil and brushy old felt pen her tools, she drew Nigel playing football in the England strip, porcine face pursed in endeavour. Running, heading, flat out in agony after a bad tackle.

'Now driving,' Toby demanded, breathing hard over the page, getting his head in the way.

Angel, a pile of clean clothes in her hands, craned to see the herd of Nigels cavorting about the large, cheap sheet of paper. 'Oh *wow*! That's so impressive! Aren't you talented?' She lingered to witness Nigel appearing on the page, a too-small sports car careering away with him, ears and pendulous cheeks pushed back by the draught, trotters protruding from T-shirt armholes and braced in panic on the steering wheel. Absently, she drew two tiny tattoos.

Toby slapped the page with a gleeful, podgy hand. 'Watty got pictures like that!'

'Really?' She selected a once-black felt pen and added curly hair blowing back from the piggy features in the wind. And stubble.

'Do the car green,' insisted Toby, so close to the pad as to almost obscure the view, his hot little arm sweatily against hers, his head smelling of shampoo and biscuits.

His approval was heady stuff. Between it and Angel's awe-struck, 'You're *brilliant*,' Tess began to enjoy herself as her crayon flew over Nigel after Nigel. Too much to notice the back door opening.

But nothing so vital escaped Toby. He jumped up. 'Look, Watty!' he shouted. 'Tess drawed Nigel, driving!'

Huge from her startled perspective, Ratty loomed above. 'Clever. Very flattering. I hope we don't have pork for lunch?' He shot her a curious look, then smiled to prove he could bear being caricatured as a pig.

Tess hadn't realised anyone else was invited for lunch, although entertaining was definitely one of Angel's things. All the time that used to be spent at the pub pre-children was now spent at Pete and Angel's house. Ratty, at least, seemed to half live there.

'Steak pie, wedges and salad. Can you lay the table, Ratty, if you've finished admiring your portrait? Tess, do you prefer mustard dressing or mayonnaise? Will Jos be very long, Ratty? I hope one of you can work this bottle opener ...'

Tess was uncertain how she felt at being so ... *included*. She wasn't sure if she was ready for it. But Jos and Pete had come in, too, and to leave when there was a place set for her wouldn't be friendly.

The page of Nigels was passed around with the salad, Pete and Jos both grinning at Ratty.

'Would you paint a proper picture of Nigel for Toby's room?' Angel asked. 'How much will it cost?'

Tess considered as she chewed her mouthful. 'Another glass of wine.'

'Wow, that's a bargain! I'll trim your hair sometime,' Angel exchanged. Her hair and beauty salon in Bettsbrough, Tess already knew, had a bubbly, brisk manager until Angel got the kids up to school age. She was always being asked when she was going back and she always groaned about how much she missed it, the prettiness and the girlie atmosphere.

After lunch, concentrating on Toby in order to remain on the edges of the adult conversation, conscious of not being part of the easy familiarity the others shared, Tess drew him quick sketches of the three now familiar Dragons of Diggleditch. Slinker, the green-backed lizard-like one with red belly, amber spines and eyes. Slider, blue and mauve with a gun-barrel snout and tongue coiled neatly behind smirking fangs, sliding on huge feet. Finally, her favourite, Winder in cheery primrose with a green tummy and crimson spines, the inept one who kept rushing his snaky body into a *knot*.

Toby was rapt at being able to order what he'd like to emerge on the page. 'Another Winder! Draw the knot.'

From the armchair, Ratty nudged Toby with his toe. 'Swap you a Spiderman comic for the drawing of Nigel in the sports car?'

Toby protected his assets better than that. 'Got Spiderman already,' he growled, clutching his drawing to his chest.

'Look, they've got the TR4 going – lunatics!'

Tess watched a noisy contraption heading up the lane towards them. Better, in her opinion, if their walk along Port Road, huddled into thickest jackets, between slapping hawthorn hedges budding already, had remained uninterrupted. Despite being included in lunch a few days ago, she still wasn't sure of her welcome with anyone but Angel.

But there was no ignoring Ratty and Pete roaring up on a 'vehicle', for want of a better description – the chassis of a sports car, apparently short of the body shell, kitchen chair seats held in place precariously by bungee elastic luggage straps and a dashboard sprouting a taped-on rear-view mirror.

Angel was obviously far more impressed than Tess by this phenomenon, circling admiringly whilst Tess rested her hand on the tandem buggy where both children – though Toby, had he been awake to ask, would declare himself too old – slept in cellular blankets.

Obviously an event, this, a landmark. Something she couldn't appreciate.

Pete bellowed over the considerable noise of the uncovered Triumph engine. 'We're going to the pub to celebrate, hop on!'

'Be sensible, how can I?' Angel indicated the buggy, throwing a yearning and, to Tess, incomprehensible look at the rear passenger accommodation, or lack of it.

Tess hunched her shoulders. 'I'll have the kids. You go.' Patchy drizzle dashed against her cheeks but the bundles wrapped up beneath their protective plastic cover in the buggy dozed, uncaring.

Angel's pixie face lit on a smile. 'But that's not fair on you, Tess! Don't you want to go?'

As the invitation hadn't been directed at her, Tess had no problems with this one. 'I can go any time. I'll go another day.'

So the car rumbled off, Angel laughing and glowing from her uncomfortable perch in the rear, waving, calling 'Owe you one!', Pete shouting 'Cheers!'

'Cheers,' echoed Ratty, with what might have been approval. 'I see you've got the Freelander back?'

She nodded.

He winked. 'Try and keep it under control.'

The drizzly period had taken most of February to clear.

But what a day, now that it had! Tess gazed up at a china blue sky heralding glorious, fresh, sudden early spring when, after the winter of long jumpers and short days, it became briefly warm enough for shirtsleeves. Her first winter at Honeybun had been good, the months passing quickly with the joy of work that was going well, with walks in wild weather, which sometimes suited her mood.

But it was great to see the sun.

By the rockery, on the crazy paving where the thyme grew through the cracks and smelt peppery, she turned her face to the welcome warmth, breathed in, sighed out. Daffodils, forsythia, busy birds singing to the breeze. She hitched up her jeans.

Her clothes were no longer tight. Away from her mother's sugar-based love she'd returned easily to her natural weight. She pulled the waistband away from her skin, marvelling at the gap that appeared. She could find her other jeans and –

'Need any help down there?'

Whipping her hands away and spinning guiltily, she found Ratty leaning on her gate. Wicked grin. Wicked eyes. Curls lifting gently from his forehead. Tattoos over the cords of his arms exposed to the sunshine.

His grin widened as she coloured.

Her hair sailed about her shoulders in the spring breeze. 'I didn't realise you were there.'

'Guessed not. Coming for a drink?'

'*Me?*'

'You said you'd come, "another day".'

'But that was only ...' When Angel had been longing to join the grown-ups for an hour in the pub, and Tess had sought something to say that would persuade her.

Straightening, Ratty shook back his hair. 'I'm going to visit Lucasta. Call for you about twelve thirty?'

'Um, right. Yeah, OK.' She answered his parting nod with a flushed one of her own. So it was true, as Angel held out. He could be nice. Amazing.

Still more amazing, when he called at Honeybun to walk her briskly up Main Road to The Three Fishes, past the run of closed doors at MAR Motors, through the Cross, past Great End and finally into the pub opposite the ford, and, in the burbling beery warmth of a village pub on a Sunday afternoon, she found herself having a good time.

Who was this stranger, buying her wine, slouching on the velvet settle, making sure the brass table was a comfortable distance from her, being good company? After their first meeting being so prickly, he had progressed to civility as her relationship with Angel grew and their paths therefore crossed. But today he was warm, he was dry and funny, interesting and interested.

And he really seemed to be interested in her work, firing questions, eyes like seawater in sunshine. 'So how do you know what a dragon looks like?'

Used to Olly's condescension, she began warily. 'I studied form from dinosaur and lizard books, sketched some exhibits in the Natural History Museum and even a fed-up lizard in a pet shop. Then a lot of character development sketches, dragons from the front, the side, lying, flying, smiling, laughing, snorting, roaring. I experimented and read the manuscript. The end of the commission's in sight now but I'm still struggling with one character. He's an enemy to both dragons and villagers, half lizard, half man. I haven't "got" him yet.'

He seemed intrigued. 'But how do you get into something like that? How does the industry work?'

Relaxing with another glass of wine she told him about her agent and friend, Kitty, her workroom, painted blue, her training at the University of East Anglia, the wolf cards.

Halfway through Sunday afternoon she was still rambling over glasses of wine and ploughman's lunch. And laughing. Apparently making him smile. Oh God, a drink or five always convinced her she was the most captivating person in the room, witty, interesting, lazy yet sharp, wine-relaxed. Wonderful. Then suddenly, from nowhere, she heard herself volunteering, 'Olly *hated* the card work, he said it was naff.'

And she was sober.

Just like that, invoking Olly's name was an ice bath and Alka Seltzer. Her words dried.

As if such an abrupt silence was unremarkable, Ratty picked up the conversational ball, telling a story she needn't listen to. She let the swell of bad feeling wash over her, recede.

Jos wandered in, dreamy eyes the colour of newly popped horse chestnuts, contributed his own view to Ratty's story, drank barley wine, smiled and drifted off to some other conversation. Ratty talked on, about his abbreviated accountancy training and his garage. She recovered enough to smile about the customer who'd whizzed along one day in early autumn and crashed into the back of his breakdown truck.

Her blood gradually stopped thumping in her ears and her fists unclenched.

Then, armed with fresh drinks, apparently privy to the scant information Tess had given Angel, he prompted, 'So. Olly was the guy you didn't marry?'

The guy she didn't marry. Tall, greyhound Olly, athletic from squash and tennis, still so vivid in her mind. Was it just the wine or did he still stir her?

'What happened to him?'

She sipped. Cold, delicious white wine, so dry it made her ears hurt; her favourite. She licked the flat-tasting condensation from the outside of the glass. 'He dumped me.'

'Ah. At least it was before the wedding.'

'Just.' She focused on the corded forearm closest to her, just above a TAG Heuer watch, where a tattoo, blue-grey, flexed as he moved. An old-fashioned milestone inscribed with the words, *One Miles*. 'That's good!' She laughed too hard, poking the tattoo, his flesh warm and only slightly yielding under her fingertip, letting herself slide away from the subject of Olly. 'One Miles! Miles A. Rattenbury. Miles Alan Rattenbury? Miles Andrew Rattenbury?'

'Miles Arnott-Rattenbury.'

She laughed again. 'You're not hyphenated?'

"Fraid so.'

'God,' she said again. 'Hyphenated. Shall we have coffee? I'm half cut. Is that hyphenated, too?'

Coffee was good, they had a second. Ratty backtracked. 'And so Olly told you marriage wasn't for him? And you wanted to leave ... London?'

'Brentwood.' She nodded, considered. 'That's a version.' The coffee wasn't working too well in the sobering-up stakes. 'I wouldn't say he *told* me,' she adjusted. 'Olly e-*mailed* me. He complained that I wanted a commitment he didn't – news to me. I was messy – I hadn't realised, but I suppose next to his computer-brain compulsive orderliness, I might be. All stuff and excuses. Like men do. By e-mail.'

That squashed feeling which went with thoughts of Olly, settled her. She gazed into her coffee. Would it ever stop hollowing her out?

'You – must – be – *joking*.' His entranced distaste recaptured her attention. 'He jilted you by *e-mail*!' If he was registering the whiff of distress, it didn't stop the dancing of his eyes.

She glared. He was trying not to laugh!

In fact, he was choking and giving in to it. 'Christ, I'm sorry! But I've never heard anything so ludicrous, so ridiculous, so preposterously brutal! It's outrageous! Didn't

52

you send your brothers round to give him a hiding?'

'It wasn't *funny*.' She tried not to let her disobedient smile evolve into a laugh. 'And I haven't got any brothers. Just my cousin Guy, who you met when you pulled his car out of the muddy field ... Could you imagine Guy meting out a hiding? And, anyway, he likes Olly.'

Ratty laughed himself sensible again. 'Pity,' he remarked. 'E-mail. What a shit. E-mail.'

Perhaps it was the wine, the relief at functioning normally in a normal situation, or just the sympathy – of a kind – from such an unexpected source. At any rate, she found herself telling him. Telling him what she hadn't confided in Angel, confessions leaking from all her deepest hurts, oozing through the thin dressings of her tenuous recovery.

'It got worse. I found out I was pregnant. Then I lost it.'

The amusement faded from his face. 'Lost the baby?'

'Lost the baby. Lost my grip. God, I lost my grip. Lost my self-respect and my confidence.'

The afternoon was nearly over. The wine had given her a headache. 'When I miscarried, I bled and bled and *bled*. They couldn't stop it, couldn't keep me conscious.' Blood on her clothes, the bed, the floor. Great scarlet splashes. She'd woken attached to a drip, someone else's blood to replace what her body pumped out so incompetently and a taste as if she'd sucked a penny. Shaking with weakness, losing control of string legs and lead-weight feet.

'It took a while to get over it. To be myself.'

'And now you're you again?'

'Getting there. But with the amount of blood I lose every month, I'm surprised I'm not two-dimensional.' What was she doing? Talking to Ratty about the Curse? An embarrassed snort and she changed the subject. She was sure she was going to regret this.

Would she regret this tipsy afternoon? His upper arm bounced gently against her shoulder as he walked her home. Angel was right – actually, Ratty was OK.

'I hear you've been calling on Lucasta?'

She laughed. 'She's amazing. Sings your praises!' Swinging back her hair that had sprung out of its clasp some time ago. '"Miles does this for me, Miles does that, Miles is such a grand chap!" Difficult to believe it's you she's speaking about. More coffee?'

They'd reached Tess's gate. Ratty was tempted. Turquoise eyes alight, her hair – he must remember to ask Angel what that colour was called – flying in the breeze, and her body neat and lithe, he was tempted to go indoors with her and see where he could make it lead.

He hadn't set out with seduction in mind. In fact, he already had a date this evening with Catriona and could do with sleeping this skinful off beforehand. Yep. Sticking with Catriona would certainly be simpler.

So he addressed the remark before, instead of discovering what the offer of coffee implied. 'My grandfather ruined her,' he explained.

'Ruined her?'

'There was a grand affair between them when they were each married to other people. It became public, Grandfather unsportingly elected to remain with his wife. Lucasta's husband, in self-righteous fury, stuck her in Pennybun whilst he continued to live it up in Chelsea. Poor old Lucasta.'

'Treacherous men.' Tess was looking sleepy, maybe the best of the alcohol had passed, for her. He skipped coffee.

'This is for me?'

Pink and edgy without alcohol for insulation and in the cold light of a Tuesday, Tess fixed her eyes on the folder open in Ratty's rimed hands, another picture of Nigel the pig, this time driving a shell of a car, black curls streaming, tattoos above his trotters.

'If you want it.' Uncertainty. She'd carried the folded card protecting the inked caricature as she'd walked up Port Road and out of the village between the hedges, almost to the next village of Port-le-bain, before turning back and making for the garage on her way home. How would he receive the little offering?

Awkwardly, feeling that Tess was showing off?

Or reluctantly, wondering if he was going to have to fend off a pass?

It was just a couple of hours' work. Because Toby hadn't wanted to part with one of his parade of Nigels, because Ratty had, in offering the innocent pleasure of getting squiffy in a village pub on Sunday afternoon, made Tess feel like any normal person. Shown outrage over Olly and put the whole thing more in perspective. In the past. She wasn't sure how much she liked him, but she felt grateful.

Hands jammed in pockets, feet shifting as if ready to race off, she watched as Pete and Jos crowded round to look, wrenches and gauges idle in their hands.

'Toby will be jealous.' Pete grinned, tossing back perennially flopped-forward hair.

'I've done his, Angel's framing it.'

Jos, looking from Tess to the picture, kept saying, 'Cool! Wicked! That's amazing. Really amazing. Cool.'

Her doubts multiplied at Ratty's continued silence. 'You don't have to keep it. But I was doing Toby's ... Anyway, you could always give it to Toby. But you asked him for the other drawing ...' Babble. Making him feel awkward, she was nearly sure, gaze fixed to the cartoon, embarrassed because he didn't want it and didn't know what to say? How stupid to take an idle joke with a three-year-old, a casual drink when he had nothing better to do, and make a friendship of it. She put out her hand. Even that felt hot and flustered. 'I'll take it to Toby, shall I?'

Bottomless eyes fixed on her. 'No! I'm going to hang it in here, in the garage.' Abruptly, he swung on her and pecked her cheek with soft, hot lips. 'It's great! Thanks.'

Relief. It was OK. A little gift from one friend to another, nothing to make a big deal over.

Pink satisfaction, relieved smile, eyes unguarded in pleasure. Ratty couldn't help feeling that she'd made it easy for him. Catriona had bored him, on Sunday evening, with her self-self conversation, not particularly interesting. Tess had more to say in five minutes than Catriona had in an hour and he'd spent the evening wishing he'd explored the situation with Tess.

He lifted his eyebrows as though struck by an idea. 'It isn't much of a thank you, but I've a pair of tickets to the Spring Ball at Port Manor this weekend. Can you make it?' Just the right amount of casual spontaneity.

And it nearly worked. A rush of something lit her eyes and her smile was shyly pleased. 'Angel told me about the ball ... It would be lovely.'

But Jos was frowning. 'Um, Ratty,' he dropped in anxiously, 'you've already invited Catriona.'

Ratty stared at Jos, swinging his new picture gently. 'Christ, how stupid of me. I'll ring Catriona ...'

'Oh no!' Tess thrust the idea away. 'Really. It doesn't matter!' A glance at her watch, a quick farewell, and she was gone.

Ratty studied the caricature, Pete studied Ratty. The

garage was silent and familiar. Ramp, fitted cabinets, lifted bonnets. A wheel against the wall where Pete struggled with a seized brake drum. The acrid smell of old oil.

Jos was gazing after Tess, trouble clouding his brow. Suddenly, it cleared. '*I* can take Tess, can't I, Ratty?' His pleasure at conjuring up a solution was written all over his face.

Ratty sighed. 'I suppose you can, Jos, yes.'

And off Jos ran, 'Tess, Tess!' Out of sight towards Little Lane.

Pete had to clutch the front of an MG, he laughed so hard. 'That didn't quite go to plan, did it?'

Ratty had never been so disgusted with himself. 'I was *amateurish*.'

'Your face! Good old Jos. What next?'

He closed the folder over Nigel and tucked it high up on a shelf. 'Don't know. Yet.' Turned back to a Mark II Jag. Thought about the Jag's timing, tried to keep his mind on the fact that if it rattled at the top of the engine when revved to 1500rpm, the chain could be adjusted there. If it was the bottom chain, it meant the engine had to come out and he'd need to ring the customer for clearance before he went on.

He took the tagged ignition key down from the row of hooks. How could he have let it go wrong? Why hadn't he lied that he and Catriona were over? He could easily have made it true. He turned the Jag's engine over and listened carefully to the rattle.

Tess. There was something graceful about her. As if she ought to walk with out-turned toes, like a dancer. Instead she strode along as if impatient to move through the countryside and see all the pretty colours, hair streaming.

Angel said Tess's hair was strawberry blonde.

Chapter Six

Tess's hair was strawberry blonde. Her eyes were greener or bluer according to what she wore, but tonight as turquoise as her silk dress, a skimming fabric sheath which bared a shoulder, hem flaring just above her ankles.

Angel had feathered the bottom few inches of her hair, whirled it into a pleat with a thick strand at the front snaking long over her bare left shoulder. Terrific.

'You *shall* go to the ball, Tesserella! Even if it's only with Jos.'

It had been quite funny, retreating from the embarrassment of Ratty being so overwhelmed with options that he'd almost invited two partners and Jos so thrilled he could relieve matters.

It would have taken a harder heart than Tess's to wipe the smile off that bearded face with a refusal. Jos was so sweet. But what on earth did a biker-mechanic wear to a ball?

Black suit, apparently, black embroidered black shirt, black shoelace tie, black tooled cowboy boots, hair smoothed into a shining pigtail and beard newly trimmed close, revealing that he did actually have a jawline. 'Jos!' She stared at a Jos bashful under scrutiny on her doorstep. 'You look ... amazing!'

The ballroom was spectacular with ruby damask curtains and snowy table linen beneath golden chandeliers. Vivid gowns, floating, swirling, set off by the marvellous, uncompromising sobriety of dinner jackets. Ages since Tess had dressed up for a good bash.

And it would have all been so lovely, so bright and friendly, if not for Catriona.

Pete and Angel, Tess and Jos were already at the table when an unusually quiet Ratty escorted in slinking, blonde-streaked Catriona, gorgeous in gunmetal satin. Expression blank, she was introduced to Tess.

'Pimm's, I think,' she husked in Ratty's direction, folding elegantly into the red plush chair. Her hair hung in a shining fall and she shook it constantly down her back.

'I hate sitting with my back to the room.' Catriona gazed at each of those who weren't.

Pete immediately took Angel, startling in fire engine red, to dance, probably knowing generous Angel would offer to switch. Catriona moved casually to Angel's seat, swapping drinks and evening purses.

'Comfortable now?' Jos looked stupefied by this little selfishness.

'Fine.' Catriona gazed past him.

Jos and Tess joined the dancing, abandoning Ratty to deal with the unlovely Catriona. Ratty looked grim and glared after them.

Apart from that, the evening was superb. Dancing with Jos – who, surprisingly, could – with Pete, all kinds of nameless men from other parties, even once with Ratty, although Catriona soon stopped that, declaring the dance a ladies' excuse me. Dinner was excellent, the speeches funny, although Tess got only half the local references.

Champagne stood on the table in a glass bucket and, returning to the dance floor under the chandeliers dimmed now in favour of a blaze of candles, Tess floated on bubbles. The band, the laughter, the pretty lights. Wonderful.

Pete collared Ratty at the bar. 'You're a bastard.'

'Well, you knew that.' Ratty finished emptying vodka into Catriona's Pimm's. 'I'm just helping her sleep.'

'Have you nobbled Jos, too? He's almost off his face!'

'Total coincidence.' Ratty looked Pete in the eye.

By midnight, he was pouring Catriona and Jos, helpless and liquid from spiked drinks, into a taxi, the driver demanding a fifty-pound bonus to deliver them home. He paid and brushed off his hands, grinning for the first time all night at an amused-disgusted Pete. 'Now I feel like dancing.'

The great thing, Tess was assured, was to make it through until five in the morning when the Survivors' Bus would take home everyone still standing.

She couldn't remember having such a great time since she was a student. So many warm hands leading her onto the dance floor, black dinner-jacketed arms escorting her back. The chatter, the music, the DJ.

Simeon Carlysle kept staring. She blanked him.

He smiled and raised his glass to her. She blanked him again.

He made his way over. When he asked her to dance she snapped, 'No thanks!'

'Oh, come on!' he cajoled. His eyes weren't on her face.

Ratty's voice from behind Tess was calm. 'You've forgotten your manners, Simeon.'

Simeon reddened. Shuffled closer to Tess and lowered his voice. 'Look, if I was a bit out of order that time, y'know, at the bonfire, I apologise. Blame it on the beer, shall we?'

And he laid his hand, heavy and strong and well remembered, on her bare arm.

Tess leapt to her feet. 'Don't *touch* me!' People looked around and she didn't care. 'Go away, stay away, don't touch me, and be grateful I haven't reported you to the police!'

His flurried retreat had been fun.

The ball was all whirling, happy, mindless, laughing *fun*. For ages she'd been so concerned with getting over everything, she'd hardly thought about fun. But *this* was Tess Riddell, dancing, dancing, having fun.

Dawn edged the damask curtains, dinner jackets on chair backs and shoes with impossible heels discarded under tables among fallen napkins. And finally, the music slowed.

Hair long since tumbled down, cheek pressed against the latest in a succession of white shirts, enjoying the feel of warm flesh through fabric, dreamily she watched Pete and Angel smooching, Pete's face against Angel's hair, hands cupping her buttocks through the scarlet dress. Angel opened her eyes to look directly at Tess, grinned, raised her brow in a little gesture of surprise.

Tess couldn't be bothered to wonder what Angel was trying to convey. She let her own eyes close, swayed within encircling arms. Nice. Light-headed. Tired. Tipsy. Nice.

'Izzat you, Ratty? How come you're not drunk?' Was it really Ratty supervising his party's retrieval of their possessions after the smoked salmon and scrambled egg breakfast with Buck's Fizz, leading them through a sunny, misty morning onto the Survivors' Bus? Identifying their stop, waving goodbye to Pete and Angel as they wove homeward across the Cross, steering Tess down Main Road and into Little Lane, arms linked. Was Ratty being so responsible? Amazing.

His voice seemed surprisingly loud. 'Key?'

She proffered her open evening purse, swaying, eyelids drooping. She accepted his supporting arm around her.

Through the green door, trying to walk with her head resting on his shoulder, eyes shut, hair streaming across his dinner jacket.

'Upstairs?'

She nodded, yes.

Breathing the warm, boozy, perfumed scent of her closeness, he took her long, turned-up fingers decorated by chased-gold rings, towing her up the turn of the stairs. Across the landing to the bedroom.

Slit-eyed, she accepted the support of his body, smiled dreamily when he dotted her face with tiny kisses, sighed when he stroked the twin wings of her collar bones with his thumbs. Shuddered when he kissed first the ear lobe with two hoops, then the one with two studs. The most carnal, promising, desirous kiss he'd ever experienced, soft lips, sexy tongue welcoming his, sending a thrill right up his body and down again.

Breaking away to shut the curtains, he left her wavering with champagne and lack of sleep by the bedside.

Spinning at the unmistakable long sound of an unfastening zip, he froze as he watched her fumble with her bra, stumble out of the pool of turquoise silk that had sunk to the carpet and kick off her shoes, sucking in his breath at the movement of lovely bare breasts. Allowing his eyes to speculate on deliciously simple, satin, stark white French knickers.

Arousal gripped in a moment. Jacket off in a shrug, bow tie unknotted, he stepped her into his arms, groaning at the exuberant buffet of her breasts. Glorious hair streamed over his hands that barely-stroked her spine and glided up her sides to her breasts as he nuzzled his lips against her neck. Her fingers dug into his shoulders as she sighed her approval and he swooped almost savagely on her mouth, hot and tasting of sexy woman. Endless, deep, tingling kisses, her nipples firm against his chest, tongue tip running mad inside his mouth. Heart racing, breath catching, sinking to the edge of the bed with her somehow on his lap. Sinking into the white softness of her breasts. Hearing her inhalation as she paused from her dizzy grapple with the dress studs of his shirt to lift trembling hands to cup his head, hearing her whimper 'Yes!' when his mouth closed feverishly on her. Struggling his shirt open, hoarse groan as her hot flesh met his. Wonderful, marvellous, lithe downiness beneath his hands, stroking, suggesting, up and down her body. The body that she arched and offered.

His delicate fingers discovering the advanced state of her arousal through the sliding fabric of her French knickers, willingly entering into the rhythm she immediately rocked against his hand. God, she was exciting! Hot as hell, unpretending, undisguised, needing – God what a need.

Spine arching, curving, hands clamped on his biceps, breasts bobbing against him, silky-skinned, her hair slithered over her breasts and his arms, spangling his senses.

Her head fell forward.

And she slumped, boneless, on his shoulder.

Lowering her gently to the coolness of the sheets, he cradled her. Then her breathing slowed. And. Every. Inch. Of. Her. Relaxed ...

Swearing horribly, he watched as her face slackened, eyes shut and she slithered into unmistakable sleep.

She'd crashed.

Sweeping back her hair from her unconscious face, he tried his lips and tongue up the xylophone of her now unresponsive rib cage. Out cold.

He gave an angry snort of laughter. 'That'll teach me!' A wave of frustration broke over him. What if he flung off his clothes and climbed in beside her anyway? Simply slept beside her, woke with her? Maybe they could take up where they left off ...?

He blew a sigh. It could be better than that.

Chapter Seven

'Lovely summer!' Angel pushed back her hair, turned her kitten face up to a sun which had, untypically, been giving England its best for weeks, and held up her arms to admire a milk-coffee tan. Tess glanced at her own arms, spangled with a million tiny freckles, envying Angel her Rich Tea biscuit complexion.

This summer was continental; long days lasting into warm evenings. Everyone spent all their spare time outdoors, the pub gardens filled with kids running between geranium tubs and people going home to barbecues. 'Are you staying this evening?' Angel's hair brushed Tess's arm as she rolled nearer to watch her trying to come up with new Nigels. Tess had spoken to the card company and they'd agreed to give her the Nigel range.

To sell cards for boyfriends, dads, husbands, brothers, nephews or sons, Nigel now played golf, football or squash. He drove a sports car, he drank pints. For Valentine's Day he clutched a pulsing heart and wore a soppy look. She tapped her pencil and thought about Christmas. Nigel began to emerge in the bottom half of a Santa suit, braces a-dangle, sharing a beer with a reindeer.

'Ever run out of ideas?'

Tess shrugged, absorbed. 'I just go on to something else.' She avoided committing herself to staying this evening. Would Ratty be joining them?

Ratty.

How the hell was she going to face him? The ball had been bad enough – when Ratty had, apparently, walked her home. In the morning she'd surfaced alone, a wake-up-in-her-make-up number. And half naked.

What had *happened*?

Back of her mind, there was the niggling memory of dancing in the arms of someone. Then nothing. Blank. What next? Maybe she muddled her way upstairs alone, drew the curtains, undressed and rolled beneath the duvet?

Maybe she hadn't needed hauling to bed. Perhaps the edge-of-the-mind memories of groans and furious curses were some head-trick, some earlier experience her dreaming mind had dredged up.

Maybe. Perhaps Simeon had cursed like that when Tess's knee found its mark ...? But she thought not.

Anyway, it paled into insignificance beside the latest humiliation. She shuddered and began to sketch Nigel balancing an entire chicken over a barbecue. A week ago, suffering – really suffering – from a flooding, debilitating period, she'd rung Angel with an SOS to ransack Crowther's shop for sanitary pads, knowing not to trust her own watery legs to walk that far. When she felt so appallingly drained she knew how easily she passed out. Some months were like this, when all she could do was slump in bed and wait for it to be over.

But, in a dire development, instead of Angel, *he'd* run up the stairs and swung into her bedroom like an intimate girlfriend. 'Angel has a problem with a pukey Jenna so I'm ... Christ, you look like crap.'

Oh, God-God, he'd gone into the shop and bought them for her! And, by his frown, hadn't particularly enjoyed the experience. Eyes down, what blood she had left staining her cheeks, muttering, 'Oh God, oh God,' she snatched the mortifying carrier bag ungratefully, paused on the bedside, plait dangling, to let her ears stop ringing, shuffled off to the bathroom in her Wee Willie Winkie nightshirt. Felt faint. Sick.

Would've have stayed closeted forever if she'd realised; realised that when she returned Ratty would've stripped the bed of, to her horror, bloodstained sheets.

'You need a clean nightie,' he suggested, without looking at her.

Oh no-o-o! She hid her eyes with both hands. 'Oh, please! Don't! Just leave me to die! I'll cope; you *can't* do this, I can't bear it!'

As he ignored her outburst and went to search the landing cupboard for fresh bedclothes, she'd no choice but to shuffle back to the bathroom to change. He glanced up when she returned. 'How do you bleed like this without dying?' Bed remade, efficient and matter-of-fact, he gathered up the soiled linen. Reached for the nightclothes from Tess, who sat with her head in her hands, in the chair.

This was the worst day of her life, worse than when Olly sent his e-mail. She was going to melt away from mortification. 'Go away!' she begged, voice muffled. 'You can't do my gory washing.'

'Shut up,' he suggested, fairly kindly. Following her very reluctant instructions he ran cold water in the bath, added a heap of salt and dumped everything in to soak. She slid under the fresh bedclothes, face averted. He fetched her a cup of tea.

'Thanks,' she managed, eyes determinedly closed. Never again, this would never happen again. Never. In future she'd stockpile sanitary towels in towers. Honeybun Cottage would become the official European tampon mountain. Oh, the indignity!

He perched familiarly on the bed, tugging her plait. 'Do I call a doctor?'

She shook her head. 'Another day or so and I'll get over it.'

'Sure?'

'Go away!'

'Stop it! What else can I get you? C'mon, sit up, drink.'

Grudgingly, she dragged herself up against the headboard aware of wearing nothing underneath her nightshirt, her frayed rope of hair and a pallor to rival the sheet. 'Paracetamol would be good, and a jug of water and a glass. Please.'

'I'll come back later and load the washing machine.' He snipped off her protest with, 'Just leave it, OK?' And he'd continued to look after her for a further two days. Abrupt, embarrassingly forthright about her needs, her mess and her condition.

She curled up with mortification whenever she thought of it. How would she ever look him in the eye again?

But then. It was comfortable, stretched on the warm grass by Angel's foxgloves that were busy with bumbling bees, roughing Nigel surfing, snorkelling, sunbathing. Toby played with two friends and a box of cars and Jenna toddled after them. Angel managed a well-earned doze.

And suddenly Pete and Ratty were wheeling out the barbecue and McLaren, Ratty's soft dog, was snapping at flies and panting revolting hot slobber. Before Tess could retreat she was surrounded by people flopping down onto the grass, delighted that the day's work was done, the sun was out and the beer was cold.

And nobody mentioned it, nobody blamed her that her body was treacherous over its simple functions and she'd, humiliatingly, needed help. Except Ratty, rolling over to inspect the sheet of Nigels, enquired, matter-of-factly, 'Better now?'

On a fresh, scalding flush, she mumbled, 'Yes. Um, thanks ... sorry for, y'know ...'

He pulled a strand of her hair. 'Don't worry about it. We both survived.'

And that was all.

Tess could relax. She realised she kind of … *trusted* Ratty.

The children did, too, she thought, leaning back on her elbows to watch Toby and his friends examining the tattoos on Ratty's arms. He shrugged off his shirt to display a tattoo that was new to her on his left shoulder blade, a car wheel. Angel would probably be able to tell her it had five-spoke alloys and a low profile tyre, or some other apparently desirable attribute. Fine dark hair covered his chest in flat whorls. Ratty never sweetened his voice for the children or crouched to their level but it was always him they selected to unknot string, make repairs or replace batteries.

McLaren opened a brown eye occasionally to flick a glance at the children capering round and round him and Ratty, who was by now comparing how-not-to-get-along-with-your-parents stories with Angel, or, in Angel's case, parents-in-law. Bickering over the rules of the game, the children collapsed to loll in Ratty's shade. Slowly, Tess pulled her pad close.

Her pencil hovered, and then began. Children. Childish movement, head-heavy proportion, every line a soft curve. Sketches, rough and feathery, began to appear for one of the final illustrations to complete *The Dragons of Diggleditch*; the childish nymphs of Diggleditch Forest frolicking unaware under the ominous and baleful gaze of Farny, half lizard, half man.

Each small head she haloed in wispy curls, eyes almond, ears pointed prettily. Small bodies naked but for artful leaf arrangements.

Farny, Farny, Farny. Lizard below the waist, man above, reptilian features. He had to look as if he was capable of turning nasty in an instant. She said, 'I need a man's body.'

And looked at Ratty.

Breaking from his conversation, his brows up, he spread his arms hospitably. 'Be gentle with me.'

They all laughed, of course they laughed, at her blush and his leer. But she was alight. *Now* she knew exactly how the elusive illustration would go.

'Would you sit? Just a sketch?' Dancing with impatience she dragged a stubby stepladder from the shed. 'Can you just ...?' She patted the top and Ratty climbed, slowly. 'On the very top, one foot here ... one there.' Stood back.

'Just wriggle back a bit ... each foot up a rung higher ...' With quick movements she arranged him, elbows on thighs, hands hanging, back curved. 'Look down at the children.' She dropped to the grass, shooed everyone else away, sharpened her pencil with a sharpener from her pocket, started rapid work.

After a few minutes Ratty sighed. 'Pete, pass me my beer.'

Tess glanced. 'Not just now.'

'My backside's numb,' he mentioned, 'and my back aches.'

'Yeah, yeah, just hang on in.' She kept him half an hour, closed her pad, sighed, 'Wooh!' And, 'Thanks.'

He landed crouched on the grass beside her like an animal, reopened the pad and flipped through to the page of baby nymphs dancing, skipping, adorable and elfin, seemingly unaware of, looming above them, the predatory presence of Farny. It'd worked really well, viewing her models from the level of the shortest, looking up at her baddie.

The stepladder became a rock. Lizard legs bent the wrong way at the knee, clawed feet turning in to clutch the crevices, flesh scaled. Torso – Ratty's own strong and hairy chest, muscled shoulders developing into extended, corded arms, elongated talons replacing mechanic's hands. To capture the reptilian essence she'd placed the eyes far back, forehead slanting steeply away into snaky curls, expression meditative, brewing trouble, as if selecting a tasty morsel.

Ratty recoiled. 'Shit! Is this how you see me?'

She stared. ''Course not, I just used bits and pieces of you. It's a kids' book, fantasy. Obviously there's no life model for a non-existent being, so I improvise. You're just a form ...'

Peering, Angel breathed, 'It's so sexy!' She touched the pencilled male torso as if feeling the power.

Tess's attention remained on Ratty. 'Don't you like it?'

His eyes were riveted. 'It's so good. But I feel ...' He hesitated. 'I feel exposed. As if you've seen every bad thing I've ever done, everything about me that's nasty or unkind. Somehow, you've drawn ... my dark side.'

Her lips curved into a smile. 'Oh, thank you!'

Dreams. Dreams again. Grope overhead, yank the light cord. Let the light banish the dreams. Get up.

Her workroom was as still as the rest of Honeybun Cottage in the summer night humidity, but she went there, opened the casement window and perched sideways on the deep sill. Looking diagonally out onto the moonlit lane and garden, she let her heart settle and the sweat cool.

Early hours. Village inert, the latest stop-out was home and the dawn risers still sleeping. There was scarcely sufficient breeze to whisper through the leafy trees between Honeybun and Pennybun, but she felt better breathing the still air than twisted in clinging sheets and dreams.

Would she never stop dreaming of Olly?

Tonight, back in bed with Olly; he'd *been* there. She shuddered. Olly's smooth hands, Olly's wide shoulders and whippy body above her, dreams returning her to a world where she still had Olly, in awe of his God-given looks, entrapped by his overwhelming sense of self. Self-belief, self-importance. Still in the thrall of Olly's self-image.

Still glad to be his.

She closed her eyes. Olly's hands controlling the movement of her hips. It had been an age since Olly and she ...

And in this night's vivid illusion Olly had left again.

Withdrawn just when she thought he'd stay. Taken her to the brink and abandoned her, unsatisfied. As he had so often, using some little callousness, calculated roughness, to stop her getting there because he wasn't ready.

But just when she groped for consciousness, escaped from the familiar frustration, a hand had reached from her sleep and pulled her back.

Powerful, tender hand, winding itself in her hair, his body rough as it brushed her breasts. He pulled her to his scalding lips, this new lover, into a kiss of depth and intensity – some shady memory refused to form – then to trail, hot and arousing, to her breasts, whilst he rocked her to a building rhythm on his lap. Stroking, kissing, loving her to a point where her pleasure was the only important thing.

She settled herself more comfortably on the hardness of the sill, rolling a pencil that had somehow jumped between her fingers, trying to make sense of the two-part dream.

First, Olly. Obviously, Olly had made love to her countless times. Automatically her mind might supply Olly to any erotic dream. And, true to form, phantom Olly had vanished when his presence was most vital.

But from what memory had she dredged up the other lover who'd taken her on from frustration? Rough velvet where Olly was glassy silk, boisterous passion against Olly's control. Generous where Olly was mean.

The old plasterwork was cool to lean against, to rest her head on, whilst she stared out into moonlight that silvered where it touched, blackened what it missed. She was becoming happy, here at Honeybun, in a little old cottage among old things. Happy on her own, without a man to account for, or to, or compromise over. It felt secure.

In the darkness was Lucasta in Pennybun. In the village centre, in Rotten Row, was Angel and Pete's little brick and stone house.

In Great End, Jos's geese would be motionless among the shrubs around his pond.

At the Cross, Ratty's garage doors would be closed in the silence. Left up Port Road, left again to Ladies' Lane, Ratty's long house stood in his garden full of delphiniums and hollyhocks. 'I'm a spiky person,' he'd explained when she remarked that all his plants seemed to grow in spears.

Yes, he was.

Would he be sleeping alone or was it Chloë tonight? Lisa? Gina?

These pretty ladies who were hardly ever included when he hung out with Jos, Pete, Angel and the kids – and now herself, of course. For the pretty ladies, he'd routinely detach himself from the domestic comfort of the group. 'Right, I'm off.'

Someone would joke, 'Leaving us for better things?'

'Clubbing with Shelli from the motor factors tonight.' Or cinema with Marie from advertising at the local paper. Drinks with Melanie something or Belinda something else.

They'd chorus, 'Be good!'

He'd quip, 'Good? I'll be *marvellous*!' One thing he wasn't, was short of company. All the Melanies, Maries and Belindas for his separate life.

But for the stuff that mattered, summer days out, the British Motor Cycle Grand Prix at Donington, the stock cars at Brafield, it was Pete and Angel, and Jos.

Now she was one of the group, too. Every day she saw

Angel and the kids; little Jenna always made straight for Tess's lap, Toby brought his comics to be shared. Pete, Jos and Ratty treated her with the same familiarity as they did Angel. Though she was ever conscious of being the newcomer, cautious of her welcome.

'I wish we didn't have to invite you everywhere twice!' Ratty complained recently. '"Would you like to come to the folk festival, Tess?" "If you're sure ..." "Yes, we're sure!" If we didn't want to invite you, believe me we wouldn't.' She must remember to accept with a certain, 'That'd be lovely,' instead of, 'If you're sure.'

Angel had advised her just to go with the flow.

Yesterday evening, Pete and Angel's anniversary, she'd done exactly that. Arriving to babysit, she'd been intercepted by Angel in the kitchen. 'Look at this!' Angel whispered, beckoning her to the door to the sitting room.

There was Ratty stretched out in the huge rocking chair that had been Angel's grandmother's, young Jenna flat out across his chest, face buried in the crook of his neck. Both of them were sound asleep. 'Ain't that sweet?' cooed Angel. Then followed the normal rush of instructions. 'Toby's already gone off so he shouldn't be any trouble. Jenna's bottle is in the fridge if she wakes up but I shouldn't think she will. Ratty'll put her in the cot when he surfaces, just watch she doesn't roll off him in the meantime. We'll be back by midnight ... just a minute, Pete. We're going to the Bettsbrough Odeon first ... yes, I'm *coming* ... and here's the phone number for the restaurant and you've my mobile.'

'Yes, but –' But they were gone, Angel laughing at Pete's impatience, kisses in the car, the engine firing, Pete driving and Angel checking her hair in her handbag mirror.

Hmm. Tess peered again into the sitting room. Apart from crooking one leg, Ratty hadn't moved. He looked peaceful, lips lightly touching, dark lashes resting thickly together. She remained, presumably, appointed babysitter. Ratty would doubtless have plans for later. Damn him, he was in the way.

Lightly upstairs to check on Toby, then she grabbed her book and made for the sofa. Tough if she disturbed him. If she had to go with the flow then so did he.

Her book was fascinating, a love story of a German officer and a local nurse on the island of Jersey during the German occupation. Riveting, the trials of warfare, the deaths, the deprivations.

But she was aware the instant Ratty's eyes opened. After several moments, he smiled, gently. 'I'm in your way.'

'Not at all,' she lied. As he made no move, she lifted Jenna and carried her up to the cot waiting with turned-down sheet to receive the baby, sleep-flushed and adorable. She watched the little girl squirm on contact with the cool cotton, resting her hand on Jenna's back whilst she settled, as Angel had taught her, waiting for the tiny body to relax.

While she was upstairs, Ratty had made coffee. He dropped back in the rocker and groaned comfortably. 'I've been to Liverpool today to get some bits. I'm shattered.'

She was now educated enough to know that 'some bits' covered every and any part of any vehicle, common or rare, small or large, easy to transport or a nightmare. MAR Motors' speciality of older cars made the procuring of 'bits' a constant preoccupation. 'Bits' for cars long out of production meant small ads, specialists and autojumbles all over the country or little engineering works that could reproduce the old. Ratty was also prepared to take on the awkward US classic market, talk the American jargon of 'trunk', 'hood' and 'muffler' which made Tess think of an elephant dressed in a duffel coat and scarf.

Coffee cup empty, still he sat on, talking desultorily about kit cars, performance marques, classic cars. Makes and models she'd never heard of, TVR, Caterham and Pagani. A fast car was 'quick', had 'poke', the engine was 'the lump'.

Sliding her cup onto the table, she asked, 'Why *old* cars?'

'I know how they work. And it's surprising how many so-called enthusiasts tire of the constant maintenance their classic vehicles demand and pay me to do some of it. Mechanics and bodywork mainly, I send the wiring and spraying to other places.

'It's all mechanical with the old stuff. You need a degree in computer programming, with the modern cars.'

The mention of computers always made her think of Olly, of his group of like-minded, goateed, suited, IT types. She tried to change the direction of her thoughts. 'Aren't you expected to be somewhere this evening?'

He lifted his wrist, glanced at his watch. 'Too late, now. Don't you want me here?'

Could hardly say, 'No, you unsettle me, I'm not sure if you just put up with me because of Angel. You're different, hazardous, sharp, not the kind of man I'm used to.' So she just shrugged and asked, 'Won't your date mind?'

'She probably will but I don't.' See, if he was supposed to be kind how was he also so ruthless?

So, instead of a quiet evening curled up with a book, safeguarding Toby and Jenna's sleep, she spent the evening with Ratty.

Ratty and a hundred questions. Was she over Olly yet, had her health improved, where did her family live? Had Guy ever paid back the two hundred?

'Guy!' She selected the easiest to answer. 'Must owe me a fortune over the years. I wouldn't mind but when his wife, Lynette, finds out, she gives me hell.' Because it saved her talking about Olly Gray she rambled on about Guy and her growing out of adolescence and into early adulthood together. 'Racing from one pub or dance or party to another in our first cars. Getting into scrapes, covering for each other. I suppose it's an old habit.'

'Did you sleep together?'

She laughed. Ratty had helped himself to a bottle of Pete's wine, a Merlot, and they were almost at the bottom of it. He'd pulled up the rocker and swung his feet onto the low table while Tess lounged on the sofa. 'Sleep with Guy? God no, even if he wasn't so hopeless with money and women it would've felt incestuous. He's like a brother.

'The nearest we got was bonking at opposite ends of the same barn, one night when the cider flowed. Talk about cringing with embarrassment in the morning!' She grinned suddenly over the memory, undoing the clasp which had begun digging into the back of her head and shaking down her hair.

'Fun,' he said lightly, watching. 'Happy days. Angel tells me your hair is strawberry blonde.'

Wrong-footed, she mumbled, 'She's the expert.' She reached for the wine bottle. Empty.

'Long hair's wonderful.' He shuffled down in his chair, eyes closed now to slits, head tilted as if ready to drift back to sleep. 'Lord give me a woman with long, long hair. Mmm.'

Casting about for a subject that was less personal, she told him about her parents, their substantial detached Oxfordshire house in Middleton Stoney with the ceanothus tree and conifers in the front garden.

'Convenient for Silverstone. And Brafield,' he said, relating the geography to racing circuits. 'And not bad for the circuit at Rockingham.'

'My mother was delighted when I turned up at home.' And horrified but capable when the unsuspected embryo gave up on the world. 'Now I've left again she's worrying like mad. She came today for lunch and to check up on me. Keeps telling me how nice it'd be if I lived near her and Dad.

She's lonely when Dad's away from home, checking out repo properties or overseeing whatever conversion he's tied money up in.

'She said that I didn't know what being a parent means. Then bit her tongue when she realised what she'd said – me having lost a baby.' Tess hunkered deeper into the sofa.

Still following the conversation, although his lids were now completely shut, Ratty asked, 'How did you get pregnant?'

She snorted. 'Don't you know what causes it?'

'Most people of our age know how to prevent it.'

She sighed. 'Oh, you know, usual stuff. After a party ... Olly thought it'd be nice to leave off the condom. A little treat to himself. Just once.'

His eyes opened for a moment.

To avoid whatever he was going to ask next, she jumped back to the safer subject of her parents. 'Dad wants me to move closer, too.'

Ratty chuckled, his foot sagging outward and resting on her knee where it jutted from the sofa. 'We all disappoint our parents. We grow from dependent babies to needy children. Then suddenly, bang, we're people. Minds, ideas, tastes that they haven't created. No more biddable kid, here comes strong-minded adult to differ and disagree, value different things and different people. Our time's ours to spend, mistakes are ours to make.

'And we make them, our mistakes, whether it's bonking in a barn or lending money we won't get back.'

She looked at him and marvelled that he could originate a thought so deep. 'Or getting jilted,' she added, as it was top of her list of errors.

Blue eyes slitted open. 'How can that be your mistake?'

'How can it be anything but?'

Chapter Eight

'Have you spoken to Tess about what happened after the ball?'

Pete was the one who understood. Jos lacked Pete's quickness, shared wavelength, intuitive understanding. Pete's marriage affected none of that, though it kind of precluded Pete from taking part in the adventurous stuff. Pete, Pete would talk and listen and accept.

Traffic had held up their return journey from Northumberland on the trail of an MG Midget gearbox. So they might as well pull off at a handy pub and eat, then lie on the grassy bank beside the beer garden and wait for the road to clear. Ratty grunted. 'She's never given any indication she remembers.'

The shepherd's pie was finished. They drank slowly, shandy because they had still to drive.

'So she was too drunk to do the business?'

'Absolutely. Looked a certainty, then looked unconscious.' He grinned. 'When she took off her dress, y'know how women do, zzzzippp! Wiggled her shoulders, stepped out of it, I thought I was home and dry. And she was so ready for it ... Then, suddenly, I was on my own.'

Pete laughed. 'What happens next?'

Ratty shrugged.

From the bank they could see, across the car park, the road still bunged up with a column of traffic. Better here in the sun on the grassy cushion.

Pete pushed back his hair. 'You know you'd do better to leave her alone.'

'I do know that, yes.'

'I mean, what happens after you've done the deed? She'd still be there, at Honeybun, still hanging out with Angel, who happens to be very fond of her.'

'True.'

'She's only just made friends here, you'd jeopardise that. Unless you're thinking of marrying her or something! Your onto-the-next-lay philosophy isn't appropriate. She's a friend, now.' Pete flicked a wasp, drunk and blindly aggressive, carefully away from his glass. 'And what about you gatecrashing Tess's babysitting?'

What about that? Gina, his stood-up date that evening, had left an obscene message on his voicemail.

A midnight-blue TVR Griffith grumbled along in the middle of the traffic. It looked and sounded amazing, he'd love to have one. Maybe he'd come across a wrecked one sometime and be able to rebuild it. They both watched the sexy sports car respectfully past before Pete continued the conversation. 'No opportunity ...?'

He shook his head. 'Just talk. Sometimes she'll talk to me. About pranks with her cousin Guy, her parents, stuff. Carefully avoiding questions about that computer oik she was with.'

'Why, d'you think?'

Another shrug. 'Who knows? Still hurt? Prefers to forget him? Still in love?' He shifted position. 'I can't weigh her up. One minute I think she's still hurting, the next that she's ready to roll.'

'Difficult,' Pete mused. 'Give me uncomplicated Angel any day. If this Olly guy wasn't still in her head, would Tess be up for it?'

'Couldn't say.'

'You shouldn't have been so bloody to her in the first place.'

'Was I, particularly?' The traffic, still thick, was moving

79

more quickly now. Probably not worth buying another drink.

'You looked on whilst Simeon tried a number on her.'

'I honestly didn't realise what Sim was trying.' Those turquoise eyes had blazed at him. Now he wanted to see them again unfocused and closing with desire, while her fingers turned to claws on his arms ...

Pete flicked grass at him. 'Wake up.'

'Thinking.'

'Be careful, people might think there's more to you than tattoos, cut-off T-shirts and jeans, stop taking you at face value! Miles Arnott-Rattenbury: interests, cars. Emotions, cars. Future, cars.'

He wasn't like that. Nowhere near so simple. Who was? He had other interests: his properties, music. And he had a huge appetite for women. Though he might not treat them so carefully as his cars.

Pete stretched, glanced over to the road. 'Angel was telling me about this bleeding-to-death-every-month stuff.'

The memory made him wince. 'She was pregnant, she miscarried, and haemorrhaged. My God, does she bleed! I thought I'd be calling the ambulance. But she said she'd be OK in a couple of days, and she was. Was she embarrassed, though.' He'd hardly enjoyed being involved, but hadn't made her mortification worse by complaining.

'And you sorted her out, did you?'

Ratty nodded.

Pete laughed. 'Nice for you. You usually only get that close to the icky stuff once you're living with someone.' Pete emptied his glass. 'So what d'you think? She up for it?'

'Don't know.'

'But you still want ...'

'Absolutely.'

It was Pete's turn to drive. Out of the car park. Windows down, hair blowing.

Hedges dusty with the harvest, a combine rolling along the ridge on the horizon, even from this distance he could taste the dry chaff in the air. 'I keep thinking,' Ratty reflected, 'if I'm just *there*, like when she was babysitting for you, it'll, I don't know, just happen. Before she has time to remember what a bastard this Olly is.'

'Of course, you're a big bastard yourself.'

'Yeah.' He scratched his head. 'But a better model.'

Chapter Nine

'Olly Gray has been. To see us.'

What? Olly's name, a jab in the chest. And her father even sounded pleased.

'Tess?'

'I'm here.' She felt the phone slide in her hand. 'What the hell did he want?'

'Just a friendly call, I'm sure that's all there was to it. He was just remembering he was nearly our son-in-law.'

Incredible. 'I haven't forgotten. Nor that he dropped me two days before our wedding. Nor that I lost a chunk from my life miscarrying his baby, which made me ill.'

James cleared his throat. 'Nobody can cope *for* you.'

'Thanks for all your support.'

Her father seemed oblivious the sarcasm. 'Anyway, darling, we had the impression that he might be coming round. Asked where you were living, in fact.'

Why not just put the phone down? Instead, she snapped, 'Coming round as in regaining consciousness? Or coming round as in calling at your home?'

'As in ... considering that something might be salvaged from your relationship.'

She spat, 'Giving me a second chance?'

'I didn't say that! Don't overreact. Darling, we don't have to talk about it if you really hate the idea, but you might even get peace of mind if you spoke to Oliver and put things in perspective.'

Upstairs in her workroom were sheaves of Slinkers and Sliders and Winders half sorted. Farny and the nymphs waited to be checked off against brief and layout and packed carefully. This afternoon the courier was calling for the results of her labour. She cut across her father's careful speech. 'I don't want a damned thing to do with Olly Gray. Not now. Not next week. Not never, ever, *ever*. OK?'

Her father's quick intake of breath was sharp in her ear. 'Don't carry on, Tess!'

'Carry on. As in continue? Or carry on with the milkman? Oh no, what I have had to do is carry on regardless!'

Her father's sigh, loud; his voice gentle, reasonable. 'You must take into account that Oliver knew nothing about the baby. And, I must say, *I* think he has a right to know. He would've been the father. It's not something to be lightly ignored.' There he'd be, she thought, behind the leather-topped desk in his study, swivelling his chair gently, looking out over the garden. Grey hair brushed back immaculately, eyes impatient, testy because Tess wasn't being malleable, thin-lipped at having to justify his opinion. '*I* think he has a right to know,' James repeated.

'And I think you're wrong. It was a failed pregnancy and I don't want him to know. I'm failure enough in his eyes. Can I speak to Mum?'

But her mother had been hardly any more comfort. 'Don't think Dad's trying to push you into anything, darling. Olly didn't let you down gently, we realise that. But he didn't know about the baby. And he didn't make you ill.'

Tess gazed out of the window. 'Mum, try not to let Dad give Olly my address. You know what he's like. His acting for the best is what most people would call meddling.'

A little pleasure went out of the final ritual of *The Dragons of Diggleditch* after that. She stewed instead of packaging her illustrations, departing into angry reverie instead of enjoying the end-of-term feeling that a commission's completion would normally provide.

Sod James, sod him. Why did she get upset? She should've stipulated briefly, lightly, coldly that she didn't want Olly and it would be pointless to tell him they almost made a child, where she was, what she was doing.

On the wall were still her three lists, the ones she'd made after taking tea with Lucasta that afternoon. She snatched them down.

Work, correspondence, walk, shopping; yes, she could tick all those fundamentals. *Stop looking back;* if only people would let her! Eat sensibly; sure, that phase was over.

SURVIVE WITHOUT OLLY! She made big, savage ticks on each of the three sheets. Easy! Survive without Olly, no trouble. She was happy in Honeybun Cottage, she was working well, she had friends. Olly Gray? Just somebody she used to know.

Early afternoon and the courier had taken *The Dragons of Diggleditch* on paper and on disc, parcelled stiffly and marked about eight times, 'Please Do Not Bend'. She shouldn't have to worry about that book any more.

There would be a nice fat cheque from Kitty. A few Nigels for the card company and some book jackets would tide her over gently until her next commission. For the first time since coming to Middledip she felt content to slither to a halt, award herself a lazy time. She yanked out the tie from her ponytail and flung back her hair. Out, then, into the sunshine!

Her feet took her next door, to Pennybun, through the gate and into a romp of roses, dahlias and late, sexy-scented honeysuckle.

Lucasta, classy today in lavender with jet beads, ushered her in as she always did, hobbling past the asparagus fern into the little parlour. 'You're looking wonderful, Middledip must agree with you!' Despite limping more than ever, Lucasta produced lapsang souchong in stubby, handleless cups like little sugar bowls and settled back to admire the view through her window. 'Isn't the garden wonderful? Miles has found a youngster to cut the grass and he moved the old bench into the sunshine last week. I'm wondering if he'd search out a new garden parasol for me. That would be lovely, wouldn't it?'

Relaxing on the cool cotton covers, Tess resigned herself good-naturedly to a conversation littered with references to Miles Arnott-Rattenbury. Despite that ritual, she always left Pennybun soothed and calm from the serene, pretty colours with which Lucasta surrounded herself and the old furniture collected from around the world as an army officer's wife. And Tess wasn't alone, half the village seemed to stroll past her gate to visit Lucasta. If they were all greeted, 'How lovely!' as she was, if they all warranted delicate china and delicious snacks and found the same comfort and tranquillity at Pennybun, it was understandable.

'I'm going to Bettsbrough in the morning, I'll collect your parasol, if you like,' she volunteered.

'Thank you, dear! Miles is travelling to Devon at the weekend so I expect he has enough to do. I'll find my purse. More tea? Something from the fruit bowl? Or,' she smiled conspiratorially, displaying faultless white dentures, 'Miles brought me some chocolate fudge ice cream …'

The ice cream was delicious, a peculiar contrast to the smokiness of lapsang. 'I used to know Miles's grandfather,' Lucasta said, suddenly, putting aside her empty bowl.

Tess nodded, and then realised she might not be supposed to know. 'Really?'

'We were … each married to other people. But we formed an attachment. It's what divided my husband and me.'

Tess nodded some more.

Lucasta's knotted hands, with the skin so soft-looking she must have been diligent with the hand cream all her life, toyed with the jet necklace where it brushed the front of her dress. She looked directly at Tess. 'I don't know that he was worth it, he didn't act particularly well, in the end. But his wife was a strong woman and perhaps that's why Lester and Miles are better men, though Miles works hard to disguise it. Don't you find him very disagreeable, sometimes?'

Tess smiled slightly. 'I don't know that I'd say *disagreeable* …'

Lucasta tutted. 'You're a saint if you don't! Some days he's as contrary as a tom cat. Even when he does you a favour he makes you feel as if it's nearly killing him.'

Wandering on when she felt Lucasta was tiring – she was really looking so faded and silvery these days it was worrying – Tess waved at Pete and Jos working in the shady garage. Would Angel fancy a bit of company, she wondered? She might be glad to escape chores, cry, 'Bliss, you've come to rescue me!' Yes, she'd pop in, see if the family fancied a stroll. Perhaps to the swings behind the village hall, Jenna loved the cage of the infant swing. The higher, the faster, the better she liked it, the more she crowed and shrieked for more. Lovely, lazy day. Her mobile phone was at home so that James couldn't ring to discuss Olly and whether he could be coaxed back.

And there was McLaren, obviously an escapee again, wagging an enthusiastic hullo and crossing towards her, his brown patches aglow in the sun, eyes bright in welcome. Tess fussed his silky ears. 'We don't need horrid old Olly, do we McLaren? Fancy a walk, sweetie?'

Angel was pleased to see her and because *The Dragons of Diggleditch* had been successfully completed she even opened a bottle of wine. Because of the hot weather they drank it quickly. Because their subsequent sunshine-drenched dawdle took them past MAR Motors they felt inclined to linger and chat, pretty loose and giggly. And because Tess felt pleased with herself she proposed, rashly, 'How about an early finish tomorrow, as it's Friday, so you can all come to Honeybun to celebrate the completion of my first full book commission in the village?'

Buying a garden parasol for Lucasta – 'blue, or perhaps mauve. With a fringe' – Tess was tempted into a little splurge on her own garden. A plain green parasol, a wooden bench, dark green patio chairs of wrought-iron ivy leaves, a table and a gas barbecue.

'British Racing Green,' Ratty approved, appropriating a chair and sending McLaren to pant and snap at flies in the shade. 'Congratulations on finishing your commission.' Astounding her, he produced a pink patio rose in a pot, a little bottle of Tendre Poison and a kiss on the cheek.

The rose was just the pink of her blush. 'Oh! I didn't expect presents! I just felt like sharing my great mood. But here you all are making it a party!'

Toby offered a silver-framed photograph of him and Jenna taken at his playgroup. 'It's very good,' he pointed out. 'That's my best shirt and Jenna's party dress. Mrs Lewis combed everyone's hair with the same comb and Mummy said she hoped no one had nits.'

Jos brought a corn dolly from the woman in the village who made them and bottles of potato wine he'd made himself. Potato wine? Could wine be made from potatoes? Not wanting to hurt his feelings by asking, Tess repeated, 'I didn't expect presents!'

Blinking hot eyes at the *niceness* of everybody, she disguised the moment by touching a little of Ratty's perfume to her throat. 'Do I smell good?'

Ratty dipped his face to her neck. 'As gorgeous as you look.'

Gorgeous. She let the remark nestle in her mind as she poured wine into new glasses from the new coolbox and brought out the new patio-ware for when the barbecue-sauce-smothered food was ready.

She'd been alone, she'd been low, she'd been uneasy in her own skin. But now she had friends to share her high and she was 'gorgeous'.

She manned the barbecue from a chair and enjoyed Pete and Angel sharing an eye-watering, wine-induced snorting giggle, the children screaming with delight as Jos gave them horse rides on faded denim knees. Ratty, grinning like the pirate king, sea-blue eyes flicking over her, smile softening.

Ratty. Funny Ratty. Snappy today, kind tomorrow. Hard, sarcastic, mocking Ratty. But also warm, teasing, laughing Ratty who shared the profits from a good deal with his friend-employees, who the children loved. Tess's eyes drifted upward from the smile and paused to collect that glittering gaze. What did it say? Offer? Would she ever ...?

'Teth-Teth!' An insistent little hand patted Tess's leg and the thought remained unformed. 'Hul-*lo*, my Jenna.' She obeyed the outstretched arms and jumped the toddler, pink-cheeked and silken-haired, onto her lap.

'Bic-bic.' Jenna showed her the biscuit, softened by being saved for some time in her hand, and settled down to gnaw it.

It was pleasant in the sunshine, swapping lazy insults, emptying the bottles of wine, breathing the summer smells of roses, grass cuttings, hamburgers and chops. Soon Jenna snuggled a hot, chubby head into the hollow of Tess's shoulder and dozed. Easy to forget that life hadn't always been so.

A sudden hush alerted Tess to a change.

Angel's 'Wow!' directed her eyes.

And there, marching up the drive over the drying thyme, chin out, was Olly Gray.

Blond hair blinding. His eyes were angry.

The power of speech deserted her.

'You might look worried,' snapped Olly, halting in front of her.

She gazed up at him, the weight of Jenna pinning her to the chair.

'I suppose this is her?'

Here's Olly, she thought, stupidly. Here, in the garden of Honeybun Cottage, was Olly saying something quite incomprehensible. 'Her?' She tried to focus through potato wine and the barbecue haze.

'I suppose this is our baby?' Had his eyes always been that cold? She didn't remember them as quite so hard.

Pete snitched Jenna brusquely onto the safety of his own lap, waking her and making her cry.

Angel's eyes blazed at the good-looking hell-man who'd burst in and ludicrously tried to claim paternity of her baby. 'Who in God's name is *this*?'

Tess stared. God. These were her friends – she must deal with this embarrassment! Jolting herself into action she leapt to her feet, lifting her voice above Angel's. 'Don't be so ridiculous!'

'I want the truth.'

'What truth?' Her hands felt clammy. 'It *is* ... Let's go inside.'

Set-faced, Olly crowded her through her own kitchen door, snapping it shut behind them to exclude possible hangers-on. He had a glower like King Kong.

'I know that's my baby, before you deny it!'

She could only gape, the kitchen table pressed against her

hips and Olly towering over her, not bothering with the how-are-yous or nice-to-see-you-agains. She tried to shake her thoughts into order. 'How on earth can Jenna be yours?'

'It's obvious!' snapped Olly. 'James let slip you were pregnant when we split up – more than two years ago. And that kid is fifteen to eighteen months old, add nine months ... My baby.'

'But ...' She couldn't back away any further. Her neck hurt from craning to meet Olly's glare. Confusion turned her tongue temporarily to wood and was useless to moisten paper lips and form a denial. Even if he ever shut up and gave her a chance.

Olly crashed on. 'James told me how long you stayed with your folks – long enough to produce my baby and get a bit of support through early infancy, collect your money from our house sale and let James set you up in a place just the right size for *two*, I'd say. Guy's evasive. Mari obviously anxious.' Hands spread in a concluding attitude. 'My baby!'

'My father has evidently been indiscreet. Guy's *always* evasive. And my mother will be anxious – because I'm getting along nicely without her.'

She ducked under his arm and backed two steps away. Such a little distance, two steps, but enough to clear her head. 'But why?' she wondered. '*Why* would you want her to be your baby? Why would Olly Gray want Jenna to be his baby?'

'It is my baby.' Two steps for her were one for him and in a second he was right back in her face.

The glower, at such proximity, unnerved her. She sniggered. A tense and probably irritating snigger. 'It's very doubtful.' She smiled. A full, mischievous gloat. 'She's not even *my* baby.'

He stopped. Eyes narrowed, feeding new information to

his mind and calculating possibilities. 'James said you were pregnant when, you know ...'

'I was. When you jilted me by e-mail, I was pregnant. Was, was, *was*! Eleven weeks, they told me. Then ... swoosh!' She made a sliding away gesture. 'Gone before I really realised it was there. And your baby was ...' Stopped. Sucked in a huge, necessary breath, searching her mind for the most brutal expression to repay him a little for the fright, pain, subsequent illness. But she hesitated. Maybe he'd ceased to touch her, if she couldn't muster enough hate to hurt him? '... Gone,' she finished, quietly. 'And in a few days I was bleeding as if it was a new national sport. I was ill for more than a year ...' She tailed off. Olly wasn't listening.

Olly was very still. Body, eyes. She could almost hear his mind ticking. Through the window she was aware of Angel and Pete on their feet, fussing around Toby, soothing Jenna.

'Did Dad tell you I'd had the baby?'

Slowly, eyes still hard on her face, he shook his head. 'No.'

'Did he tell you I'd had a miscarriage?'

He shook his head again. 'No. We were ...' He hesitated. 'I explained that I really needed to see you. He said he supposed we really ought to talk things through. Then he asked me if I'd known you were pregnant.'

Tess felt her heart begin to steady as her imagination supplied a vision of Olly taking James aside, pally-pally, earnest and sincere, persuading out of James details that Tess would rather have kept secret. 'And what did you say?'

Olly's eyes flicked round the kitchen. After a silence, he admitted, 'I was angry. I drove off.'

Tess nodded, letting her mind tick. Something had brought Olly here today. When did Olly do something for no reason? 'What did Guy say?'

Maybe because it wasn't his main focus, Olly replied unguardedly. 'He said you'd lent him dosh.' Then, 'If you miscarried, why wouldn't James tell me?'

She laughed, a small, angry sound. She never knew when James would be dependable and when he'd turn round and bite her. 'I'd guess he thought you'd turn up – as you have. He *likes* you. I'd guess he wants us to get together again. Thought I'd be pleased to see you and ...' *Dosh*. The word resonated suddenly.

'I bet you've run out of money, Olly, haven't you?' The key clicked round so suddenly that she actually chuckled. '*That's* why you so wanted Jenna to be your baby! You've screwed up and you're all out of money! You, IT wizard, can write your own cheques in today's world but somehow you've got in a financial scrape. Olly Gray, you sharky bastard! Here's me with my own house, doing OK, James in the background to run to, and you can see the answer – temporary, probably – to your problems!'

Colour hectic, breath galloping, she searched his glowering face. 'Have things gone wrong for you? Can you bear it? That *I'm* successful and solvent and *Olly's* screwed up?' She laughed, let her voice become mocking. 'Olly's screwed up!'

The furious widening of his eyes and tightening of his lips over clenched teeth gave her warning, but she was too out of practice to dodge the long hand that whipped out and cracked across her cheek.

'*Bastard*!' And it hurt! It stung! It all but made her ear pop. It wrenched humiliated, furious tears to her eyes as it had the three times it had happened before. Well, no more! 'Get out!' she barked.

She heard his suddenly shaky response. 'Tess! I ...'

And that's when the door crashed back on its hinges, glass shattering, and Tess discovered just how rapidly Olly could find himself back in the lane, leaning on his car and crowing for breath, a bloodied nose to cradle along with his aching midriff, a rip in his trouser knee where he'd landed on all fours.

But Olly obviously allowed himself to be educated by the experience. When a voice growled at his shoulder, '*Go, now*!' – he went.

While Ratty had been watching Tess's confrontation in the kitchen, Toby had begun wailing that he felt ill. Adding that to the uncomfortable situation of Olly trying to claim their daughter, it seemed sensible that Pete and Angel take the children home.

And now Angel had rushed back to check that Tess was OK, leaving Pete – and by default, Ratty – appointed babysitters.

'So?' Pete prompted, circling promising ads in the *Auto Trader* with Toby's stubby purple pencil crayon. 'What did Tess think about your heroics? I wanted to shoot back, as you were obviously brewing trouble, but Angel was upset and when Toby, with impeccable timing, threw up, I couldn't get away.'

'She cried.'

Pete drew a pleasing oval around an advertisement for a Karmann Ghia.

Ratty squinted over his shoulder. 'We've only just rebuilt a Karmann, let's do something different.'

Pete sighed, scribbled his oval out again. 'He really clipped her one, did he?'

'Certainly did. Hand print like a starfish on her face.'

Shaking his head, turning the page, Pete whistled disapproval. 'That's seriously uncool. Seriously. Smacking a woman like that.' He pushed his hair back and tried to catch the light on a dark, grainy photograph of what purported to be an accident-prone Porsche. 'Big guy, that Olly.'

Ratty grinned. 'These annoying, smooth guys with desk jobs. Pushover. And I was really cross.' He'd also taken full advantage of the surprise element, erupting into the room in a shower of broken glass. God he'd been angry. Furious. Raging. Was it Olly's contemptuous blow or Tess's humiliation? Something had exploded him into the room without feeling his feet meeting ground, lit the flashes behind his eyes. And flung the hard, maddened punch into Olly's unprepared stomach, brought the knee up into Olly's face as he doubled over, given weight to the final, satisfying, ignominious boot against the buttocks that sent Olly sprawling.

Maybe he shouldn't have been leaning against the wall outside the door where he could both watch and listen. Nor waded in uninvited. But he'd swung the odds in Tess's favour.

Pete tapped the page. 'How about a BMW Isetta?'

'No, no more bubble cars. Little bastards.'

'Low mileage, though.'

Ratty grunted. 'You wouldn't think people would be so proud of not going far.' He settled back comfortably into his chair. The beer had taken over where the wine had left off.

'What was Jos doing?' Pete ran his finger down a column of photos of vehicles for sale.

'Sitting on the wall, looking pugnacious. Until Olly took off and Tess began to sob, then he decided he had a headache and left.'

'And you kissed Tess better?'

Ratty stopped twisting to read the magazine, tipping his head back to relax his neck. 'She wasn't interested in sympathy. Well, not after the first five seconds of crying all over my shirt. Look.' He picked at a rusty smear where blood from the corner of her mouth had mixed with her tears. 'Christ, did she suddenly get enraged, ungrateful woman. Bastard Olly, bastard men, bastard this, that. Then it's "Just leave me, Ratty! Go away!" – she's always telling me to go away. So here I am, an unsung hero.' He wondered about another beer. But had to get up early in the morning to see the remains of an E-Type Jaguar in North Devon he hoped to get for silly money. Probably better not. 'Coffee?'

'Sure.' Pete tossed the magazine on a pile and wandered towards the kettle.

Ratty sent after him, 'D'you think she *knew* how she looked today in those cut-off denims and the white vest?'

The chuckle from the kitchen told him that Pete had certainly noticed.

'She should wear her hair loose like that always. And her shirts that tight.'

'Why don't you just go for it – here, not much milk left, sorry, better keep enough for the kids or I'll get scalped – is it that impossible to ask her out?'

'Mmmm.' Ratty blew his coffee. 'I think she'd refuse. Her feminine instincts would alert her, y'know, "It's a man! It's a man! Remember, men hurt!" I'm still thinking, if I'm around for her, it'll kind of just ... happen.'

'You must be dynamite in bed, Rats, if you think it'll happen without her realising! Oh hiya, Toby-boy, can't you sleep?'

'Daddy,' Toby droned drearily, rubbing his eyes with the back of one hand and scratching his pyjama'd tummy with the other. 'Daddy, I sicked again. Watty, I sicked in bed.'

'There's something gross on his cheek,' Ratty pointed out.

'I see it.' Pete sighed, abandoning his coffee and reaching out gingerly to his little boy. 'And there's another on his neck.'

Chapter Ten

'Looks like bloody chickenpox.' Pete's apologetic voice, from the phone. 'Fat blisters and a temperature. He's crying for his mum, so ...'

Tess's voice was still quivering with fury. She had to concentrate to speak to Pete civilly. 'Of course, I'll tell her.'

Angel excused herself helplessly. 'I'll have to go, Tess.'

''Course!'

'I feel dreadful leaving you, after Olly ...'

Tess shook her head, hiding her face behind a sheet of hair. 'Don't fret, I'm all over it now! Early night, double whisky, I'll be cured.'

Late into her early night, she lay wide-eyed and naked beneath a single sheet. Olly. He remained dazzling; did she still want him? Or might she have, if he hadn't slapped her? What if he'd brought roses, smiled his sexiest, asked to begin again, tried to kiss, instead of hurt her? It might've been nice to find out.

The ringing of the bedside phone jumped her out of her preoccupation. 'Fancy a trip to the seaside?' Ratty demanded, without preamble. 'I'm seeing an E-Type in Devon tomorrow, and if Pete comes now Toby's sick, it'll leave Angel with her hands full.'

Propped on her elbow in the dark, she thrust back her hair and deliberated. Wasn't she busy, chewing over the scene with Olly, beating herself up over the way trouble had come courting? Didn't she have wallowing and dissecting to do?

'Tess?'

Did she want to be cooped up in a car with the witness

to her humiliation, for a long day because Devon was a hell of a way?

Maybe she'd better leave Middledip so Olly couldn't find her again, so she didn't have to face people who were now aware that Olly thought she was supposed to put up with slaps. Olly-rage blossomed fresh in her chest. And, if she went, this time she wouldn't even tell James where she was going.

Or should she stay in spite of Olly? Or maybe he wouldn't always behave so hideously ...?

'Tess!'

No, she didn't think she wanted to visit the seaside. 'Take Jos.'

Ratty slid into impatience, anything to do with his business paramount, to his mind. 'Yes, obviously, except he's got it too!'

Tess let herself be diverted. 'Really? Poor old Jos, chickenpox at his age won't be funny.'

'Poor, poor old Jos, poor Toby, I'm dead sorry for them. But I've made arrangements to see this car tomorrow!'

'Can't you go alone?'

He made a considering noise. 'It always goes better with two to work the vendor. Someone to be dubious, baulk at the price, hate the colour. Anyway, I might need a co-driver, it's a long way and I could do with this favour, Tess.'

And I owe you one, she supplied silently. Although I didn't invite you into my quarrel and as well as worrying about after the ball, and you helping deal with my bleeding, I'm cringing that you saw me get a slapping. And if something *did* happen after the ball, why don't you say?

Maybe leaving would be best, away, far away from everyone. Up a mountain, behind a large gate, with a moat, and big, toothy dogs.

'Please?'

'Oh ... all right!' She'd tired of the argument before it'd really begun. One day; one day couldn't be that bad.

'Great, thanks! Early start, I'll be there at five. And, by the way, bring a toothbrush and change of knickers in case we have to stay over.' And he'd gone.

'Be there at five'? 'In case we need to stay over'? She slammed the phone back into the rest so hard that it jumped out again. 'Bloody Ratty! He tucked that in at the end, didn't he? Sodding arrogant self-absorbed shitty *men*!'

Tess, asleep when Ratty banged the door with an impatient fist, stumbled down the twisted staircase.

He strode in through the patched-up door. 'Forget to set your alarm?'

She pulled her towelling robe tighter and trudged back up the staircase. 'Went back to sleep.' After lying awake for hours.

He called after her, 'Sugar in your coffee?' Minutes later he opened her bedroom door, making her leap for a shirt and, with head averted, thrust the coffee mug into the room. 'Here.'

She snatched the mug, refusing to thank him. What the hell did he think he was doing, barging in like that? And not even *trying* to sneak a look.

'Five minutes,' he suggested briskly.

Despite her aggravation, she'd taken his advice and packed a few things the night before; so by pouring most of the coffee away she was ready in time, dropping breathlessly into the kitchen clutching her hairbrush.

'Great.' He walked out to the van that was waiting with the trailer hooked up behind it, leaving her to lock up and scramble after him, scolding herself for letting him rush her. Why commit herself at all to this tedious trip to see a tiresome old car?

The van began to move even as she felt for the seat belt. 'Here we go,' he said, trundling into Main Road. It was the last he spoke for some time. Smoothly he took them through Bettsbrough to the dual carriageway and onto the M6.

Gazing away from him, she brushed her hair slowly until it streamed, bright in the morning sun, over her right shoulder. Damn, she'd forgotten a band for it. No, nothing in her bag, nor her pockets, her hair would just have to remain loose and probably be a sodding nuisance. One of these days she'd just get Angel to chop the whole messy mop off. She smiled to herself. Unlikely ...

How nice it was this early morning to be able to see over the hedges from an empty road, the early sunshine making pink and apricot beauty of even the rawness of the new housing estate they passed. She wondered dreamily about those houses. At just after six, would the occupants of those roofed boxes be awake? Did they like it that their house replicated the one next door in its brand-newness, its immature garden?

She considered, in contrast, the satisfying age of everything at Honeybun, the wild little garden of pot marigolds, holly and birch, the conifers that she didn't snip into shape because her father always clipped his so formally, too tight for her taste ...

Then they were swinging off the M6 and into a service station, the radio told her it was 7.30 and she realised she must have dozed off over her thoughts. Surreptitiously, she checked her T-shirt for dribble.

'Breakfast!' Ratty slid out of the cab and stretched.

The restaurant perched on the bridge over the motorway. Ratty ate silently. Tess finished first, fidgeting and gazing through the window at the traffic disappearing in three lines either way beneath them. Why had she let herself be persuaded – no, ordered – to come? Why did she wait cooperatively for what was coming next? Perhaps Ratty would even deign to begin a conversation soon and no doubt she'd respond to his new mood and they'd be friendly again.

Bloody Ratty. Although his precious car world revered his capabilities, however you wrapped it up he was only a second-hand car dealer.

And just look at all his women; he changed them as often as he changed his jeans. Oftener. An endless queue summoned by black curls and a spark of blue eyes to take their turn on the relationship carousel, and each, inevitably, watching him move on to a fresh horse.

Traffic slid on under the bridge, lorry-lorry-van-car, car-car-lorry, car transporter.

He sometimes talked to her in a way she didn't like. He got his own way far too much, possessing a lethal dose of loveable rogue. Not that he was always loveable.

'Your face might stick like that, all cross and hissy.' His amused voice broke into her daydream.

She started, unable to prevent a guilty flush. 'I don't know what I'm doing here and why you'd ask me. What help am I, what purpose do I serve? I'm not even sure you like me!'

'Oh, I do.' He began to lead her back to the long-vehicle park. 'But I didn't at first.' Strapped in, he changed the radio station, searched out mints from the glove compartment and expanded his explanation. 'You ran into my truck and then glared round my garage. But you're better for the knowing, I like the way you help Angel sometimes, it's generous. I like your conversation and sense of humour when you relax. What's the name of that lizard-man?'

'Farny.'

'I don't like the way you look at me as if waiting for me to turn into Farny.'

He drove. She thought. Deliberated and fumed. Finally, she challenged. 'You didn't like the way I *glared round your garage?*'

He nodded and sucked his mint, noisily. 'As if it was a den of thieves waiting to rip you off.'

She shrugged, sliding down in the seat. 'When I was a student I had loads of trouble with cars, getting stuck miles from home. I'd have to find someone to sort it, sick as I wrote the cheque because it would mean letters from the bank, then, afterwards, someone would always, *always*, tell me I'd been stung, that I should never go to strange garages because they'll charge what they like!'

'Surely your folks helped you out, financially?'

'Oh yeah!' She thought about her parents' brand of aid. 'With strings attached. "We'll help you this time, darling, but you must sell the car, it's just a worry. Wait until you have a good job when you'll be able to manage properly." It became my philosophy to cope alone at all costs, dig myself out of holes I fell into – usually making myself even more trouble. Then, just as I was going through the palaver of interviews and trying to get an agent, my grandmother died and left me some capital. Was Dad mad when he found out she hadn't stipulated that he manage it for me!' She chuckled. 'I always thought Grandma considered me too dreamy, she was so switched on and decisive, but she left me quite a bit. Anyway, at least it bought me a decent car that started when I turned the ignition key.'

The motorway traffic had thickened, every variety of vehicle charging along the moving tapestry. Ratty drove with relaxed concentration. Tess remembered Olly's contrasting style of tailgating, swerving out to overtake, flashing his headlights in the outside lane and unleashing a volley of two-fingered salutes.

'And anyway,' she backtracked, 'don't you just tolerate

me because I'm friends with Angel?'

He snorted, checked his mirrors, flicked the indicator, changed lanes. 'I never tolerate anybody for such stupid reasons.'

Miles and miles, constant engine noise, small movements of his head as he continually checked his mirrors, square fingers tapping along to the radio. Mechanic's hands with the grey graining which defied any scrubbing.

'Anyway,' he remarked, ages later, when she thought the subject buried, 'I always like pretty girls.'

She ignored a little starburst of pleasure in her chest and made a rude noise. 'Truckler!'

He put on an exaggerated, gripped-by-lust groan. 'Especially when they have long, long lovely hair.'

She laughed, gathering a bunch of hers to run it up and down his forearm.

He shuddered theatrically and flicked challenging eyes to hers. 'And a gorgeous, sexy body ...'

'Don't be predictable.' She pretended she didn't want to know if that meant he thought she had a gorgeous, sexy body.

The vehicles surging around them roared on endlessly. He sang now and then with the radio, a deep and gravelly voice it was difficult to tire of. Crawling between walls of lorries to enter a contraflow, he pushed the map book her way. 'Can you look which junction I need for the M5?'

She began to flip pages. 'Where are we heading?'

'Combe Martin, North Devon.'

Miles and miles. She studied the map. 'Motorways merge. Eventually you need the A391 to Barnstaple ...'

'Not Barnstaple, it's a traffic disaster area, the coast road's better.'

Roadworks near the M4 junction, then heavy traffic as they passed Bristol. 'I'm starving, let's get lunch.' Ratty rode the slip road off the motorway and within minutes had found a pub.

The lounge bar was full of dark wood beams and small tables. As she ate a toasted sandwich dripping with melted cheese, Tess studied the print on her place mat. 'John Constable's *The Haywain*.'

Ratty grunted.

'I wonder whether pub place mats will have reproductions of Winder or Slider two centuries after my lifetime.'

'That would be interesting.' Ratty smiled at the waitress as she brought two steaming apple turnovers. 'Are you pissed off with me for charging in on the fraught moment with your ex?' He chased flaky pastry round the plate with a fingertip and his eyes waited for a reply.

She raised her eyebrows, bit her lip. If she knew how she felt, she could probably tell him. 'No-o-o,' she admitted.

'But you'd rather I'd kept out?'

'I wish you hadn't seen it happen.' And, actually, that he hadn't reminded her, now. Why did he have to spoil her lunch? Leaving trouble behind her was more her style. She ate her apple turnover as if thinking of something more important.

He slapped the table, making her jump. ''Course! How stupid of me!'

She examined his expression – irritated – and took a miniature bite of turnover.

He lowered his voice, leaning forward so that only she could hear. 'Maybe it's how you get your jollies, you two? Perhaps you *like* the rough stuff?' His smile was hard, eyes glittering. 'In which case, I apologise for butting in.'

'Don't be so ridiculous!' From the gazes swinging their way, she'd spoken too loudly. It was her turn to smack the dark wood table, making her plate jump. 'I do *not* like being slapped!'

His hands leapt, strong and warm, trapping hers. 'Good. Don't stand for it!'

She snatched back her hands. She didn't want the remains of her turnover, didn't want another drink and didn't want coffee.

Back to the van, she didn't want to talk. She slammed the door and swung her hair into a curtain between them, wishing he'd just start the damned engine, turn up the radio and get the whole horrible trip over.

She could feel his gaze, hear his breathing turn to a sigh as his hand collected the veil of hair and went on to turn her face to his. He thumbed away a frustrated tear, his voice suddenly gruffly gentle. 'So you hated it.'

Jerkily, she nodded. 'It made me feel ... weak and put in my place, exposed, humiliated! And you watched.'

His eyes glowed with compassion. 'That's what made me so angry. And the – the *righteousness* on his face, the strategic way he hit you to get his own way. I don't think I've ever seen a man really hit a woman before and no one could have stood there and just let him. He's a big guy, there's no excuse for him. Of course, you might argue that my reaction makes me no better than him and all that politically correct stuff.'

She sniffed. 'I've no objection, in principle, to Olly getting a taste of his own medicine. I just didn't ask for your help.'

He sighed. 'Call it a returned favour. You drew me a great Nigel. I sorted out someone too big for you to handle. It wasn't the first time?'

She shook her head. 'It's happened once or twice.' Then, honestly, 'Three times. He's always sorry.'

He swore. 'You don't deserve that. Believe me. Believe in yourself.' Starting the engine, he checked his mirrors before pulling away.

She searched for a tissue. 'He'll hate you. He's proud of his wonderful looks.'

The van gained speed, moved into the middle lane. 'You must've made quite a couple.' He leant forward to shrug apologies that he had no room to two girl hitch-hikers thumbing hopefully from the edge of the slip road.

So that only left pacific, quiet hours until they were undulating along by the rocks of the North Devon coastline where hedges, sliced perpendicular by the traffic, made them a tunnel.

'Will you be my girlfriend?' Slowing at each left turn, he was looking out for landmarks. 'Just a story to sell to the woman, Mrs Partridge – there's the pink and black pub.' He swung the wheel. 'Her husband's run off so she's selling this E-Type he'd stripped down. I won't get a nice price if I let on that I'm in the business, so it's better if I present myself as any old enthusiast. And if the more enthusiastic I get, the less interested you are, my darling girlfriend, she might become more anxious to sell. Here we are. If you'd be as indifferent as possible that'd be great.'

'I think I can manage that.' There didn't seem any harm in it, even if, for a heartbeat, she'd thought he meant the girlfriend bit. Ridiculous.

The Jaguar E-Type was charmless as far as Tess was concerned but she caught the gleam in Ratty's eye as he gazed down the long, nosy bonnet. Wheels off, lights blind, the car rested on blocks, boxes of bits surrounding it, and what should've been paintwork was undercoat or rust preventative. Mrs Partridge was stridently eager to make a killing, spinning tales of all the interest the E-Type was exciting.

Ratty listened politely.

In her uninterested girlfriend role, Tess answered his

artificially ardent longing with indifferent murmurs, folding her arms and tossing her hair. But she was taken aback when he took the charade so far as to grab her hand and drag her on a tour of the remains of the car. She sniffed, 'I can think of much better things to do with the money,' and reclaimed her hand.

Mrs Partridge's eyes narrowed, obviously seeing a fly in her ointment.

Arms folded, Tess concentrated on looking bored whilst Ratty made an investigation of the boxes and the car's underside, and even, after several attempts and a few adjustments, coaxed a barking response from the engine. Wiping his hands, he slid his arms around Tess, making her jump, and breathed in her ear, 'Stamp back to the van as though you're completely fed up.'

'Right!' Snatching away his hands, which had dropped casually to her bottom, she sent him a poisonous glare before flouncing away.

The old E-Type Jaguar, once probably someone's sexy, growly pride and joy, merited a long, longing last scrutiny. The bright work was OK, the rot fairly tolerable though new sills were inevitable. He leant on the nearside wing. 'Not looking too hopeful,' he warned Mrs Partridge, gazing plaintively towards Tess, po-faced in the van's passenger seat. 'How fixed are you on your price?'

He made it a very gentle haggle, stroking the car, pacing around it, convincing her she'd sell if the price dropped enough. She looked torn between a sale and greed.

Oh well, back to the van to consider her 'last word', promising to phone, sliding a pretend-conciliatory arm around Tess. He kissed her cheek. 'Be as huffy as you like!' When she twitched away pettishly, he shook a mournful head. Once out of sight down the lane he shouted jubilantly and squeezed her knee. 'Great stuff! You were brilliant!'

And he'd liked the lover-like opportunities to touch, could still feel the sweet melons of her buttocks so briefly in his hands.

Enjoying his own cleverness, he pretended not to notice her silence as he continued on the coast road, singing, to where he'd left the trailer.

Chapter Eleven

Down by the sea the swirling breeze teased Tess's hair into a dancing mass.

Ratty made a comic performance of fighting off the flying locks. 'You're a Gorgon!'

Tess got the giggles. There was something carefree about hopping about the bronzy rocks at the side of the sand, peering into pools, slipping on seaweed; mossy green the most treacherous, bulky brown ribbons unsportingly hiding pockets of seawater ready to soak careless feet. 'If I turn you to stone, here, nobody will notice. It's like a lunar landscape.' She breathed in lungfuls of the briny air, turning her face to the blue sky.

Ratty seemed to have forgotten all about the E-Type Jaguar he'd come all this way to see. He'd brought her to Combe Martin for cream tea and ice cream and was now behaving as if their only purpose in Devon was to enjoy exploring the foreshore and the tide had gone especially for them. His chosen path was taking them over mini-chasms awash with the swirling sea, adventurous but accessible to the energetic.

A giant leap carried him across what looked, to Tess, like a ravine. She halted. 'I think I'll go round.'

He turned, grinning, eyes just the same colour as the choppy sea. 'Don't be a wuss! Jump it!'

At her feet, the sea swirled and sucked. 'It's too wide.' She eyed the sawtooth rocks.

He held out encouraging arms. 'Come on, jump. Don't be a scaredy cat!'

Three seconds and a huge shriek later, Tess was groaning

from the bottom of the fissure and Ratty, sprawled on the rocks above, was scrabbling to grasp her arms. 'Don't!' she squeaked, teeth gritted and eyes tight in agony.

He hesitated. 'What have you hurt?'

'Ribs. Shoulder.' The sea was icy up to her waist and tears seeped around her eyelids. She sloshed and limped to a place where she could shamble out between the rocky sides and onto the sand, catching her breath at every movement.

'Hold onto me.'

She accepted Ratty's help, his arm strong around her waist as she limped slowly up the beach towards the elevated road. One side of her body blazed with pain.

His eyes were dull with concern. 'I'm so sorry. When you landed you kicked my foot out from under me –'

'I know,' she agreed, tightly.

'You took a hell of a tumble onto those rocks. I'll get you to casualty.'

She gasped in pain. 'For Chrissake ...! I don't like hospitals. Just get me somewhere I can rest.' It had been his fault. Mainly. Maybe. Or, at least, it hadn't been hers! Yes, OK, her foot had skidded on seaweed and bowled his leg out from underneath him. But *he* had said, 'Jump!'

'You're really hurt, those rocks are sharp –'

She yelped as she tried to lift her foot for the first rocky step.

'Let me carry you –'

'*No!*'

'Gently, then. We'll try this guest house.' It seemed like only minutes until he had booked them into a white building with a swooping red tile roof and crooked gutters and they were in her room, Ratty helping her from her torn and bloody shirt, while she tried to keep herself decent with a thin bath towel. The guest house was hardly the Ritz. The carpet was threadbare in places and the old-fashioned wallpaper had faded, but the room was clean and homely.

'Your jeans are soaked.'

'The sea was wet,' she ground out, pushing his helpful hands away from her ripped and ruined, sodden, chafing jeans – the only pair she had with her. 'You'd better try and get me something else to wear, while I shower.'

'Unless you want me to help wash any grit out?'

'Just fuck off, Ratty!' She hobbled into the bathroom and slammed the door, relieved to see that the shower was a simple electric job that gave hot water at a prod of a button and, as she let the warm stream play on her grazes, she sagged against the acrylic sides of the cubicle, alternately shivering with shock and swearing at the stinging water.

In the morning, she was so stiff she groaned aloud as she crawled from her bed. Black, brown, plum bruises were scored with jammy-red grazes from her fall into the rocks' claws.

She'd slept badly in the unfamiliar bedroom, her injuries aching and throbbing, every movement chafing her scratches into fresh smarting.

Wincing at the speckled mirror, she inspected her uncomfortably puffed flesh, then eased gingerly into a clean T-shirt and pulled on one-handed the short-shorts that were, apparently, Ratty's idea of seaside wear.

His rap on the door came at just the worst, testing moment, making her snarl, 'What?' Her shoulder pounded with every motion and tears stood in her eyes; feverish flushes rippled over her with each fresh drag of pain.

His smile faded. 'Shit, you look grim. I should've taken you to hospital.'

She shook her head and attempted clumsily to fasten the metal button at the waist of the hard new denim, left-handed. She failed and had to accept his help, his hot fingers brushing the soft, intimate flesh of her stomach.

Stiffly, she reached for her hairbrush. He took it. 'Let me.'

OK, she'd let him. As long as he was gentle, avoided the scalding throb of her shoulder, she'd let him do that small service. It was soothing, in fact, and in his silence she composed herself.

And when he'd finished and pulled gently at the fabric at her neck to inspect the pounding wound, insisting, 'I'm taking you to hospital,' she easily had the strength to snap, 'No, you're not, not unless I collapse from lack of food! Let's get breakfast before we starve.'

Chapter Twelve

'I'll phone Mrs Partridge again, see if she's thought of a new best price.'

Tess glanced up. She was beginning to feel marginally better over eggs, bacon, sausage, tomato and two enormous mugs of hot tea. The dining room looked as if it had been furnished via house clearance, but the full English breakfast was to die for. 'Your negotiations didn't seem encouraging, yesterday. I was hoping to soon head home. Mrs Partridge didn't seem to be prepared to give the car away.'

'It won't take long. I'll get it. It'll sell well when it's pretty and I'd make money even if she didn't drop any more. But she will.'

She listened in as, on the mobile, he became a wistful, would-be E-Type-owner. 'Between you and me,' he confided in Mrs Partridge, leaning back in his creaky chair, 'Tess doesn't want to spend the money. We're getting married, you know how it is.' He grinned at her.

She shut her mouth suddenly, realising her expression had frozen in muppet-like astonishment.

'I can make you an offer – but it may not be what you hope for.' But then he backed off, as if the whole project seemed suddenly overwhelming. Then waxed enthusiastic. Then thought again. A contrived negotiation; Tess preferred to savour the hot tea. But she heard him calmly offer an amount that was a little over half Mrs Partridge's 'last word' price and the conversation ended suddenly. 'That made her stutter,' he observed contentedly, closing his phone.

Then he sighed. 'I do feel bad about dropping you.'

Her shrug was stillborn on a bleat of pain but she

managed to be brave. 'One of those things.'

'You're all hurt and pale.'

She tried to make her eyebrows shrug for her.

'It was a total accident. Honestly.'

'Sure. When can we leave?'

His mobile played a fanfare, and he read the caller's number, and smirked. 'Soon, perhaps.' Sure enough, Mrs Partridge counter-offered. Ratty hinted he'd found a friend to weigh in a few hundred extra pounds so maybe it was worth another look?

'Why?' Tess scrambled stiffly back into the van that smelt of oil. Sunshine baking through the windscreen washed a flush of discomfort up her spine, sweat broke out on her forehead and she wound down the window. 'If you're already into profit, why keep beating her down?'

The black curls swung as he turned in amazement. 'I don't pay more than I need! Profit equates to success.'

'Is your business in trouble?' Ow, ow, was any other road so riddled with potholes? Each one a separate blaze of pain up her arm and into her shoulder.

'No, but it might be, one day, if I stop doing it right.' He grinned at her lopsidedly. 'Think of all my dependants.'

'Who?'

'All my illegitimate children.'

He laughed at her and she realised her expression must have been horrified.

'Don't look so disgusted, I haven't any! I meant losing Jos and Pete their jobs!'

The visit was fruitful, this time. She played the girlfriend grudgingly giving way, he acted his part with staged embraces, running his fingertips in absent-minded caress along the line of her shorts and buttock. But she was ready for him. Reaching up to kiss his throat in feigned affection, she stood hard on his foot.

His hands immediately fastened in her hair, careful of her injuries, whilst he took a revenge kiss, tongue and all, before whispering, 'Bitch!' leaving her breathless, outraged, amused, to hiss back, 'Bastard!'

The deal was soon done and Ratty produced a roll of cash from under his dashboard that made Mrs Partridge look dismayed that she was settling for such a small portion of it. She became very po-faced as he swept off his shirt, fastened dungarees over his tattoos and got down to business with a sudden onset of efficiency.

Tess dozed and sweated in the van while he worked. Two hours and the wheels were back on the E-Type, it was winched onto the trailer and chained down, the accompanying boxes stacked securely in the van. Sniffing impudently around the outbuilding, Ratty claimed several pieces of trim to lie beside them. A wave goodbye and they were off.

'I'm sure she thinks she's been done.' Tess gulped Anadin Extra with bottled water and looking at Mrs Partridge, hands on hips, watching them rumble away.

'She's right.'

More miles of motorway, darkening as they travelled through afternoon, evening and into night, the trailer rattling reassuringly behind, and Tess curled, asleep, beside him. He dropped the seat arm to cradle her.

Sleep made her look vulnerable. And desirable. He wanted to stop the van somewhere unlit and caress her soft, slack lips with his, her sleeping eyelids, the hollow of her throat. Kiss her better, kiss every inch, kiss her awake to make love. He thought of how he'd helped her to fasten her shorts, her silky belly on the back of his fingers. The strong urge to let them dip between …

It was a slow homeward journey because of pulling the

extra load but, for him, it wasn't onerous. When Tess roused, squeaking in pain as she got her shoulder moving, he distracted her by singing. One song after another, husking his favourite words into the darkness at the endless chain of headlights.

'What a hotchpotch,' she grumbled as ballads followed folk, country, blues. But she listened, tapping her foot, taking more painkillers, fretting in her seat. And when his throat was tired of singing they talked, pushing the miles by as they considered each other's lives.

How Ratty had disappointed his father with what Lester termed 'that surprising garage venture'.

Her face turned to his in the darkness; when he glanced her way he could see the lights flickering in her eyes. 'Do you see them? Your parents.'

He laughed. 'Of course I see them. They were at the Spring Ball, you danced with my father.'

Even watching the road and with only the strobe-lights of the oncoming vehicles, Ratty saw her hair swing out and settle around her left breast as she turned more fully, and felt his breath catch. '*Did* I? I didn't realise. It was a long evening.'

He thought about telling her. That he'd seen her home, they'd shared a horny interlude, groaning with frustration he'd watched her pass out and cursed his luck. 'Extremely,' he agreed neutrally, instead.

She told him about her father's proprietorial interference in her life, his frustrating reluctance to blame Olly for his part in her miserable episode. 'D'you know, when I rang to complain about Olly thinking Jenna was his, he said, sorry he didn't get a chance to make things clearer? But, if it'd made Olly interested, it served a purpose! He even *told* Olly my address when I'd expressly asked him not to! I don't know what to say to keep his nose out. Unless it's

"Piss off, you selfish bastard!"'

They shouted a laugh together, rousing themselves from the tiredness of the final hour of the journey. She clutched her shoulder, 'Ow! Ow! I'd love to see Olly's face!' Then speculated, 'Guy might know what's behind his reappearance.'

So, she was still thinking about Olly.

By the time they reached home, it was late. In the almost total blackness of her garden he moved close. 'Thanks for your help. And your company. Even if I dropped you in the sea, maybe you don't think I'm quite such a bastard now.'

'N-o-o.' She laughed, fumbling left-handed with her key. 'But you still bear watching.'

He turned the key for her.

She paused. 'What do I owe you for the guest house?'

'Co-driver's expenses. Reclaimable against tax.' He went on before the uncertainty in her expression could become a protest. 'And I'm really sorry about your shoulder and everything.'

'It's all right,' she said, before she closed the green door. 'And at least I feel as if we're friends, now. It's like having a sensible version of Guy; mates, and I know you don't expect anything ... else.'

Ratty turned back up the lane towards the Cross lit by the light in Crowther's shop window, enjoying the honeysuckle smell of the village at midnight. He blew a huge sigh and wondered where she'd got that stupid idea.

Tess slept very late in the morning, then showered and examined her bruises. The elbow was improving but her shoulder was, if anything, still more livid, as stiff and tender as a great big boil. So she ate brunch and strolled to Pennybun Cottage, pausing, as she drifted by, to admire her new patio furniture. It seemed weeks since they'd cooked on the barbecue and drunk wine but, when she lifted the lid, the shrivelled food was still on the rack. She wrenched it free and binned it.

It would be nice to see how Toby was; she'd call after seeing Lucasta. She couldn't work anyway until her pain had subsided. And Jos, she could call there too, make him a cup of coffee or something. Poor old Jos, he was used to looking after himself but it was horrible to have chickenpox erupting in all the wrong places.

She clattered Lucasta's polished brass knocker. Again. Then more loudly.

Odd. Lucasta normally answered her door like a greyhound out of a trap. Maybe she was in the bathroom. Or at the shop? Out for a drive with someone from the village? Unlikely that Ratty had taken her anywhere, the garage would already be one man short, with Jos ill.

She began to retreat, peeping tentatively through the windows. Kitchen. Sitting room.

The veined leg, when she saw it protruding from behind an armchair, jumped her back from the window. 'Lucasta?' She cupped her hands around her face against the glass. Oh God! She could see a burgundy slipper on the foot, a fold of blue-and-white dressing gown across the knee. She banged on the window. Then with both fists. *'Lucasta!'*

The door was locked. She scuttled round the cottage, clutching her shoulder, searching vainly for an open window, banged again on the sitting-room glass and yelled, in case she could be heard, 'I'll get help!'

Poor Lucasta, how long had she lain there? Was she alive? Tess raced back to Honeybun. Phone, phone, phone the garage! Engaged signal; she groaned. Wavered. Ambulance? Or Ratty? Ambulance?

Ratty first, he'd have the key. She reversed the Freelander into the lane, engine moaning, leaving the shrubs waving, first gear – 'ouch y'bastard', as her shoulder twanged. Little Lane, as fast as she dared, must get Ratty.

Late brake, glance left, ready to whip right and accelerate. A glimpse of McLaren hurtling joyfully towards her across Main Road.

'*Shit*!' She stamped on the brake and yanked the steering wheel left, '*Owwwww*!', dreading the inevitability of car colliding with dog.

She felt the bump.

It didn't seem very hard. But the Freelander was a big vehicle. And McLaren wouldn't be very solid.

On a wave of sickness, she pulled up the handbrake and turned off the ignition. No anguished yelping. Pushing the door with a trembling hand, she stepped down, hardly daring to look at her front offside.

'McLaren!' Sitting quietly in the road, he looked dreamily in her direction and away again. 'McLaren, thank God!' She dropped down beside him, wiping tears she hadn't notice start. Was there any damage? His coat beneath her tentative hands was as white and brown as always, there was no blood. Did that mean he was OK? She certainly couldn't leave him, anyway, poor lad, sitting so unnaturally well behaved in the middle of the junction of Little Lane and Main Road.

Gingerly, lip biting, praying for his customary docility, she hauled him into the back of the Freelander, 'Ouch, *ouch*,' and he stretched out slowly. He was bound to be shaken up. Dazed.

Lucasta! 'O-h-h-h, G-o-d!' she groaned, scrabbling back into the driver's seat, fumbling the ignition, driving with exaggerated care into Main Road and on up to the Cross. Ratty was on the phone near the folded doors when she drew in all anyhow and slithered out of the car.

He stared. 'Call you back,' he said to the phone. 'You're crying!' accusingly, to Tess.

Her breath was out of rhythm, nipping her chest, making it difficult to speak. 'It's McLaren and Lucasta! Ratty, Lucasta's on the floor and I can't get in! And you were on the phone, and I'm desperately sorry, but I was rushing and he just bounded across the road from nowhere, I'm sorry!' Her hair clung infuriatingly to wet cheeks, she tried to shove it behind her ears but it stuck instead to wet fingers.

She took a panting breath. 'I should've phoned the ambulance. But I thought you could get in, you've got a key, and McLaren just ...'

Ratty stilled her hands, speaking sharply. 'Wait, tell me properly, calm down, *tell* me! Lucasta first. *What* about Lucasta?'

She dragged in a deep and ragged breath and concentrated. 'I went round to see Lucasta and she didn't answer the door and it's locked and I can see her leg, she's lying on the floor and your phone was engaged. And I got into the Freelander and I was rushing to come here and ...' Her voice dropped to an agonised whisper. 'McLaren ran out and I ... I ran him over.

'I can't see any damage to him,' she excused herself to Ratty's back as he snatched at the rear door of the Freelander. 'But he seems a bit ... bemused.'

All too horrible. All too horrible, rushing back to Pennybun Cottage with Ratty's key, calling the paramedics for Lucasta whose face was darkly red, whose breathing was loud in deep unconsciousness. Then ambulance chasing, with Ratty hurling the Freelander about in complete silence, Tess snivelling in the passenger seat and McLaren shaking about silently in the luggage compartment and being a little bit sick.

Racing into the hospital. Ratty trying and failing to contact Derry Meredith, Lucasta's son, who hardly ever came to see her and lived in Mill Hill, North London.

Tess wringing her hands and saying, 'I'm so sorry!'

Ratty having to be the one that the doctors took into the relatives' room. Emerging, blinking huge eyes. 'She's gone.'

Ratty carrying McLaren into his house from the Freelander, stone-faced. Kicking the door shut from inside.

And, after a sweaty and awful sleepless night, when Tess rang timidly in the morning, Ratty was as cold and hard as marble. 'McLaren didn't wake up.'

Her mind was wool, her ears refusing to accept what she heard. 'What? What do you mean?'

'He's dead! OK?' And then, with gravel in his throat, 'I don't want to talk to you, Tess.'

Chapter Thirteen

Almost the entire village walked into church for Lucasta's funeral. Tess sidled, last minute, into the hindmost honey-coloured pew, avoiding Ratty. Expressionless Ratty, foreign in a charcoal suit, with Derry, the bearded son from Mill Hill, leading the pall-bearers, two by two slow-stepping up the flagstone nave. Black coffin, brass handles – reminding her joltingly of the brass doorknocker she'd rapped at Pennybun Cottage – a row of wreaths trembling in time.

Amazing Grace and *Abide With Me*, but she couldn't open her throat to sing.

Feeling as if she wanted to be invisible on the fringes of the service in the churchyard. She tried not to look at the ugly grave, the raw sides of the hole, the heaped earth, intending, the instant the minister was finished, to seek the refuge of Honeybun.

Of course, it didn't happen. Angel worked her way backwards to join her, whispering, 'Hasn't it been appalling? I've had to get Pete's mum to come and have the kids and Toby's just a monster at the moment. And Jos is heartbroken to be missing the whole thing.'

Gwen Crowther, black mac buttoned over her shop overall, dabbed her eyes. 'Poor Lucasta, we're all upset, I *shall* miss her.'

Of course, Pete followed Angel and, automatically, they converged with Ratty as the service ended.

Ratty, well-brushed, crisp and most unlike himself, walked alongside a man with startlingly silver hair. Dead straight, it swept across his forehead with the neatness of a bird's wing above blue eyes that held an expression of control. He was somehow familiar; maybe she'd seen him around the village.

For the funeral Tess had plaited away her hair, bought a stark navy dress which flounced around her ankles and had three-quarter length sleeves to cover her bruises. Her heeled navy shoes sank into the grass, giving her an excuse to lag. But, in the end, she couldn't avoid contact with Ratty's waiting eyes. She slid her gaze past and behind him.

'You've met Tess Riddell,' Ratty told the silver man. 'Tess bought Honeybun Cottage from The Commuters.'

'Of course.' The man extended a very clean and soft hand.

Met? Tess tried to remove the puzzled O from her lips and smiled weakly, pummelling her memory. She was plainly expected to remember. In the expectant pause for her to join the conversation, her mind went absolutely blank.

Her glance flickered back to Ratty. *I'm stuck.*

Neutrally, he cooperated. 'Tess is a very talented illustrator, Father.'

Father! And 'very talented'. Wow, very nearly a standing ovation by Ratty's standards. She was able to gather herself to respond, eyeing Lester Arnott-Rattenbury with interest. 'We met at the ball,' she agreed, as if she'd known all the time. So many dinner jackets had accompanied her around the dance floor that she'd stopped looking at who filled them.

Lester Arnott-Rattenbury was familiar for the features he shared with his son. The contrasting hair had thrown her, but the likeness was there, though Lester's expression was so careful where Ratty's was ever a mirror for his thoughts: the humour that so often lit his face, the grimness that sometimes spoilt it, concentration for those who entertained him, contempt for those who bored him.

She resolutely avoided his eyes, sure now they'd be shining with accusation, inevitable anger, even dislike.

I don't want to speak to you, Tess.

Since she'd heard them, those words had whipped around her mind, kept time with her footsteps as she walked through the village and along the bridleways where the nettles were growing long and reaching towards one another. *I don't want to speak to you, Tess.*

She had, after all, killed his dog.

Some dreary business she'd occupied herself with, that day, the day after Lucasta and McLaren's deaths, brushing away, blotting away, wiping away the sliding tears. Somewhere, sometime she'd heard it was an actor's trick to prompt tears by telling themselves, 'My dog is dead.' As she ironed jeans and shirts, her mind kept helplessly supplying, 'His dog is dead. I've killed his dog. Poor, poor McLaren!' The tears slid on.

And obviously the pleasure in belonging in Middledip would be short-lived if Ratty decided she was 'out'. So vivid, so central. Hostility from Ratty would close the ranks against her, Angel's friendship would shrink into a daytime thing when Ratty wasn't around, Pete and Jos would merely wave as she passed. And she'd *enjoyed* being a part of a crowd with in-jokes and shared experiences.

She'd actually begun to enjoy Ratty's friendship, the talks over the babysitting, the van on the motorway with the trailer rattling behind. His friendship was pivotal to the rest.

But she didn't see what she could do to prevent it from coming to an end.

She remembered how Olly had never let her be truly included with his friends, although he'd somehow contrived to separate her from her own. Sometime, Olly must've had a heart bypass. Which had made it easy to ignore the apology for his recent behaviour he'd left on her answering machine. Apology from Olly? That was a first.

The 'afterwards' for Lucasta was in the village hall and they all walked there from the church together.

Middledip owned a marvellous village hall, large and proudly kept up, with pairs of green-curtained French doors down each side. Today, blinding white tablecloths set off solemn lilies and the last of the gladioli. She thought of the gorgeously scented ruby roses at the door of Pennybun and Lucasta's cheerful collection of daisies.

The tea she was handed was too weak and she abandoned it in favour of more sustaining wine. Angel and Pete were across the room. Ratty, brows down at the son from Mill Hill, all rapid sentences and terse hand movements, in the middle. He appeared absorbed, but, as she ventured past in search of another drink, he leant out of his conversation. 'Can I have a word, later?'

She nodded. Yuk, he probably wanted to tell her exactly what he thought of her and she didn't feel up to it. He'd accuse her of driving likely to endanger village dogs, failure to dash successfully to the rescue. He might even sue, because pedigree dogs were valuable.

The caterers began to circulate little kits of plate, napkin and fork ready for the bun fight. Fine. Good opportunity. She glided four backward steps towards the green floor-length curtains, one sidestep and she was hidden.

The French doors behind her opened smoothly and she was out, free. Car park, Cross Street, Port Road, skirt the Cross to Main Road, Little Lane, Honeybun. Safe.

Staring at Ratty across her kitchen, she wondered how she could have been so stupid as to think that going home and discarding funereal dress would award her sanctuary. He'd simply come after her in his expensive suit and black tie, onyx cufflinks snicked in the cuffs.

Inconsequentially, she thought about that dream. *That* dream. That hand, taking her to the heights.

Ratty looked drained. He threw the black tie across a chair, tipped his chin to unfasten his top button and hung his jacket on the cupboard door. 'I hate funerals.' He scrubbed at his eyes with the heels of his hands. 'Hate, hate, *hate* funerals.' A dark curl peeped from his open collar.

'Deadly,' she agreed. Then screwed her eyes shut suddenly as she realised what she'd just said. But, seeming not to notice the howler, Ratty just dragged out a chair and flopped onto it.

She supposed he must be waiting there for something, brooding, staring blankly at the knotty wooden table. 'Coffee?' she offered.

A bored face.

'Beer?'

His face considered. 'I'd really like a good, fat whisky. I don't suppose ...?'

She had only the silly, thimble glasses that'd been her grandmother's and filled two to their fragile brims, wishing he'd get off his chest whatever he'd come to say.

He rested his temple against his hand, heaved another huge sigh. 'Poor Lucasta. I'm going to miss her like hell.'

God. God, she was so hideously selfish, gearing up to have a row with Ratty if he turned arsey. They'd just buried Lucasta! A long, interesting life had ended, a bright and caring person faded to memories and here she was, jittery in case Ratty called her nasty names.

Still, she chose a chair that kept the table between them. She licked her lips. 'You must feel dreadful.'

He refilled his glass. 'God, yes. I've always had Lucasta to turn to. Her reality, her wisdom. She'd always make me feel better, listen, know the right thing to say.'

'Yes. She had a gift for pointing you gently in the right

direction.' Uneasily, she watched as Ratty topped up his glass, rose to refill hers, then settled in the next chair. She jumped when he touched her hand, very lightly, with one fingertip.

'When you rang, was I utterly bloody?' He looked rueful.

The beginnings of relief spread her shoulders. Oh joy, perhaps he hadn't come to quarrel! 'I'm so sorry about McLaren. But he just ...'

He squeezed his eyes shut. '*Don't*! Don't apologise any more, I should never have let you.

'It was all me, Tess, my fault. I shouldn't have let him escape to cannon into motorists and I should've taken him to the vet. But, with what was happening with Lucasta, I just let his brain swell or something until he lapsed into a coma, and told myself he was asleep.

'Then you rang just when I was detesting myself most, so I took it out on you. It's been such a crappy week.

'Derry Meredith is a self-serving bastard. The funeral would've been sing-a-hymn-and-let's-go-home if he'd had his way. I've fought him every step to get her a decent send off and paid for most of it. Can I switch to coffee? My head's splitting.' Ratty looked strained.

She sent him into the sitting room. When she joined him, carrying a little circular tray with the cafetière and china mugs, a non-matching saucer holding two paracetamol, she apologised lightly. 'Not up to Lucasta's standards, I'm afraid. She always offered me tiny eggshell china cups and a gracious coffee pot.'

Ratty left his blue moquette chair and joined her on the bandy little sofa. 'Me, too.'

Halfway down his coffee he evidently began to think about other things. 'How's the shoulder healing?' Delicate but familiar, he hooked the neck of the grass-green T-shirt to one side. She imagined the brown, red and yellow flesh, and the scabs flaking off. Yuk.

'Gruesome. Forgiven me yet?'

Ignore it! Ignore his casual familiarity, his hot and gentle fingertips, his warm breath. It's just his way and means nothing.

She answered lightly, 'I forgive you, if you forgive me for McLaren.'

Side by side they sat on the softness of her sofa, he rumpling his suit, after-shave blending with his warm, comfortable maleness. Relaxing into his company she made a sandwich and fresh coffee, put some music on in the background.

'So, that was your father,' she observed.

'Lester Arnott-Rattenbury,' he agreed.

'Not friends?'

He shook his head. 'We don't always understand each other, it's a different thing. I don't dislike him but it's difficult to feel warm. He's looked at me as if I was an alien since I was about fifteen. He disapproves.'

The little black curl that lay snugly in the hollow beneath his Adam's apple moved slightly when he spoke. She moved her eyes up to his face. 'Of you?'

'Just disapproves, it's what he does best.' Another coffee cup emptied, he put it down on the table. 'We don't laugh at the same things.'

She settled more deeply into the cushions. Ratty obviously wanted to talk; maybe Lucasta's death had, in a way, made him lonely, needy of somebody to fall into the category between man-talk and pillow-talk. She prompted, 'That's sad, if you never laugh together.'

He grinned up at the ceiling. 'There *was* once ... I took my driving test the minute I could, but failed. You can imagine how pissed off I was! So, having a motor cycle licence, I bought a Reliant Robin.'

She snorted with laughter. 'Bet that impressed the girls!'

'Actually, there was plenty of room in the back ... Anyway, the police stopped me one night in Bettsbrough when there was a whole gang of people on board. I passed the breathalyser but gave them loads of attitude, so they took us all in; vehicle dangerously overloaded, blah, blah.

'And they kept us there for hours! God, they must've had some axe to grind that night, frightened the girls to death, the bastards.'

The music CD needed changing but she couldn't be bothered to move; she was enjoying envisaging a young attitude-laden Ratty wowing the girls with his Del Boy Trotter-style three-wheel fibreglass van.

'Predictably enough, I was released last. They impounded the three-wheeler, so I walked home and arrived about six o'clock, just as my father was getting up. And he just *exploded*! It was brilliant. He was absolutely on my side and made huge waves.' He grinned again, savouring the memory. 'He got onto a senior officer and let off real rockets about police officers with nothing better to do.

'Following Sunday, my parents were entertaining friends at a boozy lunch on the patio – and up turns an inspector, to apologise.' Ratty stuck his chest out, tucked an imaginary cap under his arm. 'And he, *personally*, would ensure that there would be no repetition.

'My father was propped up against the mantelpiece, clutching a massive whisky, listening intently. He considered his response carefully, then said, "It's no wonder the children call you pigs!"'

'No!' Tess breathed in delight.

'It was a magical moment in father-son relations. He's OK but we're not that close. I think he's waiting for me to grow up. Sad. Long wait.'

Late into the evening of keeping Ratty company in his unhappiness, Tess plucked up the courage to present him with what had been intended as a peace offering or a conscience salver. From a photograph supplied by Angel, with pastels on black paper, Tess had captured McLaren, long ears listening, tongue lolling from his wide doggy laugh. Feathery coat van Dyck brown and burnt sienna between the white, eyes brightened with a starburst into a knowing expression.

She watched him stare. 'Almost too painfully good,' he murmured. And he dropped a kiss on her temple.

He'd made himself at home, shoes off, feet on the table, head tipped back on the sofa cushions. She looked at his throat, the upward thrust of dark hair. Once, it had been one of her favourite things, when standing next to Olly, to look up at the smoothness of his throat and tiptoe to kiss it. One of her favourite things. Sometimes he'd twitch away, sometimes he'd accept the caress and rest his hand in the small of her back.

To replace Ratty's silence she began the latest instalment in the story of Olly, because she could always change the subject if he glazed over.

'I rang Guy.' He turned to listen; she tucked her feet up and burrowed sideways into the sofa to face him. 'He claimed he hadn't heard from Olly for ages. 'Course, he would say that. I threatened to insist on all my money back, which made him laugh, so I said I'd tell Lynette about his girlfriend.'

'Foul play!' He grinned. 'Did he cave in?'

She thought about Guy's alarm, palpable even across the wires. 'Immediately. Hell hath no fury like Lynette! So now I know.' His eyes enquired, so she went on.

'Apparently, in the last months before the supposed wedding, Olly met someone.'

'Ah!'

'Dazzling, apparently. But more importantly, *loaded*, a

company director with responsibility for a large IT department!'

'Aha, a better bet?'

'*Tons* better. And loads of consultative work to outsource, potentially lucrative. But, unfortunately, the contract proved to be a little over Olly's head and he'd never admit it. So he just ploughed on, getting in a horrible mess and covering up.

'Meanwhile, the wedding date loomed and he began to wonder whether I was the best he could do. Dazzling Director was, as you pointed out, a much better bet, so he hooked himself up with her. But, presently, Dazzling Director realised what a bollocks he'd made of her precious intranet. She shunted him off to a contract with a subsidiary north of the border whilst she tracked his errors.

'Before long, he was axed, both his companionship and his services dispensed with, and his invoices ignored. Panic, panic, for Olly. *And* the loaded lady, muddied by his mistakes no doubt, wasn't too fussy about spreading the word.'

'Bad situation.'

'Right. Funds didn't materialise and other contracts were slow to develop, but Olly still had his lifestyle to be serviced. So, he thinks, *maybe* ditching reliable old Tess was an error of judgement. It might be naff, earning her living scribbling piccies for kiddies' books, but it is a living and she owns her own house. He has a chat with good old James, gets half a story, steams up here with the mistaken impression he has leverage in the shape of a shared baby. Because he wanted somewhere to regroup. And where better than somewhere that's free?'

He shifted beside her. 'You're better off without him.'

'That's what I keep telling myself.'

Ratty linked his hands behind his head. 'I don't suppose

you feel like letting me spend the night here?'

Spend the night? Her heart tripped up, her mouth opened but her locked brain refused to supply any words. His smiling eyes held a message she knew she ought to be able to decipher, but the thumping in her chest spread to her head, confusing her.

'I'd be no trouble,' he coaxed. 'But the thought of a comfortable bed is very attractive. Mine seems a long way away, through the cold, dark night.'

She squeaked, stupidly, 'But I've only got one bed!'

'I don't mind sharing.'

'Oh.'

He watched her for a few more moments before his grin widened. 'OK. Through the cold, dark night to my own cold, lonely bed it is.' He began to gather what he'd left in a trail behind him: shoes, tie, jacket.

She sat on for some time on the squashiness of the sofa. Wondering. He'd just been teasing. She supposed.

Chapter Fourteen

Mondays and Thursdays were village clinic days, up Port Road in a building used by various peripatetic health services. Angel wanted Tess, sitting at Angel's kitchen table, chilled through with the Curse and legs like washed rope, to consult the GP there. 'It can't be right that you suffer like this every month, Dr Warrington will sort you out.'

Tess made a face like a bloodhound. 'I don't like doctors.'

'He's really nice. Don't be so defeatist!'

When Tess finally made the effort to go a week later, she was pleasantly surprised by Dr Warrington, forty, blunt and kind, talking through her options with casual sympathy.

After childhood ailments and before falling into the clutches of Dr Flowers, her parents' GP, she'd rarely seen a doctor. Nearing retirement, never looking at her, Dr Flowers had spoken about 'female workings' and scribbled hasty prescriptions. She'd felt a flubbery mess.

Much better was easy-going Dr Warrington, who listened and offered practical help. 'There's Mefenemic Acid, which works on the muscles of the womb, so there's no weight gain or lethargy, I promise. Or, there's the low-dosage contraceptive pill – what form of contraception do you use?'

Her breath caught in her throat, sent a flush across her cheeks. 'I haven't, um, y'know, needed it. Recently.'

'Might you?'

She thought about Simeon's onslaught, of getting tipsy, the possibilities. Or even if Ratty's offer had been serious – which surely it hadn't been – and she'd wanted to ... 'Might be an idea,' she muttered.

'It's good protection. Doesn't replace safe sex, of course.' He could've been talking about three different ways to cook beef, with his direct looks over the desk, rather than the prospect of Tess admitting someone into her body.

Clutching the prescription she'd need to go to Bettsbrough to fill, she felt hopeful and in control, and decided to skip in to Rotten Row to see how Toby was.

Toby, she discovered quickly, was scabby, itchy, bored and looking for trouble and he'd found it in tormenting Jenna, who was hugging her bowl of potato, fish and peas to avoid big brother's thieving fingers.

'No-no!' she pleaded, red-faced, when Toby advanced on the high chair at the side furthest from Angel.

'But it's *my* lunch!' howled Toby in an ogre's voice.

'No-*naaaaah*!' Jenna shrieked, screwing her head frantically as Toby slunk behind her high chair to avoid Angel's vengeful hands.

Wading into 'No-no-no!', '*Stop* it, Toby!' and renewed groans of 'It's *my* lunch!', Tess intercepted the uncharacteristically horrid Toby, swinging him into the air. 'Hey, what's your problem, spotty boy?'

'Madhouse! Madhouse!' Angel wailed, frazzled, hair sticking up. 'Toby still can't play with other children and he's bored out of his skull. Jenna's fed up with being cooped up indoors, particularly with Toby being a demon from hell. But I can't keep them apart!'

This was where Tess came into her own, this was where she knew, smugly, she excelled. 'Tess to the rescue! I'll take him upstairs for a few minutes.' She jogged Toby strenuously in her arms as she carried him up to his room. 'C'mon, you, I need you.'

'What for-for-for?' he yelled, letting his head snap back with satisfaction at such delicious violence.

'I need a new drawing of Nigel,' she improvised. 'Nigel

with chickenpox, for a Get Well card.' Behind them, Jenna's tortured screeches subsided as she was left in peace with her potato and peas. 'Where's that Nigel? Where's your pad? C'mon, fetch the crayons!'

They snuggled together on Toby's pillows. Nigel, perched on Toby's legs, modelled and Tess began drawing a large, grumpy, sorry-for-himself Nigel, who had nasty itchy scabs exactly where Toby did. 'In his *ear*, and up his *nose*,' Toby stipulated.

As the drawing progressed his interjections became fewer, his fidgeting stilled and, after twenty minutes, he let his head tip back in sleep. She eased away, leaving his pad propped so he could see poor old poxed-pig Nigel when he woke, and crept back downstairs to where Jenna avoided the facecloth by snatching her head from side to side and craning backwards.

Angel had to pin the small, chocolate-smeared head fiercely against her hip to win the round.

'Teth!' Jenna shouted, arms up, all grins now she was full, happy and clean, crowing with joy that it must be her turn to be swung into Tess's arms.

Flushed with success after her efforts with Toby, Tess helped her out of the high chair. 'Toby's asleep.'

Angel sighed in relief. 'You're a blessing! Toby's a horrid monster. I'm sure Pete's working later than usual to avoid the Toby From Hell. All I need now is for Jenna to nap for an hour or two and I'll be in heaven,' she hinted heavily.

'Wrap her up, I'll walk her.'

'Tess, I could *kiss* you.' Angel raced for Jenna's jacket.

Proud of the talent she was unexpectedly discovering in herself with Angel's kids, Tess volunteered airily, 'I'll keep her for a while, give you a break. Wanna walk, Jenna-babe? With Tess?'

'With Teth,' Jenna agreed, unfolding the arms she'd

clamped to her chest when her jacket appeared.

And it was a lovely walk, through the ford as the stream was low, up the lane edged with hawthorn heavy with red berries. A loop to rejoin Main Road at Great End, then Tess paused at the garage to display her sleeping cherub before going home.

Brake on, buggy turned away from the wind, she could work up a few ideas for her new commission. Jenna could stay there just outside the kitchen door until she woke. No point bringing her indoors to overheat, sleeping in her coat. She'd be fine.

Tess ran upstairs for pencils, her pad and the brief for the Bavarian folk tales book, then checked outside that Jenna was still sleeping peacefully. This would be a good time to try out ideas for decorative borders, she decided, and ran up again for a pot of coloured pencils, watercolours and a couple of fine brushes. She filled a little pot with water at the kitchen sink, glancing out to check once more on Jenna, and finally settled down.

As usual, she began with her list of things associated with the stories. Feathered hats, horns, cows, flowers, mountains, bells, snow. Plenty to work with, there. Soon she was absorbed in an overlapping pattern of cowbells twined with ribbon. Yellow? No, better green, the green of mountain grass. She played around with the colours at the side of her pad then spent some time trying different combinations to get the beaten look of the cowbells just right. After an hour she felt she'd earned a bathroom break.

When she came back, she peeped out once more to see whether Jenna was stirring yet.

And the buggy was empty.

The blanket was flipped back and the reins hanging.

Tess jumped so hard that she actually banged her forehead on the glass of the window. 'Jenna?

OhmyGodohmyGod!' Unable to believe the evidence of her eyes, fumbling with the awkward doorknob, she raced outside, heart hammering. 'Jenna?'

At that moment, a moment that seemed to take a month, Angel, Pete and Ratty strode through the gateway, deep in some laughing conversation, a more cheerful-looking Toby being piggybacked by his father. And Tess heard a voice from the lawn beyond the rockery.

'Tess,' said Olly.

'*Teth*! Down!' yelled Jenna, from his arms.

She jumped around to face them.

Olly stood at the far end of the lawn, his hair blowing in the wind. Next to him, the rail fence separated the garden from the small rear drive where the Freelander stood. Jenna craned to look at Tess, cross and bewildered, face still creased with sleep. She shouted, 'Down, down!' Oh. God.

The group entering the garden halted suddenly, silence descending as if they'd all been fitted with an 'off' switch.

A silence shattered by Jenna's first wail as she cast herself backwards, straining to escape. Olly tried to hold her more tightly against him, awkward with inexperience, wincing when Jenna's furious head collided with his. Jenna clutched her forehead and began to scream. 'Mummeeee! Mummee-eee-eee!'

Angel, horrified, cast frantically between Tess and Olly. 'Christ, what's going on?' She leapt for the stone steps that led up to the lawn.

'*Wait*!' Ratty halted Angel with a swift hand, swinging her round before she made the first step. 'Don't let's spook him into doing anything more stupid than he already has.' His gaze fastened on Tess. 'Tess is the best person to sort him out.'

Tess swallowed, throat dry, prickles of sweat starting on her face. Oh God. Olly had Jenna! Stupid, idiotic bastard

Olly had Jenna! Her mind went blank. She gaped hopelessly across the garden where Olly struggled to hold onto an increasingly distressed Jenna. Her gaze moved to the fence. So low, so easily stepped over by someone Olly's height. Then he'd be away, out of sight, with Jenna. His car was probably there in the lane ...

'*Tess*!'

She looked back at Ratty. His mouth was a grim line, his eyes holding hers.

'Do it,' he suggested, quietly.

Her voice, when she tried to use it, faltered and floundered in her throat. She had to cough, and even then it emerged quavering and squeaky with horror. 'What on earth are you up to, Olly? What are you doing with Jenna? Put her down!'

He smiled thinly. 'I need your full attention. This way I'll get it.' Jenna prised herself away from his chest, feet kicking into his stomach. He had to raise his voice above her shrieks. 'We need to talk about us, what's happened, how we can sort everything out. We need to be truthful with each other.'

Tess hesitated, her mind spinning. She flung another glance at Ratty as if for inspiration. Beside him Angel was clutching Pete, who was staring, as set-faced as a lion waiting to pounce, at Olly.

Everyone was giving her time to act.

She must do something. Think, think, think, how best to steer Olly through this wobbly. Olly didn't usually have wobblies. He was acting out of character. That meant dangerous levels of stress, didn't it? She looked back at him, suddenly realising how to wrong-foot him. Calmly, she said, 'No, sorry.'

It surprised him into coming a step closer. '*No?*' he repeated.

She shook her head, folding her arms. 'I think we'll just let the police deal with it. Child abduction's too serious for me.'

'Don't be stupid, not if it's my child.' Olly sounded as if he meant to be bullish and immovable, but the first threads of uncertainty were already lacing his voice.

She licked her lips. The trick would be to defeat him with cold logic, undermine his uncharacteristic, impetuous action.

'*Your* child?' She hoped she sounded scathing.

Angel's gasp was loud in the quiet of the garden. 'But you *told* him! Didn't you *tell* the stupid bastard that Jenna wasn't yours? She's ours. Tell him, she's *ours*.' She swung again towards Olly. Both Ratty and Pete shot out a hand to halt her.

'Jenna's *ours*!' Toby shouted angrily. 'That man's got our Jenna!'

Olly frowned at Angel, biting his lip.

Tess claimed his attention again, making her voice weary. 'Olly, Jenna's not our child. She's Angel and Pete's daughter. I've never had a child. All I had was a miscarriage.' Then she paused. 'Did *Dad* tell you Jenna's our child?' A terrible, ferocious anger burst over her at the thought.

'No,' Olly admitted sulkily. 'But I thought, well, he might be shielding you.'

Tess snorted. Then, instead of closing in on Olly, she took a step backwards to the kitchen door. 'I'm phoning the police, because you've gone mad. You've stolen a child and it's too scary. I don't want to be involved.'

'Tess!' A shout to stop her. A pause. 'Isn't she? Ours? Truly?'

'Don't be so pathetic, you weasel.' Deliberately, she turned her back, reaching into the kitchen for the phone.

She could hear him clicking his tongue as he did when his brain was speeding. The trouble with Olly was that he was so unused to acting emotionally that he was rubbish at it.

Jenna's screams were persistent, desperate, pleading. Tess had to grit her teeth not to hurl herself across the garden to snatch her out of Olly's arms. God alone knew how Angel and Pete were feeling. A sweat of fear trickled from her temple and down beside one eye. Hoping the tremor in her hands didn't show, she began to dial.

Focus. Jenna must be claimed back unhurt at all costs. Olly mustn't be frightened into running off with her. No opportunity must be created for him to become crafty, as he could. She could do this, she just had to out-cool him.

Tess paused as if struck by a thought. 'Last chance to hand Jenna over. If you do it now, I'll try and get Angel and Pete to keep the police out of it.' She glanced over at her friend. 'I'm really sorry, Angel. She might be with an idiot but he's not dangerous.'

Angel returned a glare of pure acid. 'He'd better not be!'

Ratty's gaze was still directed at Tess. She paused to connect with it. He nodded slightly. She was doing OK.

Tess returned her attention to Olly. 'Well?' she asked, coldly.

After a long moment, he began to walk towards her. Jenna was still arching her body to try and escape his clutches. Tess's heart flipped in anticipation. Bliss, bliss, he was going to cooperate! She moved rapidly to intercept him, aware of Angel shadowing her.

But Olly halted again, ignoring Jenna's screech of outrage. His eyes flicked to Pete and Ratty. 'I suppose I give the baby to you, then your caveman mates rough me up, right?'

Oh no, he was having second thoughts! Tess stopped, shrugged, turned away. 'OK, I'll phone the police, we'll do it that way.'

Pete spoke for the first time, scornful and angry. 'Nobody will rough you up, weasel.'

A silence. A stand-off. Tess again picked up the phone.

'All right!' Olly completed the distance between them with an animal-like scuttle. 'All right, here, take her.'

Tess dropped the phone as she found the hot and furious weight of Jenna thrust into her arms by Olly and plucked out again by Angel almost in one movement. Olly turned and sprinted across the lawn, scrambling over the rails and out of sight.

He'd gone! Jenna was safe. The garden executed a fine pirouette around her. 'Oh thank God, Angel!' She flung open her arms to hug her friend in joy that it was all over.

But then recoiled. Because Angel, Angel her best friend in all the world, was looking at her with a stranger's eyes and yelling, 'Why couldn't you look after her? Why did you let that lunatic get his hands on her?'

And Pete demanding gruffly, 'How the hell did that happen, Tess?'

Defences down with the shock of attack from such an unexpected quarter, Tess felt tears well from her eyes. 'I – I stayed right in the kitchen, pottering about with ideas at the table. I only spent a couple of minutes in the bathroom. When I came back, he'd got her.'

Aghast, she gazed at Angel, desperate for her to understand. But Angel tossed her hair and swung away, clutching Jenna, leading her family to the safety of home, Pete carrying Toby and pulling the empty buggy.

They wanted to get away from her.

She turned beseechingly to Ratty. 'Leave them,' he advised, economically.

The backlash of horror that washed over her was so intense that blackness threatened the peripheries of her vision. She turned and cannoned blindly into her kitchen, kicking the door shut behind her and locking it. She huddled there for most of the evening, through trembling anger that clenched her chest and into an enormous stillness, sitting in the dark, gazing at the clouds passing over her garden, glimpsing the stars and a half-moon. It was a long time before she got up and rang her father.

'Remind me, Dad. Why did you tell Olly my address when I'd asked you not to?'

An uncomfortable pause. 'Sorry.'

Tess gripped the phone. 'Why?'

'I just felt … well, the name of the village slipped out, so I decided he might as well know the whole thing. I thought …' Another pause. 'There's never any point in trying not to face up to things. You two ought to talk.'

Tess put down the phone.

Not a *bad* summer. Not if you took everything into account.

Tess sat, her back to the ford, finishing a painting of The Three Fishes that the landlord had commissioned and, she suspected, wouldn't really want to pay for. Even if her new commission to illustrate Bavarian folk tales was underway, though not as much fun as *The Dragons of Diggleditch*, these crisp days as summer faded into autumn should be savoured; and this was an opportunity to sit outside, even if swaddled in a fleece jacket.

Tess did a mental review. In some ways, she fitted in Middledip now; said 'Hello' to everyone she passed in the street, gossiped at the shop, strolled into the pub alone.

It was all much better than the days when she hadn't known a soul she encountered when she walked up Main Road.

She rolled a sable brush number nine between her fingers, looking from the pub to her watercolour, waiting for the shadows she'd painted at the gable end to dry. Her work was going well.

And it could've been a great summer – if Lucasta hadn't died. If Tess hadn't killed Ratty's dog and hadn't let Jenna be snatched by Olly.

She began to feather in colour on the rowan tree that bowed over the brindle slates of The Three Fishes. It was just beginning to turn to rust and jaundiced yellow, the rowan. Shortly it would burst into the flames of its full autumn cloak. It would be a shame to miss that. And if she wasn't going to finish the work until then, it was a good excuse to stop now. She had her sketches, anyway. She cleaned her brush, laid it back in the wooden case, poured away the water and screwed the lid on the jar.

Sometimes she just didn't feel up to working and this morning was one of them. Since mislaying Jenna, the light had sometimes gone out of her days abruptly and for one enormous reason.

Angel hadn't attempted to patch things up.

Tess kept to herself, worked long hours, taking her walks across the footpath over Carlysle land to Port Road so she needn't pass the garage. Though, unavoidably, she'd run the gauntlet this morning – it was either pass the garage or walk across the fields to the ford, which was just stupid.

There had just been Jos, de-poxed presumably, bending over a Jeep on the forecourt, throwing back his ponytail and casting her a grin and a wave.

Now she walked home quickly, hiding herself behind her board with the paper taped on.

Being ostracised was a lonely business.

Chapter Fifteen

'I don't know what to think.'

'You do,' he needled, watching Angel washing lettuce irritably at the kitchen sink. Her sleeve kept slithering down and she had to jerk it up with her teeth, making little *urrrgh*! noises of aggravation. Toby propelled a fully laden toy car transporter carefully in and out of the chair and table legs. 'Vrumm, vrumm, beep,' he played softly, managing somehow to hotch on one knee and pinch Nigel against his body with the other.

Angel tossed the lettuce down and began an energetic assault on the cucumber. 'You haven't got kids, Ratty.'

'No.'

'You don't understand how terrifying it was!'

'I can only guess. And sympathise.' Angel had always been super-protective. He'd known her since she was a teenager berating strangers about leaving their dogs tied up too long outside shops and crying when her grass snake died. All that caring had, naturally, devolved upon the kids to make her a tigerish mother. Jenna's recent escapade must've constituted her very worst nightmare.

Snick, snick, Angel cut matchstick carrots with aggravated precision. 'What if he'd actually disappeared with her? You hear about these things.'

'I know.'

The handle of the food mill, being wrenched round to grate cheese, broke mid-turn, and Angel slammed it down with a tiny scream. The glass worktop saver snapped. After a pause long enough in which to count to ten, she shook out a bin bag and tipped everything in; cheese, mill and three pieces of worktop saver. Began to unwrap substitute cheese slices with such a murderous expression that Ratty felt his chest tuck up on a silent laugh. Dear Angel. Normally too nice to be successfully angry, this time she was mega-pissed off.

He got the better of his laughter and asked dispassionately, 'Was it Tess's fault?'

Angel threw a cheese slice onto a plate. It landed with a flap. 'Who else's?'

'Was it Tess's?'

Toby, from under the table, asked, 'Is Tess coming?'

'I don't think so.' Angel answered her son. 'Yes, I think so,' she flashed at Ratty.

'How?'

Indignant hands on hips, transferring cheese crumbs onto black trousers, Angel stared. 'She was *supposed* to be looking after Jenna!'

'Right, she took her out. With your permission?'

'Yes, *but* ...'

'And to Honeybun?'

'Yes, but ...'

'Then she left Jenna outside the kitchen door, strapped in her buggy, till she woke. Don't you do that?'

'Yes. But ...'

'She went for a pee whilst Jenna was still out there, do you do that?'

'Occasionally, but ...'

'So. Tell me – *how* was it Tess's fault?'

Only a small woman, Angel, but she could slam drawers shut with surprising resonance, it quite made Ratty's ears ring. 'She ought to choose her company more carefully, for one thing! That moron Olly, thinking Jenna was his, taking her. He wouldn't have been anywhere near, if not for Tess!'

Ratty felt the car transporter collide with his boot, heard

it shed its load and Toby mutter, 'Oh fishcakes!'

He shifted his position, tucked his feet obligingly under the chair. 'And she controls him, does she? We all heard her tell him quite clearly that Jenna wasn't his, nor hers. As I understand, Olly's in financial straits and looking for access to Tess's bank account. Tess asked her father not to give her address to Olly but he did, and I suppose if her father hadn't then her dappy cousin would have. And that, and Olly's leaping to conclusions, if anything, set the whole catastrophe in motion.'

'Vrumm, vrumm, Northampton, Pederbowough,' intoned Toby.

With deliberate movements Angel wiped down every work surface, washing out the cloth beneath the running tap. Surfaces finished, she began on the cupboard doors. 'She could come to see *me*,' she hedged.

Ratty snorted. 'This is Tess we're talking about. Since Olly dumped her she thinks rejection is her bag. So she's hidden away, stewing. As far as she's concerned you hate her deeply, which means we all do. You, Pete, me, Jos, all Middledip. If it gets too bad you'll see her house on the market, you just watch.'

Angel smirked. 'Ha! That'll stuff your plans, won't it?' She began on another door.

He rubbed his chin. Gazed out of the window. Examined his motives. Was he meddling out of a genuine desire to heal the needless rift between Tess and Angel? Or was it just too uncomfortable to have the discord interfere with his measured, foxy pursuit?

He stood up abruptly. He didn't need to explain his motives to anyone. 'When you've got a cogent argument that she acted stupidly, remember to share it with me.' He pushed his chair in and heard Toby tut as the car transporter shed its load again. 'I'll be interested. Because it looked to me as if she was put in an impossible situation. And rescued it.'

He wondered if she was even going to let him in, the way she stood back, returning his gaze speculatively through the newly glazed back door. He waved a reassuring hand. 'Hi, only me.' After a moment, she unbolted the door and let him through it.

'Isn't it about time you grew up?' he asked, gently. Her hair was loose. It needed brushing. He tugged it gently, forcing her eyes round to his. It felt good, her hair.

'Don't you think you owe Angel and Pete an apology? It's up to you to be big about this. I *know* you couldn't foresee what was going to happen but I think you ought to speak to Angel.'

She snatched her hair back. 'She didn't look as if she wanted to hear!'

He dragged out a kitchen chair and dropped into it. 'So – what? Shop in Bettsbrough instead of Gwen Crowther's in case you run into each other? Become a hermit? And do I get a coffee or shall I just die quietly of thirst?'

She threw instant into mugs, took milk from the fridge. Her voice small. 'She was so furious.'

'Can you blame her? It was terrifying!'

'I know.'

'But you can't pluck up the courage to make up?'

Back to him as she poured the scalding water, she shook her head vehemently, making her hair jig.

They drank silently. Tess avoided lifting her face; Ratty watched the top of her head and reached the bottom of his cup, out of ideas. 'Oh well,' he sniped, abandoning the empty cup. 'If you decide to sell Honeybun, will you give me first refusal? Lucasta's left me Pennybun, owning both properties might be an advantage.'

Sidetracked, Tess whistled. 'Has she? What does the son from Mill Hill feel about that?'

'Hopping mad. She's left him most of the contents, aside from minor bequests. But she left most of her liquid funds to a donkey sanctuary and left the property to yours truly!'

'Bless her.' She almost smiled. 'She obviously thinks more about the donkeys than Derry. But she appreciated you, you were good to her.'

He replied gruffly. 'Don't go spreading stuff like that around. Bad for my image.' Walking through the door without closing it behind him, he shouted back, 'But you're a disappointment!'

Rotten Row; a medley of brick and stone. Some time in the last century fresh bricks had built up the part between dormer windows where thatch had once dipped between and the existing tiles had been added.

Off the kerb, then back on it, she looked up and down the road then back at Rotten Row. Picked out what, precisely, belonged to Pete and Angel's property, once two. Sitting room two windows, dining room, window on the stairs, Toby's room, two windows in Pete and Angel's room. One stained door with thick black iron strapping, a ring to twist instead of a handle. She turned away; maybe she'd just walk on up Port Road today. Hesitated, and turned back.

The stained door crashed open suddenly and Angel stood in the opening, hands on hips, hair in bunches, which made her look thirteen. 'For Christ's sake!' she yelled. 'Don't be so *wet*! Either come in or go and throw yourself under a bus but don't skulk about out there like a muddy dog!'

In the kitchen where she'd sat fancying herself part of the family so often, they hugged. 'I'm *so* sorr—'

'No!' Angel snipped her off.

'But –!'

'No. It's all over.'

Tess hugged Angel harder, beaming. 'I feel as though elephants have dismounted from my shoulders!'

'Hi. Only me.' A dark, wet evening, he shifted foot to foot outside the kitchen door, shoulders hunched. When she opened the door he bent forward into the warmth, dripping coldly onto her quarry tiles, and kissed her. 'Well done.' Turned and went back into the night.

He'd gone, and her lips were still wet from his rainy kiss when she touched her mouth with her fingertips.

Chapter Sixteen

'You're a gorgeous, sexy woman.'

It was Christmas in the sitting room at Rotten Row, the first time he said it. After the children had finally gone to bed, hugging their best new toys, the adults had collapsed among rags of wrapping paper and half-dishes of nuts to watch Christmas shows and eat what they'd already had plenty of. The fire danced, smelling sooty and woody, redolent of the season.

Jos left to 'meet some people'.

And Angel, lounging on the floor between Pete's feet, shot Ratty a look of mischief. 'Not going with Jos?'

Ratty sank lower as if too comfortable to move, and grunted.

'Slowing down, Rats?'

'Must be.'

Pete and Angel laughed and looked at one another. Ratty looked at the television. Tess looked at everyone else. 'What's funny?'

Angel leaned over and tapped Ratty's knee to make him look. 'You know what? You and Tess might as well be married.'

'*What*?' As Tess's mouth opened her eyebrows flew up in her hair.

'You two. Don't pretend! Round here, the pub or Honeybun, every evening together, these days.'

'Not every!' Tess disclaimed hotly.

Ratty's concentration remained on the set and his can of Ruddles County, as if the discussion had nothing to do with him.

'*Nearly* every. You babysit, in comes Ratty, and here you'll both be when we come home. If I ring Ratty in the evening and he's not home, I find him at Honeybun. If you have a meal with us he stays, instead of leaving after the brandy to go tarting about the nightclubs!'

Tess scoffed, 'Rubbish!' Gulped two steadying mouthfuls of wine.

'He plays with your hair, for Christ's sake! Him and his Rapunzel complex. Plays with your *hair*! Doesn't he?' Angel appealed to Pete.

'Sure. Another beer, Ratty?'

Tess felt Ratty gently disengage his hand from the ends of her hair as he reached for the new can.

'Bet he bought you a Christmas present.'

Tess rolled her eyes as if the question was too stupid to answer. Beneath her jumper, the delicate silvery star on a chain around her neck felt suddenly heavy. Riveting suddenly hot eyes on the television, she sniffed. 'You're just overtired with horrendous cooking and dealing with excited kids and going mental at the thought of doing it all again for the in-laws tomorrow! Take your frustrations out on someone else.' Angel's needling had begun a couple of days ago when Ratty invited them all for supper and Tess, unwary of his seasonal speciality, got squiffy on whisky-soaked mince pies drowned in hot Advocat and Ratty had had to cart her home.

'Leave her alone, Angel,' Pete said, gently.

Maybe recognising that she'd gone far enough but determined to have the last word, Angel muttered, '*Just* like a married couple. And thanks for reminding me about the in-laws, by the way.' She cast A Look at Pete, who grinned, winked and blew her a kiss.

Turning slightly from his corner of the sofa, Ratty joined the conversation. 'Anyway, we're not like a married couple.

We don't have sex.'

Whisky before lunch, two wines with, champagne in the afternoon, beer for variety before the evening session. That must be why, when she turned to Ratty, Tess's face went as red as if she'd stuck her head in the whispering coal fire. 'But you wouldn't want to, would you?'

'Yes.'

'No, I mean ... We're not, romantic or anything. You've never suggested –'

'I have.' He sipped his beer, he watched the programme; he glanced at her and away.

What was that expression in his eyes? She could *almost* believe him serious. If she didn't know him better, anyway. 'Have what?'

'Suggested.'

'You weren't serious!'

'Wasn't I?'

Infuriated with his stupid calm monotone as if discussing the work on some old car, she shifted crossly. 'So what if we spend time together? Relationships between the sexes don't need to be sexual, do they?' And if he wanted to say something about that he should come out and say it. 'I don't even know why you'd want to!' she grumbled, meaning 'I don't know why you'd want to alter the status quo.'

He turned on a leer, said gently, as if enlightening a fool, 'Because you're a gorgeous, sexy woman.'

So outrageous, his expression so lewd, she began to laugh. 'You idiot!'

'I must be.' He turned back to the television.

Angel never knew when to leave well alone. 'You're not telling me you're happy with just a friendship?'

'Oh, shut up.' Tess fidgeted irritably, hung up on a reply. If she said no, it would sound as if she was making a pass at Ratty. He'd probably take her up on it, in his casual way, and nothing would ever be the same again. Couple of weeks of bed, till Ratty fancied someone fresh, as he always did. Yes, two weeks seemed his average. Gone would be the companionable outings, the discussions about Pennybun, the warmth, the respect for her work. 'It's a great friendship, I value it,' she said weakly. 'It doesn't mean Ratty can't go on as before.'

Ratty stirred again. 'Then why do I feel I'm being unfaithful if I take someone else to bed?'

She felt her face stiffen, the way it did when she was desperate not to show her thoughts. 'Don't let me stop you.'

'I try not to.'

It was an unsatisfactory conversation, ambiguous and unsettling, not leading anywhere but with the potential to undermine something she couldn't name. She saw Angel open her mouth, face animated as if about to burst out with some secret, saw Pete shush her, pull her onto his lap, kiss, whisper.

The programme ended, Pete flipped through the on-screen menu, Ratty became absorbed in *Classic Car*. And when Tess yawned a strained half-hour later and decided she was going, he prepared to walk her home. As usual.

'Come on, you gorgeous, sexy woman, where's your coat?'

'Stay if you want,' she muttered, searching for her gloves, compelled to question what had previously been simply accepted.

'I would, if I wanted.'

It wasn't very Christmassy outdoors. No snow, no visit from Jack Frost to transform the village into a silvery picture, just peevish gusts to carry chill mist into their faces. Amber street lamps wore haloes and reflected on glistening pavements. Tess could feel her hair scrunching damply into candyfloss around her face.

'So.' At her gate he hunkered into his jacket. 'Still friends?'

''Course.' What else was on offer? She wished he'd be specific.

No, she didn't. Everything was great as it was, wasn't it? Great friends, life was easy, no risks, no emotional demands. And if she had to squash down her sexuality when it awoke, she could cope; her libido could cartwheel about her dreams without consequence. Reality brought tranquillity and she could live without passion. Probably. For a while, anyway. Though sometimes, just sometimes, she looked at a young fit guy – like Ratty – and knew she was still fully functioning.

It seemed only casual curiosity when he suggested, 'Still hot for Olly?'

She looked away as if thinking carefully, not wanting him to see into her eyes. 'Not hot.'

'Do you wish things had been different? That he'd never pulled back from the marriage?'

Smoothing her hair down, she shrugged. 'How can I say? Things aren't different. It's difficult to stay in love with someone who starts acting like a shit.'

'So there's nothing stopping you hooking up with someone else? A hypothetical someone?'

'But why should I?' The words were out before she could consider them. She crunched her toes up in her boots, shivering. 'I mean, I'm OK as I am. I'd have to be really sure before I started out with someone new, and what could make me sure? If I knew a hypothetical someone well enough and would really hate to be without him ...'

'Don't you want sex? Or maybe there's an arrangement you keep private?'

'There isn't.' She hesitated. 'Perhaps I can live without it.'

'I can't. Goodnight, gorgeous, sexy woman.'

Uneasily, Tess laughed.

So, like friends do, they had a running gag, a gentle joke to carry with them up to The Three Fishes the next evening.

'When are you going to pay this gorgeous, sexy woman for the picture?' Ratty demanded of Harry Tubb, red-faced, sauntering landlord, who could spend all evening leaning on one side of the bar mirroring his regulars leaning on the other. The interior of the pub was warm, humming with chatter and laughter and smelling strongly of beer. Tess's painting of the pub hung above the roaring fire.

Unmoved, Harry watched his barman ring a sale into the till and give change. 'Don't worry, duck, she'll get her money.'

'By the end of the month?'

'Leave it!' Tess muttered, not enjoying this discussion in front of the whole pub.

'She'll get her money.' Irritation flickered across Harry's florid face and he pushed back the wave of hair that had been left marooned as his hairline receded. Regulars referred to the single serpentine lock as 'The Sperm'. He smiled at Tess. His teeth sloped backwards into his mouth and she didn't like his smile, turned-in, turned-down, like a shark.

Ratty let the subject drop as Lester strolled in, brushing rain from his waxed jacket. 'Gin and tonic?' he asked his father.

'If you twist my arm.' Lester smiled at Tess, hung his jacket up near the door. 'Merry Christmas.'

Tess smiled. 'And to you.' Soon, Ratty and his father were deep in conversation about Pennybun Cottage and the work that was required, until Lester spotted friends across the room and wandered off to join in a game of solo whist. Ratty was soon arguing with Garry from Port Road as to whether Audi had the edge over BMW and the evening sidled comfortably by in the beery, noisy warmth.

At last orders, Ratty closed his mouth around the last drops of bitter, passed Tess her coat, then unhooked the yet-to-be-paid-for picture from the wall.

Tess stared.

Ratty raised his voice, grinning crookedly, as he did when being his awkwardest. 'We'll bring it back when you're ready to settle the bill, Harry, all right?'

Harry's red face darkened as his eyes rested on 'his' picture tucked under Ratty's arm. And, as the mellow clientele began to shout 'Pay the woman, Harry!', his mouth narrowed into a turned-down slit. 'Don't worry, here it is!' He snatched notes from the till, 'The Sperm' jiggling hectically.

Well-used tens and twenties were slapped down truculently by Harry Tubb, intercepted and counted gleefully by Ratty and finally pressed into Tess's palm.

Ratty rehung the picture, extending his hand behind him to assist Tess through the crowd that had developed behind the bar stools, saying, 'C'mon, gorgeous.'

'And Merry Christmas to Harry!' she hissed.

Ratty just laughed. 'He'll be OK. Don't suppose you could follow me to Bettsbrough tomorrow and bring me back? I've got a Lotus Europa, now with new brake drums, to deliver to an owner freshly returned from Christmas with the in-laws. It would save asking Pete or Jos when they're on holiday.'

Outside, Tess closed her jacket against the December drizzle. 'Can do. I need to visit the art supplies shop in Bettsbrough, anyway.' Her Christmas duties had ended when she sent her mother a Marks & Spencer voucher and her father book tokens. She was content to idle her way through the useful elapse between Christmas and New Year with errands and jaunts.

The owner of the Lotus proved to be Graham Poole, accountant, son of friends of Lester and Elisabeth Arnott-Rattenbury. His house, on the outskirts of Bettsbrough, was called The Old New Inn because it used to be a pub.

'Isn't she a darling?' cried Graham, uncombed and creased in having-a-day-off cords and fleece shirt, running his hand across the Lotus's roof.

'If you like a car without rear vision,' Ratty ribbed.

'Nonsense, won't hear a word against my Lotus! Come and have a cuppa, I'll write you a cheque.'

So Tess obligingly lined the Freelander up, about twice the height, behind the Lotus Europa with its gold coach lines, and followed the two men into a tiny corner conservatory, facing the courtyard. At least, whilst Ratty explained to Graham when best to do an oil change and scribbled the address of a firm in Mansfield who undertook nickel and chromium plating, she could gaze through French doors and admire the rockery and the gabled lines of the old stables. It was preferable to facing Graham, who laughed bad breath into the small room and answered every remark with, 'I hear what you're saying,' eyes beaming from behind dirty little specs. Like Lucasta had and Lester did, he addressed Ratty as Miles.

Tess wondered whether he cleaned himself up for his office. Or were there clients desirous of an unwashed accountant with filmy teeth and hair that parted at the back? Maybe pig farmers appreciated a money person they felt at ease with in their work clothes?

Whilst Ratty drew Graham a wiring diagram and offered to get hold of a new loom for him, Tess waited patiently, watching an old black Labrador lie on his back in a slice of winter sunshine by the bronze-look water feature. Customers were customers and this was one of Ratty's.

But oh, to be floating among the myriad, gorgeous

colours of the oil pastels and watercolours, enjoying the papery smell of the art supplies shop!

And surely, when she'd made such superhuman efforts not to look at her watch, Ratty could just take his cheque and go, now he was at the handshaking stage? But no. Outside, Ratty stopped on the modern-day substitute for proper cobbles. 'Graham, is a computer kept at home but used for the business an allowable expense? Or would the taxman claim duality of purpose?'

She sighed, but prepared for another wait.

Graham laughed halitosis over them, probably remembering gleefully Ratty dropping out of accountancy; he rubbed his chin and rebuked, 'After free advice, Miles?'

Tess's brain clicked abruptly back into the conversation. She smiled sweetly. 'Does professional advice always have to be paid for, Graham?'

He smiled smugly. ''Fraid so.'

Words thrust themselves well in front of brain activity. 'So you'll expect an invoice for the hour and twenty minutes *Miles* has just spent advising *you*! Don't look so shocked, I expect his hourly rate is well below what you covetous bastards charge!'

Silent, on the way to the pay-and-display in town, she checked the road to the left, daring a glance at Ratty who was gazing uncooperatively out of the window.

'I'll apologise to him if you want me to!' she sighed when she'd reversed into a parking space. 'I shouldn't piss off your customers –'

Ratty turned to her, grinning brilliantly. '*Don't* spoil it! You were right! People are always doing that to me, usually accountants or solicitors, gits who charge you just for picking up your file. You were fantastic, standing up for me like that.' Her jaw slackened with surprise and was mashed against his jacket as he squashed her into a jubilant hug. 'And you know what? I *am* going to bill the bastard!'

A celebratory lager, then she finally got her anticipated treat of selecting pens, pencils, pads in three sizes, acrylic paints, a rainbow of watercolours and soft, new sable brushes, all rustling in paper bags in the back as they drove home.

Ratty was ready to line up another jaunt. 'By the way, I'm going to pick up some bits from Oxford next week, if you want to come?'

She was quite positive. 'No.'

'I could drop you at your parents' house, see the guy, pick you up?'

'No.'

She felt rather than saw his shrug. She added, 'They're not talking to me.'

He nodded. 'That Jenna stunt of Olly's?'

She changed down and edged the Freelander over to let a clodded tractor, the big-wheeled kind, between herself and the hedge. 'I phoned my father about giving Olly my address and swore at him. He took offence. My mother was "shocked and disappointed" – at me, I presume, it might've been Dad or Olly, she didn't say.

'Since I was sixteen I seem to have been battling them over something – the right to grow up, maybe. God knows what they'd have done if I'd actually been difficult. All that for someone who never got in a fix! Or hardly ever.' She didn't mention disappearing during her A levels. She had, after all, come back. 'When I was ill I kind of fell back into their clutches and they're reluctant to let me go again.

'It would be nice if I wanted to see them more, there must be some mileage left in the relationship. But while they're so prohibitive I avoid them like a diabetic avoids sugar.'

Ratty eased down into his seat. 'We should introduce

mine to yours, they could have a disapproval party. Perhaps watching through glass as we romp naked on the lawn.'

'I don't think I'd want anyone to watch!' Then she realised that sounded as if she wouldn't object to the romp. And blushed.

'Sorry about Angel,' Pete apologised when he returned to work in the New Year. 'She thinks you need a shove.'

'I don't.'

'I told her. No broad hints, no secret words with Tess, no heavy-handed manipulation. Really, she'll behave.'

'She'd better.' Ratty flipped over job sheets and wondered if the guy with the Ford Anglia Super would remember his booking for a new gearbox and clutch assembly this morning. He'd blanched at the estimate. 'Or I'll ring your mother and say Angel needs some advice about the children. Angel would like that. Jos, can you check over the jobs for the next few days against the stock bits? Particularly, the headlights for the Bristol. And the Lucas electronic ignition we're fitting on the MGB.'

Jos nodded. 'What's Angel been up to?'

'Helping out,' Ratty answered ironically. 'Good Christmas?'

Eyes shining, Jos nodded and smiled his shy smile, tucked stray hair behind his ears. 'Got a new woman.'

Ratty had known this through the grapevine and suspected for even longer but he steered Jos through admissions that yes, they were sleeping together and yes, she was quite pretty. Discovered Jos wanted to get off early, she was at his place and had promised to cook.

Later, when Jos was safely on the phone, Pete re-emerged from beneath the bonnet of the white E-Type, now on blocks, looking as if he wore black gloves. 'Everybody's doing it but you.'

'Yep, I get that feeling.' Ratty lifted his head and looked thoughtful. 'But I do have a plan. Or, at least, I'm planning a plan. I'll need a bit of backup from you and Angel, though.'

Chapter Seventeen

He knew how to plan. He'd planned projects for the garage or funding the rent-accruing properties he owned round the village.

First, he must establish what he wanted and how he intended to get it. What would be the consequences? The ramifications? Could he manipulate the personality and emotions involved?

Mmmm. The tricky bit.

'Shall I tell you my plans for Lucasta's house?' Ratty burst into Tess's kitchen. 'Sorry, am I stopping you working?'

Tess blew out her lips and tossed down her pad. 'I'm struggling anyway, attempting to be authentic, traditional *and* innovative. It's like rubbing your tummy and patting your head.'

Ratty turned her sketch pad and studied the roughs of cowherds and meadow flowers. 'Aren't lederhosen shorter?'

'Various lengths, according to the books. Tell me about your plans.'

Ratty dropped into a chair. 'Now that Lucasta's obnoxious son has cleared the house of everything not screwed down, it's time Pennybun had a bit of attention.'

Derry Meredith had been with a big truck to clear his mother's cottage of everything possible. Had needed reminding, in fact, that there were individual bequests to come before his claim on the remaining contents. Ratty, and then Tess, had made offers on japanned cabinets, the bed frame, the boxed ornaments and crockery that formed Derry's inheritance. But he'd turned them down, saying he preferred to take his chances at auction.

'The survey's arrived.' Ratty waved a thick envelope. 'If you could spare me an hour ...' So, huddled in jackets, they let themselves into Pennybun's empty-house chill.

It always took Tess a minute to orientate herself to Pennybun, being a mirror image of Honeybun.

In the little sitting room, outlines on the wallpaper reminded her of where Lucasta had stood the drinks cabinet, the oil painting of Singapore, the ivory tusks carved with a train of trunk-holding-tail elephants. Even the carpet and curtains had gone. Tess sighed. 'Bleak.'

Ratty touched her shoulder. 'I try not to think she's gone, just remember her dispensing lapsang with one hand and WKD with the other.'

He changed the subject. 'Look, as well as the cottage, she left me this.' From the mantelpiece he picked up a little pewter-coloured cigarette case a few inches across and flat. 'Evidence of old sins.'

At the window, they crowded close, Ratty stooping so that Tess could see his new treasure. 'She kept it all these years, a gift from my reprehensible grandfather. This side, see, their signatures have been engraved and then gilded. *Lucasta* and *Jerome*.'

Tess ran her tapered fingertip over the old, engraved *Lucasta*. 'Bless her. All these years.'

The case looked small in his capable hands, gleaming with dull light. He turned it. 'Then, here, *Adored Lucasta, my life, my love* and *Jerome, reason for living*.'

Tess sighed mistily. 'What a love!'

He grunted a laugh. 'What a sizzling affair, maybe, what terrific fun. He dumped her when the scandal threatened his real life.'

Ratty's warm nearness countered the room's chill and Tess inched closer to take the case, revolving it in her hands.

'You men. Bastards all.'

He took it back, searching with blunt fingertips for the catch. 'Evidently he was.' The catch was stubborn, he had no nails.

She flicked it open for him. 'Like you're not a bastard with women!'

'I've never said "I love you" if I didn't. Here they are – Lucasta and Jerome!' Inside the case, tucked in the corner, a small golden heart opened locket-style to cradle a tiny sepia in each half. Photographs when photography was young and Lucasta and Jerome were flung about by illicit passion.

Gently, Tess took the case back. 'There they are. So tiny.'

Ratty's cheek brushed her temple as he craned to see. 'Not very clear. Could be anyone, if we didn't know. See the words, inside? *Lucasta, holder of the heart of Jerome Arnott-Rattenbury*. Do you notice, on the outside, where it might be spotted, it's only first names? Inside he feels secure enough to be revealed – but refuses to use her married name?'

'Cynic!'

'No. But I think he was.' His warm hand smoothed her hair down to the small of her back, one of those absent, affectionate caresses of which Angel had exaggerated the importance. 'And hard, to allow the affair to be so torrid, then turn his back at crunch time.'

She laughed. When she turned her face, his was very near. 'Whereas you're as moral as a priest and as faithful as a puppy.'

He stared down at her for long moments. She tried to read his expression as he slid the case into an inside jacket pocket. Was he going to say something significant? He had that look, thoughtful, considering. No. He'd turned to the surveyor's report. 'What do you think of this?'

It was a long time since the cottage had been updated. Ratty intended to give it the full works, he explained. 'Damp proofing first. Rewiring. Replastering after the proofers and electricians. A lot's unsound.' Tap, tap.

She followed him into the kitchen, missing his warmth. 'And you've got the funds?'

'More or less. I'm hoping to get some grant money. I've been in touch with the council and the heritage people. No, I'm wrong, new windows *then* replastering.' He flicked the report.

'Where do I come in?' She leant against the old pot sink with him, surveying Lucasta's kitchen: an inappropriate free-standing electric cooker, space where the table once stood against the wall, two oak dressers Ratty had screwed down to become fixtures before Derry could claim them as moveable estate.

'Two ways. I wondered if you'd let people in occasionally, when I can't? Take messages if I'm out chasing bits somewhere?'

'Should think so, yes.'

'Then design. I'm going to have a kitchen handmade round these two dressers.'

'And the sink?'

'Is it worth keeping?'

She wrinkled her nose. 'Think how stainless steel would look, in here!'

'Right. Dressers and sink, then. Range in the chimney breast?'

Tess nodded.

'Tiles behind, hand-painted china doorknobs ... I thought, maybe, you'd help with the design – you've got the eye. I want your picture of McLaren up *here*.' He rubbed his chin again. 'Maybe I could commission you to do something bigger for above ... I don't know quite what.'

Brow furrowed, chin rasping, he got caught up on this minor point.

She threw back her hair and put her head on one side, stroked her own un-rasping chin, suggested, 'Portrait of your father?'

His eyes gleamed as he turned his grin on her. 'He'd love that! It *would* be nice to have a portrait of Lucasta.'

'Can't be done,' she denied firmly, reading his sidelong, hopeful look accurately. 'No sitter, no up-to-date photographs, I couldn't do her justice.'

Opening the under-sink cupboard, releasing a smell of dampness and Ajax, Ratty came out with a bubble-wrapped parcel. 'There's this.' From a monochrome photograph hand-tinted with watery colour, behind the glass Lucasta was just beginning to smile. A much younger Lucasta with glossy hair piled high on a head tilted on a long, elegant neck. A curving crack marred the glass and the mount was damp-marked and buckled, the frame parting at the mitres.

'That should've gone to Derry!'

'But I stole it. Like it?'

She leant against him to get a better look. 'I wouldn't want to copy that, the original's too good. I'll remount and frame it, if you want.' What would make it special for him? She considered. 'If the mount is very broad,' she indicated a size, 'it can be decorated. Pencil sketches of Pennybun? Lucasta's favourite flowers? What d'you think?'

He took several moments to reply. 'I think,' he returned eventually, 'you're a very clever lady.

'I also think that, if you rest your delectable chest on somebody's arm like that, you'll give somebody the wrong message altogether.'

She leapt away, flaming. 'I didn't notice!'

Carefully, he replaced the photo in the polythene. 'Thanks a lot.'

As work began on Pennybun Cottage, Ratty's moods varied. He was missing Lucasta, of course, Tess understood that. So when he turned up at Honeybun seeking her company on a jaunt, she generally went along.

'So,' she puffed up the sloping grass, watching her footing where the cows had lately been, trying to keep up with Ratty's strides. 'Why move into Pennybun when you've got a perfectly good place?'

He waited until she'd caught up. 'I like Pennybun, it was Lucasta's. The house at Ladies Lane is somewhere to live but I think I could be at home in Pennybun.'

She paused to look behind her, across the field to the old orange tile roofs of Pennybun and Honeybun, surrounded by trees behind the six-foot wall that marked the beginning of the farmland. 'You sure we're allowed in this field?'

'The farmer won't mind, I don't know about the bull ... Don't be such a wimp, there's no bull! Wasn't it you who said you were sick of being indoors, sick of travelling by car, and needed to blow the cobwebs away?'

'But this is a cross-country hike. I would've settled for a brisk walk to the pub. Ouch!' For about the fifth time she turned her ankle on the clumpy grass.

'What a princess you are sometimes!' His voice slid from impatience to cooing sarcasm. 'Give Watty your lickle-ickle handie, let me help you up this nasty steep slope, Pwincess Tessie.'

She grinned and blew him a raspberry. His hand, a grimy layer over the usual oily layer because he'd been shovelling old plaster into a skip, closed firmly over her ink stains and golden rings. Walking in the same beat was much easier and her breathing steadied. Her huge jumper kept her just about warm enough and it was half pleasant to shake the fidgets out in a kind of a canter over the grazing land that encircled the village.

Work at Pennybun tended to eat up time. The damp proofing company had left a God-almighty mess; the electricians had rewired, fixed a plentiful amount of sockets and a shower unit and made more. Now Ratty was fuming over a letter from the heritage people disagreeing with the replacement of the windows.

'Anyone would think I was going to replace them with PVCu, not hardwood to match the existing! Some bossy bloody bureaucratic bitch has decided the old *glass* should be used, would you believe? Has she tried salvaging and reusing glass of that age? It's not original anyway, probably replaced about a hundred years ago. Any window frame less than one-third rotten she wants *repairing* instead of replacing! A bloody inspired idea, eh? Half the windows replaced and half repaired.

'Anyway, the joiner got her sorted. "I don't do bodged jobs, duck." Brilliant! Mind that cow-do, Princess.'

She could hardly reply for the furious pace, but at least they were swinging downhill now, towards a stream. She'd never struck out across the farmland since the early run-in with Simeon, always keeping carefully to footpaths. Ratty had no such qualms. 'Have you got permission to replace the windows, then?' she gasped.

'Bureaucratic Bitch has gone away to consider but I think she's run out of steam. The man from the council was told-you-so-ing, he's got no more patience with impractical idealism than me. The Commuters got your windows replaced. I only want to do the same.'

Good job it was The Commuters who'd modernised Honeybun Cottage. Though if they hadn't, they might not have sunk in financial sewage and wouldn't have sold and she'd be living in a different house in a different village with a whole load of different friends. Different shop, different pub ...

'Can you manage eight steps across this tree, Princess, or shall I whistle up an alabaster-white winged horse to purvey your delicateness?'

'I think I can manage.' She achieved the necessary steps across the fallen tree over the stream, pausing to watch the water rush in paw-prints across the shale bed, an excuse to get her breath. Her hand was still in Ratty's. It was warm, so she left it there.

He seemed to have rushed some of the frustrations from his system and they strolled the bank, snapping twigs, looking out where the land rolled away from them combed in brown furrows. She shivered in the uninterrupted wind and he pulled half his fleece jacket across her back as they moved on, away from the sharp smell of nettles.

Crossing the second of two lanes, he remarked, 'Carlysle land from here. If you cross the stream and go right through the coppice you'll find the stile and the footpaths back to the village.'

The memory of being shown off Carlysle land halted her. 'Should we go back by the lane then?'

Ratty shouldered his way through the hawthorn, the thorns catching in his curls. 'They won't mind. My father and Carlysle are matey. Used to want me to be friends with Simeon when we were little.'

'And were you?' Cautiously, she followed.

'Sometimes. Their chauffeur used to let me wash their cars, a black BMW and a red Mini Cooper.' They followed the stream to a bridge, sturdy, functional oak, grey with age and green with algae, climbed two steps and paused to watch the water. Clearer here, it had a bed of rounded rocks and last year's leaves. The wind scuttled along with the stream, funnelled between the coppice and the hawthorn hedge.

Tess sank her head to huddle deeper into her jumper, turning her back to the breeze.

'Is lickle Princess still cold?' Ratty stretched his fleece jacket a bit further, trying to get the other side around her as well, shuffling closer.

'That's better.' She looked up to joke about him behaving himself, but she saw such desire flare in the brightness of his blue eyes that the words died in her throat. For a long second she was transfixed, washed by flashes of want and half-understood expectation.

Her hair writhed about them both in the breeze.

Then his arms tightened, his head dropped. And he kissed her.

A hard, hot kiss, his wind-roughened lips scalding her as his body pressed hers back against the handrail. Questing, his tongue tip caressing, promising, making her think of things she usually tried not to. Lovemaking. Wanting. Pleasure.

Slowly, he lifted his head. Slackened the clinch. Waited for her reaction.

She took a long shaky breath and slid from his embrace, four measured, backward steps towards Carlysle's coppice.

Chapter Eighteen

His eyes followed. Waiting.

She licked her lips, remembering where his had been. How his kiss had felt. Had made her feel. 'I thought ...'

He was very still.

Thoughtfully, she licked her lips again. 'I thought ... it was the *princess* who did the kissing. Not the frog.'

He gasped. His blazing glare of incredulous outrage rewarded her. 'You bitch!' He threw himself. She ran.

Leaping, two steps, racing from his pursuing footsteps, his curses. Dodging through the birches and conifers, shrieking and panting with laughter, one bare stride ahead, ducking, zigzagging, to avoid his grasping hands. Sideways to slide by the fence he had to jump, glancing back and laughing harder to see him trip.

Exploding through the tree line, yelping as she heard him gain on clearer ground, swinging right with bursting heart up the greensward, away from the little lake the stream widened into, aware of a large gazebo ahead. Right with her! Jump left, stop dead, double back, belt downhill.

Then she was yanked back mid-stride and spun against his chest, his arms clamping hers by her side. Chests heaving together as they crowed for breath.

Her laughter faded. The maleness of him, the overwhelming maleness, the plaster dust smell, his heat.

The whisper, 'Bitch!' His head dipping, lips hovering; her heart jumping in anticipation.

The round of applause from the gazebo.

Heads up.

'Oh, hullo Mother,' said Ratty.

Through a slither of anticlimax Tess heard him sigh, 'An audience!' Saw him pushing back the black curls from his eyes, felt his hand guiding her up the slope, ignoring her reluctance.

God, she must look like a tramp in her enormous jumper. She pushed her hair back over her shoulders, trying to sort out which bit went which side of her parting. She felt caught out, like Toby when she'd found him pinching Jenna's chocolate.

'There's no telling where you'll turn up, Miles,' remarked Elisabeth Arnott-Rattenbury. Her hair was dark steel-grey, but her face beneath contrastingly smooth and youthful. She accepted Ratty's peck on her cheek.

'I'm sure you had that all arse about face,' Lester rocked his brandy balloon gravely. 'Far better to let her do the chasing.'

'Unfortunately, she wouldn't be able to catch me.'

Hot and confused, Tess shook hands with Lester and Elisabeth, glared at Simeon who looked injured, and was introduced to his parents, Christopher and Cassie Carlysle.

Christopher had a bone-shaped head and a lugubrious face beneath sparse brown hair. 'Our local artist! Nice to meet you. Shouldn't have left it this long to call!'

Wrong-footed, she felt resentful and difficult. Her face stiffened. 'Oh? I didn't mean to be rude. Simeon threw me off the first time I wandered onto your property. I did attend the bonfire party on your farm but that's best forgotten.'

Christopher looked nonplussed. Cassie shrieked and raised plucked eyebrows into blonde streaks, clutching a thin chest dramatically. 'Don't tell me! Simeon has gone that colour that tells a mother that her child is in the wrong!' She laughed a tinkly laugh, louder than anyone else's. Tess didn't laugh, but inspected the interior of the gazebo.

Like a stubby bandstand, open all round in summer, it was made usable in the chillier weather by being glassed in. How pleasant to dine in one's gabled manor house then stroll across one's park for brandy and coffee in the gazebo, to be out of the wind, with the weak sun magnified through the panes. Civilised.

For a family with a son who used his size and weight to crush a girl against the side of a van and force his kisses on her. She shuddered to remember the beery smell, the scary suffocation, the intrusion.

She was passed both brandy and coffee by Ratty, chatting to his parents as if he'd arranged the meeting rather than just happening across them. The only seat free was a fixed wooden one somewhere between a big armchair and small bench. Ratty squashed in beside her, clutching his brandy, talking about Pennybun, the garage, Pete and Angel.

Tess was silent.

The transition from a hot kiss and a crazy game to this social supping and the animosity that automatically reared near Simeon, unsettled her. Ratty's thigh was hard against hers, his arm moving with his gestures. She watched his mother watching him and wondered. Did Elisabeth feel hurt that they rarely met? That her son didn't go home for Christmas? Or had she come to terms somehow with their tepid relationship? Immaculate from her sleek hair through the golden silk shirt and trousers to soft leather moccasins, she made Cassie's mint-green short-skirted outfit look overstated yet ordinary, Tess's knotted mane and paint-spotted khakis feel wild and scruffy.

Simeon topped up her coffee. 'I didn't know you two had a thing.'

'We *don't*.'

Silence at her sharp reply.

Then Ratty, smooth, suddenly cold. 'Violate Princess

Tess? *You* ought to know better. If you remember the bonfire –'

Cassie again affected shrieking protest. 'No, no, I believe we're back on the misdeeds of my offspring, change the subject quickly!' Another plinking laugh.

Simeon leaned closer and whispered, 'I *did* try to apologise ...'

'Piffle!' She turned away, letting the conversation go on without her, about the Village Feast, which was looming.

Christopher seemed OK, exhibiting a dry sense of humour and not much patience with his son. Cassie was silly and just the opposite.

'I'd lend a hand with the Feast, myself,' Cassie pointed to herself with every long, scarlet-nailed finger on her left hand. 'And I know the upkeep of the village hall is the responsibility of us all. But I just can't envisage working with that formidable woman!'

'Carola,' Ratty supplied. 'We've been summoned to her house tomorrow evening to be given our instructions.'

Tess roused herself. 'Is that what Angel's roped me into?'

''Fraid so, Angel's involved every year, she says you'll love it. Everyone's very keen on the village hall and it being available for all of us. The Feast attracts people from miles around and raises funds to support the hall for the next year.'

'And is Carola that really tiny, really blonde woman who's always shoving charity envelopes through my door?'

'That's her.'

Tess longed suddenly to be at home instead of here, talking about a meeting she knew she wasn't going to want to attend. Suddenly she was exhausted by the hike, the chase, the listening. Marvellous if she could click her fingers and summon the winged horse Ratty mentioned and be swept home for a hot bath. Bed seemed very attractive. Of course, she still slept alone.

And had done for such a long time.

The walk home was serene. Ratty took her hand casually to help her over the fence and the tree-bridge. 'You'll go to Carola's meeting tomorrow, won't you? She's a pain but the Feast is important to the village and she's dying to involve you.'

'I suppose so.'

He provided his cupped hands to vault her to the top of the wall behind Honeybun.

Tess paused on the top, groaning in disgust. 'Oh no, Guy's waiting for me!'

Immediately, Ratty backed away. 'Lucky ol' you. Tomorrow evening, then, Princess.'

Chapter Nineteen

'Bloody Guy! What a bloody day!' This was what having friends was about, this walking together to Carola's house and not wanting to. Up Main Road past The Three Fishes, left into Great Hill Road and left again into New Street and Bankside, which must be referred to as the 'new village', not 'an estate', where the houses were large but too close, drives were long enough for two or three cars and four standard house designs were varied only cosmetically.

She'd wandered through Bankside once or twice before but found nothing in the newness to make her linger. The 'proper village' was more to her taste, where the ironstone cottages had stood for a couple of centuries.

'Guy turned up yesterday. His wife has discovered his affair, inevitably, and flung all his stuff on the lawn. So Guy makes a beeline for Honeybun Cottage, complete with boot full of muddy clothes!'

Arm round Pete, hand tucked chummily in his back pocket, Jenna on her hip, Angel grinned. 'Did you take him in?'

''Course, that's what I'm for, so far as Guy can see. Then I spent all evening listening to his problems – mainly how expensive it's been to have a long-standing mistress and a non-earning wife!'

'Where did he sleep?' Ratty allowed Toby to hang onto his belt and take giant strides behind him.

'Sitting-room floor. *Not* up to his standards, apparently. And first thing this morning, up pops Lynette!'

Absurd, the day, and though she was making them laugh about it now, pulling her jacket tight against the dusky chill, she'd been infuriated at the time. Guy, typically, had been safe in the shower when Lynette rapped hard on the back door.

'Don't let on I'm here!' He had sounded apprehensive over the gargling water.

Tess sighed. 'And your car just drove itself into the drive, did it?'

'Shit. Tell her I've gone for a long walk.'

'She won't believe that!' She hadn't, but pushed past with a snort and a sneer, dark hair yanked back into a ball, lips pinched to stop them trembling. 'I suppose I'd better sort the silly bastard out. It's not you he's humping?'

'Absolutely not!'

'I've always thought he might. He'll bonk anything.'

'Thanks. Why don't you come in and sit down?' Tess had glared at Lynette, who'd already flounced herself down at the kitchen table. And suddenly *she* was the one arguing with Lynette, whilst Guy skulked on the landing. Maybe Tess should keep her great beak out of Guy and Lynette's marriage? Or should Lynette try to avoid being such a carping, miserable tyrant, for a change?

Losing patience, Tess dragged Guy down to quarrel with his wife, leaving them to it while she shut herself in her workroom to check and parcel the Bavarian tales commission. Thank God there was another *Dragons* anthology on the horizon, she was sick of lederhosen and cocky hats. And thank God she wasn't saddled with a man like Guy.

Staring out of the window, she thought instead of Ratty, the greatest possible contrast. What was happening there? The fabled 'just good friends'?

So why did he kiss her?

She looked at the mossy roof tiles of Pennybun, wondering if he was there.

Why *did* he kiss her? It hadn't been a kiss of mere friendship. Was she fooling herself that she was unaffected by sea-bright eyes and a wicked smile, gypsy curls? He stirred her. She'd tucked her feelings away, after Olly. Was that changing? Were they going to have a thing? And when it ended, what then? That was the bit she couldn't get her head around. No going back then to the old friendship, drinking at The Three Fishes, long hikes, babysitting.

Why did he kiss her, reminding her how it felt to be pulled hungrily against the hardness of a man's chest? Not that Olly had been hungry. Olly had been measured, thoughtful, controlling.

Whereas Ratty was very real.

Voices rose, downstairs. Guy progressing from a conciliatory murmur to a raw bellow, Lynette beginning on a raucous shriek and going on from there. She turned on music to drown them out.

When the package was ready for the courier, Tess began to sort through her materials, filling in time rather than enter the kitchen warfare. She sharpened several pencils, rotating them slowly as she shaved them to a point with a scalpel. Fag ends of superseded acrylic paint tubes, a pile of them, old. She dug out a couple of brushes that had seen better days and, splitting the crumpled tubes, began idly to paint a creeper over the blue walls. Twining, inching, leaves like hearts and spades, through an airbrick in the corner, around the pipework which dropped through the room, to writhe across the top of the window and into the window reveal. She added pink-cream trumpets of morning glory. And it stopped mattering that she felt obliged to hide herself away in her own home, time just wandered by until the slamming of the back door shook her window.

Good. One of them had gone.

It was Guy who remained, drooped against the dresser,

shoulders slumped, head down. 'She's gone.'

'Didn't you grovel enough?'

'Not really.' He stroked the length of his nose, a familiar gesture. She felt a sudden twang of yearning for the happy young days with Guy, before he turned into a bit of a liability and failed to answer life's call to grow responsible. Days of mates, crowds, pubs, clubs, when Guy had stroked his nose and chuckled, not gazed at the floor and jutted out an unhappy bottom lip. 'I suppose I'm not very nice to her.'

Hungry, she propelled him to a kitchen chair to get him out of her way. 'Humping other women definitely comes under that heading. Doesn't she want you back?' She made him a cheese and pickle sandwich, which she knew very well he didn't care for.

'I told her she was crap in bed.'

'Ouch.' Watching him chew his sandwich, eating her own, thoughtfully, leaning against the china sink waiting for the kettle to boil, she gave in to prurience. 'And is she?'

'She is now. Lights out, Granny nightie. Doesn't actually say "Tidy up when you've finished", but might as well.'

That didn't sound much fun. Should she feel sorry for Lynette? Or Guy? She made tea, ate some fruit, considered. Decided it wasn't her problem. 'Well, whatever,' she remarked, 'your days here are numbered, Guy, there's no room and you're a pain in the arse.'

Ratty laughed at this account of her cousinly candour. 'So, has he gone?'

'Has he gone?' echoed Toby from his new perch on Ratty's shoulders. They'd slowed their approach to Bankside to hear the end of the story.

'He has, now.' When he'd behaved badly enough for her to insist loudly he ring Lynette and try harder.

Malicious bastard, Guy. Despite everything that happened, despite Tess howling down the stairs, uncaring who heard, 'Don't let him in! Don't open the door!' Guy *had*. 'Hullo, Olly!'

She stamped. She'd seen Olly draw up. It would've been simple to ignore him until he went away, if Guy hadn't opened the door and sounded pleased to see him!

Down the stairs, she jumped into the kitchen, hands on hips, hair flying into her face and faced Olly. 'What?'

Smiling his best, burning smile, Olly offered a single red rose in a ribbon-wound polythene sleeve. 'How are you?'

She folded her arms uncooperatively. 'What do you want? Run out of children to steal?'

His hair was shorter, slid like strands of silk when he shook it back. His eyes still that compelling Arctic blue, lips still thin and sensuous, he still towered above her. The base of his throat still emerged smoothly from his collar.

'I'd like to talk.' His smile continued to be beautiful.

Today didn't seem a good temper day. The Pill, every bit as brilliant as Dr Warrington had said it would be at reducing her erratic monthly deluge to a manageable flow, hadn't altered her occasional premenstrual fury. Her cottage, generally a peaceful sanctuary, now seemed *teeming* with *people* who were really, *really*, REALLY irritating! She didn't usually suffer from gritted teeth, stiffened shoulders and clenched fists. On the whole her words were mild enough. But today she seemed to have lost all equanimity.

'*Pity,*' she spat at Olly, who jumped slightly. 'Pity you didn't have the urge to talk before you jilted me – by e-mail!'

Guy hooted, half admiring. 'I didn't know that! Did you really?' Tess glared to wipe the smirk from his face, wounded that he could find it funny.

'Or when I lay in gory sheets and lost a baby! Our baby, Olly! Pity it wasn't when I was living with my parents, feeling alone and lonely and unloved. Pity, Olly. Because then, *I might have listened*!'

Lips straightening, Olly stuttered. 'But surely ...'

She pushed past him, snatched open the kitchen door. 'You – get out. And, *you*,' she snarled at her cousin. 'Phone and sort your wife out. Don't witter on about her sexlessness, you damned well take her to bed and make it happen!'

Olly's turn to laugh. 'Don't you make it happen in bed for your wife, Guy? OK, *OK*, I'm going! I'll call again when you're feeling less stressed. I really do want to talk to you.'

Spiteful, sulky, Guy called after him. 'Should've made it a dozen roses, Olly, she might not have realised how broke you are!'

Guy left very soon after a long telephone conversation of 'been inconsiderate' and 'work everything out'. Before he went, he ratted on Olly with thorough rancour. 'He's in really deep poo, basically. Ran up God knows what bills when he was doing well, then surfed from one credit card to another, applying for them all, moving the balance and taking advantage of the free credit period. Then new card applications began to be refused. Do you *know* what they charge on unpaid balances?'

She had some idea. And it reinforced her suspicions about what was bringing Olly back into her orbit. He needed somewhere to live and someone to subsidise him for a bit. She felt a moment's sympathy. It couldn't be easy for him, he seemed to be paying pretty dearly for his mistakes. Then she hardened her heart.

No sympathy from Tess Riddell, today!

Hoisting Toby into a more comfortable position, Ratty matched his pace to hers, rubbing shoulders. 'You know something, Princess, I love you when you're angry.'

'You should have heard me when my father rang ... Good God!'

Carola's house. Decorated barge-boards, repro-medieval front door, bullions in the bay window, pierced ridge tiles, statues, a koi carp pond and bridge guarding the front door, an arch and a pergola.

'Wait till you see the inside,' hissed Angel, as Carola opened the door.

'You're the last,' Carola reprimanded gently, towing them across the hall to the sitting room like a tiny blonde tug. 'Come and join us!' Tess, gazing around from the back of the group, felt her lip curl. As a compulsive viewer of how-to television programmes, subscriber to every glossy home monthly, Carola obviously fancied herself as a designer and decorator.

The intensity of the effect was difficult to absorb. Rugs hand-hooked, embroideries and tapestries on walls that were dragged, ragged, marbled, stencilled and sponged, doors scumbled or crackle-glazed, curtains swagged-and-tailed, scalloped, fringed or valanced. Tess's artistic soul was offended.

Carola suggested Angel leave 'the kiddies' with her 'brood' in the playroom. Formerly the dining room, until Carola and her husband – who commuted and very sensibly spent as much time at work as possible – extended the sitting room to football pitch proportions, it was manned by a 'village girl'. Carola called her children 'honeee' and never told, always asked. 'Now, can you play nicely? Can you do that for me, honeee? Mmmm? Oh, I expect you'll do as you like, as usual!' The grinning face of the eldest girl as she rolled backwards into a toy box suggested that Carola was right.

The meeting gathered round an oval dining table big enough to host a conference. Carola took the head, dispensing with the formality of being elected chairperson. 'I've put the extra leaf in so there should be room. Does everybody know everybody? Does everybody know Tess? I'll just go round – Elaine Tubb, from The Three Fishes, Kelly, Hazel and Sarah from Mums 'n' Tots, Ida, Hubert, Rose and Grace from Church. OK? Now ...'

Tess exchanged smiles with Gwen Crowther then sighed deeper into her chair, almost slipping from the taut Regency-striped fabric, and only half listened whilst Carola ran through details of the upcoming Feast. 'Sponsorship – Ratty?'

Ratty saluted. 'One stall, ma'am.'

'Elaine, can we count on The Three Fishes for another? We've got corn dollies, hand-knits, tombola, white elephant, candles and aromatherapy oils, and then the table-toppers.

'Raffle – a hamper (ta, Gwen), half-a-doz bottles of wine from The Three Fishes (thanks, Elaine), oil change and service from MAR Motors, cut-and-blow from Angel, hand-knitted Dennis the Menace and Bart Simpson, half a day's gardening from the landscape man. And hand stencilling from me.'

Ratty whispered, 'Hope I don't win that!'

Oblivious, Carola ran on about erecting the stalls, decorating the stalls, filling the stalls, manning the stalls. Dismantling the stalls and turning them into tables for the finger buffet at the evening dance.

'Now, Tess, I'm relying on you.'

Having been concentrating on avoiding Ratty as he tried to pull loose the laces of her Doc Martens with his feet, Tess stumbled. 'Me? Pardon?'

Carola's hair was even blonder than Olly's. With the waxy transparency of skin and lips that were nearly colourless. If she ever got a commission to paint a ghost, Carola would be a great sitter – if she'd sit still for more than five minutes!

'As our resident artist, would you be prepared to paint a picture for us? An original "Nigel" perhaps?'

'Copyright,' Tess intercepted hastily, although copyright rested with herself.

'Oh dear. I was hoping yours could be top raffle prize? I was seeing you signing the work for the winner? For the photo to go in the evening paper.' She made a rectangle with her hands and looked through.

It wasn't a bad idea. She could send the clipping to her agent. Tess agreed cautiously. 'But I'll create something new, specially.'

Carola clapped. 'Wonderful! It could be the start of something, a character just for the Feast every year! Perhaps something to reflect the agriculture all around us. A sheep?'

'I come up with my own ideas.'

'Oh, oops! Whatever!'

Interminable, the meeting, with disgusting refreshments in the shape of sesame-seed toffee fingers, herbal tea and home-made wine. A long evening full of Carola's enthusiasm and everyone else's long-suffering cooperation.

'Good job it's for the village – and no one else wants to do it,' Ratty observed as they marched back down Main Road, laden with sleepy children, hurrying to keep warm. 'Or I'd have to pull her head off to shut her up!'

Gwen brought Milky Bars out from her shop for the children and everyone shivered on the garage forecourt whilst the adults chose between Wagon Wheels and Mars Bars.

And then it happened.

One minute Tess was enjoying being part of the group, teasing Angel about whether or not she'd babysit on Friday evening, Ratty's arm warm against hers as she opened the chocolate wrapper for a suddenly wakeful Toby, Ratty grinning down at her and calling her Princess.

And then his attention was whipped away like a magician's tablecloth. 'Christ!' he breathed.

'Franca!' Angel exclaimed in an odd voice.

Toby was thrust into Tess's surprised arms and Ratty stepped slowly towards a woman who was hovering outside the shop, grinning madly. Astride a bicycle, a steadying foot to the kerb, elbows on the handlebars, her chest was very much in evidence and her fair hair plaited into knobs above each ear. Her body looked as if she spent every day eating sensibly and working out.

''Ello,' she called, accent French and sexy. 'I am welcome?'

'*Franca*!' Ratty threw out his arms and homed in.

Franca squealed as she was lifted clear of the cycle and swung into his embrace.

'Here comes the mushy stuff!' Pete joked. 'They'll be at it like knives again, you'll see.'

So. They had been at it like knives before. Which would explain Ratty's turned back as he crushed Franca to him, the long and thorough kiss whilst one of Franca's dainty feet curled up to her taut bottom and her hands locked behind Ratty's neck.

Angel and Pete, the children and Tess, waited like spare parts until Franca broke away from the embrace and waved. Ratty whispered in her ear, made her laugh, pulled her back for more kisses. 'Tomorrow?' she managed, giggling as Ratty pursued her lips. 'Now I am busy!'

And then Ratty was stooping to pick up the cycle, shouting, 'See you!' throwing his arm around Franca and hustling her around the corner and out of sight.

'Fancy Franca coming back.' Angel turned to take Toby, who was nodding again now. 'I didn't think we'd see her again.'

Pete shifted Jenna in his arms. 'Looks like she intends

finding out if Ratty's any less set against commitment. He looked pleased to see her, anyway.'

'Very affectionate,' Angel agreed. An uncomfortable expression passed over her face. 'Coming in for coffee, Tess?'

Tess looked over at the corner. Seeing once again Ratty disappearing without a backward look, pushing a cycle with one hand, squeezing a buttock with the other. 'No,' she said. 'No thanks.' She tried to think of something to add about an early night or a hot bath or making sure Guy hadn't reappeared. But failed.

Chapter Twenty

'Thanks for landing me in the shit with Angel.' Pete stepped into his overalls, shrugging on the sleeves, flipping out the collar. 'She sends you the following message: "You'd better have made the right choices, you unremitting bastard." She's not happy, Rats, with you for doing it, or with me for going along with it. I'm not thrilled about it myself.'

Ratty kept his eyes on the radiator hoses he was examining, turning them towards the light, picking at possible rot spots with stubby nails.

Pete pulled out the drawer of a tool chest. 'And how was the night with Franca?'

'Much as you'd suppose.'

At the back of the garage Jos lifted his head sharply. 'Is Franca back? You spent the night together, Rats?'

Ratty selected a new jubilee clip, tested the screw. 'She's back at the Peterborough office for a month or two.'

He could feel Jos's stare like a prodding finger, before Jos returned to his work in silence. A silence he kept up more or less all morning.

Until Ratty was on the forecourt and Jos must've thought him out of earshot. His voice came hollowly from under the ramp. 'So he and Franca got it together again?'

Muffled, Pete's voice emerged from the foot well of a Rover. 'Certainly looked that way last night, when Franca appeared. All over each other when last seen.'

'Must be two years?'

'About that. It was hot at the time.'

Jos sighed. 'I thought ... I thought he and Tess were heading for each other like a train crash.'

186

'Looked that way sometimes, didn't it?'

'Was Tess upset?'

'A bit quiet. Have you got my feeler gauges?'

'Haven't even got my own feeler gauges, look in Ratty's box. She's bound to feel ...'

'... a bit left out? Probably. Yes, probably.' Pete tucked his hair back and straightened his back. 'But you know Ratty.'

The waste bin overflowed. Tess gazed down at her pad and hated the succession of cavorting hedgehogs. She wasn't in the mood, that was the trouble; creative people depended on being in the mood. And she wasn't.

Or was it only the creative? Perhaps, some days, keyboard operators' fingers were stiff and stupid, perhaps supermarket staff served only rude customers, perhaps butchers suffered from imperfect chops or lumpy sausages and bank managers felt like strangling their staff and machine-gunning the customers?

She pencil-slashed at her page of hedgehogs, back and forth, until she'd spoiled the page and about eight beneath. She turned them, slowly, until she came to where the sheets were still unblemished and fresh. Then, skimming the pad violently against the wall, quite likely spoiled them, too. For a month now she'd been uptight, unsettled and irascible. Life had changed and she didn't like it.

Didn't like acknowledging that Ratty's infatuation with Franca had removed him from the position of 'friend'. Well no, he was friendly when they met but he was no longer there for Tess, tugging her hair, calling her 'Princess' or 'gorgeous, sexy woman'.

It was Franca; Franca who walked hand in hand with Ratty and on whose temples kisses dropped. Sickeningly attractive, unfortunately, with her sexy French accent and pneumatic body, clear skin and pretty hair. Stupid, hateful hairstyle, why didn't Ratty worry her to leave it loose? Or perhaps it was enough for him to see it loose at night. In bed.

Worse, Franca had a history with those Tess considered her friends.

Her friends. And though they remained her friends, she couldn't shake off the feeling of becoming the second driver in a one-car team.

Long days. Disregarding earlier intentions she bought a television and spent more time at home. Got into *The Bill*, a series of Channel Four documentaries and read *Ceefax* for hours. She even considered subscribing to satellite television.

Then she could watch all day and all night, all those repeats and pathetic adverts appealing for charitable donations.

And never do anything.

And never see anyone.

And never go anywhere ever, *ever again*.

Someone at the back door. Tess ignored the rapping the first time, but when the five rapid knocks sounded again, she trudged downstairs, pulling her jacket on. She'd stepped down into the kitchen before seeing, through the glass, that it was Olly. She snorted. 'Bugger!' And opened the door.

'I'm just going out for a walk. What do you want?'

Olly took a step back. 'Oh. Right.'

They stared at each other. Olly looked more relaxed, the frown that had drawn a sharp line between his brows was missing.

Then he managed a smile, softening his face. 'I still want to talk to you for a few minutes. I'll phone.'

Tess stepped through the door, closing and locking it

behind her. 'I shouldn't think we can have very much more to say to each other.'

'Right.' He trailed back down the drive to his car parked in the lane. Tess pushed her way past it. She'd walk out of the village today, walk for a mile or two on the verges, gazing over the hedges and into the fields. Just this once she didn't feel like threading her way through the village, having to wave at everyone at the garage or decide whether to call on Angel.

She set off, hands in pockets, head down.

'Where are you going?'

When she looked behind, Olly was standing looking after her. 'A walk,' she tossed back, without pausing. Then she heard his running footsteps, catching her up.

'I'll walk with you for a few minutes.'

She stopped abruptly. 'Why don't you just piss off?' She strode away, leaving him standing in the road again.

By the time she got to the first curve she'd begun to wonder uneasily what he could be up to. You never could tell with Olly, tricky, crafty Olly. Maybe it would be smart to know? She glanced back. He was still standing where she'd left him, slapping the fob of his keys against his palm and watching. She shouted, 'All right, then! But get a move on!'

With the length of his legs he caught up with her in seconds. Gazing away from him, over the fields, she snapped, 'So? What?'

He tucked his keys into his pocket. Took a deep breath, then sighed. 'I decided I'd better say sorry.'

She gave an incredulous laugh.

Olly bit his lip. 'I know it all ended in crap but I was thinking ... when we were first going out, it was magic, wasn't it?'

And he actually seemed to be waiting for an answer. Tess

shrugged, ungraciously, it *had* seemed like magic to her but she wasn't going to admit it. 'A bit late to realise that.'

A car came up behind them and they hopped up onto the verge out of the way. The car stopped, a navy-blue Triumph Stag. Ratty leant over and wound down the passenger window and raised his eyebrows at Tess. 'Are you OK?'

'Fine.'

'Sure?'

'Yes!'

After a long, appraising look at Olly, he turned back to her. 'I expect you've got your mobile?' He held his own mobile up to show her.

She nodded, pulled her phone out of pocket.

Ratty grinned. 'Should the screen be blank like that?'

She grimaced and switched it on. After a long look Olly's way, Ratty drove off.

Olly gave a half-laugh. 'He made it quite obvious he doesn't trust me.'

'Some people don't like violent men.' Bastard Olly. Fresh disgust flooded in at the memory of how he'd slapped her. She let the gusty little breeze push her into a crosser pace and watched the birds waltzing on the wind above the fields while Olly paced in his thin-soled, unsuitable shoes beside her.

'I hadn't really thought …' he began. He paused, then tried again. 'It didn't seem like …' He sighed and shook his head. 'I wouldn't call myself *violent*.'

Tess sighed. 'Olly, you hit me!' She turned ready to take out more of her frustrations on him.

'Oh hell,' he said.

She let her mood carry her along. 'If you touch me again I'll see you in court.'

They tramped on in silence, Tess pushing back tendrils of hair that the breeze teased free from her plait. God, she didn't want Olly with her. And neither did she want to paint the raffle prize picture she hadn't even started, but it was probably too late to get out of it. God. She needed a holiday.

'I am sorry.' Olly suddenly halted.

Tess turned to face him. 'It's a bit late for that.'

He inched closer. 'But I am sorry. It sounds feeble, now, but in the heat of the moment ... I was frightened, I'd just been threatened with bankruptcy and I lashed out. It didn't seem like violence, precisely. And now I sound pathetic.'

Tess said, flatly, 'It is violence. You are pathetic. What about the other times?'

She watched his lips thin. 'I suppose you counted!'

'I remember them all.'

They glared at each other, defiance and guilt flashing across Olly's face. It might be that standing up to him – now, when it was too late, secluded here in the leafy lane – was foolhardy to say the least. But Tess almost wished he would crack her one. She was ready for him this time. If his hand so much as twitched, she'd knee him so hard he'd still be spitting his balls out this time next week.

But when it became obvious the silent staring contest wasn't going to provoke him, Tess turned back towards Middledip. 'And are you bankrupt?'

He followed. 'No, I scraped out of it. So, how's work going?'

Oh, right, that'd be it. She swung on him, teeth gritted. 'Look Olly, it's *my* work and it's *my* money that I earn from it. It's not going into your pocket or Guy's. I'm not looking for any non-fee-paying lodgers, either! OK? So you might as well sod off.'

Olly almost smiled, his blond hair lifting in the breeze. 'I'm not on the scrounge.' He looked away, looked back. 'In fact, I've got a job, done what I always said I wouldn't do and gone to work for some huge faceless firm at the same desk in the same office every day, to do as I'm told. I'm a project leader in a soft drinks company. I've given up everything I was so intent on but I'm getting paid OK and others take the strain and the shit. I'm making enough to live. Most of my equipment's gone back to the leasing companies and I've started paying off the credit card companies. Those bastards are remorseless when they're clawing their money back.'

Olly's eyes were still a brilliant colour when he smiled. He was smiling now.

She scowled to avoid her face breaking into the congratulatory response he obviously wanted. 'So you've had a personality transplant, you're not sponging and you're not here for a fight – what's brought you up country this weekend?'

Olly fidgeted. Then his mouth lifted at the corners, lighting his eyes with new brilliance. 'I miss you. A bit.'

'Posters ready? Got to get them up around the village, in Port-le-bain and this side of Bettsbrough. Can I see? Are they nice?' Carola closed the door and was in Tess's kitchen, fine white hair shining, eyes alert, buttons buttoned, neat from top to bottom.

In an old sweatshirt, hair corkscrewed up in a butterfly clasp, Tess felt like an old conker husk. 'Ah.' She shifted feet and felt her colour bloom. 'I'll bring you them tomorrow.'

Carola cocked her head, firing off rapid guesses. 'There's a problem. You're too busy. You've forgotten. You hated the idea but were too kind to say. Shall I go away and get them done quickly somewhere else? And does this jeopardise the raffle prize? Because the bulk of the tickets have already been sold and to be honest *that* is a difficulty.'

Huge guilt, partly because Carola was right that she hadn't really wanted to do the posters, partly because Carola was prepared to give her all to the Feast but was totally understanding when other people weren't; it made Tess feel humble.

She shook herself. 'Let's rough out what you want.' Pulling the ever-present pad off the dresser, she fished in her top pocket for her pencil. 'Won't take long to do something on the Mac and print it off.'

'Oooh, can I see how? I've only ever used a PC.'

So they were up in the workroom designing a poster.

Middledip Feast 6th May, Tess typed in. *Stalls, competitions, bouncy castle. Village Hall 2-5 p.m. Don't miss the Buffet Dance and mega-raffle, 7.30 p.m. till late.* She let Carola choose fonts and colours.

Carola, childlike, soaked up the new information, full of energy. 'How big can we have these?'

'A4,' firmly. 'Any bigger will get ripped by the wind.'

'OK, can we have sixty?'

So that was how Carola got people to do what she wanted, she simply asked and never displayed disappointment if refused. A lethal combination, difficult to resist. So, as well as doing damage to her ink cartridge supplies, Tess found herself driving off to Port-le-bain with ten posters for telegraph poles and shop windows. Then there was still the raffle prize.

The Feast profits this year were for the village hall exterior decoration. She scribbled 'village hall' and 'maintenance – decoration, cleaning, painting, preparation'. Tapped her teeth with her pencil and thoughtfully began evolving sketches of animals in overalls or smocks. Badgers painting, deer wielding blowtorches, rabbits on ladders clearing gutters.

She took a board and stood on the cricket pitch to sketch

the side view of the hall. For the first time in weeks she sank into her work, right until she lost the light. Then she felt the familiar urge to call at Rotten Row. Which was a good move or bad, depending, because there was Carola drinking coffee, poring over lists of jobs to be matched with volunteers.

'Ooh! The very person!' Carola exclaimed. 'I'm looking for a darling artistic type to be in charge of decorating the stalls. We normally get some of the village children to help.'

After hugging Angel briefly in unspoken apology for having been so reclusive recently, Tess flopped down at the kitchen table. 'Cutting out leaves from green card and posies from crêpe paper, that sort of thing? OK.'

'And you know where to get the materials, I expect?'

'Yes.'

'So can you?'

'Yes!'

'And the raffle prize ...?'

'Give me another week.'

Carola added a series of ticks to her list. 'Now, it'll need to be framed ...'

Tess laughed and held up her hands in surrender. 'OK, OK, I'm sure that's my job, too!'

And she actually began to feel real interest because Middledip was fortunate to have a wonderful village hall and every villager expected it to be available for wedding receptions, funeral teas and engagement parties.

'And,' beamed Carola, 'you might book it for your wedding reception!'

So when Ratty popped his head round the back door and smiled, Tess was laughing at such a preposterous idea and didn't have to coax her facial muscles to work, at all.

'I wanted to, kind of, apologise.'

Tess tapped the end of a brush on the table and adjusted the phone in her hand. 'I thought you had. Kind of.'

'Yeah. Well.'

Silence. Tess listened to nothing down the phone. 'So what's on your agenda today? I'm busy.'

'How many times am I supposed to say sorry before you speak to me nicely again?'

Tess threw down the brush, which spattered tiny flecks of cobalt around it. 'To be honest, you being humble is too weird.'

He laughed, and she was suddenly transported back to the days before they'd even been engaged, when Olly had laughed quite a lot, and been fun. She heard him take a deep breath. 'I'd like to take you out to dinner.'

'No thanks.' She didn't even have to think about it.

'Come on! Let me redeem myself, make amends. A nice restaurant, a meal, a few drinks. Have you got plans for tonight?'

She let the words revolve in her mind. Plans for tonight? Not many. Like eating at home and sitting in front of a television to avoid calling on Angel and Pete and having to watch Ratty slobber over Franca.

She rubbed the tip of her finger over the specks of paint that were drying already, comparing staying in alone with going out with someone she'd once adored. 'There's nothing in it for you. No money, no home, no bed to sleep in or have sex in.'

'Just a meal. Old friends, no hard feelings,' he confirmed.

And it was OK, in the end.

All the tense, condescending parts of Olly seemed to have wandered off somewhere. He picked her up, took her to a reasonable restaurant where she felt OK in her blue fitted dress with a cobweb-lace shrug thrown over. He didn't try to change her mind about what she ordered, he didn't choose something himself that would take extra time to prepare, he told her she looked nice without suggesting some way she could've looked better. He asked how her parents were and told her a bit about his job.

It almost began to feel familiar, being out with him, with his not-a-hair-out-of-place appearance. She even enjoyed talking about all his mates in London who she'd once known.

'So,' she said, after he'd ordered her a brandy and she felt pretty relaxed. 'What's this all about?' Her gaze caught on his fine lips for a moment when he smiled.

'Don't be so suspicious.' He glanced across the tables covered with red cloths and all the chattering diners clustered around them and became serious. 'This is the new me.'

She laughed. 'When did you realise you needed renewing?'

His smile faded. He shrugged. 'Partly because of our recent encounters, I had a look at myself. I didn't like the way things were going, so I looked for a solution.' He would do. 'I'd got surly and nasty and suspicious of everyone. But things are better now.'

Tess let her disbelief show on her face. 'Incredible. What did it take?'

He sat back, met her eyes. 'I admitted to myself that I couldn't do it.'

She shook her head. 'Do what?'

He spread his hands. 'The whole freelance thing. Finding my own work, setting my prices, dealing with the problems, debt collections, insurance, repairs, taxes, accountants. I tried hard, but it didn't come off. I networked and I back-stabbed, the whole thing, but I made a balls of it.' His hands clenched briefly on the tablecloth. 'It's impossible to properly explain. You can't appreciate the amount of crap you have to wade through, unless you do it.'

Tess sat forward so suddenly that she rocked the table. 'What do you think I do? Wave a magic wand? I'm freelance just as much as you were!'

'It's not the same,' he said automatically, his chin going in the air, the old hardness reappearing suddenly around his eyes.

She let her eyes blaze into his. 'It. Is. The. Same.'

He stared for a moment. Then dropped his eyes. 'If you say so,' he muttered.

Tess downed her brandy and returned to the wine. 'You've got a little way to go with the new you, Olly.'

After a moment he laughed again and she joined in.

So, it was OK. OK with Olly, an OK kind of evening. She went home feeling happier than she would have been spending the evening in front of the television. And some people made do with OK all their lives. OK was OK, especially if you'd made up your mind that friendship was safer than a heart that cartwheeled and hands that grew clammy whenever a certain someone crept into your thoughts.

Chapter Twenty-One

Nice to be working with Slinker, Slider and Winder again now the second anthology had been given the go ahead. Tess could pin up the layouts and study the brief, pin up earlier character sketches for the sake of consistency. Pause at sketches of Farny, the broadness of the lizard-man's chest fanned with dark curls. Look out over at Pennybun.

Lucasta's rhododendron was lovely this May, its blatant vermilion glowing above other shrubs. Ratty's rhododendron now.

At Pennybun, most of the remedial work was finished, damp proofing, rewiring and plastering. The new windows were lovely. Yesterday, she'd let in the joiner to measure up for the kitchen just as Ratty growled up in his Caterham. She'd turned to watch as he levered himself from the austere lines of the open-topped sports car he'd built, dark green and quirky. It seemed a long time since he'd driven her anywhere in it, flying and bouncing along like a fart in a hurricane, two inches from the floor.

Must he really look at his watch as he rapidly selected mouldings, finish, worktops? The Pennybun project had been fun, before, but it was a bit of a bind now. OK for Franca, safe in conference at a chemical works on Peterborough's outskirts, with no danger of being asked to let people in.

Ratty finished with the joiner, checked his watch again, tossed his keys and smiled at Tess. 'So, Carola involved you with the Feast, in the end?'

'It was more fun than I'd expected.'

'Thought it would be.' He'd checked she was well, how

work was going, that the Freelander was behaving itself. Folded himself back into the Caterham, reversed, and was gone.

He hadn't mentioned seeing her being driven out of the village by Olly, when he'd given a wave, a quirk of the eyebrows and carried on down Main Road, apparently unsurprised and undisturbed by her choice of companion. She'd quite expected her mobile to ring, to hear his sharp, 'Are you OK?' It hadn't rung, though she'd made sure it was on.

If he'd shown any interest at all she would've mentioned that Olly had just been on the phone before she'd broken off to let Ratty's joiner in. 'I'm ringing you from work. That's cool, isn't it? I can stop work and doss about and it's not me losing money.'

He'd enjoyed dinner, he said, he'd enjoyed her company, was regretting more and more the way things had ended. Eventually he wound up to, 'So, how do you feel about doing it again, sometime?'

After several moments she'd answered, 'Maybe. OK.' After all, her dance card was hardly full.

She shook herself into the present as Ratty's Caterham blasted out of sight. Time to meet Carola at the village hall to check the decorations. The making of them had been jolly, shrill kiddies cutting leaves from thin green card, the defter mastering crêpe roses to make into swags.

The raffle prize picture was awkward under one arm; she shifted it as she walked. Spring had sprung, would it be dry on Saturday? Spring showers had been more like torrential deluges lately. More people would turn out if it was dry. So much effort, the Feast deserved success.

'She's got it, she's got it! I knew she wouldn't let me down!' Carola ran across the hall, clapping pleased hands. 'Look, look, everybody! Isn't it marvellous?'

Tess stood back and let them drop their swags and skirts for the stalls and gather to exclaim. A nice bit of whimsy, the watercolour was of the hall worked on by a band of animal tradesmen. She grinned as they found 'themselves' – a badger in a brown smock like Hubert's, a tiny white rabbit with Carola's thin and geometric bob, a deer with Angel's hair but wielding a blowtorch instead of a hairdryer.

'Grace, this badger's got your flowery overall!'

'The rabbit with the bucket's got Sarah's new perm – and that one has Kelly's bandaged finger! Isn't it wonderful?'

'If you want me to sign it as it's presented, the glass will have to go in later.' It might be shallow but Tess got a kick out of their admiration. Feeling respected and wanted had kept her at the hall when she'd wanted to run over the hill and far away.

And anyway, despite initial misgivings, she enjoyed helping, had begun to understand Angel's pleasure in community activity, the kiddies racing round and getting in the way, the giggles. The alliance.

So she agreed meekly with Carola's suggestions that she help erect and decorate the stalls on Saturday morning, man the door on Saturday afternoon when it was all (hopefully) happening, be early – so Carola had one less thing to worry about – in the evening when she was, of course, presenting the first prize for the raffle.

Angel was the next to find her a job to do. 'Any chance you could babysit on Thursday evening, Tess?'

Toby and Jenna, bless them, were a comfort. Tess loved entertaining them. Babysitting was fun: crazy bath time, a pyjama'd wrestle, a bedtime story (or eight). ''Course. Going somewhere nice?' She peered down from the stage where Carola had insisted she stand to 'get the feel of it'. Actually, she didn't like the feel of it at all. Too high, too exposed.

'A meal at The Pheasant.' Angel looked unenthusiastic, though normally she'd be wild to dress up for the expensive and over-booked restaurant.

'Posh! What have you done to deserve that?'

'It's a bribe,' Angel shifted uneasily. 'I have to do something unspeakable – pretend to like something I don't.'

Tess rolled her eyes. 'Wish *I* had a sex life like that!'

Angel giggled. Then stopped, suddenly.

Ratty looked up as Angel rocked the buggy and swung Toby's hand, gazing down Main Road as Tess disappeared in the direction of Honeybun Cottage. 'She agreed to babysit on Thursday,' she said. It was obvious where Angel's sympathies lay.

He commiserated. 'Hell, isn't it?'

Angel switched her baleful gaze to him. He was her husband's best friend and employer, her children loved him, she probably cared for him best in the world apart from Pete and the kids. But she covered Toby's ears to declare, 'You're a shit, Ratty. You could've done things differently. You better be right.'

He stared down at the coked-up spark plugs in his oily hands. 'Yes, I better had.'

Angel sniffed and covered Toby's ears once more. 'You know she's been seeing that ultra-arse, Olly?'

'I saw them together.'

'He's promised never to slap her again. He'd better not.'

Ratty looked up and met her eyes. 'I don't think he will.'

Angel tugged the buggy round, angrily. 'You realise she might sleep with him again?'

Silence.

'He's bad for her. I'll bet you didn't think he'd be back on the scene, did you?'

Ratty rolled the spark plug from one hand to another.

'No. They're not sleeping together, are they?'

'They might be.' Angel glared for several seconds, then softened. 'OK, they're not. She says that'd be far too far, far too fast.'

Ratty sighed. 'Well. She's got a lot of sense.'

Tess wouldn't have agreed to babysit if she'd known. OK, she'd have had to agree, but at least she *would've* known. It wouldn't have been such a shock. Or she could have pretended to be ill, with something horrible, like shingles. In fact, shingles would've been nicer.

She'd been lounging on the grey sitting-room carpet, drawing on a magic slate, watching Jenna wiping Toby's drawings half done, laughing at Toby's outrage, chatting as Pete waited patiently for Angel to appear. When, from upstairs, Angel yelled, 'They're here!'

And Ratty waltzed in, hand in hand with a radiant Franca.

Tess's flabbergasted eyes met his, were held to their brilliance until he looked away. Hair trimmed, he must've wet shaved to subdue his customary stubble to that degree of smoothness. Pretty powerful.

Behind him hovered Jos and new girlfriend Miranda, a shy dab with oval glasses and an Indian print skirt.

Franca broke the silence in her really excellent English, complimenting Tess on her kindness in babysitting whilst everyone else went out.

'Always the bridesmaid and never the bride,' Tess muttered, then forced a big smile to show it was a joke. Very still, she lay on the rug with the children, dowdy in old jeans whilst Franca looked *stunning* in tall black boots under a long black skirt split to her thighs, dawn-pink angora jumper clinging in a way that, Tess thought despairingly, must make every man long to touch.

They left in a flurry of phone numbers, reminders, instructions, thanks and, probably, sighs of relief. Tess lay back on the carpet and glared at the ceiling. 'Well, if that doesn't just about take the shitty biscuit.'

Toby clamped a gleeful hand to his mouth. '*Tess*, you said ...!'

'Bi'cuit?' asked Jenna, looking expectantly towards the kitchen.

Tess sprang up, fuelled by anger and anguish, half blind in her own glistening hot-eyed world. 'Why not? Biscuit for Toby, biscuit for Jenna! But none for Tess because she said a bad word! OK?'

'*Yeah* ...'

She relieved her frustration by stamping into the kitchen, jarring her legs against the unyielding stone floors and the children stamped happily after, swinging arms and waggling behinds.

The adults returned late, replete, well-oiled, over-relaxed. The children had been in bed for hours. Grabbing her book, unwilling to be caught staring into space, Tess met Franca's smouldering gaze with a carefully casual smile. She was too slow to stop Angel making her a cup of coffee and had to sip and blow rapidly, wanting escape.

Ratty was quiet. Maybe he was the designated driver, the only one sober. 'Are you OK?' he asked her twice. He chose an armchair and, when Franca prowled across to sit on the arm, exchanged a peculiar look with her, hesitating before taking her hand. Maybe they'd had a row. Good.

'Shall I walk you home?' He jumped up when Tess zipped herself into her jacket.

'No!' Too loud. More softly, 'Thanks. I can manage.' She left them, silent, behind her.

In the morning she did something she thought she'd never do again. She rang Olly.

'Hi. I thought I'd just try your direct line, as you gave me the number.'

He sounded pleased to hear her voice. 'I was thinking about you, you must be telepathic.'

'Shouldn't think so.' She heard a few keystrokes from a keyboard, and the big-office hum in the background, wondered what it was like to work in the same building as several hundred others, how much space must be given over to canteens and restrooms, how many people Olly now knew to shout hullo to. 'What were you thinking about me?'

More keystrokes. As Olly was speaking on his company line when that company was paying him to do something more productive, she really ought not be irritated that he was obviously not giving her his entire attention. The keystrokes paused. 'I was wondering if you fancied coming down this weekend?'

'Back to London?' Olly lived in North London now, had to tube into work. She tried to picture him rocking down the Northern Line every morning, strap-hanging. 'I'm busy on Saturday.'

'Sunday?'

Something inside her recoiled. 'No, I can't really be bothered, just for the day.'

'Then stay longer.'

The old feeling washed over her, frustration and impotence that she had to remind him. 'I have to work!'

He drew in his breath. 'Yeah, sorry. The new me needs a lot of reminding, doesn't he?'

She laughed. Olly wasn't all bad. 'Maybe some other time,' she said.

'Or maybe I'll whiz up to see you,' he said, unconvincingly.

The next day, too doleful to achieve much real work in the hour or two before she was due at the village hall, she went on with the painting on her workroom wall.

Morning glory trumpets, proudly open on the earlier lengths of creeper, now became withered blooms like empty socks.

Above the window overlooking Pennybun she painted a heart, a faithful technical representation: left ventricle, right ventricle, left and right atrium, pulmonary trunk, vena cava. On the blue background the colours darkened, making the heart look dead and disused as she painted the creeper choking it. Strangled by winding stems and dead flowers.

Basic, callow. A portrait of her feelings.

She stood back and assessed her dark work. 'You're sad, you are, plastering the wall with your most mediocre stuff. Sad woman. Can't get to grips with what you want, not prepared to risk your emotions like anybody else.'

At least today would be busy and full. Decorating stalls, manning the door, dismantling stalls, rearranging them for the evening dance. Raffle drawn at nine, the final prize her picture. She must mount the stage to present it to the winner, make light-hearted remarks and smile for the photographer as she flourished a signature across the corner. Then she could go home.

A busy morning became a long one. Tess and Hubert took pairs of stepladders around the hall, festooning roses across the stall tops under the sponsors' signs. The Three Fishes. MAR Motors. A. & G. Crowther.

On automatic pilot, Tess tried to ignore Carola dashing about with fanatical eyes and a handful of lists, discourage Toby, Jenna and friends from climbing the steps behind her, act normally with Angel and wield a staple gun on the navy and white skirts at the front of the stalls.

It was stupid, childish, to feel excluded because her

friends had gone out with Franca. And naïve to have assumed that her friendship with Ratty would continue forever unchanged. Obviously their special friendship had suffered the instant he found somebody more special still. If she'd wanted more, she should've ...? Done something or other, anyway. Taken a chance. Taken him up on one of his casual smutty suggestions, returned his kiss, been first to clasp hands. Allowed herself to react to him instead of suppressing her libido until it surfaced only at night in vivid, spectacular, erotic dreams.

Tack, pin, fetch, carry, sweep, dust, until lunchtime finally arrived, and they broke until one thirty.

Through the kitchen door she shucked out of her jacket and picked up a letter from the mat. The handwriting was familiar. Showing a rare sensitivity in realising e-mail from him might not be welcome, Olly had sent a clipping from the *Evening Standard* about Kitty and some client who'd won an award. And on a fold of paper, written, 'Thought you might like this. Hope you're OK.' She was staring at it, acknowledging sinkingly that Olly was making an unlikely amount of effort, when Ratty tapped and strolled in.

Familiar in his soft fleece jacket, his jaw was shadowed because he only shaved when he felt like it. Under his arm was a bottle wrapped in a crisp white cloth. 'I wish you'd let me see you home the other night. I wanted to know you got here all right.'

'You were with Franca.'

'Franca wouldn't mind.' He looked out of the window, putting his bottle down on the sill. 'Am I disturbing you?' He nodded at the letter.

'Olly.' She threw the envelope at the bin. It missed.

He pulled a face. 'I hope he's behaving? How's it going at the village hall? Anyone quarrelled with Carola and stormed out yet? Were you going to offer me coffee?'

'Yes. OK. Nobody. Yes, OK.'

So they sat across the table, as they used to, talking about the Feast.

'You're doing your famous local artist bit, tonight?'

'Carola would throw herself under a bus if I backed out. She thinks her idea's wonderful.'

'It is.' He ate an apple, she watched the square whiteness of his teeth crunching through the rosy peel and into the flesh. Then he glanced at his watch and got up. Sod. 'Don't mind if I leave this in your fridge, do you, Princess?' He opened the fridge door, slid the wrapped bottle onto a shelf, winked at her and grinned his most brilliant, lascivious grin. 'Special plans tonight.'

Gone. So. Special plans. Too busy to nip home to unload a bottle of – she opened the fridge door and peeked – champagne. Moët. She wondered when he anticipated retrieving it. The old, easy ways were still there, but obviously his priorities had altered.

She sighed. Climbed the stairs to shower slowly, brush and plait her hair, slide into a blue dress because Carola thought jeans were for gardening. Time up. She had to go and take twenty pences and smile as if she was enjoying herself because everyone had put in so much that she couldn't let them down.

Tomorrow, maybe, she'd stay in bed all day. Or camp in front of the television with assorted chocolate bars. Or get forgetful-drunk. And she'd surf the Net and get a last-minute deal, because now would be a good time to take a couple of weeks out. Somewhere that was already hot, a blue sea, a blond beach, walks along cliffs. She could almost taste the sea on the breeze already. The freedom.

But, today, she had to get on with the Feast.

Tess took money as quickly as people could push through the door and the village hall filled and filled. The stalls looked cheery and pretty. Table-toppers did brisk business with old china and unloved CDs, outgrown toys and books, the corn-dolly lady put on a lovely display, Angel did makeovers. At the counter that would become a bar later, Hubert, Grace, Ida and Rose dispensed tea and coffee in proper cups. A team of teenagers constantly ferried in trays of clean cups and saucers, disappearing reloaded with dirty ones. In the corner by the tea stand Ratty perched on a stool and played acoustic guitar whilst Franca drank coffee close by.

A constant stream of people chattered past, shoving coins into the plastic box that was Tess's till, bringing in the smell of fresh air and making her wish she was out there, tramping about the lanes.

'Been roped in?'

Meeting the calm grey-green gaze of Elisabeth Arnott-Rattenbury, Tess tried to look as if she hadn't been looking at Ratty. 'You know how it is.'

'You're being kept busy.' All the Arnott-Rattenburys spoke the same nice, accentless English.

'It's slowing down now, but they're still coming.' She shook back her pigtail and delved in her box for change. Elisabeth moved aside to let a family pay.

Tess glanced at her. 'Ratty ... Miles is playing.'

'Yes, I see him.' Elisabeth smiled.

Tess watched her make her way to where Ratty was making music on a beautifully inlaid twelve-string guitar, throw coins into his guitar case. Ratty laughed and challenged her; she pantomimed exasperation and shook her purse upside down, to show that it was empty.

Tess took her eyes away to take more door money, and suddenly Elisabeth was back with a china cup of tea. 'You must be parched.'

Once she thought about it, she was. 'Well, thanks,' she muttered, easing a back pleated from standing so long, resting her behind on the table edge, wishing someone could turn the volume down on all the exclamations and laughter that seemed to fill the old stone hall up to its wooden rafters. 'That's lovely.'

Elisabeth lifted her own cup. 'Do you know whether Cassie and Christopher Carlysle have been, yet?'

'Been and gone I'm afraid.'

Elisabeth smiled. 'Good. I can relax. Are your parents coming today?'

Good God, she hoped not. 'Not that I know of.'

'No moral support required when you do the raffle prize, tonight?'

Tess took sixty pence from a woman with two kids. 'I can manage.' Relations weren't that warm, yet, though Tess had at least rung home.

Elisabeth looked around. 'I see my son is doing his own thing, as usual.'

'He plays well.' Tess thought of Ratty playing in the sunshine in the garden at Rotten Row or Honeybun. Singing in the rattling van pulling the stripped-down E-Type back from Devon.

Elisabeth sipped. 'He's not a bad sort.'

''Course not,' she agreed cautiously.

'Has his own ways. His own way of getting people to fall in with his plans. Circuitous ways. Rather than negotiate, he navigates himself into the position he wants.' She sighed. 'I wish he'd make things simpler for himself. But, that's Miles.'

Elisabeth ran a long-fingered hand over neat hair, watched her son play, curled around the guitar, left hand sliding over the frets. 'Look at his precious cars. His results in business studies were so good Lester and I felt it was the obvious way to go, accountancy or something, and Miles agreed, yes, it was only sensible. Applied to the right places and off he went.

'Instead of saying, "But it's not what I want, I want to do something else," he went along with us till he could change it. Then turned up one day saying he'd finished with the course. He'd been buying cars, doing them up and selling at a profit in the holidays and evenings. He'd accrued enough capital to strike out full-time, and rented a "place" – a shack really.

'I can see him now, standing there so pugnaciously. Showing us that he'd made it happen. Lester doesn't react very well to Miles in that mood. He was hurt at the way Miles had gone about things. Lester tends to withdraw when he's hurt, which Miles calls disapproval. Pity it couldn't have been different.' Elisabeth's cup was empty.

Tess took it absently, brow creased in thought. 'He's his own person, you have to take him or leave him.'

Elisabeth looked at her curiously. 'Take him or leave him,' she agreed. Then, 'Your picture is very good. Miles said your talent shone out.'

Her face went hot with pleasure. 'Flattery!'

'He never flatters. He feels things strongly, passionately, there's no one I'd rather have in my corner. But Miles does not flatter.'

Tess stared after her.

The day got longer and drearier. The hall was slow to empty, leaving little time to dismantle the stalls and relocate the decorations for the dance. Through the middle of their muddle the DJ and his mate trucked all their stuff, and calls of 'Where's this going?' were overlaid with 'One-two, one-two,' through speakers the size of fridges.

Chilly from standing in the draught from the door, Tess

dashed home for another shower, Carola calling after her, 'Dress up – make us look important!'

There was a message on the answering machine from Olly. 'Just ringing to see you're all right,' he said.

'I'm sodding busy,' she snipped, hurling her clothes at the laundry basket in her bedroom and watching them bounce off, supposing bad-temperedly that she'd have to wash her hair. The shower was hot, ran into her eyes, making them boil. Just like tears.

Life wasn't always kind. Although she felt strained from making an effort all day, now she had to go back and do it again, when all she wanted was to crawl in bed and just lie.

And there was the back door again, rap-rap, probably Ratty wanting his champagne back for his specially planned night. Damn, blast and bugger him. Bastard. Maybe she should phone Olly back. Get him lined up to go somewhere tomorrow, away from the village.

But it was Angel who peered back at Tess through the glass. 'I've come to do your hair!'

Tess opened the door. 'Do my ...? I don't need –'

'Carola wants her star to be just right!'

Angel chivvied her upstairs, bullied her into a short black skirt and a gold-shot lace top which made her hair blaze. 'Got to make the effort, it's for the village!'

With Angel that bright and bouncy, Tess gave in. It wasn't worth the energy she'd expend arguing, so she slumped on her stool and submitted her hair to being blow-dried.

'I'm putting it up,' she said ungraciously.

'Oh no, you don't want ...'

'*Up!*' Silly tears pricked. Must be overtired. Yes, all tomorrow in bed.

Silently, Angel swept Tess's hair up on the back of her

head, Tess felt the spike slide through the curved black barrette. Felt the cool spray of lacquer on her nape. 'No need to get upset,' Angel said, giving her a quick hug from behind.

The hall looked good and sounded better as Tess stepped back through the door. Gently rotating lights, crêpe, velvet bows around the bar where the optics twinkled and glasses were stacked, businesslike, tray on tray.

'Now, you look *marvellous*,' Carola encouraged. 'Your piccie's on its easel up on the stage, look! Nothing to do but circulate and enjoy yourself until raffle time. After that,' she gusted out a sigh and clasped her forehead, 'we can *all* relax and get sozzled.'

Tess felt suddenly small over the way she was dragging her feet. Carola worked like a horse to keep the hall up to its wonderful standard, full of energy and ideas, expecting no thanks, accepting others' excuses.

Right, she'd give Carola her all these last couple of hours, circulating, buying people drinks and generally doing what she could to make jolly. She'd do her piece at the raffle with huge smiles and twinkles, make a great impression.

Then she'd go home to bed.

As if reading her mind, Pete and Angel dragged her off to start the dancing, Jos cornered her to meet his dear, shy Miranda properly, and soon the hall was jumping and she was tripping over people, whisked from conversation with Tubb from the pub to chat to Lester Arnott-Rattenbury, attractive silver hair alight beneath the lights. Hubert introduced her to the vicar, Grace wanted her to meet her mother, Gwen Crowther asked her to sign a card for Carola. 'It's one of yours, duck!'

Almost everyone in the locality turned up. Christopher Carlysle asked her to dance, using the opportunity to badger, 'I wish you'd tell me what went on with Simeon.'

'I don't think I will,' she called, over the music. She didn't need reminding. There was Simeon, in fact, beer in one hand, some poor female in the other, his face red and movements loose, already. She looked away.

And if her gaze kept drifting to the door as the hall filled up, nobody would've noticed, what with dancing and chatting and having such a good time.

It was inevitable that Franca would shimmy in, gorgeous in a shiny pink skirt and top. Tess turned to the barman, not wanting to see Ratty follow.

She didn't get a second to eat any of the bits of pizza or sausages on sticks, never seemed to finish a drink before putting it down and losing it, but at least that way the first part of the evening was quick and painless. Fairly, anyway.

Chapter Twenty-Two

She was glad to leave the stage.

It was over.

They'd put on a very creditable performance, she and Carola, getting the clutching-ticket-stubs audience tiptoeing to see who'd won the whisky and who a cut-and-blow-dry. Carola, clutching the crêpe-covered box of patiently folded tickets, laughing replies to the catcalls of 'Shake 'em up!', called on Tess to present her picture of an industrious animal kingdom to a shiny-looking estate agent from Bankside.

Tess flourished a signature in the corner with her fountain pen, and posed for the papers. 'Congratulations!' she beamed brightly at the estate agent for the benefit of the scruffy, spotty local photographer.

Then it was three cheers for Carola and all her hard work, Carola holding onto Tess's hand whilst she thanked everybody for their support and hoped they'd all have a marvellous evening. 'And now, ladies and gents, this is our first "slowie". Gents, if you never get up to dance again this evening, *please* lead the lady in your life onto the floor for this one!'

Grin stuck on, eyes hurting from looking the wrong way into the lights, Tess finally freed herself and made for the wooden-treaded steps at the front of the stage.

It was over. Now she could melt away. Go home. Hibernate.

But, as she reached solid ground, a warm, square hand slid into hers and an arm scooped her in the direction of the dance floor. 'Dance with me, Princess?'

Accepting the hands on her waist, automatically resting hers on Ratty's broad shoulders, she looked up at him. He smiled. Pulled her close.

'This is supposed to be the dance for wives and girlfriends! Where's Franca?' she whispered.

His eyes were fixed on hers. 'Dancing, with Darrel.' He nodded to where Franca was wrapped around a dark man. 'Her husband.'

'Husband? I didn't know –'

'I know.' He kissed her temple, a gentle feather-light kiss that brought thoughts of the Ball sharply to mind. One of these days she'd ask him ...

The dance floor was so crowded that it was only possible to shuffle, cocooned by other warm bodies, and enjoy the heady mingling of perfumes. Her mind churned: Franca had a husband, and that husband was right here. And Ratty was engrossed in – and, she presumed from the indications, very physical with – Franca.

Oh, right. She sighed, examining a little spiral of disappointment inside herself. 'I'm your cover, so that Darrel doesn't suspect?'

He balanced his forehead on hers for a moment. 'Absolutely *not*.'

Hmm. Oh well, not her problem. For whatever reason here she was, here they were, and it felt good, for the first time in weeks her heart lifted. It felt so *nice* to be drawn against the heat of Ratty's hard-muscled body as they danced; she'd almost forgotten how it felt to feel a man's heart pulsing against her through his shirt, to breathe his aftershave, move in his rhythm.

The dance ended too soon. The music changed to happy-boppy party stuff and Ratty, voice very deep, breath very hot on the side of her head, said, 'Can we talk?'

She allowed herself to be towed through the dancers and

across the foyer into the tiny office where there was a window seat, an armchair, three shelves, an old school desk with a typist's chair, a mop and a bucket. He closed the door behind them and leant against it.

Legs aching, she looked around for somewhere to sit. But the armchair looked dusty and the window seat full of splinters and she'd feel just too ridiculous perched on a typist's chair. 'Funny place for a chat.'

He smiled his long, lazy, quirky smile. 'You could run away from my place or throw me out of Honeybun. Here, you'll have to listen.' He paused. 'The prospect of this conversation's been buzzing round in my head all day.'

His voice was gentle. Her hands were somehow trapped in his, his thumbs slightly rough in her palms. At the open collar of his black polo shirt one crisp, black curl moved as he spoke. She fixed her eyes to it, and the way his throat rose. Slid her gaze upwards to his lips as they moved; and she *was* listening, she was, but her untidy thoughts were skittering up their own route. Franca was married and not, evidently, separated. Not, therefore, such a cut-and-dried issue as she'd assumed their affair to be. Franca had no prior claim.

All's fair in love and war.

His lips paused. She remembered his kisses. And felt herself swaying forward, body extending, heels lifting. Until their lips touched.

His arms sprang around her like a trap, bringing her powerfully against him, his tongue found hers and she was jolted by a charge worthy of the national grid. His kiss was thorough. Lengthy. And the second was better even than the first.

Finally, he drew back. '*That* makes things easier.'

If it was wrong to lean against his body and feel his heart trotting as fast as hers, funny it felt so right. Even while her brain was trying to raise problems about being hurt and being second best, her heart and her body were drifting along on a puffy cloud of dawning exultation and anticipation.

His gaze was fixed on her with – yes, she was sure it was with tenderness. 'I'd better tell you the story,' he murmured, 'but I don't know where to begin.'

'Cut to the chase,' she suggested. The soft kisses he kept dropping on her face were delicious, made her half close her eyes, feel carefree and loopy. Maybe they *would* have a thing. Go to bed. It would be fun.

'OK, bottom line – Princess, I love you.'

It took a few moments, to open her eyes again and focus. Her mind supplied her with a riot of responses, but her vocal chords failed her. She swallowed, tried again and whispered, 'Love me?' Not just a thing?

'Really.' He pulled her harder against him.

But she felt a flash of sudden anger. Why did he have to spoil things, just when she was building up a delicious hot, horny anticipation by saying something so insulting to her intelligence? She pulled sharply away. 'And what about Franca?'

He sighed, clasping his hands behind the small of her back so that she'd really have to fight to remove herself. 'Franca was ... a way of making things clear for you.' His grip tightened as she began to try and force his hands apart. 'Tess, you're going to listen to this! Listen!

'Franca and I were together a couple of years ago. She was working here for six months, when her time was up she wanted something permanent, I didn't; she went home.

'Then she met Darrel, who's much better for her. They married recently.

'When she wrote that she was coming back for a couple of months – well, I could see how she would be useful.

Listen! Darrel took a bit of persuading, though, Frenchmen are terribly mean about lending their wives.'

'Unsporting!'

He laughed, looked at her face, and stopped. 'Anyway. She agreed to ...' She could see him struggling for the right phrases. '... Give the impression ... pretend ...'

'... that you were passionately in love and couldn't keep your hands off each other?'

'I suppose. Yes. That was the plan.'

She stopped listening. She'd been moved and manoeuvred, manipulated, and it made her bloody furious! A plot! 'Who knew about this precious plan?'

He sighed. 'Angel and Pete, who've been calling me every kind of bastard and telling me I was all wrong. Franca and Darrel, of course.'

She felt her fingers curl into claws. They'd all been watching, assessing her misery, knowing they could end it! 'That's outrageous,' she hissed through wooden lips. 'That is just about the most outrageous thing I've ever heard in my life!' She again tried to break away, her eyes beginning to burn. 'It was all a plan, no, a *conspiracy* against me! Let me *go*!'

Contrarily, he jerked her inflexibly against him, his breathing fast and hard, his eyes angry sparks. 'No, listen! Just listen! What am I supposed to do? You sent me crazy with your safe, no-risks, no-pain philosophy! Your sterile "Don't touch me, we're only friends!" OK, you've been hurt, but it was Olly Gray who hurt you, not the rest of the world. Not me! I'm not Olly Gray! And I've known, I've *known* I love you, I'm pretty damned sure that you feel something for me! Would you admit it? Would you react when I made a move? When I kissed you?' He kissed her mouth, hard. 'How was I supposed to make you admit what there is between us and confront your feelings?' He began to punctuate his words with hot rough kisses, temple, cheeks, neck. 'Tell me how it made you feel, me with Franca. Anything like it felt when I saw you driving off with Olly? Like free-falling without a parachute?

'Admit it hurt! Tell me you missed me! Be honest with yourself, be brave, *break* out of your safe world. *Feel* again. Tell me. Admit the truth, Tess, and don't you dare tell me you only want to be my fucking friend!'

He stopped, his blazing gaze searching her face. She knew he was waiting for her. But she was afraid.

She'd loved before and it had hurt, it had hurt! It had led to hopelessness and helplessness and humiliation, illness, the loss of a baby. She allowed herself to think of her lost baby, feel the grief; grief from love.

Was she ever going to be ready to expose herself, ever, ever again?

But, with Ratty's eyes boring into her, seeing past her fears, she thought about being without him again. Ow. About the disdain she'd see in his eyes if she denied what she felt. For what, anyway?

Safety's sake.

Safety's sake? The deadness and woeful isolation she'd experienced watching him with Franca?

She swallowed, whispered, 'And afterwards? When it's over?'

His whisper was a caress. 'Why should there be an afterwards? Why shouldn't it last?'

Would it? Was that relevant? She'd shrunk from the deeper relationship to protect the friendship – but, as he'd quite brutally demonstrated, if he got close to someone else, the friendship would change anyway.

Maybe she owed it to him to admit she loved him back. The feeling welled, strong, imperative.

She let it.

219

Her eyes shut, fists clenched, she whispered, 'OK.'

Fingers bit into her arms. 'OK, what? *Tell* me, you chicken!' His voice was dangerous-amused, strangled, exasperated, in her face.

Right, she would. One-two-three-*go*! She opened her eyes, took a big breath, met his gaze, half shouted, 'Yes, I love you!'

'I believe,' he murmured, when he came up for air. 'I believe there's a bottle of Moët chilling at your place?'

'You devious bastard,' she marvelled. 'You and your circuitous routes.'

'Where's your coat?'

Hand in hand they flitted across the foyer, the dancing still in full swing through the door to the hall.

Outside, into a breezy spring evening. Ratty admitted he'd almost pulled out of his machinations at the eleventh hour, when he'd kissed her on the bridge and chased her through the coppice, when he'd caught her and thought her defences finally down. Before discovering their audience. 'Then,' he complained, bringing up her hand, which he was holding very hard, to kiss it, 'Simeon suggested we were an item and you snapped his head off, as if the idea was poison. I had to reduce your options.'

'It's Simeon who's poison.'

At Honeybun Cottage, after retrieving the champagne, Ratty fished two napkin-wrapped crystal flutes from the side pockets of his jacket. Uncorking the champagne like a waiter, he cradled the bottle's mouth with the linen cloth, turning the bottle not the cork, *tutt-shushhh*, not wasting a single bubble. Handing one pale sparkling glassful to her, he touched it with his. 'Us.'

She sipped. 'To us.' She let her tongue lick the delicious

crisp dryness from her lips, groaning happily as he sent his tongue tip chasing hers. Champagne-chilled kisses dotting her jaw, she shuddered as he nuzzled the electric spot immediately below her ear lobe.

He suggested softly, 'Upstairs?'

She nodded.

Up the dogleg stairs, hands clasped, clutching glasses, Ratty holding the bottle neck between strong fingers. Watching him set down the bottle and his glass, light one lamp to a soft pink gleam, turn to her, a tall outline.

And reach for her.

She twitched away, breath racing. 'God, look at my clothes thrown everywhere! You'd think I'd be able to use a laundry basket at my age, wouldn't you? Just let me tidy up.' She knew she was babbling. But the washing! And how fresh were her sheets?

He caught her, swung her against him. 'Don't worry, Princess. Everything will be fine.'

For goodness' sake, she was trembling. She could actually feel herself vibrating like an idling car. His head was just above hers, face tilted towards her, his hands running up and down the backs of her arms. Her voice cracked as she gazed into his face. 'It's been so long.'

'I know. Just let me love you. Tess.' Face touching hers, lips skimming her forehead, down to her mouth. 'It'll be fine. It'll be marvellous. We're going to be wonderful, together.' He held her to his kisses and his caressing hands until she felt secure again, able to melt against him, let him slide off her outer clothes. It was going to be OK.

He reached behind her head and unspiked the clasp in her hair. Because Angel had put it up without the thirty-four grips Tess would have rammed in, her mane swung down with a rush, slithering about her back and her arms and her breasts.

His breath hissed between his teeth. 'You're beautiful!'

He stroked her back, her neck, stroked, stroked, until she was aware of nothing but his hands. On her collarbones, shoulder blades, down her ribs at the back and up again at the front. Nuzzling the crook of her neck, making her gasp and rock, the balls of his thumbs a gossamer touch on the sides of her breasts. Breathless with his kisses and hot with anticipation she reached for his shirt buttons. Soon his naked chest was against her and his movements became urgent, hot hands on her breasts, fumbling for a second with a clasp, flinging her underwear across the room.

Hand winding in the thickness of hair at her nape, holding her for his demanding kiss. His sigh rasping, 'You're a gorgeous, sexy woman!' Neither of them laughed.

Scooping her up, swinging her onto the bed, Ratty rolled down beside her.

He was right, it was going to be marvellous.

She might even faint from it. From the scalding of his mouth on her breasts, from the roughness of his hands, from the excitement of his flesh on her flesh.

When she reached for him she held her breath – this was where Olly would have refused to let her participate, and her pleasure would be compromised as he twitched away, insisted upon complete control, withdrew until she acquiesced.

But she laid her hand on Ratty and he bucked like a pony, groaned, sinking back onto the pillows.

'Is that good?' she breathed.

'Jeez! It's ... incredible! Don't stop.' His eyes rolled back and he moved with her touch, gasping and clutching as she explored, desire rocketing inside her because she could make him feel like that. And when he reached for her again it took him only seconds to coax her, quivering, to the end of the roller coaster ride.

When the darkness showed the first hint of dawn, he woke her, pulling her nakedness against his body. This time he made love to her with silent urgency. Because at last she was there! He could claim her; pull her body, warm and yielding against his. And love her. He'd made it happen. He deserved to cradle her in his triumph and revel in her response.

Chapter Twenty-Three

Awake. Soaring, glorious, rushing joy.

Tess was in love. The grainy hand that cupped her breast belonged to him; the chest against her back was his, the legs following the crook of hers, the heavy arm across her ribs. The tattoos, the 'One Miles' milestone and a car she seemed to remember was a Porsche Speedster.

How incredible she should be in bed with a man with tattoos, Ratty, an unlikely product of a comfortably-off family of lawyers and Army officers. In love with him and his cars and his tattoos and the whole thing.

Rain at the window; she didn't care! Nor that the floor was strewn with clothes, some of which was yesterday's laundry. If the sheets hadn't needed changing before, they did now. She was free to spend the day doing nothing or making love or walking through the woods in the soft, gorgeous, sexy rain. Or making love.

'What're you smirking about?' Gravelly voice, just behind her ear. She wriggled round to face him, his hair tumbled to quills on his forehead like an Angora goat. Kissed the stubble on his cheek. Pressed the flat of a hand to the fan of black hair on his chest.

'I'm happy.'

The smile began in his blue eyes. 'Told you it'd be wonderful.'

'Smug bastard.'

'Happy bastard.' Kiss. 'Lucky bastard.' Two kisses. Under the quilt, his hand trickled across her stomach. 'Horny bastard.'

She laid her hands over his. 'But I want a shower. I want

to be clean and smell good, have breakfast.' She looked at the clock. 'I mean, lunch.' She rubbed her cheek on his bristling one. 'Before we do it all again.'

He followed her nakedness into the bathroom.

Facing away from the hissing hot water, she closed her eyes as he stroked shower gel across her shoulders. 'Yesterday, your mother gave me the benefit of insight into your character, how you navigate yourself into the position you want, rather than negotiate.'

His hot, soapy hands worked deliciously down her spine. 'Yeah? I don't do her credit.'

Combing out the heavy length of her wet hair, she paused. Men's voices. Her driveway? She wandered to the top of the stairs. But it was Ratty alone at the kitchen table waiting for the kettle to boil, with only the *Sunday Times* to defend his nakedness, when James Riddell tapped and entered.

James was mid-sentence. 'These things need to be talked out properly, fences need to be mended ... Who the bloody hell are you?'

Tess slapped a horrified hand to her mouth. Her father – and Ratty naked!

Peeping down the stairwell into the kitchen she watched Ratty freeze, unfreeze. Stand, *Sunday Times* judiciously placed, offer his right hand and, manufacturing a precarious dignity, produce the handle he seldom bothered with. 'Good morning. Miles Arnott-Rattenbury.'

James ignored the hand, mouth a furious slit beneath narrow nose. 'Where's my daughter?'

'Here.' She traipsed down the staircase. James's expression was a study in outrage. Olly Gray stood slightly behind him, staring at Tess's bare feet, wet hair, towelling robe. And Ratty. Oh crap, she could've done without Olly.

She looked from Olly's dismay to James's disgust. Ah

well, she was entitled to keep a naked man in her kitchen if she wanted to! Laughter began to simmer somewhere around her breastbone.

And the naked man looked so ... tense. Her mouth curled at the corners. 'The sitting room, I think. Let's leave Ratty to dress.' She motioned her guests to pass into the next room on the *Sunday Times* side of Ratty, listening as he leapt the stairs and thudded into the bedroom. 'Coffee? Tea?'

Leaving her father and ex-fiancé waiting on the blue moquette, she boiled the kettle and set out white china mugs. Ratty, swiftly dressed, jumped down warily into the kitchen; she grinned and kissed him.

'I'm only putting up with this for your sake,' he hissed.

She smothered a spurt of laughter and gave him the tray with four china mugs and a cafetière. 'My hero!' Then she raised her voice. 'Fancy some toast, Dad?'

'No, I bloody don't!' James's annoyance was obvious in the straight lines of his face, the colourless pinches around his lips. Hating it, hating catching his daughter very obviously with her lover, a lover *he* hadn't OK'd. Just when, she supposed, he'd thought she'd dipped her toe back into Olly's waters. Presumably Olly had told him that he and Tess were getting along now, and James had decided to see what he could do to promote Olly's cause. When had James turned into the kind of father who saw his child as a vehicle for his own preferences? 'Eggs and bacon then?' she suggested evenly.

From the sudden light in Ratty's eyes and the lift at the corner of his lips, she saw that his sense of the ridiculous was beginning to kick in.

But poor Olly looked winded, body tight with it, face slack. She sighed. 'Sorry, Olly. I don't expect you'll be staying very long.' Settling down beside Ratty on the sofa, she sent her ex-fiancé an apologetic look. She really would've preferred Olly not to have been hurt. Wouldn't she? Yes, she would. Although he had hurt her quite badly ...

Olly's features rearranged themselves as he visibly pulled himself together. 'How long has this been going on?'

'Long enough.'

When he looked down his hair slid forward. She studied him, the clean-shaven beauty she'd thought so bright, insipid now beside Ratty's dark, stubbly strength and glittering eyes. He lifted his suddenly angry gaze to Ratty. 'You?' he demanded bitterly. 'What d'you want with her, Caveman? You don't know her.'

'I know enough.'

'You've hardly known her five minutes! You know enough? You don't know her like I do! Bet you don't even know ...' He cast around for an example, conjured up, feebly, 'You don't even know what "Tess" is short for!'

Ratty shook his head, sipping his coffee and stroking Tess's bare feet with his own. 'That's true,' he agreed amicably. 'Teresa?'

'Therese!' Olly said triumphantly.

'Really? Very glamorous. Very suitable for a lovely, talented lady.' Dangerous, rigid, bland courtesy. 'Don't you think it's time you went?'

Olly switched his gaze to Tess. 'Really? Him?'

She shrugged. 'Sorry.' The mug rattled on the tray, the kitchen door slammed behind Olly Gray.

Tess met her father's eye. Grinned. Oh dear, in its way this was fun. Fun! It was lovely to have Ratty so obviously in her corner. 'You haven't, by any chance, lent Olly money?'

James broke the eye contact, leant forward to replace his empty mug on the tray. 'It's quite a small matter.'

She crowed with delighted laughter and slapped the arm

of the sofa. 'I thought somebody must have, he had more to chuck around than he ought to considering the job he's got. You've seen the last of that, then. Olly's financial control has slipped a bit – ask Guy!'

For several seconds James glared ferociously. Then the lines of his face softened, he looked down, examined his tie. Almost smiled, reminding Tess how he could be. 'I had thought you might feed me,' he suggested, changing the subject.

Ratty slid in. 'Perhaps you'll join us for a meal at the pub?'

James turned on him a glare that should've melted steel. 'Thank you. Are we dressing for lunch?'

It might have been thoroughly uncomfortable, the tension. Tess might have felt anxious, torn, burbling herself stupid to cobble together a conversation.

But not today. Not with Ratty's knee pressed against hers; closely shaved, sharply dressed, sleeves-down Ratty across the brass-topped table. Not now she was in love, not in *her* local where people tossed her congratulations about the Feast – was it only yesterday? Hadn't it gone well? Which evening was the photo due in the paper, wasn't Carola brilliant? Warm and safe, she belonged. James, in a buttoned-up shirt and a V-necked sweater, looked beige and out of place.

And where she might have felt worried by her father's pensive silences, tried to coax conversation from him, now she shrugged, held Ratty's hand across the table and listened to him talking to Bren from Port Road as to whether it was possible to drop the gearbox out of a Vauxhall Cresta without a pit. Thought about how good he'd been in bed with those hands which looked as if they ought to feel like sandpaper, but didn't. Watched his lips. Felt her legs go funny.

James wouldn't be ignored for long, of course, sipping Perrier and awaiting his roast chicken. And, as she anticipated, sure enough he launched suddenly into a snap of questions, palpably designed to discomfort Ratty. 'I understand you're self-employed in the car trade? Where? Your own premises? Rented or owned? *Wholly* owned? Really?' James, of course, was pretty much into property himself.

Ratty stepped into James's pause for breath. 'Plus my place, Pennybun and three houses rented out.'

James lifted yet-to-be-convinced eyebrows. 'Tick and a gold star,' he mocked, leaning back to allow Janice from behind the bar to set a chicken dinner before him, cutlery in a red gingham paper napkin. 'Forgive my enquiries,' blandly. 'But you seem close to my daughter.'

Ratty grinned. 'I forgive you entirely. And, just to ease your enquiries on their way: yes, I love your daughter – enough, even, to suffer this interrogation.'

James gave a puff of outrage.

'You might also like to know that I'm brave enough to communicate with her directly – not by *e-mail*. I won't belittle her and particularly I won't be *slapping* her face. I consider her entirely loveable, gorgeous, talented and able. Just to cover all your *enquiries*.'

James's sharp laugh splintered the following silence. 'You cocky young bastard!'

'And I love her enough to have a *go* at getting along with you. Shall we have a Chablis with this?'

'I'm driving. Well, perhaps just a glass.'

A spectator at this joust between irritation and staunch self-belief, Tess chewed slowly. This was good, she was enjoying it.

She turned the conversation. 'So, how's your development of the old tied cottages in Middleton going?'

James ever enjoyed an opportunity to talk about his own affairs. 'Good. Only one left unsold, plenty of interest, won't be long.'

She folded her napkin. 'How's Mum?'

'Worrying about you.' James leant in to exclude Ratty. 'I *hope* you're not going to be sorry over Oliver.'

She slapped the napkin down in exasperation. 'I've finished being *sorry* over Olly! When he dumped me I was *sorry*, when I miscarried I was *sorry*. Though, with the way things have gone today perhaps I ought to be singing "Who's Sorry Now?"' She tried not to smile at Ratty's sudden snort of laughter. 'Stop poking your beak in, Dad. There's no future for me and Olly.'

'You can't blame me for trying to hint if I think you might be making a mistake, Therese ...'

She met her father's gaze. 'Happily, in common with everything I say, and everything I do, I don't need your permission to make my choices. If you want to ally yourself with Olly, that's your privilege. It might be nice if you'd respect my choices, though.' Colour high, she picked up her cutlery from the middle of an astounded silence.

Ratty covered her hand. 'More wine, Princess?'

'Thank you.'

'Mr Riddell?'

'No!'

Ratty tilted Tess's chin, meeting her furious eyes. 'I love you when you're angry.'

She couldn't help but smile. It took charge of her mouth and her eyes and floated her heart.

The chicken was crisp then succulent, the roast potatoes golden (peppered liberally to make the punters drink more) but Tess couldn't wait for the meal to be over, for James to get back into his Volvo and go. *Go!* So she could wrap her arms around Ratty and feed on his strength, his maleness and the heat he radiated, which made her want him. After all, she'd only just gained the privilege.

But now James was frowning. He cleared his throat. 'What's this about slapping?'

She glugged the last of the wine and waved the bottle at Janice to be replaced. Oh no, she wasn't getting into the slapping thing at this late stage. 'The cherry pie is good, if you're thinking of dessert.'

'Slapping?'

'Or perhaps fresh coffee? Revive you for the drive home.' Please go.

'*Slapping*, Therese?'

She groaned, smoothing back her hair and screwing up her eyes. Sight easier to be calm if James would stop winding her up. 'Yes.'

James placed his cutlery very precisely together. 'I don't believe it.'

Her eyes opened to slits. 'Now, why doesn't that surprise me? Why ask when you'd already decided what to believe?'

'Don't you be like that with me!'

She made her voice ultra-low and soft, disguising the fury that was bubbling in her chest. 'I'll be anything.' She sat forward, seeing him sit back. 'I'll be anything I please. Yes, Olly used to slap me to win an argument, he's bigger, see, could hold me with this hand and hit me with that. Like this. Look, hold with the left, slap with the right. Quite hard. Enough to make me cry. Then he could make it up to me, once I was back in line. That's your Olly! Of course, he said he's sorry, now.'

Only Ratty finished his meal, watching Tess, freeing a hand to cover hers. Solid, silent, ready for anything.

The thought made her smile and his smile flashed back. *I'm with you, Princess*, said the lopsided twist of his lips, *you're doing fine*, was the gleam in his sea-like eyes. She relaxed. What did James matter? What did Olly matter? Or Guy, who'd remained traitorously close to Olly when Olly had been behaving badly? None of them mattered.

She had Ratty.

This man, dark and sexy, strong and decisive, was on her side. It was in his reach across the table, in his eyes, in his expression and in the hand that gripped hers. James couldn't spoil it.

Ratty held out his glass as she refilled her own. 'You'll be drunk.'

'Would that worry you?'

'No, I can carry you.'

He probably would, too. With his grins and leers, his mechanic's hands, even his obstinacies and sarcasms, he was a hundred times Olly. 'You're very real,' she told him suddenly.

'If he slapped you, why on earth didn't you tell me?'

Impatient at the interruption, she snapped back round to James. But saw something in his eyes, unhappiness, a flicker of guilt, to make her pause, make her voice reasonable, rueful. 'You'd have said something like, "He must have had his reasons".'

James was silent. He stared into the fireplace. Until he was ready for a sudden, cold, vicious about-turn. 'I think I'm going to have to see him.'

'Chop his head off,' agreed Ratty, encouragingly.

'For God's sake!' She freed her hands from Ratty, who was turning each of her rings around to inspect the patterns, and gripped her father's arm instead, speaking slowly, calmly, emphatically. 'I don't want you to. *Don't* act on my behalf, unasked and unwanted. Stay out of it, OK?' She softened her expression and her voice. 'If it makes you feel any better, Ratty's already evened up the score a bit. Right? Stay out.'

'I am your father.'

Her fingers tightened on his arm. 'Too late! When I needed that, you were ambivalent. When I craved sympathy, you divided yours with Olly. But I've found my own way. Just ... just remember I'm an adult. Respect me. Maybe we'll get along. I'd like that.'

He wasn't surprised when, as soon as Jos went out on the breakdown, Pete appeared at his side. 'Unexpected day off, yesterday.'

Spanner in his hand, Ratty tightened a series of bolts, beginning the round again, methodical, measured. 'You know how it is. One of those days when I just couldn't seem to get out of bed.'

Pete laughed, clapped him on the shoulder. 'So it all worked out?'

He heaved an exaggerated sigh. 'I'm *shaking*, it worked out so well.' He returned to each bolt for a final time, that last crucial check.

'I had to physically restrain Angel from ringing, she was gagging to know what happened!'

Straightening, Ratty finally let Pete meet his eyes. 'I'm glad she didn't.'

'So ... no complaints?'

'None.' Ratty let the pause develop. He knew his grin was smug.

'Everything you wanted?'

'Sure.'

'Rats! C'mon, share! Was it worth the wait?'

He threw his head back and laughed. 'Christ, it was! She's wonderful, she's fantastic, we're fantastic together. I just can't get enough of her. *Yessss*, it was worth the wait!'

Pete went back to the distributor on the bench, chuckling. 'I've never seen you like this before.'

'Never been like it before. The real thing's just ... amazing!'

Amazing that he should admit it, too, he who'd played the field at Olympic level, careful never to get too tied up, cynical about his best bets, ruthless when he got tired.

And now it was him surfing this tidal wave of passion after such a frustrating wait. Nobody, not even Pete, knew quite how bad it'd been, waiting for Tess to realise she loved him. How he'd struggled to give her space, how it went against his character to admit to himself that he, *he*, having finally bestowed his love, must machinate like mad for reciprocation.

How he'd held it together he didn't know, when she'd persistently slid her eyes away and pretended not to feel the spark. The torture of the near-miss after the Spring Ball; how he hadn't gone out and laid everything in sight, he, who thought sex had been invented especially for him. And whenever she laughed off the idea of romance, how he'd prevented himself from flaring up and shaking sense into her.

But he'd done it. Coolly played himself into being a winner and now his prize was this wonderful, magnificent love, this desirous lover. This gorgeous, sexy woman, the hang-on-tight, never-known-anything-like-it sex.

It had been worth it, yes, it had. But nobody realised how desperate he'd been; how frantically he'd had to hope.

The phone was greasy from a thousand oily hands when he lifted it from the bench where Pete had left it. Astounding that James Riddell should phone the garage. What the hell? 'Yep?'

'Is Tess all right?'

'Fine.' He listened to James's hollow breathing.

'As her father, I feel I ought to ... Her mother and I love her very much.'

He raised his eyebrows, searched for a response. 'I'm sure.'

A scratching, fidgeting noise, as if James was scribbling whilst he chose his words. 'I feel I've let her down.'

Ratty let the pause stretch itself, because what could he say to contradict that?

'Are you still there?'

'Yep.'

'I want ... I'm ringing ...'

Ratty looked at the clock on the garage wall whilst he waited for James to order his words. What would Tess be doing at 2.33 p.m. on the first Tuesday they'd been together? Working? He pictured her bending close to her paper, wielding a delicate brush or making feathery strokes with a pencil. Would her mind be on him? Perhaps on their lovemaking, new and fresh and consuming. And exhausting. Or walking? Maybe with Angel, Jenna and Toby, maybe through the village, maybe they'd call in.

Or she could be out in her beloved Freelander. He wasn't, to be honest, wild about driving with her. It unnerved him when she was distracted by the magic colours of a deep lilac bush lit by horizontal sun against a leaden sky; he could see exactly how she'd arrived in his life by smashing into his truck.

Maybe he'd phone her in a few minutes. Just for the chance of hearing her voice. Whisper, 'Hullo Princess, I love you.'

He switched his attention back to James, who was blowing out a long sigh. 'If you and Tess are, um, together now, I want you to ...' He listened unhelpfully to another hesitation. 'We want her to be happy.'

'So do I.'

'We don't want her to have more trouble.'

'Neither do I.'

Another pause. 'D'you think things will work out between you?'

'Yes.'

James laughed uneasily. 'That's uncompromising!'

'I am.'

'Young man, you're making this very difficult!'

Through the door he noticed the trees were budding again and the birds were busy. He returned to the conversation. 'I don't know what you want me to say. I don't suppose you want me to comment on your behaviour? I certainly don't want you to comment on mine. I accept you love Tess, if you want reassurance, I love Tess, and I'll be good to her.'

'That's something, I suppose.'

'We're going to be good together. Don't concern yourself.'

Chapter Twenty-Four

She still did it, made to turn in at Honeybun Cottage. Had actually pulled up in the wrong drive on occasions, then remembered that she'd moved to Pennybun and giggled aloud before reversing into the lane to drive fifty yards to the next gate. Next door. They lived next door, in freshly plastered rooms, colours they'd chosen together, a mixture of her furniture and Ratty's.

Honeybun could be rented out, earn its keep like Ratty's properties, when she got round to it, when she adjusted herself to letting it go and finally moved the last of her things from Honeybun to Pennybun. When she was used to living at Pennybun, had finished grumbling, 'It does my head in! Everything's back to front here.'

'You'll cope.' He'd grin, catch her, snatch her close, making her yelp at his suddenness. Kiss her, hands pushing past elastic, flicking open buttons. 'It can't be that difficult to sort out a mere five rooms.'

'But,' she tipped her head back as his hand pulled gently at the length of her hair, shivering when the scratchiness of his stubble nuzzled the delicate skin of her neck, 'they're five *back-to-front* rooms.'

'Tess Through the Looking Glass.'

'That's exactly how it feels.'

It did feel odd in Pennybun, turning left to the stairs from the kitchen instead of right, or arriving in the bathroom instead of her peaceful blue-painted workroom. It didn't yet feel like home.

Through the kitchen door that opened the other way, then she put the kettle on the range – where the stairs should be – shouting, 'Ratty?' Just in case he might already be home. The tiny wood-framed sofa in the corner beckoned. She dropped into its familiar comfort, clutching hot chocolate. There wasn't room for a sofa in the kitchen really but Ratty insisted a chair wasn't enough. Where she might sit he wanted room to squash in.

McLaren laughed down at her from one wall, young Lucasta smouldered from another.

They lived together. Ratty and Tess. Just the two of them at Pennybun.

A beatific existence of exploring each other, shut off from the rest of the world whenever they wanted. Or out together, supplying the wine for Angel's terrific meals, babysitting, borrowing the children occasionally. No ties to stop them attending a hill climb, camping out at the Cambridge Folk Festival, mixing with the petrolheads at the grand prix, walking hand in hand up the road to The Three Fishes. They even visited each set of parents, occasionally, and, once, risked both sets together at a meal in a restaurant by the river.

But best was being here, the two of them, at Pennybun.

She felt as if she'd recovered after flu. Ratty had cured her, woken every nerve end, wooed her into delicious, watery-legged libidinous intimacy. Whenever he reached for her she was ready and whenever she reached for him ... Joy to be a partner instead of a puppet.

She checked her watch, he wouldn't be long. Shedding his overalls at the door, trying to hug her without contact with his half-cleaned hands, talking about this Ford Anglia Super and that Wolseley, drawing her up the stairs with his conversation, to be there whilst he showered. Towelling black curls, one step, two step, all damp and hot from the shower, scooping her up for a proper, minutes-long embrace. 'Kiss me,' he'd whisper into her neck. Tell her how he'd been thinking about her, melt her with his hot breath, gentle hands, urgent lips.

How often they made love, then, when he'd been those eight or nine hours away from her. How often he smooched her over to the bed in their green-and-gold bedroom, swung her feet up and dropped down beside her into the depths of the duvet. 'I love you, sexy woman.'

Home soon.

If she sat there dreaming much longer, wondering what was going to happen, unfold, change, he'd be home.

Disappointingly, he phoned instead. 'I've got to take the wrecker to Oundle. Tubb's in trouble with his Daimler Sovereign.'

'It's a nice run to Oundle,' she remarked hopefully.

'Squashed in with Harry Tubb?'

Sweaty. Funny smile. No, maybe not. She liked stone-built Oundle, if not for Harry Tubb they could have snatched a bar meal somewhere, been alone in the darkness of the cab of the wrecker to drive home. She could have told him.

And by the time he did stroll in, hanging up his keys, Guy had turned up, and Ratty just kissed her and said easily, 'Dinner guest?' Which meant Guy felt invited to stay, desultorily washing salad whilst Tess made spaghetti carbonara.

Then Guy lingered, talked on and on about that holiday in Munich when he and Tess had walked the tall streets among the statues and monuments, supported the German way of setting out benches and tables at every gathering and calling it a Fest. Did she remember applauding the gold-painted mime beneath the Glockenspiel? Standing on the very steps where Hitler gave the Munich Address, attempting a polka in a bierkeller, swaying to drinking songs they didn't understand? And remember that man who'd refused to say 'Prost!' with Tess because, to counterbalance prodigious amounts of alcohol, she had water in her *Maßkrug*!

They'd lost their way and taken directions from a German Scotsman in a swirling kilt. James had exploded down the phone because Tess rang home drunk at 4 a.m.

Guy had had to borrow money. 'I don't know what happened to mine.'

'You spent it!'

Guy nodded as if the idea hadn't previously occurred. 'Probably.'

Then Guy got round to asking Ratty whether he'd be interested in a TR7 going up for sale. Tess loaded the dishwasher whilst they concluded that Ratty wasn't interested unless it was black and gold, a good seller. But he wouldn't want to pay a lot.

She tuned it out. Ratty got on with everyone, when he chose. He'd offer unstinting hospitality because Guy was her cousin. As long as Guy behaved, he was welcome. If he displayed any of his occasional tendencies to use her, Ratty would turn on him like an unpredictable Alsatian.

It was wonderful to have someone sticking up for her and she never ceased to appreciate it. And it was nice to see Guy. But she wished he'd go.

'I thought he'd never leave!'

'Certainly made himself at home. Did he ask for money?'

'Not this time. He wanted you to buy that car.'

'P'raps he'll get a drink out of it if he sells it. Are you ever coming to bed tonight?'

'In a minute.' She shook her hair from its clasp.

'Here, Princess.' He held out his hand for the hairbrush. He never tired of sitting behind her, brushing until her hair lay like rose gold down to her waist. Then pulling her down beside him, letting the hair slither through his fingers, pulling her against him.

Now was the time to tell him.

Or maybe not right now. *That* was too good to postpone.

Whilst their breathing slowed, she snuggled in the crook of his arm, her hand on his chest. It was time.

A jump in her chest. She must tell him but her mouth seemed suddenly reluctant to open and let the words out.

Possibilities turned over in her mind, his likely reactions chased after. If only she could know his reaction *first*, it would make selecting her approach so much easier.

'What's up?'

She jumped, wrong-footed. He caressed her cheekbone as he waited. Seeing through her.

So, time to tell. Feverishly, she re-revised her openings. Women had to tell men this all the time, there had to be ways to make it important, welcome news.

But, if it wasn't? What if it was a catastrophe?

Blue eyes were turning wary, black eyebrows straight-lining above them. He was wondering. 'Tell me,' he suggested, mild, but with that hint of hardness which reminded her that people didn't mess with him. He could be difficult, though not with her, never with her. Yet. She bit her lip and narrowed her eyes, hovering between two opening gambits.

'Tess!'

She took a deep breath to deliver the news in a reasonable, measured manner. But unrehearsed words pushed past her planned phrases, tumbled past her lips. 'We've been a bit careless.'

The eyebrows shot up. The arm around her tightened, gave a slight shake. 'What?'

Heat rose to her face, she half smiled, half laughed. 'Um,' and 'Well ...' She tried again. 'When I was ill, you know, that night, the curry, remember?' He nodded, dawning suspicion in his eyes. Her gaze dropped to the twin fans of black hair on the power of his chest, her hand rose to smooth them. 'If you read, if we'd read, the instructions with the contraceptive pill ... Well, we should've taken other, um, precautions.'

She cleared her throat, flicked a glance at his poleaxed expression. 'So what happens, you see ...'

'Holy crap,' he croaked. 'We're having a baby!'

'Mmm.'

Expression ludicrous, incredulous, he stared into her eyes. 'Really?'

'Mmm.'

'How did that happen?'

'I just told you.' She must be composed. It was vital not to give too much away until he'd reacted, committed himself.

He was very still. Apart from the ridiculous incredulity, she couldn't read his face. Distaste? Fear? Disappointment? Dismay? Let it be joy! Or, at least, acceptance.

He blinked. 'You *do* want to keep it?'

Relief made her head buzz. 'Of course *I* want to! Do you?'

'Why wouldn't I want to? Tess!' He dragged her off her elbow and into his arms, burying his face in her hair, hugging her too tightly. 'I love you!' Laughing, kissing, rolling over her, 'Oh my God,' and, 'I can't believe it,' and, 'Oh my God,' again. He kissed his way down to the abdomen where it was all to happen, began a silly one-sided conversation with what he called 'his foetus'.

Eventually, he just cradled her against the hot flesh of his body. 'Have you seen a doctor?'

'Dr Warrington, today. He said, "Aha! The incredible baby-producing tummy bug!" And gave me a stack of leaflets showing veiny breasts and screwed-up babies. He's doing a test to make sure.'

She watched Ratty's lips descend slowly until her eyes closed and her lips opened to reciprocate his kiss.

Against her mouth, he murmured, 'Is everything going to be all right this time?'

'He says there's no reason to think it'll go wrong again. But, be very sensible.'

Ratty gripped her. 'We'll be more sensible than anyone has ever been before. I love you. We'll love our baby.' Kiss, kiss, 'Everything will be wonderful,' kiss, 'because nothing bad is going to happen,' kiss, 'nothing could – happen to – spoil – this.'

Chapter Twenty-Five

Nothing could spoil it. Certainly not so soon. How should she have known that carrying the mail up to open with that first cup of tea, would do it? Suspect, when he opened his eyes, smiled his sexiest and joked, 'Hullo, Mummy,' that she shouldn't have giggled back? There was nothing, then, to stop her abandoning the tray and bouncing in beside him, agreeing that the baby would be their secret for a few more weeks. It was only sensible.

Then, the unexploded bomb was just one of a dozen envelopes waiting for attention.

So she knew the love was still on her face, the tenderness in her eyes when she opened her bank statements, the laugh in her voice when she repeated a remark about her credit card and he didn't answer.

But she deflated abruptly when he began to swear, softly and continuously.

'What?' she reached for the pages in his hand. She gazed in dismay as he leapt up and turned his back. 'What? Bad news? Rats?'

Two of his strides across the tiny landing and the bathroom door shut. She heard the bolt slide.

She sat, stunned, among the junk mail, the envelopes, the statements, in their bed, her heart hammering blood round her veins, forcing cold sweat through her pores. Fruitless questions swarmed around her mind. Sitting on their bed like a mermaid washed ashore, she felt sick, wondering frantically what had caused Ratty to dive for cover. Had to be something bad.

He was white, when he emerged, hair damp at the front as if he'd rinsed his face. Hesitantly, he sank down beside her, cleared his throat, slid his arm around her.

His eyes, his troubled eyes, it had to be something bad, bad. This was how people were when they had to impart awful news, with gentle sympathy and a grave expression.

'*What*?' She trembled when his gaze faltered and dropped to a thickness of papers clutched in his fist beside him on the bed. She couldn't take her eyes away.

'It's ... a problem. My Christ.'

She waited, swallowing back the rising in her throat. Fresh sweat broke on her swimmy head.

'The Child Support Agency says ...'

'CSA?' Stiff lips, rubber tongue. A voice which sounded something like hers.

He wavered a sigh, wiped his forehead with the back of his hand. She watched the sheaf of printed paper as his hand moved.

'They say there's a child.'

Her heart thumped right up in the back of her throat as she sifted frantically through his words for the meaning. Could this be something to do with *her* child, the collection of cells which was apparently inside her, waiting to be their baby? She didn't see how. And in his face she saw guilt.

'You've got a *child*?'

'They say so. I didn't know, no idea!'

She shook off his arm, battling waves of nausea. Morning sickness. How humbling, how intolerably humiliating if she barfed it all up, here in their bed, in front of him whilst he told her the incredible news that he had a child!

She took a grip on herself. 'Who? I mean, the mother?'

'Madeline Gavanagh. Madeline and me ... a couple of years ago. I promise you I didn't know there could be a baby. Well ...'

He tailed off. His face, that face she'd loved so wholly, was chiselled with misery. And guilt.

A deep breath. She waited for the thudding in her ears to subside. It was imperative that she get this straight. 'This baby is more than a year old?'

'Apparently. I don't know why she's waited to make a claim.'

'And it's your baby?'

'Apparently.'

'You had unprotected sex with her?'

He barely nodded. 'Once or twice.'

She felt a ferocious red tide of anger erupt inside her. 'Don't you even know *which*?'

His eyes were filled with misery.

She gripped her temples with her fingertips. 'Just let me clarify. After you had unprotected sex with this Madeline, which of you ended the relationship?'

She could see him thinking about lying. The indecision was written on his face as he looked down at the paperwork in his hands, then out of the window. Then at her.

'Me.'

'Without knowing she'd fallen pregnant? So,' she sank her face into her palms. 'You didn't bother to find out. You left her up to her neck in it!'

Suddenly she had to get away, off their passionate bed. Such a mockery. She swayed to her feet.

He protested, 'It was only a couple of times!' Then, bitterly, 'I'm usually careful.'

She swung round. 'Do you really think so? When we got it together, I don't remember *condoms* figuring in your Great Plan!'

His eyes were hunted, anguished, hair curling down to thick, dark brows, pallor accentuated the shadow of his day-old beard. 'I assumed you'd say something if you wanted me to take care of it.'

'Bloody big assumption!'

'But with Madeline it *was* only a couple of times, when I was boozed up! It was unlucky.' Expression desperate, he moved around the bed towards her; she backed off.

'Unlucky! I'd say they were persistent little bastards, your "guys"! A boozy session for her, a tummy bug for me and bingo!'

'It doesn't have to change anything.' Desperation, panic in his voice. 'Don't let it change what we've got, we don't have to suffer for this. It was before us, before we'd met, even!' Desperately, 'If it helps, I won't see the baby.'

'Is it a boy or a girl?'

He hesitated. 'Boy. It'll just be financial.'

'What's his name?'

'Jason. I won't see him.'

Step by step he'd backed her up to the doorway. She stared at him as if she'd never seen him clearly before, held up her hands to stay him.

A deep breath. *'You won't see him?'* She was screaming, suddenly she was screaming and she couldn't help it, screaming because she felt screaming was the only means of communicating such disgust, fury, pain. *'How can you not* see your son? Christ, last night you lay there,' she flung a hand to the bed, knowing tears were making her nose-running ugly and not caring. 'Carrying on an entire conversation with *your foetus*, nothing more than a bunch of cells hitching a ride on an egg. And you think you'll be able to stay away from a living, breathing, loving baby? *Your son*! And why would you, anyway? How can you suggest it? Does Jason deserve being ignored by his father? And doesn't Madeline deserve help with the parenting? Do you think that you *ought* to be able to have your drunken sex and then sail on your merry, selfish, I'm-all-right-Jack way, leaving a child and a changed life behind you?'

She dragged in a huge, ragged breath. 'If you can ignore Madeline's baby, you can ignore *mine*! Is that what I've got to look forward to?'

'Of course not!'

She watched fury flash across his features, before he collected himself, forcing himself to be calm, concentrate. Search for a solution to the problem, ways of gaining ground. Eyes casting about, he located the tissues beside the bed and held out a handful for her.

And when she reached for them he snatched her hand, as she'd known he would, and pulled her towards him. She could almost feel his comforting heartbeat across the few inches remaining between them. Yes, let him soothe her, wipe her face with clean, cool tissues, stroke back her hair where it plastered wet cheeks. Enable her to breathe again, see properly to be disillusioned by his remorseful, hunted, wary eyes.

'Don't cry, Princess.' His hands sidled gently up her arms as if sneaking a halter onto a nervous pony. Inching closer, he slid his arms around, letting their bodies gently touch, pressing a delicate kiss against her forehead, each swollen eye, the tip of her nose, cheeks, and so slowly to her parted lips. A kiss to feel his way, to bridge the chasm the bomb had caused, to coax her that everything would be all right.

But when his mouth fastened onto hers, his tongue quivering, probing with all his usual tenderness, she forced herself to stand indifferently immobile. Arms clamped to sides. Lips passive. Tongue flaccid and mouth unaccommodating. The most insulting, contemptuous action, far more hurtful than simply fighting him off.

He jerked away.

And finally, she was free to make for the bathroom to heave over the toilet bowl.

When he knocked, she asked him wearily, calmly, quietly, to go to work as usual. 'I need a shower, time to think. Space. You mustn't crowd me. I've got a lot to come to terms with.'

And he said, 'OK.' She heard him. And then, 'I love you.'

But when she emerged it was to find him waiting in the bedroom, gaunt and haunted. She recoiled as he rose from the bed. 'I thought you'd gone to work!'

He brushed her words aside, brows down, eyes intent. 'We have to talk! I can't just go to the garage and leave this unresolved between us, you're treating me like a monster, some bastard who gets his girlfriend pregnant and then scarpers –'

'But you are,' she said, quietly.

Black anger clouded his face. '*I. Didn't. Know*!'

'You should have. You had unprotected sex. You should have checked out any consequences.'

'Tess, it isn't always just the man's fault –' He reached out, took her arms.

She slapped at his hands, yanked her arms away. 'Get away from me! I don't want you near me – you've turned into Olly Gray!'

'You all right, Ratty?'

'Don't ask.'

'You look like ...'

'Don't *ask*!'

The garage became unnaturally silent. He fumbled through his work somehow, between phone calls on his mobile from the privacy of a forecourt car. To the Child Support Agency, calm and non-committal and all-in-a-day's work, who sent him to their website to read about DNA testing. 'But if there's a possibility that Jason Gavanagh is your child you should be prepared –'

He snapped, 'There's every possibility, but I deal in certainties!' And clicked off.

Madeline had to be tracked down, wasn't on her old number. He had to ring five people, each either reluctant or avid, before discovering her at her parents' house. After a guilty pause, she confessed, 'I wouldn't have put them on to you, but I've had to leave my job, I'm in a jam. Mum can't look after Jason while I work any more because she's ill, we've had to go on benefit, it's horrible, managing like this! They stop some of my money if I don't name the father.'

'Couldn't you have approached me first? Privately, perhaps?'

She was flustered, awkward. Hardly the bubbly Madeline he remembered, always in a rush to get to the next party and buy the next dress. 'You get these immense *forms* and you have to answer all these questions! The father is obliged in law ...'

'And you're sure it's me?'

'I think it's likely, don't you?'

'Are you sure it's me?'

'We did ...'

'Have you any idea how this is affecting *me*? Did you give that any thought at all? *Are you sure he's mine*?'

'Deal with the CSA.' She hung up.

He hardly had any idea of what he did, after that. Pete dealt with three men who stopped to admire the red Pontiac on the forecourt, kept the work flowing and made sure Ratty was left alone. God bless Pete.

A hundred times he almost rang her.

A thousand times.

To beg forgiveness, understanding? To check she was OK? Just to hear her, overlay the morning's memory of her scorn? But she'd asked for space. She always needed space, acres, when something ugly happened.

But God, she'd been so angry. He cringed at the memory of the fury and contempt in her eyes. The letter had caught him so unawares, so cruelly destroyed their joy in Tess's pregnancy that he'd made a complete hash of the argument that followed, feverishly casting about for things to say, anything to drag them away from the abyss he'd suddenly glimpsed at their feet.

In blurting out that he wouldn't see the child he was alleged to have fathered, he'd had some half-arsed idea of demonstrating his commitment to Tess, to their baby. Instead she'd leapt to the conclusion that he was a heartless bastard, wriggling out of his paternal responsibilities at the first instant.

... You've turned into Olly Gray ... You've turned into Olly Gray.

He wandered to the open doors to gaze out, longing to see her as ever, strolling with Angel and the kids or striding off on a wild walk to make herself feel better.

He could go home. It was a few hundred yards away. The urge was almost irresistible to run down Little Lane to Pennybun. To drag her into his arms and plead with her to see her unfairness in blaming him, it happened all the time, the drink, the carelessness. He'd just been unlucky, surely she could see that?

But she'd asked for space.

All day he was stupid and clumsy with apprehension. Skinned every knuckle on his right hand, dropped his spanners and gauges, which immediately rolled into the least accessible corners.

Time crawled by without his mobile ringing, without Tess trailing up the road to rest her sad face on his shoulder and wrap her needy arms around him, telling him they'd work it out together. To agree that their love was too great to spoil.

It should've occurred to him earlier but it didn't – until he walked up the path and saw the space where the Freelander had been.

The kitchen door swung as it always did, everything was where it always was, the range, the green tiles and Tess's paintings. But he only had to stand still and listen for reality to break around him like a freak wave, turning his legs to string as he stumbled up the stairs.

He lost control long enough to yell, pointlessly, 'You better not have gone!'

Apart from that he was stonily calm, opening the oak wardrobe, the chest of drawers. Inspecting the workroom, the bathroom.

No clothes that smelled of Tess, no dresses, no jeans, no sexy underwear. No lotions, no shampoo, no make-up. No paint, no paper, no pencils, no box files of correspondence, no books containing her work.

No Tess.

Except for the note in her handwriting stuck to the dressing-table mirror: *I need to get away.*

Chapter Twenty-Six

Through the small landing window he stared out at the drive. Could almost see her stumping up and down with boxes, clothes, suitcases, portfolios, drawing board, stacking the back of the Freelander until her rear vision was obscured and she'd have to drive on her door mirrors. Her computer would have been a problem; the big-screen monitor needed strapping to the front passenger seat with a seat belt. That's how it had been when he'd first met her, when he'd towed the Freelander into the garage and it was stacked out with her possessions.

But then, Tess was used to packing. Never got completely *un*packed, when he thought about it; there were still boxes left in Honeybun for her to get around to.

'I should've expected this,' he spat aloud, uselessly because she wasn't there to hear. And suddenly a great rage swelled around, above, inside his head; temple-buzzing, vision-shaking fury. He flung himself into the workroom, crashing the door back against the wall. 'I might've known you'd leave! Why couldn't you stay and work things out? *Why?*' He picked up yesterday's coffee mug, all she'd left.

Through the window. Yes, through the ... there! That was better! Stoking the violence boiling inside with that sharp splintering of glass. Much better. He needed more.

'*Why?*' Wildly into the bedroom, heaving at her wardrobe until it clattered over. '*Why?*' Dressing-table stool at the mirror still bearing that hateful note, which splintered, hesitated, then hissed to the floor in a curtain of light. '*Why?*' The heavier the furniture, the more satisfying the crash to displace the roaring in his head.

Best was everything which smashed and shattered into irredeemable shards, chinking, cracking, jingling, littering the carpets, scarring the walls. Brittle, dangerous, widespread debris.

'I smashed up the house.' He listened to a silence over the phone.

At least Pete, when he finally reacted, reacted positively. 'Shall I come?'

'Please, Pete.'

Three minutes, then Pete entered the kitchen, crunching, awed, through the pulverised glassware from the dresser, the mugs from the tree. Dead quiet, dead calm, dead still, Ratty watched Pete crouch into his field of vision, heard him as if he was calling down a lift shaft. 'Where's the whisky?'

He squinted from his bottom-step seat. 'Sideboard.' Saw Pete crunch his way to the sitting-room door, peer in. The only room to have escaped.

Pete's voice down that shaft again, sombre, warily coaxing. 'In here, Rats. You need a drink. C'mon mate, drink.'

He allowed himself to be steered by the elbow like an incompetent to a seat, accepted the whisky bottle by the neck, supposed drearily that there was nothing much left to drink from, swigged twice, gagged, returned the bottle.

'More.' Pete pushed it back.

It was completely the wrong thing to do. He drank anyway. 'She's left me.'

Pete wiped the bottle with his sleeve, drank, wiped, passed it back, whistled his amazement. 'No shit? Christ, I'm sorry.'

Ratty's throat was on fire and it didn't matter. Good to be senseless, destructive, to choke down the raw spirit without giving himself respite. Let his eyes water, let his voice crack as he forced out, hoarsely, 'CSA are onto me. Madeline Gavanagh's had a kid and says its mine.'

Pete sucked in his breath. 'Is it?'

'Could be.' He took back the bottle, swigged, retched, swigged again. 'Could be. And Tess has put into action The Tess Riddell Coping Mechanism. She's fucked off somewhere else.'

It was all he could do to breathe between gulps.

Pete's voice, 'You've had enough, now.'

And his, 'I haven't.'

Sometimes Pete spoke and sometimes he was silent and that was good. Good old Pete. Pete was the best.

And in twenty minutes he wasn't safe to be left, Ratty understood that. His head clamoured at whisky on no food. Not safe to be left in a house full of broken glass, shattered crockery, splintered furniture, only sensible to let Pete help him through the garden, up the village to Rotten Row, clutching the whisky bottle, staggering but willing enough, dragged along by Pete's fist wound into the fabric of his jacket. Up and down the kerb, zigzag stumble into their sitting room where Angel shifted from foot to foot, hands to her face in horror.

'She's left me,' he explained amiably, swaying, probably intimidating, close. 'Run away. Didjer know?'

'No, Rats. I didn't know. Get him up to the spare room, Pete, I'll make him coffee.'

'I don't need *coffee*. I've got *this*!' He shook the whisky bottle in front of her anxious face. 'Drink with me, Angel. Drink to my runaway, drink to my children. Let's drink ourselves sober like we used to when we were young and stupid. And Pete and me can share you, you're safer.'

'You're an obnoxious drunk,' she scolded gently.

The sofa caught him behind the knee and he buckled

gracefully down into its embrace. 'Aw, don't be like that, Angel. We'll drink to weak women and unlucky men!'

From the darkness swirling at the peripheries of his vision, from the whisky bottle sliding through his fingers, from Angel's worried face swimming too colourfully above him, he was passing out. 'Sorry,' he said, letting himself go.

But he did hear Angel, gargling through the spinning darkness, 'What the hell are we going to do with him?'

And Pete, 'Dunno. But he couldn't stay there. It looks as if there's been an explosion.'

Very ill, terribly ill he felt, but sober. Completely. Seeing things so clearly it hurt.

He lurched into the kitchen. 'Sorry about last night.'

'Don't be.' Angel left her vegetables and sat him on a kitchen chair, anxious but looking pleased that he was at least walking and talking. Pete eased his way in, leaving Toby and Jenna on the floor engrossed in cartoons, pushing the door shut behind him.

Explanations, it was reasonable that they'd expect them. He raked his fingers through his hair, which felt uncombed and clumpy. 'The CSA say this kid, Jason Gavanagh, is my child. I got this big form, yesterday, asking whether I accept paternity. You remember Madeline Gavanagh?'

Nods.

'And he could be mine. Probably is. There were a couple of times, y'know after a drink.'

More nods.

Angel had made him a slice of toast and he nibbled minutely at the corner. He really ought to eat. Did he eat at all yesterday? Probably not, probably part of the reason why he felt so bad. He managed half a mouthful, chewing food that he didn't actually want to touch.

'So Tess has left?'

'Run away!'

'Left,' corrected Angel, gently. 'Do you think she'll come back?'

'Believing that is the only thing keeping me sane. It just seems that the only way she can deal with a problem is to run and hide.'

Angel frowned, rubbed at the edge of the table with her finger to erase a crayon mark. 'Madeline was *previous* to Tess, wasn't she? Tess presumably realised you'd had sex before.'

Ratty picked up another morsel of toast. 'You're missing the point. The *point* is that I *had* unprotected sex and I didn't bother to enquire whether I'd left behind more than I'd bargained for. As far as Tess is concerned ... well, she said I've turned into Olly Gray.'

Olly Gray. Olly Gray. Ratty's strides back to Pennybun Cottage spoke the name. Turned into Olly Gray. You've turned into Olly Gray.

Reaching the cottage, he had other things to worry about. 'Oh *Christ*.'

Angel squeezed into the kitchen beside him. 'You're absolutely barking mad, Ratty, d'you know that? Where do we start with this lot?'

'Oh Christ,' he repeated, barely able to bring his eyes to settle on the havoc, from the gaping of the burst windows to the mulch of smashed china and glass. The fallen dresser, the upturned chairs, one broken.

The pictures of McLaren and Lucasta peering back oddly from behind glass spiders' webs.

They could only start at the top and work down. Knock out the remaining glass from the sashes and sweep up, right the wardrobe, remove the door with the broken hinge until it could be repaired.

257

A screw had ripped from the frame of the dressing-table stool. Two bathroom tiles were cracked.

'This is like clearing up after an air raid.' Angel picked splintered glass from her fingertip. 'Overwhelmingly depressing.' But mainly she and Pete worked alongside him in silence, doing what had to be done. And he was grateful for their help. Grateful that Pete rang the joiner and, because Ratty was a fast payer and realised he'd have to pay top rates, got an agreement to re-glaze the following morning. Grateful that Angel had asked Pete's parents to have the kids so that she could collect empty boxes from Crowther's to fill with the millions of glass crystals.

And then all he wanted was for them to go away.

So he could be alone, alone in the empty shell of a home with the night wind blowing the curtains in empty windows.

Chapter Twenty-Seven

'Bit more compromising now, aren't we? My God! Aren't you the chap who was confident everything would work out like a dream? No chance of unhappiness, not with you looking after her?'

Asking James if he knew where Tess was because he seemed to have lost her, was bound to cause a furious eruption. It was precisely what he'd expected. Ratty let him have his rant, then lunged in when James took a breath. 'Did you hear from her, yesterday? Today?'

Fresh heights of outrage emanated from the phone. 'Don't you think I might have *mentioned* it?'

'Not necessarily.' He stretched wearily and listened to the joiner and his mate knocking, upstairs. Apart from the unavoidable hammering and chopping, they worked in awed – or disgusted – silence. So much damage, no explanation. He'd shut himself in the sitting room with the telephone.

'... It was *you*, Mr Five Houses, who said you'd always be fair ...'

'I also suggested you didn't comment on my behaviour! Listen ... just a minute ... *listen* ...'

Hopeless; he closed his eyes, gritted his teeth and waited for James to run down from a fresh tirade of 'What d'you think you're' and 'How dare you'. Fought to resume in a neutral tone of unnatural courtesy. 'Please, Mr Riddell. If you know anything, anything at all, just tell me she's all right. If she doesn't want me to know her whereabouts, OK. But,' he swallowed, hearing his voice hoarsen, '*please* let me know she's safe!'

James blustered. 'Why shouldn't she be? She's surely capable of taking a hotel room or something? She always has been before!'

Through the window the shrubs nodded, dusty green. If only she was still the other side of them, busy in her workroom at Honeybun. Why had he pushed her to join him at Pennybun? At least if she'd stayed in her own place she could've locked the doors against him and he'd know she was there. Know she was safe.

'She's pregnant. Just.' The phone was beginning to slip in his hand. And then, in a sudden burst of fear, 'What if it happens again, the bleeding? What if she's alone? She could bleed to ...'

'Oh, you *stupid* young bastard!' Bang. Phone down.

He called back. James exploded afresh. 'Now what do you want?'

'Telephone numbers. She hasn't left them here.'

'You've got some nerve!'

Must keep a grip. A hold, even if precarious, on his temper. Focus only on the important. 'OK, I'm next best thing to an axe murderer, if I had a brain I'd be dangerous. But let's make sure she's OK. Shall we?'

James retired into silence, sighed, creaked his chair. Eventually he spat, 'Who?'

'Guy. Kitty, her agent. Olly. Old friends.'

'I've been trying her mobile,' James offered grudgingly.

'Pointless, isn't it?'

'So that's the picture. She's vanished. If you know anything ... I need to know she's all right.'

Guy's disembodied voice was careless. 'Haven't heard a thing! Disappeared whilst you were at work, did she? What about her mobile?'

'She's obviously changed her number. Look, Guy, I know

she's your cousin but for Christ's sake, let me know if you hear from her. You don't have to go into detail, as long as I know she's safe.'

'She'll be OK, when she scarpered during her A levels she came home when she ran out of money.'

'That's not going to apply now, is it?' He squashed down impatience, it was vital that he kept all avenues of communication open. 'Anyway, if you come up with anything ...'

'Well, well, well!' Olly was going to be difficult. Going to adore being difficult, in fact. Ratty could just imagine his wide, thin-lipped smirk, his delight that Ratty had fucked up.

'Yeah, yeah, have your little gloat.' Desperation was threatening. He felt distant and unwell, and needed to eat. The joiners, at the kitchen window now, pounded their patterns on the front of his skull. He'd cease to function competently if he didn't eat something. But his throat kept closing at the prospect.

He picked up a pen and stabbed it at the little pad he'd searched out, hoping to have lots of information to list on it. Apart from the stab marks, the page was blank. 'Is she with you?'

'So you think she might come here?'

Stab. Stab-stab. 'I don't know. Is she there? Do you think she might turn up?'

'If she was coming to me she would've been here by now. James will know.'

'Apparently not. Can you think of anyone she might've gone to? Friends?'

Ratty persisted and Olly, with a show of reluctance, read out some numbers. Ratty could envisage him scrolling through a list on his personal organiser. 'But don't waste your time. She won't be with any of them, they haven't heard from her since we split. They were people we knew together. I tried them before James coughed up her address.'

Ratty bulldozed on. 'But if you do happen to hear, call me? Or at least James?'

Olly laughed. 'I might.'

If he pressed the knuckles of his hand between his eyes hard enough, he might be able to burrow into the hammering and stop it. 'You fascinate me. I don't understand why you ever got together when you so obviously couldn't give a toss.'

'In actual fact I do, of course I do! Tess looks great, I like to go to bed with her and she's good at looking after me. I thought being married to her would be comfortable, then I met someone else and lost the plot for a while. It happens. But if I get another crack at her, it won't happen again. And, from what you say, I might be getting my next crack any minute.'

'You give blokes a bad name.'

Unseen, through the French doors he watched his father turning papers, box file on knee, chin on knuckles. Pressing the door handle, he stepped inside a room that never changed. Parquet, pale wallpaper up to the moulded cornice, ornate plaster roses, a five-armed light fitting matching the one visible through the arch to the dining room. He wished, irrelevantly and irascibly, that his parents could have one single, pendant light in the house, with an ordinary cotton shade.

'Miles!' His father jerked up, flitting through surprise, pleasure, and into wariness. 'What's up?'

And suddenly he couldn't speak, couldn't loosen the knot in his throat to confess. He felt like a child who'd smashed a window. More than a smashed window though, this time.

Lester closed his file. 'Come through. How about coffee?'

Follow. Follow grey trousers and leather moccasins, his own boots leaving the parquet with a sucking noise. Through into the spacious kitchen with oak units and a peninsular breakfast bar. He slid onto a tall wooden stool, propped the heaviness of his head on his palm while Lester bustled with the kettle. When the coffee came he looked down into the steam until his eyes smarted. Glanced at Lester and away.

'What is it?' Lester's voice was kind.

Clearing his throat, he watched the little island of foam spin in the centre of his coffee. Mustn't cry, too ridiculous, a grown man! Deep breath. 'The CSA are alleging that I'm the absent parent of a little boy. Tess has left.' It became easier, whilst Lester listened intently, to talk about Madeline and the bits of heedlessness that had jumped up to bite him, Tess's extreme reaction, his endless, fruitless attempts to find her.

Thank God, Lester, sympathetic hand on his shoulder, was going to be reasonable, helpful. 'You know, Miles, if she doesn't want to be found it's simple enough. People do it every day. Hotel, motel, rented house. Disappear into an unconnected part of the country. I'm not sure there's anything to be done.'

'And she's pregnant. And in the past she miscarried, had a massive bleed that put her in hospital. I prefer her not to be alone somewhere, in those circumstances.'

'Jesus, Mary and Joseph!'

Ratty ground his teeth. 'Is plural blasphemy the thing in legal circles these days?' Why did Lester always make him sarcastic?

'Well, you are rather springing grandchildren on me, Miles!' Lester laughed shortly. 'So, what have you done to find her?'

And he went though it all again, drinking coffee which was somehow strong yet tasteless, wearily enumerating the prolific phone calls. James, Guy and Olly. The frustrating chain of unreturned calls to Kitty, Tess's agent, culminating in a curt refusal to discuss one of her artists. The pointless wading through the list that Olly had provided, every Melissa and Melanie, Jack, Samantha, Clare, all vague or surprised or uninterested.

'It'll have to be the police, then.' Lester became businesslike.

Ratty looked up. 'Will they help?'

'Might. Depends who's on duty.' Lester drummed his fingers and thought. 'But they're reluctant to intervene in a domestic. We'll have to be very concerned for her health, stress her history and that her parents haven't heard from her, that sort of thing. 'Course, the police will automatically approach the Riddells and they'd be obliged to be frank with them in a way they might not with you, if they did happen to know anything.'

Glumly, he sipped the strong yet tasteless coffee. 'Her father says I'm a stupid young bastard.'

'Yes, well. List all the phone numbers of the people you've approached, all that. See what the boys in blue can do if you're nice to them.'

Ratty grinned faintly, remembering *it's no wonder the children call you pigs*. He'd be nice. Too nice for words if it got him somewhere. Some of the tension rolled away. At least he was getting the sensation of travelling positively instead of careering round in squawking circles.

Lester rubbed his chin. 'The other baby. The mother?'

'Madeline Gavanagh.'

'Oh, yes. Dates fit?'

The obvious question. He let his elbow slide along the breakfast table, taking his head with it. 'Couple of times

264

we dispensed with condoms. It's a possibility. Probability, even.'

He mustn't be impatient that Lester was gazing at his garden, frowning. Odd not to be sure, he realised. Ratty's son? Lester's grandchild? Was their blood circulating the little body of Jason Gavanagh, a stranger?

So he explained about attending the Child Support Agency for interview, prior to arranging an appointment for a pinprick blood sample to be taken by a local doctor and sent to the DNA testing company. The two passport photos, so that Madeline could check the right person had provided the sample. Then all he had to do was wait a few more weeks.

'And if he's mine, I'll be supporting him financially until he's eighteen, I suppose.'

Lester rubbed his eyes. 'What about ... meeting him. Will you want to be in his life?'

The stool screeched the tiles as he flung it back. 'How the hell do I know? This is all new to me, I don't know how it feels to be a father!'

Extending that sympathetic hand again to sit Ratty back down, Lester observed gravely, 'It can be a hell of a job. Finish your coffee. Let me think.' He tapped his terribly clean fingertips on the bar.

Ratty watched, sipped. The old man could be a great asset when he chose. It hadn't apparently occurred to him to distance himself. There he was, bending his considerable intelligence to the problem without giving a second thought to all the wary years between them. Was that fatherhood?

Lester stopped tapping. 'Why do you want to find her?'

He stared. How was he supposed to answer that, articulate the hugeness of his need?

Lester offered prompts, dotting his finger on the

worktop. 'Because she's pregnant and you're genuinely worried for her safety? Because it's her turn to pay at the supermarket? Because you love her desperately? Because you feel she ought not to leave without permission? You need her to cook your tea? What?'

'Love her,' Ratty croaked eventually. 'I thought we'd be together. And the pregnancy. And the danger is real. All the rest –'

'– is rubbish. Yes,' Lester nodded. 'But think of it from the standpoint of the police. So our line is: you're worried to death because she's newly pregnant and has a history of miscarriage, followed by haemorrhage. You're desperate to establish her safety. You realise they'll ask if you gave her reason to fear you?'

'What?'

'Bashed her about.'

'No, I bastard didn't!'

'Threatened to?'

'No!'

'Good. Come on, old son, let's see what we can do before your mother turns up.'

And Ratty climbed thankfully into his father's silver, leather-seated BMW, pathetically grateful to be taken in hand, home to shower and shave three days' growth, climb into fresh clothes, be driven into Bettsbrough.

As well as moral support, he would benefit from the fast mind, quiet reason and inside track of a solicitor.

A solicitor who proved handy for the procedure that went just how Lester obviously knew it would. A civilian desk clerk greeted them, and was interrupted by a sergeant materialising from behind a door. 'Are we expecting you, Lester?'

'No, it's just something that's come up. Who's the duty inspector today? Alan Rose? Would he have a minute for me, do you think?'

And they were in, shown into the inspector's office with such speed that Ratty watched closely to see if there were any funny handshakes. But no, it seemed simply a matter of the contacts of a local criminal lawyer, built up over the years when Alan was a sergeant in uniform and then CID. And Lester having once defended a friend of Alan's who'd been very, very stupid.

Lester, relaxed and friendly, ran through the facts of their problem unemotionally and he and Alan agreed philosophically that women will sometimes pack and go, it came under the heading of 'choosing to leave'. Difficult for the police to interest themselves.

'And I wouldn't be wasting your time, Alan, but there is a genuine fear for her safety. If she hadn't required urgent medical intervention after miscarriage in the past, if she wasn't pregnant now ...' Lester made a 'tricky one' face.

Alan Rose lifted his eyebrows and nodded gently. 'OK, let's see what we can do.'

With a sense of unreality Ratty watched Inspector Rose fill out a 'misper', missing persons form. Heard himself agreeing to drop in a recent photograph of Tess. Became aware that the inspector, behind quiet grey eyes, was exercising a fine talent in extracting information without committing himself.

No, arguments weren't a feature of their relationship. She hadn't left him before but he understood that she'd run away during exams, as a teenager. He couldn't imagine why she'd claim benefit because she was self-employed and well able to support herself. He had put together all the details of friends and family who might be helpful.

Alan Rose neatened his paperwork. 'Leave it with me. I ought to be able to find something in this lot. I'll get back to you.'

Then they were back on the bustle of the pavement and

Ratty deflated, as all the purpose and sense of progress that had carried him there soaked away. He mulled over the inspector's list of steps that people took to cover the tracks they left in their finances or with their phones. And the electoral roll wouldn't be renewed for months.

Painful realisation. 'They're right. She can disappear indefinitely, if she wants to.'

Awfully, Elisabeth turned up at the cottage that night with swimming eyes to clasp his hand and rake over it all again. 'Just leave me to it,' he kept suggesting, wishing desperately for her to take her disabling sympathy and leave.

'But you were happy!' she protested. And, 'Babies! The oldest mistake in the book – and there's no excuse for it these days. I wish you'd taken responsibility, Miles!'

Yep. That would've been good.

Chapter Twenty-Eight

Every night! Every night this hell, tormenting, making him taut and restless, giving him no peace.

As if things weren't bad enough already, with Tess still missing and nobody admitting contact with her. One of them knew, one, because the police had turned her up in nothing flat. Alan Rose had rung Lester, cagey about an address obtained through the back door from contacts made in his years tackling fraud. And confirmed by someone else.

Ratty had been urgent that his father might talk the police inspector into indiscretion; but Lester had been philosophical. 'He'll mean the tax office, I should think. She's self-employed, they'll have an address for her. Anyway, the local boys sent a bobby round and Alan's satisfied she's fit and well, but she doesn't want to be found. And that is her prerogative.' He must understand it was as much as could be divulged.

She didn't want to be found.

Daily, a thousand reminders pricked him; empty workroom, empty bed, Tess's mail. Daily, he passed Honeybun Cottage serene behind its gate, occasionally made himself go in and check that all was well, pick up more mail for Tess and see images of her in every corner. He stood very still for a very long time before the painting of the choked heart on the blue workroom wall, straining to get some feeling for where she was. Hopeless.

And at night, those damned dreams! Vivid, juicy dreams, leaving him completely aroused, equally frustrated. She'd once told him about similar lurid dreams after Olly, before him. She'd thought their truncated encounter after the ball had been one of them. He hadn't understood, properly.

Memories dressed up as dreams – walking into their bedroom to find Tess standing by the chest of drawers, reading a book's final chapter. He sucked in his breath every time he remembered. Soft white shirt not quite covering low-rise panties he promoted instantly to be his favourite. Bare legs. Newly brushed hair flowing over one shoulder, brush still dangling from her hand.

Jerked out of her book by his appearance, she'd squeaked, 'Look at the time! I'm supposed to be with Angel!' She shut the book, hasty, guilty.

'I know you are.' He hooked her to him, wanting to feel her in his arms, her hair running through his fingers.

She lifted her face for a quick kiss. 'I'm late,' she pointed out, pushing gently against him.

'I know.' He tightened his arms, kissed her again, more thoroughly, dropping his hands to cup her buttocks.

Her soft lips whispered against his. 'Angel will be wondering.'

'I know.' He leant back to lift her feet clear of the floor and drifted to the bed, let the edge catch her behind her knees, lowering himself down to her. Flicking open the neat buttons of the white shirt, following his hand's progress with his lips, hearing her breath catch, feeling her shudder. Ignoring another breathy, absent reminder that Angel would be waiting.

Pushing the soft white shirt off the bed.

Her chuckle as she traced his throat with her lips. 'Angel'll be *furious*!'

'I *know*.'

Her smoky, sexy laugh laced dreams full of slender, smooth hands on his body and the tissue softness of her skin. He groaned in his throat as he broke from the dream just before the exquisite moment, sweat cooling as another bitter disappointment raced his heart. He thought of her willingness, eagerness, his longing to bury himself. Of when he had Tess and every night was an adventure.

Unable to fall asleep again, he went over and over the same ground. Where was she? How could he find out? God knew he'd tried, but everybody hid behind confidentiality. She must be meeting her tax bills and National Insurance contributions, must be in contact with her bank.

But catch any of those bodies letting fall a clue? No. Would the family tracing organisations get involved in a domestic? Not a chance.

So he'd reach the garage, out of sleep and out of sorts, to work his way through another day of Cadillacs and Pontiacs, Lotuses and MGs, hunting down spares, replacing piston rings, reboring, rebuilding front wings that had corroded around headlights, making the occasional killing from a rebuild, his mind shaking the problem around like a terrier.

Out in the wrecker to pick up a vehicle, every song on the radio reminded him of her, every road they'd driven. The old poster on Port Road she always noticed, *Massive Shoe Sale*. He'd hear her giggle, 'How many people wear massive shoes?'

And, despairing, he'd glare at the empty seat beside him. 'Where are you? Are you alone? How does it feel? Do you know how crazy this is? What a waste?' Had she ever loved him? She couldn't have, could she, to do this?

Though she'd certainly seemed convincing.

Was he supposed to be going after her, carrying her home, making up?

How?

So he passed the days, introverted, worried, tripping over people willing to prop him up. Angel and Pete offering meals, Jos pointing out stock car racing meetings, Elisabeth and Lester ringing or calling almost every day.

However touched, he was ungrateful. He told Elisabeth, 'I haven't seen you so much since I was fourteen!'

'You haven't needed us much, since then.'

Another letter.

He'd been angry before, was acknowledged to be impatient and acerbic with people who irritated him. When he'd careered through Pennybun Cottage, destructive as a tornado, it had seemed a level of rage that he was glad to think he'd never again experience.

But no craziness, no demolition was sufficient to discharge the violent, ballooning fury the fresh letter brought. He stood in his kitchen and simply roared at it in rage, feeling his throat crack and his temples pound at the awful, absolute, extravagant pointlessness of everything.

If Tess had suddenly reappeared he wouldn't have trusted himself in the same room in case he took it out on her.

But no such outlet for his feelings presented itself and so he drew his wrath into himself, where it could bubble and brew, and hammered off up the road to MAR Motors.

He waited for Jos to go off and telephone his Miranda before breaking the silence that seemed a feature of the garage these days.

'I'm not the father.'

Pete withdrew his head from a wheel arch and stared. 'Of Madeline's ...?'

''Sright. Got a report this morning.'

'Oh my God. Oh my *God*! So you won't be paying maintenance.'

'That's the least of my problems! Money! But what about Tess and the baby?' Uncharacteristically, he began to attack the wooden bench with a screwdriver, gouging out savage scars of fresh, splintered wood.

Pete always dared to ask him what nobody else would. 'What *about* Tess? If she turns up?'

He gazed out towards the Cross, narrow-eyed, reversing the screwdriver to let the handle bang against the bench, the chisel head digging into his palm. 'I don't know. I could strangle her!' The banging quickened, became louder, his hand hurt more and he stopped and looked down at blood as if surprised. Examined the puncture, laid the screwdriver carefully in the tool chest. 'Shit. I loved her.'

He'd loved her. It obviously hadn't been enough.

The night was dark and the breeze, right up there on the bridge, was warm and buffeting. It teased her hair in dancing strands across her face and she kept lifting her hand to shove it back.

She raised her eyes to look downriver towards the docks where lights burned like sparks from a wood fire above the floodlights, reflected in amber scribbles along the black water.

Below, the water lolled, as if waiting, and she wondered how it would feel to climb the steel, riveted edge and hurl herself down to meet it.

No. Of course she wouldn't.

But she imagined the poor, unfortunate police officers dealing with the husk she left behind, tramping down her parents' gravel drive past the over-trimmed conifers to squash the brass bell push. Inviting themselves in, grave-faced.

She tried to picture the reaction from her parents. James angry, angry at being made to feel grief. Mari sinking into a boneless heap, blaming herself, endless tears. 'We should've persuaded her to stay with us,' she'd weep.

And James would point out righteously, 'She wanted to

be left alone. She's done it before, taken herself off without telling anyone.'

They'd ring Ratty ... Would they? From the soft darkness above the sparky lights she conjured up dark curls and blue eyes. The grin. Where was he now? What was he doing? He had a son.

She'd have to get back. She was somewhere in Yorkshire; she'd driven for three hours up the motorway because she couldn't bear being indoors. She had to get back to the rented terraced house in Northampton, a tight street behind Wellingborough Road, slotted in amongst the others in the maze.

She hadn't run very far, in fact it felt half-hearted and attention-seeking. Having once again run from a tricky situation and started over, she had no idea what to do next. The police had found her. If she was going to become a hermit she should've done it properly, on a farm on the folds of the Pennines or a craggy cliff top in Cornwall. She really ought to have got more than an hour away.

She began walking back to where the Freelander waited in a lay-by, letting her elbow bang-bang-bang against the parapet. She missed him, missed him, missed him. Missed his company, his love, his loving. Her lover, lost. No – thrown away by her own reactions to trouble.

Up into the driving seat, throwing back her hair, she wondered if there was room for manoeuvre. Maybe she could go back. Face Ratty. 'OK, I ran,' she'd say, 'but I've come back because I love you and I want us to try to work through this together.'

How incredibly badly she'd handled things. It'd be a challenge to find a way to reverse this particular instance of starting over. She twisted the ignition key savagely.

'So,' began Lester, conversationally.

'So?'

'What now?'

He shrugged. Stretched his feet towards the fireplace as if a fire burned there.

'You've spoken to Madeline, I take it?'

What a phone conversation that had been. 'I wouldn't say "spoken". I shouted. She cried. I shouted louder. Then I was sorry.'

His father grunted. 'All over now.'

'It is, isn't it? And she did say she was sorry, for the trouble. "Don't worry about it," I said, "I've only lost my girlfriend and my child".'

'It won't help to be bitter.'

'Hardly matters, now.'

'So,' said Lester, again. 'Have you figured out who's in touch with Tess? Who the other party was the police found to be in possession of her current address?'

He closed his eyes. Shook his head. 'If somebody's in touch, they're being too clever for me. Her family keeps ringing to see what I know.' And how he loved those conversations, James insisting, Mari pleading, surely, surely, *surely* he knew where she was? Too much time had gone past now; she'd never been away this long before. It was only two strides before they'd be suggesting he'd done her in and hidden her body under the floorboards. He shook his head. 'Christ, her mother can cry! "Every knock at the door, every call on the phone, I think they've found her dead," bleat, bleat. If the police got their information there, I'd be amazed.'

Lester nodded. 'So there's got to be another explanation,' he agreed, meeting Ratty's eyes.

Ratty blinked, sat up. 'What? What do you know?'

Lester broke the eye contact, studied a fingernail. 'I wouldn't say I *know*. But you're just not thinking.'

God, it was like struggling with homework, when Lester would try and make him puzzle things out for himself. Irritation, his constant companion, reared up and made him snap, '*What*? Who?'

'Think, Miles! Tess needs to live, doesn't she? Eat, pay rent? Therefore, needs to earn money ...'

'The agent! *Kitty* – of course! My God, I'm so thick sometimes.' Palm against the flat of his forehead. 'Of course, of course,' he repeated. He reached over for the occasionally growing stack of letters addressed to Tess, flicked through them for the cream envelopes which normally arrived monthly. 'Nothing from her, her statements have stopped coming here. Of course, you're right – if she knows where Tess is, Tess can keep working.' He pictured her setting up a new workroom, perhaps in a rented flat somewhere. Maybe she'd get permission from the landlord to paint it her favourite, peaceful blue. He flung the pile of letters away, jerked to his feet.

'I'm expected at Pete's.' Moving automatically, he handed Lester his jacket, wanting him to go.

Lester jiggled his car keys. 'Take care, son.'

But, at last, he felt energetic and alive. The evening was soft and warm and he dashed through it to the house at Rotten Row, hope rising inside like good news.

On Angel's face he saw a sudden mirroring of his own smile, together with relief at the hint of more than black moods. 'Dinner in ten minutes,' she grinned. 'I thought you were going to be late.'

Toby shouted, 'And I'd have to eat yours!' Clean and fragrant in Spiderman pyjamas, he made forking motions with a toy lorry. 'Pie and chips, yum!'

'It's lasagne,' corrected Angel, laughing, tossing salad.

'Yuk!' groaned Toby. 'Wanna play cars, Ratty?' Toby had recently conquered the letter R, and Ratty quite missed being called 'Watty'.

Brumming toy vehicles up and down Toby's mat of the road, patiently going over the rules of the highway, Ratty kept thinking of Kitty. Kitty who Tess had worked with for years, Kitty who always combined meetings with Tess with long lunches in wine bars, and had Tess's best career interests at heart. He'd spoken to her himself on the telephone. A London voice, fast, economic verbal delivery, enthusiastic, switched on. Kitty who must know where Tess was hiding.

That evening seemed like old times.

Children full of giggles, every remark a joke, a meal, a beer, the mateyness. A new light-heartedness. He must've been bringing everyone down with his foul moods and misery. Maybe things were going to change, though. Maybe.

Jenna fell asleep on his chest as if she was still a baby and he carried her up to the pine cot she'd more or less outgrown. Sliding her between smooth sheets and a fluffy blanket, he watched her flushed face, smoothed her drakes' tails into the crook of her neck and thought of when he and Tess had shared the babysitting. The ache of missing her bit him suddenly in the chest and he gripped the cot rail. What about his own baby? Surely Tess wouldn't be so cruel as to keep the birth a secret? In his fantasies he was fond of constructing an emotional telephone call: Tess, in the throes of labour, begging him to race across the country to be with her, hold her, to love their baby into the world. They'd realise nothing else mattered, the birth would put everything into perspective, make her prioritise. Maybe. Or maybe he'd have to search registers of births to find proof that his child existed.

Or maybe she'd decided she couldn't bring a child up alone. There was always abortion. He swallowed.

One last touch of Jenna's warm, satin hair, and he

clattered down to read to Toby, eat apple crumble and feed Toby bits when Angel wasn't looking. Agreed to tuck Toby in, then finally back to an armchair.

Pete consulted the telly page, Angel folded clothes. 'I was looking at Gwen's new card stock today,' she said, too casually, as if having just remembered.

He felt his head snap round.

Angel glanced at him, then back to her folding, took away the ironing basket and returned with a cellophane-wrapped card.

Ratty reached out. The card, he noticed absently, trembled very slightly in his hand. He studied the illustration. Two lizards in evening dress, cheek to cheek, dancing a slinky tango. The T and the star, very tiny. *For Both of You on Your Anniversary*. He turned it over to read the name of the card company. Looked inside, closed it precisely. Although there was no way of knowing how long the card company had held the illustration, it tended to support the theory that she was working – what else would she do?

Angel sat next to him and slid the card from his wooden fingers. 'No news, I suppose?'

He turned to Pete. 'Can you cope without me tomorrow?'

'If you want.'

'You'll be rushed. That Morris Minor has to be collected from the spray shop. Someone from the new village is booked for a pre-MOT check, you might be able to postpone them. There's something else in the book I can't remember.'

'OK. You'll be all right, will you?'

'I'm taking a day out.' He tried to rediscover the hope that had bubbled, but it seemed elusive now. Funny to think that whilst he was dragging himself through the agonies of hell, losing his head in that appalling way, pestering the cops and almost everyone he could think of, Tess was out there somewhere, drawing lizards that tangoed.

Good job he'd changed the Caterham for a Mark II Jaguar. He wouldn't have fancied leaving the Caterham, with all the vulnerabilities of a convertible, in a London car park, because he'd decided to park at Finchley Central and go on by tube. She used to live in Finchley, it would be amazing if ...

No, she wouldn't be there, the flat was long sold. Hadn't he stopped that kind of clutching at straws? Like calling unannounced at Guy's Towcester home in vain hope. Lynette coldly amused, Guy at work at the bank which, amazingly enough, employed him as a financial adviser. 'Come and search,' Lynette invited, thin-lipped, flinging back the door. 'You're more than welcome to her if you can find her.'

And the one and only visit to Tess's parents, when James glowered and Mari kept lifting her palms. 'Why is she doing this? To us, I mean, to me? I can understand why she's doing it to you!' Diving up her sleeve for a tissue permanently at the ready for the easy tears. 'But why us? Have you really heard *nothing*?'

No, that kind of hopeless stupidity was behind him now.

Drizzle at the tube station as he waited for the underground that was, here, overground. Not busy, plenty of seats. Other passengers' rocking faces were reflected in the glass when they entered the tunnel, colours of hair, of skin. Shoppers, teenagers with personal stereos, a loud scruff in his twenties leering and making women uncomfortable. A woman with hair matted like a black doormat down her back staring into the darkness.

Was Tess back here? In London? He couldn't imagine her, somehow, turning her shoulders to pass so many strangers in the crowded streets. Where would she walk properly? Where could she let her hair whip out behind her and stride as she did along the bridleways around Middledip?

Yet, she had once.

When she was with Olly and before, this was where she'd lived. The flat in Finchley, he remembered her saying, was a converted house in a street of converted houses, under the railway bridge from the main road, pubs on each corner, and two rows of trees which heaved up the paving as they grew. In fact, she'd quite liked London, told him about sitting on the steps of the Alexandra Palace to watch a silver, city dawn, taxis still waiting on the hill.

She was adaptable.

King's Road. As he hadn't made an appointment, he had to wait outside her titchy office, rented from someone else's office space, for Kitty to return from a meeting. She was neither surprised to see him, nor welcoming.

She was almost as tall as he was and wore a floppy cinnamon suit, untidily. Her hair, streaked blonde, urchin cut and tucked behind her ears, didn't suit her Amazonian proportions. Piles of portfolios. Cabinets. Framed book jackets on the walls.

'Right.' She sat, indicated the chair across the teeming desk. She tidied aside two piles of paper to give her room to plonk down her elbows and clasp her hands, raising belligerent eyebrows, assessing him through direct grey eyes. 'Right.'

He smiled. He was used to achieving something with women with his smile, but Kitty's expression remained steely. He reminded her who he was, and she nodded. 'You must have an address for Tess,' he suggested pleasantly.

'I'm afraid I can't comment, Mr Rattenbury.' Leaving off his 'Arnott' was presumably to cut him down to size. 'I can't and won't discuss the personal life of one of my artists. Although I will tell you that I've already told Olly Gray that.'

His stomach departed like an express lift down a pit shaft. He had to force his lips to work. 'Olly's been here already?'

She nodded.

He stared. She stared back. 'Was that long ago?'

'A while.' She nodded again.

Oh God. Oh Christ. He'd been so stupid. Olly had thought of the Kitty connection ages ago, right away, perhaps. While Ratty had been circling madly trying to pick up the scent, Olly had followed the line straight here. 'But you didn't tell him where she was?'

'I'm not able to tell anyone anything.' This time she shook her head.

'You're her agent.'

'I'm both her agent and her friend and in neither capacity am I prepared to discuss her.'

He persevered, his voice strengthening as his heart steadied with the knowledge that Olly had made no progress through Kitty. 'Tess must be working?'

She looked steadily at him. Let her eyes go deliberately to the wall clock and then back to his face. 'Sorry.'

'Is she all right? Please?'

'Sorry.'

'Just ...'

'Sorry.'

He felt the last traces of hope soak out as if through the soles of his shoes. Stared blankly, through a window that needed washing, at a busy pigeon community picking and pecking around their encrusted colony. 'OK.' He felt so drained, so inert that he could have sat there forever, gazing through a streaky window at grey pigeons on a grey roof.

It took a great effort to drag his attention back to Kitty. 'OK. Thanks.' He began the huge climb to his feet.

Another thought slid into the greyness of his mind.

'Could you send a letter on for me?'

Her lids dropped slightly, guardedly. He thought her eyes held something – compassion maybe. But her voice was still neutral. 'Agreeing or refusing would indicate whether I hold an address, wouldn't it?'

He sat back down. Bent his brain. Think, think. 'OK.' He tried the smile again, just in case. 'If I write a note, would you hold it, *in the event* that you're ever in a position to pass it on?'

He watched her considering. Come on, come on, how can it hurt? Say yes!

She nodded suddenly. 'I don't see why not. I'll hold it on those terms. Here,' she tossed him a pad. 'Use that little table over there.'

Away from her desk, he noticed. She obviously didn't intend to leave him alone with her card index!

Chapter Twenty-Nine

Dear Tess,
Please get in touch. I've missed you. I love you. What we had was too good to ... Rip the page from the pad, screw it up, drop it in the brown plastic bin. No. He wasn't going to plead.

Tess,
Hope you're safe and well. The baby must be well on the way now and, naturally, I'm anxious to know ... Crap. Emotional, weak.

Tess,
There are things that must be sorted. I have a right to know the fate of my baby and have some input, financial and otherwise to its ... Businesslike and brutal. Perfect to keep her forever hiding.

Princess,
Madeline Gavanagh's baby has been proved not to be mine ... No, why should he tell her? So she'd feel her flight had been perfectly justified, could condescend to return now he'd sorted things out? *I hope you don't fall out of love with our child so easily.* Couldn't be more wrong! What the hell did he want to say? Head on left hand, tap the pen impatiently with the right. Begin again. *Don't you think this has gone on long enough? What do you think is going to happen to you if you come back to Middledip?* Rubbish. *I love you. I love you. I love you. I miss you. I thought our love was huge.*

He stared at the wall. Loosed the page gently from the pad, folded it and slid it into his pocket. Dug in the wastebasket and fished out everything he'd just tossed, cramming his pockets with the litter.

He handed Kitty her pad and pen, drearily. 'Thanks anyway,' he muttered like a browser to a shop assistant. 'I've decided not to bother.'

Her mobile phone sang.

Tess swung away from bride and groom lizards to pick up quickly. Kitty was the only holder of the new number and her new e-mail address. 'Your hyphenated boyfriend has just left.'

A sudden thumping in her head. Ratty had been in Kitty's office, in London. She could picture the office, picture him there.

'He was asking after you but I claimed confidentiality.'

Silence. Kitty waiting for a reaction. Tess not knowing how to react. 'Oh?' she mumbled, eventually. Then, as Kitty was obviously not intending to spout news, 'What did he want? Exactly?'

Shuffling of papers. Kitty's sigh. 'Information. Do I have an address, are you safe? Had I given information to Olly the Fink? He asked to leave a note for me to pass on if I could. I agreed.'

Gripping the receiver, she felt the beginnings of excitement. Relief. Joy! Were things going to work out? 'What does it say?'

A pause. 'Tess, I'm sorry. In the end he decided not to bother.'

She could've cried. 'Not to bother?'

'He gave it enough tries, used half my pad. Then gave up, stuffed all the attempts in his pocket too, so I can't even scavenge in my bin, though I'd love to! So. Thought I'd let you know.'

Tess spoke to stop her from breaking the connection. 'How did he seem?'

Kitty puffed a sigh. 'Pretty pissed off.'

End the call. Cross to the window. Gaze at similar houses across a road jammed with parked vehicles. Pretty pissed off. Could mean anything. Cross. Hurt. Fed up. Lonely. Disillusioned. Let down.

All of the above.

She rang Kitty back, suddenly hungry to hear another human voice in this silent, empty house. 'If he comes back,' she began eagerly. But then her resolve dissolved. 'Ring again, won't you?'

Kitty gave a tiny sigh. 'Of course.' Then, 'Tess, if he wants to communicate with you and you want to know what he has to say – don't you think it's time you talked to him?'

Despite feeling dismal all the way up the country, once he got home in the twilight he felt a sudden restless energy.

What a fucking waste of time.

What a waste of his life, rotting away here in Pennybun Cottage, like Lucasta had.

But he was no old lady discarded by love, he was Miles Arnott-Rattenbury, single, free, well funded! Life was out there waiting, so was his previously awesome social life, pubs and clubs, race meetings, concerts, a world of women. Days gone by, he'd had sufficient choice of them. He would again.

Shower, shave, cool blue shirt.

Fill the Jag up on the way to Bettsbrough. Pete? No, not fair, he was going to pull, big time, and Pete had Angel.

Jos? Too many questions, too much explaining.

Just himself then, wallet, car keys. Drive straight past The

Three Fishes, not thinking of Tess.

He chose a town centre pub where women in short skirts drank bottled beer, shots and alcopops. Easy enough to put himself about, test the water, meeting eyes, smiling, noting telltale increased vivacity as he drifted by. He added himself to someone's crowd and went on to the new Irish pub where the drink was Guinness. In the tremendous crush by the bar he let his arm rest behind a tall ash-blonde with hair past her shoulders and eyes outlined in vivid blue.

'We want to be there before 10.30,' she called into his ear, over the hubbub. 'Or we'll have to pay full entrance fee.'

He nodded, not needing to know where 'there' was. 'Just time for one more, OK?'

The club, when they got to it, was big and loud and filling up fast. He detached himself from the group, did a complete circuit, up and down changes of level, drinking the driver's allowance of one beer from the bottle, browsing.

The ash-blonde followed his progress with her gaze, pouting and giving a twinkling wave when he looked over. He held her in reserve. She was pretty, she was tall, but young and avid.

Another blonde in a short, shiny skirt blazed an interested look his way. Hmm, a possible.

Three together, already on a dance floor lit from below, one dumpy but with a nice smile, one ill at ease, one dancing as if everyone watched, making sure her chest was moving, tossing back well-kept hair and glancing about for talent. She met his eyes fearlessly. And smiled. A banker.

He finished his beer, got just ahead of the sudden influx as the pubs closed, bought a bottle of water. His eyes caught suddenly. Wow, that familiar *yes*!

The blondes seemed suddenly insipid, other dancers amateur as he watched dusky breasts bustle under a lace top over a full bra, dark hair gleam down a sinuously moving back above the curve of her bottom. Such smooth, coffee skin, how could such subtle colour be described as 'black'? Abandoning drink, he went into action.

Easy. Closer and closer until he matched her beat with his and within an hour she was laughing up at him beneath incredible lashes. Melting eyes, sensuous lips, beautiful white teeth. Mesmerising body touching his and filling his arms in the slow dances, breathtaking. Her name was Milly.

This was it! He was over Tess and back to the old life of serious fun. None of his talents had deserted him. He concentrated intensely on her, bought her drinks and asked her life story. And she became affectionate.

He drove her around the edges of Peterborough to her flat in a modern block, window frames stained in many colours, and parked the Jag under a lamp. Fingers crossed it would be OK. Up to the first floor, fingers linked with hers as she led him through a green-stained front door.

Back to the happy old routine: coffee on, jacket off. Music. Laughter. Expectation. Kisses, experimental and exploratory, becoming deep and arousing. Maybe, just maybe, he'd be able to leave in the morning with a smile on his face and some hope that he was getting over Tess.

Half an hour later he was sinking with her onto her bed, the quilted gold satin fabric chill on his naked back. Her nearly-black hair was beautiful, heavy and thick when he tangled his fingers in it. Just as good as strawberry blonde.

Luscious chocolate eyes were full of promise. Forget turquoise. Forget! *Forget*!

He kissed her neck where it met her shoulder. 'Where's the bathroom, um…?'

'*Milly*!' She frowned at him in mock reproof. 'Next room. Don't be long.' She stretched suggestively.

He kissed her nose. 'I won't.' Once in the bathroom he

took his mobile from his waistband and rang Pete. 'Extricate me,' he whispered.

He'd barely climbed back onto the gold quilt when his phone sang for his attention. 'Sorry, sorry, should've turned it off!' he apologised to her frown.

In his ear, Pete recited blearily, 'What am I supposed to be saying? The police are here, somebody's been trying to break into your house. And Angel says, don't wake us up to play silly phone games from bathrooms, you bastard!'

'What? Oh no! Really? Will I? OK, I will. Thanks, Pete.' He reached around his nearly bedmate for his shirt. 'This is *terrible*! I've got to go! Somebody's disturbed intruders at my place and the cops want to speak to me.' He hurried into his jacket. And then, seeing her woebegone expression, 'But I can have your number, can't I?' That would make her feel better. He watched her scribble on a piece torn from the corner of *Red* magazine and tucked it into his wallet. 'Really sorry!' Backing out, he apologised to her sulky expression and folded arms.

Then he was clattering down the stairs, turning down his collar. The Jag was safely where he had left it and he was on his way.

Once home, he awarded himself a whisky to take upstairs. Bedtime ritual: watch, small change, wallet. He threw away Milly's number. She wasn't his type, after all.

Apart from not being able to chase Tess from his thoughts, life went on. Some day, he told himself, he'd be able to shrug her into the past. For now he fixed cars, fetched cars, studied the small ads for bits and raked through autojumbles. Tried to regain the old satisfaction of running his business, of his name being known among classic devotees, of the E-Type fetching serious money.

He drank at the pub and ate Angel's glorious meals and

played with Toby and Jenna who'd stopped asking, 'Where's Tess?' Only Carola still asked, so he avoided Carola.

Occasional calls came from Guy or Mari or James still puzzled or hurt or annoyed. His parents' concern continued; Elisabeth had taken to dropping in at the garage for a cuppa, perching her neat self incongruously on the burst-open stool by the tool chest.

And he, the man who thought sex had been invented just for him, wasn't getting any.

Tess's heart bang-bang-banged and her throat clamped shut around her breath. There was someone down in the kitchen. She could hear man-sized footsteps. Now the sitting room! Was there time to get downstairs and out whilst he was in there? Slow steps back to the sitting-room door told her there wasn't.

Silently, fearfully, backing away from the stairs, she crossed the landing to the bathroom, perhaps the least likely place he'd look. Pushed the door to.

Heart hammering, she eased into the gap at the side of the airing cupboard and hid herself with the folds of the shower curtain. It might suffice, if he didn't put on the light.

What did he want? Her? Things from the house? What was lying around to give her away? Not much in the kitchen, nor the unfurnished sitting room that she hardly used.

His steps travelled upstairs, pausing on the landing, travelling on into the back bedroom. But no sound of a shutting door, no chance for her to creep past. Ages, it seemed, quivering against the cold, glossed cupboard, the roll of the bath edge digging into her leg, until the unnaturally quiet movements of the intruder stole back to the landing, stopped outside the workroom. She struggled to bring her breathing under control as she clenched shut her eyes, willed him, *go, go*.

And he did. The same measured footfall on each tread and down onto the quarry tiles. Then, finally, the blessed, welcome sound of the kitchen door opening and shutting.

Tess let out her breath. 'Thank God!' He hadn't found her. He'd gone without doing more than look around.

She slid past the clinging shower curtain, wiping sweating palms on her jumper. Fearfully, as if unable to quite believe she'd heard him leave, into the bedroom, to shut the door and light the lamp. Bare and tidy, just as she'd left it.

Relief. She'd live to fight another day. She went down to secure the kitchen door, thinking she'd have to get into the habit of being more careful about locking it. A good strong cup of tea would calm her, then she'd come back upstairs to read, listen to the radio, continue her solitary, silent existence since last time she visited the supermarket and spoke to the person on the checkout.

She turned the back door key, reached for the kettle.

And he was there.

Not safely out into the twilight as she'd supposed. But there. Leaning in the sitting-room doorway. Locked in with her.

A scream, it must be hers, a banged elbow as she leapt backwards, water spilling and splashing from the kettle in her hand.

Even as she madly computed the probabilities and possibilities of scrabbling for the back door key, turning it, opening the door and getting away from the expression in his eyes, she realised there was no real escape. He was a few leisurely strides away.

He straightened up and stepped silently nearer, close enough to touch. His eyes glittered and she was scared.

'Hullo, Princess,' he said. 'When did you get back?'

Chapter Thirty

His eyes pinned her, like a rabbit in the headlights. He broke the contact first, let his eyes travel over her. Size ten jeans where the bump should have been. 'No baby,' he observed neutrally.

She gulped, tried for normality. 'I'm going to have a cup of ...'

'No you're not. No baby?'

Her eyes shut. 'No baby,' she whispered. She shouldn't have come back. Or she should have gone straight to Pennybun and risked whatever reception waited. Not slunk back to Honeybun the way she had yesterday, squeezing the Freelander in the hut, hoping the shrubbery between the two cottages would hide her for just a few hours more until she'd screwed up the courage to face him. She opened her eyes at his silence, dared to look at his impassive face. 'There wasn't a baby after all.'

'You lost it?'

She shook her head. 'My period just arrived.' Tears crept out between her lashes.

'I don't suppose,' he mused, stepping forward so that she shuffled nervously back until the door handle jabbed her ribs, 'that you lifted a few too many boxes?'

Tears stilled in shock. 'That was nothing to do with it!'

'No?' His eyes, which used to be filled with love, now accused. '*What* were you doing just before your miscarriage?'

Heart flip. She gazed at the wall to avoid his eyes.

He answered himself. 'Carrying boxes! Running away. Something's wrong, Tess must pack up and go. And flush a baby!'

Her voice was hoarse, choked with disbelief. 'There was no baby this time!'

'How did you know? When you took your bold decision to clear out whilst I was safely out of the way, when you felt the only thing to do was scarper, when you stuffed your little world into boxes and loaded the Freelander, when you carried that monster computer monitor downstairs, did you think you were *being very sensible*?

'Tell me.' He moved forward, crowding without touching. 'Why Princess Tess couldn't just say, "I can't cope with your past, I'm leaving". Did you think I'd beat you up? Tie you to a stake?'

Tears raced each other down her cheeks, her chin, jumped for safety as she shook her head.

'But it didn't occur to you to simply tell me it was over?'

Another wild headshake, gagged by her throat muscles. This was awful, worse even than she'd imagined, because he was right! It had been blind reaction. So hurt, so angry that *he'd* been the bastard, left a relationship after unprotected sex without bothering to find out ... just like Olly. Fuelled with self-righteous indignation at his treachery, she'd run, fled. It wasn't until she stopped that she wondered why.

And he was accusing her of killing their baby in the process! 'I rang ... after. Dr Warrington said the test showed I wasn't pregnant after all.' She covered her face, the choking sobs burst out in an ugly volley at the memory, at the disappointment, and she shuffled towards him. She was so *sorry*! And oh, to feel the strength of his chest and arms!

But Ratty stepped back, leaving her marooned and foolish, drowning in her own tears.

His voice, when it came again, seemed distant. 'When Olly's child was conceived,' he asked, 'it wasn't rape, was it?'

Her sleeve was scratchy and non-absorbent when she struggled to use it to wipe her tears. She gasped, tried unsuccessfully to sniff. 'Of course not!' She shook her head.

His head levelled with hers and she looked down to hide the red, blotchy, swollen mess of her face. 'How *did* that baby happen? Maybe you got carried away? Got unlucky?'

Put like that, there was a startling resemblance to his own scenario.

'Get out of the way, I want to leave,' he said.

'Tess's back.'

'Shit!' Pete banged his head on a raised bonnet. Rubbing the sore spot, he stared, astonished. 'When?'

'I called at Honeybun last night to check everything was OK. There she was.'

Pete reconnected a battery, careful not to over-tighten on the soft terminals, shook back his hair. 'So, everything's going to be all right?'

'No.'

'Getting back together?'

'No.'

'Don't you want?'

'No.'

'What about the baby?'

'There wasn't one.'

He looked away from Pete's shocked eyes. Pete had children, knew how loving them felt. Ratty's baby may not have really existed but he hadn't known that and had still to grieve. Feel aggrieved. For a stupid moment his eyes boiled. He blinked.

Only the relationship debris remained. He must get used to seeing but not loving her. Realise that they wouldn't be falling into bed together; he wouldn't revel in her body, the intimacy she loved. This horrible, hollow, missing-her feeling would continue to gape in his chest.

Her furniture would have to travel from Pennybun to Honeybun, but the finances were simple. Tess had kept herself distressingly separate.

A colossal lot of bridges had to be rebuilt.

Anxious at the prospect of a welter of problems, to settle her nerves Tess made a list, Lucasta-style. *To Face – village shop, the pub*. Oh, ouch, too horrible to contemplate, all those people; go back to that one later. *Angel, Pete, Jos, Ratty*. God he'd been so angry! How could she have thought for even a microsecond he'd want her back? But then why had he been looking for her?

She touched her abdomen and wished that she had been pregnant; would everything have been different if she'd come back swollen and heavy with their child?

She bit her pencil and watched the trees tossing in the lane. A walk beckoned. But … meeting people? Milk was needed, bread, fruit, coffee, supplies were dwindling. She pictured Gwen and Julie's keen expressions, the avid 'Are you back?' and 'Where've you been?' if she called at the village shop – opposite the garage for God's sake! Maybe Tesco at Bettsbrough would be easier.

Wasn't this where she came in?

Wasn't this just how it'd been, the square peg in the village's round hole, avoiding people in case they spoke to her? Or in case they didn't? She wasn't going there again.

Actually, it wasn't at all as she'd expected.

Gwen said, 'Hello, stranger,' and rang up the purchases. Julie the assistant just carried on wiping tins. Flattening, really. Flattening.

When she emerged, clutching two blue-striped carriers, she jumped to see Ratty wiping something with an oily rag, obviously waiting for her. Polishing whatever it was, cut-away sleeves revealing his tattoos moving over his muscles, he stepped nearer.

'What are you doing this evening?'

A heart trip, a mushroom of joy like a nuclear cloud. It would be OK! He'd blown off steam and now they'd be able to get on with patching things up! She beamed. 'Nothing, if you're asking.'

His eyes shifted from her plaited hair to her face. 'Can you come and sort out your gear and leave your key? About eight?'

Oh ... Falling without a parachute. Stomach leaping to her mouth. 'Well, yes, I suppose –'

'Let's get it over with.'

'OK, I'll –' But there was just his back as, buffing whatever the hell bit of car it was, he left her standing.

So. Little sofa and chairs back up the lane to Honeybun, a couple of tables, a cabinet. Ratty offered his key to Honeybun and waited stoically whilst she fumbled and fluffed unwinding the Pennybun key from her ring. The door shut behind him as he left.

She flung herself on the bandy little sofa, which somehow held the scent of Ratty, too miserable for tears. She felt as if a hole had been blown in her chest and the wind that blew through her was very cold.

Her status in the village changed.

Ratty had withdrawn his – what? His patronage? Stamp of approval?

It felt collusive, as if the residents of the village were silently ganging up on her. Except they weren't, because nobody was paying her much attention at all. Passing the garage, Pete and Jos would say 'Hi!' neutrally, Ratty would glance and nod. And they'd all carry on diligently with their stupid cars.

But worst of all, and what for some reason she hadn't anticipated, was Angel, with whom there seemed to be no going back.

Her greeting, when Tess tapped on her door, was a tepid, 'Wondered when you'd show.' But there was no picking up where they'd left off, no tearful hug and matey confession. Just the last echo of the old affection, heavily coloured by Angel's disappointment. 'Were you expecting to be welcomed with open arms? We were supposed to be friends! You left without telling me, and hurt Ratty.'

'It wasn't calculated.' She was miserable with guilt.

'Maybe not, but you can't be so ... arbitrary! If you were going to end the relationship over a bit of bad news from the CSA, you shouldn't pick the most hurtful, misery-making way of doing it and expect us to lump it.' She reached into the cupboard for flour, shaking back her fair hair, a shorter, scraggy bob. 'I thought I understood you. But this? Tell me, truthfully, why did you have to come back in such a sneaky way?'

Tess fiddled with her ponytail. 'I was gearing myself up for the confrontation.'

Angle sniffed. 'So you couldn't just turn up at Pennybun and tell Ratty you were alive and well and living next door, right?'

Tess said, unconvincingly, 'I was going to.'

'Why couldn't you ring? If he'd bellowed or whatever it is he does that makes you totally unable to face him, you could've put the phone down.'

Tess heard herself go all croaky. 'And hear his voice? Angel ...' She struggled for control, had to get up and get herself a glass of water before finishing inadequately, 'I missed him.'

Adding margarine to her mixing bowl, Angel frowned. 'So why didn't you stay away? Start over somewhere else?'

What? Never see Ratty again, never feel the heat of his body, the strength in his hands? Tess gulped more water, stating contradictorily, 'I had to see him.'

A pause. Angel's hands worked methodically at her baking, but the eyes she fixed on Tess were narrow and accusing. 'You wanted it the easy way. You wanted him to discover you, throw his arms around you and love you better. No effort required on your part.'

Tess simply couldn't answer.

Angel dropped her eyes to her work. 'What do your parents think?'

She felt her face heat up. 'I haven't, um ... I'll ring them.'

Angel thumped her pastry down, whistling in scandalised admiration. 'My God, you're wonderful! All the upset you caused, have you any idea? Your poor mother has been expecting your body to be recovered from a ditch, and *you haven't even told her you're back?*'

'I'll phone! They know that I need to get away from things, sometimes!'

'*For months?* And why phone? Why not break the habit of a lifetime and face them? Suffer their recriminations, put up with the shit. Go for it!'

'My mother will be in fits,' she sulked.

'Yes, won't she? And your dad will be insufferable and say why didn't you stay with Olly? And I'm beginning to wonder the same thing – perhaps you two deserve one another. And while you're at it you could face Lester and Elisabeth. They've had a terrible time with Ratty!'

She didn't, as it happened, have to, because the Arnott-Rattenburys pretty soon faced her, knocking at her kitchen door and stepping in for a brusque visit. 'Just to clear the air, rather than avoid each other,' said Lester, grim-faced, refusing a flustered offer of coffee.

Elisabeth's attractive smile was absent. 'It's a shame you

and Miles have to live in such proximity. But as it seems you're going to, we might as well be civil.' As they left, she remarked, 'Good job about the baby.'

Tess trailed upstairs, heart bruised. Coming back, far from solving everything, had left her in a place she hadn't bargained for.

In the wrong.

She'd gone away. Left Ratty going bananas. Failed to cope with the facts of life, that sex causes babies and accidents happen. Which was, as it had been bluntly pointed out, exactly what had happened between her and Olly. Unprotected sex to which she hadn't objected, at the time.

Landmines she'd laid kept blowing up under her feet.

And now she couldn't expect to be welcomed back by her friends with their arms open, nor to rekindle the love between her and Ratty.

Although, well, yes, actually, she *had* kind of expected both those things.

She drove down to see James and Mari through an evening of ragged apricot and pink clouds flung across the sky.

Her mother dropped a hot plate and screamed when Tess walked into the kitchen. *'Tess!'*

Tess flushed. 'Sorry I haven't ...'

'Therese!' Her father actually ran downstairs at Mari's scream, ashen-faced and ludicrously hopeful.

To Tess's acute discomfort and guilt, James gently placed his arms around her, drew the still-stunned Mari into the circle and they all stood there clutching each other like American kids doing a 'group hug' thing on telly. She almost died when she realised that the tears plopping down onto all their clothes originated with James.

And if she'd earned a quid for each of their questions

after the initial touching moment, she could have taken six months off on the proceeds.

Mari kicked off, holding Tess's arm as if she might disintegrate. 'Why didn't you just send us a card, for God's sake? Did you have to put us through this? Where have you been for so long? Have you been all right? Did you lose another baby?'

'I needed space,' Tess muttered. 'Sorry I didn't get in touch but I didn't feel like speaking to anyone. It was a false alarm with the baby.'

Then she was dancing back in shock as James suddenly lunged forward and roared in her face, 'For God's sake have you *any* idea what we've been going through? Couldn't you have just phoned us *once*?'

And then she sat there in cold horror while Mari sank down at the kitchen table and, head in arms, gave way to sobs, and James knelt beside her, saying, 'Shush,' and, 'She's back, she's back, she's OK!'

Looking up at Tess, suddenly he was older. 'One of us must telephone young Rattenbury. He's been out of his head.'

The blush that crackled into Tess's face was like an inferno. 'I've been in touch,' she said, shortly. Then she found herself muttering, 'Sorry, I'm sorry' contritely, as she realised that life had not been fun for her parents whilst she hid herself away.

At the end of two hours of joy and recrimination and sticking up for herself, Tess climbed back into the Freelander.

'*Please* keep in touch.' Mari hesitated. 'Are you sure you'll be OK in Middledip? So near to … him?'

'It'll be fine,' Tess declared touchily. 'I made a mess of everything, but it's my mess and I'll sort it!'

Her phone was ringing when she got home. James had

wasted no time in passing on the good news to Olly. 'You really piss me off, you do. You could've let me know you were OK.'

'I suppose I could.'

'Are you and Caveman back together?'

She caught her breath on a jab of pain. 'No.'

'Good.' He put the phone down.

It rang again a minute later. 'When I'm not quite so pissed off with you, how about dinner?'

Dinner with Olly? She could. Odd, but Olly now seemed to represent safety and familiarity; if she went out with him, it would be a break from the hostility and accusation from everyone else. But he would still be Olly. 'Thanks,' she said. 'But no.'

Later, just as she was trudging up to bed, it was Guy's turn to phone. He, at least, seemed to feel no need to scold her. 'I said you'd show up! I told Uncle James you weren't doing it on purpose, you just don't always think of other people.'

She winced. 'It must run in the family.'

'Good one! And Ratty's kicked you out of bed, has he?'

She felt tears queue up in her throat and spill out of her eyes.

Middledip's pathways and lanes were still there for her to stride, watching the countryside, the men in the fields and toy-like machinery.

Her work was still there to bury her, her workroom with her paints and pastels, pencils and ink. Something to take over from the lizards must be dreamt up, the brief for her new commission read through. She stuck the old sketch of lizard-man Farny – Ratty so grim and sexy – underneath the choked heart on the wall, defiantly. Sod them all, no one was likely to see it.

And, happily, there were the kids. Toby and Jenna soon warmed to her again, eager-eyed whenever she appeared. Toby was ready for school in September and Jenna for playgroup. Despite the coolness between her and Angel, she still volunteered to entertain the kids whilst Angel did someone's hair, still went in smelling of Dior and left smelling of buttery toast.

The first time she offered to help, timid and tentative, Angel stared. 'You don't have to.'

'But I want to!'

So it was permitted, as a daytime thing if Ratty was at work. Because, evenings, it went without saying Angel and Pete had to choose between her and Ratty. And they chose Ratty.

Even her offer of babysitting one evening when Angel's regular girl was busy, was treated gingerly.

'I didn't want to ask you.' Angel folded mouse-strewn pyjamas.

'Don't you trust me any more?'

Angel's eyes confronted hers. 'It's not a matter of trust, it's awkwardness. We're going out with Jos, Miranda, Ratty and "partner". D'you see?'

In the sofa, an arm around each child and a book across her knees, Tess shook her hair forward. It took several breaths to stay a sudden giddiness. 'I hadn't thought of that,' she admitted unsteadily. 'How stupid of me. How *stupid*!'

But she still agreed to babysit because she loved the kids, bath time, the bedtime story, the cuddles. They loved her – a rare thing these days. Angel assured her that, unlike the days of The Great Franca Plan, Ratty's girlfriend would not be paraded under the babysitter's nose.

'But, Tess, it's not a repeat performance of the Franca thing. It's a date, like it always was. Ratty's hitting on someone. It's not an attempt to make you jealous. The days when Ratty would scheme to make the world what you wanted are over.'

Ow-ow-ouch. 'OK. Got it.' Did she sound breezy? She meant to sound breezy.

'I'll understand if you don't want to sit. I'll wait until Kelly from the village is free.'

'Don't worry,' she declared, staunchly, falsely. 'I'll cope.'

But, in Angel's pretty, comfortable home, the children asleep upstairs, she was overcome with memories of the days when she would have been glued to Ratty's side while he played with a strand of her hair and called her Princess.

The worst thing about staying in Middledip was Ratty.

But she was going to stay, just because she wanted to prove that she could do it.

Though it meant constant toothache in her chest, watching him pass her house, seeing his set face through folded-back garage doors. Exactly as when she first came to Middledip. Smiles for everyone else, wary tolerance for her when their paths crossed.

The only person who called on her as friendly as ever with her charity envelope, was Carola. 'Funnily enough,' she said, plonking herself down. 'I'm collecting for women seeking refuge. I know you'll give generously!' She grinned.

Tess accepted the irony and delved in her purse, relieved that someone mentioned her antics without condemnation. 'Everyone's so damning, Carola. What can I do?'

'Sit it out, they'll forget. Mind, I don't suppose anything will wash with Ratty now, will it? Bringing a man like him to your side once is an achievement. Twice? Impossible. I'm having a coffee morning on Tuesday to raise more money for the refugees, can you come?'

'No. Well,' she corrected herself, thinking about the honesty everyone seemed to want from her, 'I can but I don't want to!'

The last bastion was the pub. The chattery, beery warmth.

Right, a test. Walk in and buy a drink, say hello, and if there was no welcome, well fine, she'd drink alone. Scary, but it had to be regarded as a challenge rather than a problem.

It was warm, smoky, the cosy groups were made up mainly of men. Ratty and Jos were slouched in the seat just by the door. Well, they just would be. She skidded to a halt. Her feet almost acted independently to spin and rush her back out but she got a grip. She knew her colour was up, but coughed and said, 'Hi.'

Then she saw Lester in a further corner and sent him a small smile. He nodded before his eyes flickered to his son.

A sudden hush as she approached the bar and Tubb slunk forward to serve her himself. 'Where the hell've you been, then?'

'Working away.'

He laughed. 'Is that what you call it?' With a sneer that showed his sharky, backward-slanting teeth, he nodded in Ratty's direction. 'Forget to tell him, did you?'

Cutting him off, she snapped loudly, 'What do you have to do to get a drink in this pub?' The drink arrived in silence, a frosted half-pint of lager. Why hadn't she ordered wine? She could've drunk it more quickly. She gritted her teeth and stuck it out until her drink was gone. Several people managed a hello. When she left, both Ratty and Jos nodded goodbye.

Back down Main Road she pondered what it was she'd just seen in Ratty's expression, something that had lately been missing. Respect, maybe.

Chapter Thirty-One

In the lee of the Freelander, accepting its shelter from the blustering wind, Tess watched the water hurrying along the deep drainage ditch at the roadside. Beyond, the Fens unrolled themselves in a grid-work of fields and hedges, a pastiche of greens, browns and golds marred by steel pylons marching along with their nasty little arms out. A bridge crossed a dyke in the distance.

Gulls, wings spread and bills gaping, formed a chaotic wake behind a methodically ploughing tractor. What could instil such greedy urgency? Seed? Fishy fertiliser?

Though she'd been brought up with a living carpet of farmland around her, Tess had never learnt much about it. Nothing more than the basic facts, anyway: oilseed rape makes fields brilliant yellow, other crops ripen green-to-gold. Tractors and combines are out until ten at night during the harvest. Silage stinks and so do cows. Bulls are dangerous. Farmers' sons usually have money and a car.

'In trouble?'

She whipped round, holding her hair back. The wrecker had pulled up facing the Freelander and Ratty was leaning out of the window.

'Car trouble?' he asked again at her astounded silence.

Mind racing, she nodded. He'd get out. If he hitched up her vehicle she'd get a ride in the cab of the breakdown truck. With him. 'Completely dead,' she sighed. 'Any chance of a tow?'

Jumping out, rolling on the top part of his overalls from around his waist, he opened her door. 'Try it.'

Hell. Impassive face, strong, stubbled chin, bright eyes.

The whorl of hair in the hollow of his throat, the tattoos where his sleeves ought to be. She swallowed, surfing such a breaking wave of wanting and longing that she could hardly think straight. 'Sorry?'

'Try and start her again.'

She bit her lip. It would start, of course; she'd only stopped to look at the scenery. Then he'd shrug, 'Bring her in sometime and I'll check her out.' Climb into the cab alone and proceed with whatever errand she'd interrupted. No ride in the wrecker for her.

'It won't start.'

'Try it,' he repeated impatiently.

'It won't start,' she declared defiantly. Snatching her keys out of her pocket she hurled them into the bustling water of the drainage ditch and watched the bright green algae close up as if the keys had never passed through. 'See?'

He looked from her to the water, and back, frowning horribly, with the once-familiar air of trying to weigh her up. 'Have you gone quite mad?'

A big shrug and she stuffed belligerent hands into her pockets and waited to see what he'd do, certain he wouldn't abandon her. 'How about a tow home?' she suggested again.

Gazing into the drainage ditch, he seemed hypnotised by the scurrying water. 'Unfortunately,' he said at last, 'I'm on my way to fetch a car. You'll have to ring someone to ferry you. Or,' he offered, tepidly, 'tag along. Got to get this car so it's the round trip or nothing.'

'Round trip, I suppose.' She left the Freelander unlocked, waltzing ahead of him to the wrecker, skipping up into the cab, moving a leather holdall from the seat and into the space behind. And, as he buckled himself in, she dared, 'Thanks for stopping.'

The radio came on with the ignition. He grunted, turned

305

the truck, and they pulled away towards Peterborough, past piebald ponies grazing a scrappy paddock of yellow weeds, thistles and rusty sorrel and a farmhouse huddled behind a tree windbreak.

She gave him ten minutes to get used to being put upon. 'How are things?' she began tentatively.

'OK.'

'Plenty of work?'

'Yep.'

He didn't ask, but she told him about her latest commission. He nodded in between checking mirrors and waving faster vehicles past, changing gear, watching the traffic.

They were safely on the A1(M) before he asked roughly, as if he couldn't hold the question back, 'Where did you go?'

No point in pretending she didn't know what he meant. Fresh sweat sprang into her palms. She cleared her throat. 'Northampton. Hotel then a rented terrace.'

His fingers tapped thoughtfully. 'Why Northampton?'

'It was handy.'

He nodded as if at a perfectly sensible reply and began singing along with the radio under his breath. A new silence lengthened. Her breathing caught at the thought of how she must break it. But break it she must, or be condemned forever to this distant excuse for a relationship.

'Ratty ... I'm very sorry. I'm sorry I left the way I did, and I'm just, just *slaughtered* there was no – baby. Really.' Her voice wobbled and she coughed twice. Stole a glance, was unnerved when their gazes coincided. 'You're right. I shouldn't have leapt to the moral high ground. And I shouldn't have left without telling you. Or at all.'

If her soul baring had softened him at all, he hid it well. He listened and nodded, and when she'd finished, responded surprisingly gently. 'It's all water under the bridge now.'

That wasn't right! Her imagination had obligingly supplied her with pictures of him reacting with joy to such repentance, letting his emotions spill, admitting he still loved her. But, no, he just kept his hands on the wheel, watching the traffic, checking his mirrors.

Her stomach sank. For the millionth time, why hadn't she found some other way of coping with his paternity of the little boy? Jason. And what was Jason like? Did he have dark curly hair and blue eyes? Would he grow to be his own man with his own ways? What was his mother like, was Ratty in contact?

But when courage was the currency, she'd soon overspent. She couldn't ask.

Early evening. White headlights, red tail lights, blue dusk. Tess stretched, glad Ratty had finally swung the wrecker into a motel car park. She could kill for a cup of tea and a plate of chips. 'Where on earth is the car you're fetching?'

Ratty pulled the leather holdall out from behind her seat and locked the doors. 'Brighton.'

'*Brighton*?' She scurried to catch up with him as he strolled to Reception. 'That's miles!'

'Yes, it's an overnighter. There's a foyer shop here, I think, you'll be able to buy a toothbrush.'

'Godsake! You didn't say we were going to *Brighton*!'

'You should've asked, if you were fussy. But your options looked pretty limited to me.'

She stumped off to the shop while he booked them separate rooms.

He handed her the punched card bearing her room number. 'I'm going to crash out for an hour or two. I'll knock on your door eightish, we'll eat.' He walked her to the door by his, pointed out, ironically, 'Next door neighbours!'

It was OK, the room, for a separate room. A little shower, a double bed with the bedspread tucked under and around the pillows, as only ever seen in motels, two armchairs, a kettle with coffee sachets, a TV. After all the practice, she shouldn't even notice when she was by herself, let alone feel lonely.

The usual free shampoos and gels made her spend a long time in the shower. She untangled her hair as best she could with the inadequate brush from the shop's travel pack, blew it dry with the wall dryer, brushed it again and dressed. Oh, for terrific clothes and brilliant make-up and mind-blowing perfume so that she could knock Ratty's eyes out! But, she supposed, dejectedly, she might just as well be in khakis and a shirt, rather ordinary, for all the reaction she had been getting.

Still only 6.47 p.m. She watched some television. 7.14. Hopped channels. Played with the satellite stations and got lost in the radio channels. 7.37.

Checking her reflection, she smoothed her eyebrows. Then studied her hands and tried all her rings on different fingers. 7.55 – nearly 'eightish'!

Except that Ratty didn't knock on the door until 8.29, by which time she'd stuck her head out to look about six times and brushed her hair another twice.

In a clean shirt, hair still damp, he looked fresh and self-possessed. 'Let's get off the motorway and find a pub.'

He found one ten minutes away with a very brightly coloured carpet and a jukebox. They ate pizza and drank beer, made stilted conversation about Angel and Pete and the kids and how Jos seemed to have moved Miranda in but was too shy to say so.

Ratty was pleasant, but not friendly. There were no sexy

grins to make her feel like the only woman in the room. On the contrary, she caught him twice noticing the talent and noticed three women noticing him.

To gain his attention, she told him that Lester and Elisabeth had been to see her. He knew. And she'd seen her own parents who were relieved and furious and exasperated. He could imagine. Olly had told her she pissed him off. How outrageous. Even Guy had said she ought to get a hold of herself and grow up. That was rich. And Guy and Lynette wanted to start a family. An unlikely plan.

By the time they returned to the motel, she'd talked herself out and he was just as polite and impassive as he had been since finding her at the roadside.

She hesitated outside her room.

He walked straight past. 'Goodnight.'

Chapter Thirty-Two

Here she was again. Firmly escorted to her separate room, and dumped.

Bedtime. Bathroom, hairbrush, she sat up in bed, brushing absently. He was right behind that wall, doing his own well-remembered bedtime stuff. Watch off, shoes kicked under the bed, teeth brushed with rapid efficiency.

He didn't want her back.

Reality slapped her. He didn't want her back. Here they were with all the ingredients for joyous reconciliation and he was treating her with courteous reserve. God, he really didn't want her or he would've engineered it: a nightcap in her room, a late film in his.

She tapped the hairbrush, thinking, remembering Elisabeth's contention that Ratty believed in making things happen. If he wasn't prepared to make *this* happen, then what? She smiled nervously at her reflection.

Then she'd have to!

Maybe bravery, or rather bravado, would win him.

With no choice of clothes, she wriggled into the undies she'd bought in the foyer, boring cotton but clean and her long shirt all crinkled at the bottom. Shivering on her nerves she thrust her arms into her jacket, remembering to stuff her key card in the pocket. One last fluffing of her hair – he loved her hair – and she marched into battle.

He answered the door in only trousers, raised his eyebrows at her shirt-cum-very-mini-dress and let her in, shutting the door behind her. Said nothing.

Smiling felt stiff and peculiar. 'I, um.' She looked past

him, at his shirt over the chair, *Classic Car* magazine on the bed, darted a glance back to his face.

He shifted impatiently on bare feet. 'What's up? Problem with your room?'

'Sort of, yes.' Deep breath. 'I don't want to sleep there.' Licking her lips, she stuffed her hands in her pockets, withdrew them, shifting on bare feet. 'I want to sleep here.'

The sentence rang around her head, echoed as she watched expressions ripple across his face. Surprise, curiosity.

Then – unmistakably – fury, blazing in his eyes.

She flinched. This was why she wasn't that good at confrontation! Heart thumping, she studied his naked chest and shoulders, his jawline. Oh for the safety and pleasure of being embraced against that torso, revelling in his heat and strength!

Ignoring his murderous expression, she closed her eyes and reached for him.

And Ratty went berserk.

'*What the fucking hell do you think you're doing?*' He thrust her hands away and lowered his voice to a hiss. 'Barging in and demanding to sleep here? Aren't you the one who ran away and left me half-demented, not knowing if you were alive, even? And now you just say sorry and expect I'll forgive the lot?'

She recoiled, wavering, but forced herself to stand firm and meet his eyes. 'But I love you! I still want ... Don't you love me any more?' She couldn't seem to control her hands; they lifted, supplicating, and fluttered towards him again.

He grabbed her arms hard. 'Do you think I've got no feelings?' His fingers were inflexible, his eyes frightening as they blazed at her. 'You tell me you're pregnant then you abandon me! It was a false alarm – but you don't tell me. I was merely the father!' His strong fingers dug into the complaining muscle of her arms. 'Do women seriously think they can just bring us into play when it suits? You didn't *tell* me!'

He let go of her abruptly.

She teetered, as if only his hands had been keeping her upright, tears burning in her eyes. 'I'm sorry!'

He seemed in no mood for apologies. 'You came back and let me find out accidentally! You're hopeless,' he spat, bitterly. 'Hopeless, helpless, useless. When are you going to learn to deal with life properly?'

She rubbed her arms, wincing at his contempt as he turned away.

It was her chance to escape, but she doubted her legs would take her. Even if she wanted to. Which she didn't. Anger was beginning to uncoil in her stomach.

'Oh, I'm sick of saying how sorry I am,' she snapped. 'But you told me you had a son, one you'd never made the least effort to take responsibility for! I freaked out, OK? I'm sorry if the mighty Arnott-Rattenburys deal with crap like that better than I do! I thought I was pregnant and I reacted badly.

'Yes, if you want, you could say I ran away. But I *did* come back and try and mend fences and I *did* come here tonight and even suggest –'

He swung back, one arm shooting around her, his other hand capturing her head, snatching her to him, the length of her body crushed bruisingly against his. 'Is that all you came for? Fine!' His hands became callous and irresistible, pushing her jacket down her arms, wrenching her shirt up, bending her arms to pull the sleeves off, rough, careless.

'If you're here to drop your knickers, let's do it! You always were good value in bed.' His hands yanked her briefs down, his hard mouth pounced on hers, stifling her protests.

312

It was awful, it was terrible! Swooped off her feet she crashed to the bed, knocked breathless as he landed half on top of her, pinning her, dragging his jeans off with furious movements. 'I can oblige, if this is what you want!'

No, it wasn't right, it wasn't what she wanted. He was taking, there was no love in it and she didn't have the strength –

... Oh, just let him.

Suddenly, she felt powerless, drained.

This wasn't Ratty, this spiteful, vengeful, punishing stranger. This was some monster she'd created. A monster that was going to have sex with her as a primitive act of reprisal.

'She asked for it,' he would be justified in saying. Nobody had ever asked for it more than she just had. Literally, tramped into his room and asked for it.

Let it happen, let it happen. It would soon be over. Afterwards she could retreat to her separate room, make her way back to Peterborough by public transport. She'd think again about staying in Middledip. But if she left, she'd do it in her own time, with purpose and dignity. Appoint an estate agent and choose somewhere rather than accept the first place she stumbled across. The Outer Hebrides sounded good, a nice long way from this room of smashed dreams and harsh comeuppance.

He was naked before she felt him pause. She could feel his breath on her clenched face. Her heart, which she'd thought had taken all the punishment it could, folded up with one huge, wretched squeeze as his hand lifted and she cringed.

But, when they touched her, the fingers were gentle again, peeling sticky hair back from her face. Smoothing. Soothing.

He sank onto his back, breath grating in his throat,

pulled her sad head onto his shoulder. 'I'm such a terrible shit!' He pulled a sheet over their bodies.

Tess listened to her own breath slowing, the madness, the crisis, slowly passing. Relief, relief. She was left ridiculous with her shirt around her neck and her knickers at her knees. Cautiously, she tried to wriggle back into her clothing.

His hand stayed her, sliding underneath the sheet to rest familiarly on her naked hip.

Quietly, bleak but unthreatening, he told her how enraged he'd been when she left. 'I wrecked the house. The windows, the furniture, even your grandmother's glasses and the pictures of McLaren and Lucasta.'

Fresh guilt humbled her. 'I'm sorry,' she whispered for the hundredth time.

He shushed her. 'No excuses. It was self-indulgent lack of control. I regret that as much as what I let you think I was going to do a minute ago. Nothing like that will ever happen again, I promise you.

'And then there's Jason.'

The silence went on so long that she lifted her head and flicked a glance under spiky lashes. 'Have you seen him?' Her voice was throaty from tears. 'Or doesn't his mother want you to?'

'I haven't seen him.' Something in his voice. Some ... regret? The hand on her hip moved upward and the thumb began absently to stroke her lower ribs. 'He's not my child.'

Thud. Then her heart began to race. 'Not?' she croaked.

'No. DNA testing proved it.'

'But she claimed you as the father?'

'I was the most likely candidate. But she had a ding-dong with someone else at the same time, he's not mine. I suppose she had to do the CSA thing again with whoever's second on her list.' He sighed. 'Christ, the game's weighted against the man. She tells me I've got a child, and she says, "Let's wait for the result of the paternity tests before you see him". Then he's not mine, and she says, "Sorry if I caused you any trouble"!' His fingers ceased to stroke, just rested on her ribs as they must've done a hundred times. She felt a fairy ring of goosebumps rise around his hand.

'All for nothing.' She shuffled to fit the lines of her leg more comfortably against his. Nothing. The whole, unbelievable mess had been for nothing. Love beyond anything, thrown away. For nothing. A nothing which had brought them to this hideous physical fight here in a motel room near the M25. Bedspread scratchy; half naked; relationship in shards.

And now she had to extricate herself. To do him the courtesy of leaving him to his justifiable brooding. To face a realistic future with him as a neighbour or, in time, maybe a friend, forgetting what could've been.

Tentatively, she crept her arms into the sleeves of the shirt ridged absurdly around her neck, to ease her underwear back to its proper place, ridiculous and undignified.

Just when she thought she'd achieved some haphazard semblance of decency and was rehearsing, 'This was a mistake and I'll go now,' he turned his head.

'Don't go.'

Don't go? Her heart tripped up.

He sighed and tightened his arms, claiming back the inches she'd withdrawn. 'Shit, Princess, there's no car to fetch from Brighton. I was on my way home when I saw you.'

Funny that her heartbeat should increase to deafening proportions when she seemed to have stopped breathing altogether. He levered himself up above her, the darkness of his hair bobbing in ringlets against thick eyebrows. A naked leg slid its way between hers and sent shock waves up the middle.

315

The expression in his eyes softened. 'I want you,' he whispered, dropping a tiny kiss on her face. 'I always want you more than I've ever wanted anyone. Or will ever.' His lips trailed along her jawline. 'When you left I went mad. I wanted to kill you for your unfairness. I wanted bloody revenge for the pain. But through all that, even on my worst, spiteful, days' – he let his fingertips drift over the sensitiveness of her belly, carrying the by now well-travelled fabric of her shirt up again – 'I'd indulge myself with wild fantasies of making love to you again, Princess. You.' His hand – iron, minutes ago – found her breast with velvet touch. His breath hissed in between his teeth.

She clutched him fiercely. He still wanted her! 'I love you! I've never stopped. And I've missed you so much!' In a moment she was wriggling smartly back out of her shirt, pressing eager breasts against the hot breadth of his chest.

With a groan and a compulsive movement, he finally reacted as she knew she could make him. 'You gorgeous, sexy woman!' His hard, scalding body weight pinned her, trapped her, felt delicious. 'Christ, I want you!'

His head dropped to her breast and her heart hammered. His lips travelled the upward length of her throat, the ticklish crook of her neck, *that* place below her ear lobe. And she knew her hands were clasping his back frantically as her mouth awaited his soft and considerate lips, hips lifting in invitation. Never had she felt quite so heated, so sensitive, so ready for him.

'Love me,' she suggested, grinding her pelvis against him, abruptly aware of her own desperation to end the long months without his body, uncaring whether he thought her overwhelming or demanding or impatient. 'Love me!'

He bit her neck, lifted himself above her. 'Of course I love you!'

Epilogue

He parked the wrecker and strolled across his forecourt and into his garage, where Pete was busy at the back of yet another VW Beetle.

After the first flash of relief, Pete shook his head and complained, 'You don't know where I can get a good mechanic, do you? Short-handed today, I had to send Jos to pick up Graham's Lotus.' He selected one of the array of spanners arranged about his feet.

Ratty grinned. 'I've been busy. Can you manage if I take a few days off?'

Pete raised his eyebrows as he worked. 'Anyone I know?'

Ratty sank his chin on his fist and muttered, 'Tess.'

Pete's spanner clanged to the concrete floor. 'Did you say Tess? How the hell did that happen?'

Ratty accepted a punch to his upper arm with a sheepish grin, wincing, and decided to pay Pete the compliment of the truth. 'On my way back, yesterday, she was standing at the side of the road with the Freelander. She threw her keys into a ditch so I'd tow her home. I pretended I had a car to pick up from Brighton and that it was an overnighter, got rooms in a motel.

'I gave her the cold shoulder. She came to my room in knickers and shirt and asked to sleep with me. I tried to beat her off, and we had a fight. She won me round.'

'All right, all right!' Pete pretended to be huffed. 'You don't have to make things up. I suppose some things are too private to be shared. So, now you're going to spend the week in bed?'

'That's about it.' Ratty laughed.

'Angel will be tickled to death, anyway. Let us know when you've taken the *Do not disturb* sign off the door.'

'I'll be in touch. We will be, I mean.'

Back towards Pennybun in the last of the slanting sunshine, Ratty let his mind return to Tess and last night, as they'd rumbled back up the motorway, encased in the wrecker's comfortable familiar road noise. 'We won't rush things this time,' he'd suggested. 'Maybe it'd be better if you stayed at Honeybun. I thought of it, after you'd gone. We can spend as much time together as we want, but keep separate bases, maybe you'd feel more secure.' He'd felt for the warmth of her hand, as he drove. Wanting to reassure her. To be reasonable, adult, cautious. Sensible.

'Oh, Rats!' she'd complained. 'I was going to ask you to marry me. Are you scared?'

He turned into the gate of Pennybun Cottage.

Tonight, they'd celebrate quietly. A restaurant, a bottle of bubbly, bed like a couple of rabbits.

He could show her again how much he loved her and tomorrow, he thought, they could fetch the rest of her boxes from Honeybun.

He could help her unpack.

About the Author

Sue Moorcroft is an accomplished writer of novels and short stories, as well as a creative writing tutor.

Her previous novels include *Family Matters, Uphill All the Way* and *A Place to Call Home*.

She is also the commissioning editor and a contributor to *Loves Me, Loves Me Not*, an anthology of short stories celebrating the Romantic Novelists' Association's 50th anniversary.

www.suemoorcroft.com
www.suemoorcroft.wordpress.com
www.twitter.com/suemoorcroft

Coming Soon
from Choc Lit

Persuade Me, Juliet Archer's modern take
on Jane Austen's *Persuasion*.

Boy meets girl, falls in love, asks her to
sail round the world with him.

Girl loves boy – but listens to the Voice of Reason,
an old family friend, and says no.

The words 'forgive and forget' aren't in
Rick Wentworth's vocabulary. The word 'regret'
is definitely in Anna Elliot's.

When they meet again eight years later,
he seems indifferent and intent on finding happiness
elsewhere. Can she convince him that their lost love is
worth a second chance?

Introducing the Choc Lit Club

Join us at the Choc Lit Club where we're creating a
delicious selection of romantic fiction for
today's independent woman.
Where heroes are like chocolate – irresistible!

Each month we have author interviews and feature
books that have been recommended and rated by our
readers and the Choc Lit Tasting Panel.

If you have a favourite novel with
an irresistible hero, then let us know.

We'd also love to hear how you enjoyed *Starting Over*.
Just visit www.choc-lit.co.uk and give your feedback.
Describe Ratty in terms of chocolate
and you could be our Flavour of the Month Winner!

More Choc Lit

Why not try something else
from the Choc Lit selection?

The Importance of Being Emma by Juliet Archer
is a modern retelling of Jane Austen's *Emma*.

With its clueless heroine and entertaining plot,
it stays true to the original while giving fresh insights
into the mind of its thoroughly updated
and irresistible hero.

The Importance of Being Emma was shortlisted for the
2009 Melissa Nathan Award for Comedy Romance.